SOUL FLIGHT

SOUL FLIGHT

AN OUTCAST
ADVENTURE

WILLIAM ALBERT BALDWIN

Copyright 2019 William Albert Baldwin
All rights reserved
ISBN-13 978-1987731590
CreateSpace Independent Publishing Platform

Cover design by Linda Judd.

SOUL FLIGHT

To the outsiders,

The people who don't fit in,

Who straddle the boundaries

And celebrate the interplexities.

"Negroes are deemed as good as white people in Venice, and so this man feels no desire to go back to his native land. His judgment is correct."

    – Mark Twain, *The Innocents Abroad*

"*Hier bin ich Mensch; hier darf ich's sein.*"

    – Goethe, *Faust*

FLIGHT

ONE

In his mind's eye he'd seen them, after the blinding flash: The planes striking the buildings; the fires breaking out; the dense black cloud rising into the bright blue sky. He'd heard the terrified screams. Now he heard only the landing gear deploying.

Alan hated the visions. Even the ones that came true omitted any specifics he could have passed to authorities. No one would have believed him.

But why two planes instead of one? He usually saw only the plane he was on—*that* was paranoia. *This* was different.

He'd been leaning over his three-year old daughter in the window seat to watch the ships trailing wakes on Lake Michigan. Then the plane had dropped below the tallest downtown buildings and headed inland past the skyscrapers. The bright July sun had glistened suddenly off glass and steel—the blinding flash. Then the planes and fire, the smoke and screams. What had he seen? It was 1995; airplanes didn't crash into buildings.

Landing in Chicago at last: Halfway to Virginia and his parents. After four hours squashed between his little daughter and an overly-cheerful stranger—the window and aisle seats—Alan looked forward to stretching.

He stuffed his newspaper into the pouch below the tray table, now in its upright, locked position. The article on page seven had confirmed Alan's fears: *China Sentences William Bao To Ten Years For Spying*. A week earlier Alan might have helped him, but Alan had been fired from Human Rights International. Alan's church would no longer help; he'd resigned as president and congregant. The Bao verdict hit Alan hard; Alan's HRI group had hosted Bao's last public appearance before he left for China.

"You from Chicago?" The question startled him from his reverie. The woman beside him had lowered her book and was looking at him. A stylized silver fish hung from her neck.

Alan forced a smile. "No, I'm just visiting…." She was staring at his ringless hand. "I'm visiting a friend."

The woman returned to reading. Little Lavender stared out the window as the runway approached. Alan closed his eyes and then, as wheels met concrete, relaxed. "Praise Hermes!" he said to himself. He always thanked the God of Journeys when they landed safely.

But had he spoken only to himself? Sometimes he spoke out loud without meaning to. He glanced at the woman beside him: She was tucking her book—something inspirational, Alan couldn't catch the title—into her purse. He worried too much. She couldn't see the pentagram under his shirt, or the wedding rings he wasn't wearing. But could he be sure? Some people can sense the invisible—Alan could.

But even if she sensed it, his neighbor would deny that Alan was a witch; he didn't channel deep basso demons or hurl ectoplasm like the witches on TV. How could he be a witch when he belonged to a church (though he didn't anymore—and could she imagine a church that included atheists and witches? No—it was inconceivable).

As for polyamory, the woman would simply stammer: "Poly…whatery?" Polys were an utterly insignificant, unknown minority in America; more unbelievable than witches and pagans. If he tried to explain, she'd simply declare: "You can't fall in love with two people at once. It's all about sex." And how could he explain? If he couldn't explain his opera obsession, how could he explain his attractions to people, the way he…loved?

But Alan had reasons to worry. Forty-five with beard graying, he knew he was growing old. He was tired of sitting and had forgotten to bring his opera recordings. But he'd reached Chicago and was ready to debark. Gayle might have the Wagner tape he'd sent her. He stood up, grabbed his two small duffles, and led Lavender off the plane. Businessmen around them tucked *New York Times* under their arms. As they entered the passenger lounge the humidity hit them. The afternoon sun had drenched the terminal in oppressive light and heat.

He spotted Gayle waiting across the lounge. Thirty-five, short, and sturdy, she erupted into a broad smile, waved, and ran towards them, her hip-length blond hair trailing down her back. Her headband reminded Alan of English Morris ribbons, and the bells on her belt jingled like an English Morris dancer. It made Alan laugh: Morris Dancers with their ribbons and hankies and bells! He remembered how Vicki beamed when she leapt into the air with her dancing team. Had Gayle started learning English folk-dancing too? She plunged into Alan's arms and raised her mouth to his.

"You taste good!" she cried after their kiss.

A long hug. Lavender jumped gleefully around them, shouting "Gayle!"

"Lavender was perfect on the flight."

The three-year old beamed.

"But the woman beside me! I don't think she liked us."
He instinctively checked for the pentagram under his shirt.

"Any news from Vicki?" Gayle asked. "It was the funniest thing: I saw a woman who looked just like her run through the terminal awhile ago. Must have been late for a flight. But of course it wasn't her."

"Of course. She's in the Northwest with Claire." He glanced at Lavender. "She even took her passport—I brought mine too out of spite. For all I know they're in Canada. Where's the hotel?"

"Just across the street. Let's get your luggage."

He pointed at his duffles. "This is all I've got; I'm only going to my parents."

Gayle scowled.

They headed for the parking garage, Lavender jumping and singing. Alan caught Saturday headlines on newspaper stands and snippets of news reports on overhead monitors. The Balkan war was heating up, the Oklahoma City bombing investigation continued.

"Are you happy to see me, Tumblebug?" Gayle laughed and mussed Lavender's hair.

Twenty minutes later they'd settled into the hotel room and Lavender had started complaining. She'd attached herself to the couple's intertwined legs.

"No more hugging! I want to eat!"

"It's too early to eat. I need to rest."

"I'm hungry, Daddy. I want dinner."

"Let's see what's on TV. We'll eat pretty soon."

He found a program with cartoons, then crawled onto the bed beside Gayle—Lavender now had forgotten them.

"I've missed you, Alan," Gayle whispered.

But he couldn't stay awake. His pentagram had tumbled from his shirt; Gayle lifted the chain, kissed the star and the two attached rings, and tucked it all back in.

"Thanks," he mumbled drowsily. Alan was thinking of dancers…and airplanes…and the woman with the book and the necklace, regarding him curiously.

"She never said anything about leaving me. Not until Sunday, on the way to *Cirque des Étoilles*." From the bed they could hear Lavender snoring in front of the television. "She left with Claire Monday morning. Said they'd be back in a few weeks. Said we'd talk when they got back."

"Who's Claire?"

"A friend from the coven. Married to a Sicilian."

Gayle scowled. "How can you talk about covens? I call *myself* pagan because I grow a vegetable garden; I love digging in the soil. But *covens*? Covens and *Witches*? Why use words that people will laugh at? I want to make a difference in the world. When Nelson Mandela got out of prison, I organized a celebration on campus; that's what *I* do. I—" She seemed at a loss to express her incredulity. "Covens and Witches!"

"So call it a prayer group. Preston, Janie, Claire, and us; we're the coven. We've been practicing Magic for years." Gayle grimaced again. "Don't want to say 'magic?' Call it meditation. Role-playing and visualization in a support group. Preston and Janie—" But the bitter memory stopped him.

"Is Claire poly?" she whispered.

"I doubt she knows what it means. The word's only been around a couple years. Claire probably thinks it's just swinging or slutting or cheating; nothing to do with *love*. She's attracted to other people, but Tomie won't hear of it: *No one touches my wife*."

"You think Claire and Vicki are getting it on?"

17

"They like each other, and they're both bi. But Claire promised Tomie—"

"People don't always do what they promise."

"Nice," Alan whispered as the hostess led them to their surprisingly large table—extra room, no doubt, for the toddler. Gayle had driven them into downtown Chicago. The restaurant was suitable for Lavender—but classier than any place Alan had eaten for several years.

"Sean and I used to eat here when we first got married, when we came to Chicago for Cubs games." For an instant Alan sensed anger.

"Alan," she went on after they'd been seated, "Why won't you come up to Janesville? There's plenty of room. I thought you were coming to visit, but now you're going to Virginia."

"But wouldn't Sean mind, at such short notice? I've got to meet him sometime, but—"

"He's off to England for a month. All last week he was in Yellowstone; wanted some time alone. He came back last night and stayed with me here—did you notice the look the maid gave you?—then he flew off again. I wanted him to come back sooner. I had to bring down the extra stuff he needed for England." Lavender was coloring with her crayons.

"Alan," Gayle continued, lowering her voice, "What happened to you last weekend?"

Alan scowled. He remembered the embarrassed disapproval on the maid's face. "I resigned as church president and quit the church. HRI fired me, and Vicki left with Claire. I told you on the phone."

"You made no sense on the phone. And you hung up once I said I could meet you here."

"The church refused to run my remarks in the newsletter—three little lines about polys! I thought they'd understand. It's not like UUs are Christians; we haven't been Christian for a century!"

"Yeah—You reject the Trinity."

"That's over-simplistic. We've got our own trinity: Love, Truth, and Service. God and Jesus are beside the point: Unitarians follow their conscience. They shouldn't have a problem with polys; poly ethics are built on consent and respect! But when I lit a candle for the four of us— you, me, Sean, and Vicki—people thought I was crazy."

For an instant he was back in the church, with its gleaming stained glass and beautiful dome. He loved that building and those people, whether they liked him—and the nail polish he sometimes wore—or not.

"Does Vicki think you're crazy?"

"She's tired of being a misfit. She wants to be normal."

"And HRI?"

"They called that afternoon, rejected my resolution on sexual freedom, and asked me to stop wearing the pentagram. I was 'making the Christians nervous.' I refused, so they fired me."

"But the Chinese case—"

"Nothing to do with me, really. I'm just the last HRI person Bao saw before he left for China. I can't do anything to help him; he's in jail for ten years now, for taking photos of labor camps. At least I've still got my faculty position at the college—but who cares about history these days?"

Gayle regarded him a long moment.

"Is Vicki leaving because of *me*?"

19

"No," snapped Alan defensively, "she likes you. It's Preston and Janie—" He stopped, embarrassed. "The four of us were involved for five years, then Vicki got pregnant. They panicked and broke it off." He stared down at the table. "We were utterly devastated; we never expected they'd *dump* us. That was 1990. Vicki's been a wreck ever since. Nearly had a breakdown." He glanced around nervously. "But she likes *you*," he continued in a whisper. "She's jealous now and then, that's normal; but she let us sleep together in the cottage. She let us take the honeymoon in Monterey." Lavender was coloring on her menu. "I know she's hard to talk to—"

"Well what if she leaves you, Alan? Look: Janesville's only two hours away and Sean won't be back for weeks. There's room for you and Lavender." Lavender was playing with her macaroni. "Do you have to go to Virginia *tomorrow*?"

"I need to talk to my parents. I need to ask them about…" He groped for words. "Did I tell you they're interested in another couple? They've always been interested in others, apparently. They just didn't think—." His voice faltered. "But now I've inspired them, it seems. It's hard to believe." He laughed awkwardly. "Vicki's unhappy, but not because of *you*. She's in denial about…" His voice dropped to scarcely audible. "She's in denial about what we are. She knows I'd never leave her, but I don't want *her* to leave *me*! I need to talk to my parents."

"But I've hardly seen you, Alan!" Gayle said, dropping his hand. Lavender had dumped her crayons all over the table. "Everything's been online—our whole relationship! Except for the week I came to visit. We knew each other for ten months before we met! Emails and phone calls aren't the same as being together." She leaned forward and whispered: "Though I *love* the phone sex!" Lavender was building a mountain out of the pasta, apparently hearing nothing. "California's so far away," Gayle went on in a normal voice, "it's amazing we ever met. And it was only because you posted that poly message…"

"I think we should do a reading," Gayle said as they drove back; Alan didn't reply. Alan had studied Tarot but divination was not his focus. More often he invoked the Greek god Hermes for safe driving, lit candles for aid at the appropriate planetary hours, and made the sign of the pentagram to bless dead animals along the road. And he used the Pagan names for the days of the week.

He'd been practicing Wicca—the religion of Goddess and God—European ritual Witchcraft—for over ten years; peppering his practice with Greek, Celtic, and Nordic additions; Eastern and Tribal religion; and his own Unitarian Universalism.

His parents had always encouraged him to think for himself; it wasn't surprising he'd ended up Unitarian. Unitarians believe you should develop your own theology. In Alan's case early interests—Jesus, Wagner, Shakespeare, and T. S. Eliot—had drawn him towards the visionary; not surprisingly he'd stumbled into Wicca.

"Gods," said Gayle, "you look tired!"

"I feel lost," he told her as they parked. "I'm afraid I've screwed up everything."

"A reading might help."

The long day of travel had caught up with Lavender. Alan carried her into the hotel room and tucked her into the second bed.

Gayle pulled the Tarot from her bag. *Ribbons and bells by her suitcase…* Alan shuffled the cards.

21

The spread included four of the Major Arcana, the most significant subset of the deck: Death, the Devil, the Hanged Man, and the Tower; plus several Cups. Alan turned pale.

"The four worst cards," he muttered. "Four Major Arcana! And the cups: An emotional disaster. Last Sunday. Last Sunday."

He paused for a moment, then gasped.

"What?" asked Gayle.

He felt himself shriveling in front of her. "I've lost my soul."

"You shouldn't rush to an interpre—"

"My soul is gone."

She looked at him, puzzled.

"It's abandoned me." He sounded pathetic. "How can I get it back?"

"What do you mean?" she asked. "How can you lose a soul? You can't misplace it like a watch, then find it again!"

Alan shrugged.

"No, wait," she went on. "I remember. Soul loss and retrieval. Joseph Campbell and Carl Jung both talk about it. It's shamanic. A psychic crisis can provoke a loss of soul." She considered a moment. "But shamans can retrieve lost souls." She took him in her arms.

"But what do I do?" he pleaded. "I'm not a shaman; you laugh when I say I'm a 'witch.' How do you find a lost soul?"

She pondered again. "Try anything that might work, I suppose. Like the knights who sought the Grail, in the medieval legends."

"But I don't know how."

"You improvise then," she answered emphatically. "You've studied this more than me. You know the Teachings: It's impossible to say what the soul or Grail is—

but you'll know when you find it. It's something within; the essence that sustains you." She kissed and hugged him tightly.

"Meanwhile," she whispered, "come to bed. I want to feel you inside me."

TWO

"Love you, Grandma. Love you, Grandpa."

Lavender crawled across the sofa one grand-parent to the other; laughed; then plopped down exhausted between them.

Alan and Lavender had arrived in Virginia late Sunday afternoon. Alan hadn't been home since Lavender's birth. He looked forward to meeting the couple his parents were interested in; he could hardly believe they all might be poly—it seemed so fantastical, and how do people realize such things anyhow?—but at the last minute the couple had decided not to come over.

Alan thought he'd stay a few weeks. He'd discuss the Tarot—he'd already described the Reading. His parents were broad-minded about religion. His father had adopted Buddhism while living in Japan when Alan was a boy; his mother had grown up Quaker—and they attended a Unitarian congregation. Alan figured he could think things over, spend some time alone, enjoy Lavender and his parents, and return to California clear-headed.

After carrying Alan's duffle bags back to his old room, Mr. Horne had slipped into his *yukata* (not a "kimono") and *zoris* (not "flip-flops"), and they had settled into the living room. Water was heating for tea; Lavender would soon be out cold. His father's bookshelf caught Alan's notice.

"Jazz albums?" Alan asked. "I didn't know you liked jazz."

He turned from the records, the small wooden Buddha, and the books on Buddhism and Emerson, to his father sitting across the room. His father looked trim for seventy.

"Your mom, you know—the Louis Armstrong and Pete Fountain got me interested."

"I'm still a Wagner guy," Alan quipped, grinning.

Mr. Horne rolled his eyes. "You're too cerebral, Alan. Wagner's so damned long-winded—in my opinion. Except for the 'Ride of the Valkyries.' Classical music's good, but jazz is a lot more fun. I appreciate Wagner, but Bach's a lot more lively—and jazz is a lot like Bach."

Alan pulled a few albums from the shelf.

"I've listened to Mom's records. I'll try some of your new stuff before I go to bed. I'm still on California time. Where's the headset?"

Lavender had passed out on the sofa. Alan carried her to their room. His parents followed with the stack of LPs.

Lavender smiled drowsily as Alan tucked the blanket around her. His parents beamed as she snuggled into the pillow.

"Adorable," whispered Mrs. Horne.

"The smile of an angel," said Mr. Horne. "An angel or a Buddha."

"I always appreciate your wooden Buddhas," Alan said. "So serene." The teapot whistled, and Mrs. Horne ran to the kitchen. Alan sighed. "I wish we'd gotten to China."

"But we lived in Japan. We lived in Germany. You got to your Wagner festival. Not the typical American experience. I wish they'd had Japanese lessons on the airbase, you would have been fluent by now. Your languages amaze me! Are you still studying Mandarin?"

"Not since Tian An Men—what's the point?"

"It's been forgotten like the Tibetans," his father said bitterly. "Alan, I'm sorry about HRI. I admired your work for them."

"I learned from you and the Red Cross."

"I was lucky. We lived on military bases, but did humanitarian work. Twenty years overseas, forty-some years altogether; starting with the Philippines and MacArthur. Those prison camps. If Mao hadn't taken over China... Are you still doing Tai Ji, you and Vicki?"

"No. Quit that too."

Mr. Horne glanced down the hallway. "Any chance you'll move back to Virginia?" he asked softly.

"No. In California we can be ourselves. We can't do that here."

"But the earthquakes…"

"We survived the '89 quake. It's worth it to have more freedom."

"Tea's ready," Mrs. Horne yelled from the kitchen.

"Better get back to your mom." Then: "Alan, I'm sorry about Bao."

"I'll be out in a minute," Alan said. "I want to change clothes."

"Do you like my new outfit?"

Alan's parents ignored the question. Since Lavender had gone to bed, their tone had grown increasingly adamant.

"You shouldn't spend your time here, Alan," his father said, "while Vicki's travelling with Claire. Lavender can stay but you have matters to settle. You've lost a job, you've quit your church; Vicki's probably leaving you. The Tarot reading…"

"In Australia," his mother cut in, "the traditional Aborigines—when a man comes of age he goes on a 'walkabout.' It helps him understand his place in society."

"I'm forty-five years old, Ma."

"You told us a couple of years ago that you'd studied with a shaman in the mountains. You mentioned a vision quest."

"But I didn't go, I just did some drumming—a weekend workshop. A genuine quest can take days, weeks. You fast and keep a vigil. You wait for a vision…in an isolated place, like the Badlands in South Dakota."

"Traditionally, yes," said Mrs. Horne. "But you've never been particularly traditional." They regarded one another uneasily. "And how is Gayle?" his mother asked. "How is this new lover?"

"She's fine," Alan answered, taken aback. "Comfortable with herself—and expresses what's on her mind."

"You still love Vicki?" Mr. Horne asked.

"I love them both. Vicki and I have been married fifteen years." He paused then added: "Preston really hurt her."

"Maybe *she* should do a Walkabout," Mrs. Horne ventured.

"I think she *is*—with Claire."

"It may not involve walking," Mr. Horne quipped. None of them laughed.

"Sex can be a Walkabout too," said Alan quietly.

"A non-traditional one," Mr. Horne replied.

"I don't love Gayle because of the sex; it's the way she integrates it into her life. For Vicki sex is just something you *do*. For Gayle sex is something you *are*."

"They'll call her a slut," said Mr. Horne, struggling not to smile.

"She must be very wise," Mrs. Horne countered, a glint in her eyes.

"You impress me, you know; both of you," Alan said. "You don't walk on eggshells anymore. You've learned to respect your differences. How can Vicki and I learn that?"

"*You're* the Witch, Alan." Her tone suggested disappointment. "I thought you and Vicki were getting along."

"*I* thought we were getting along; then she went off with Claire. I told you what happened when Preston and Janie dumped us: She wouldn't eat, she couldn't sleep, she wasn't interested in sex. Refused to talk. Something inside her died. I thought she'd gotten over it; now I don't know. It's okay for her to go off with Claire; the trip will do her good. I just don't want her to leave me."

"Does she want to keep Lavender?" Mr. Horne asked.

"She didn't say. They just drove off."

"She doesn't seem very stable."

Alan sighed. "I wouldn't be surprised if they sailed off a cliff somewhere. They headed for the Northwest, but didn't take any maps."

"Why would she leave you?" Mrs. Horne asked.

"My continued existence reminds her of Preston and Janie. If the poly support group gets going, *that* will remind her. She'd rather forget. She feels ashamed and betrayed."

"So go back to monogamy," Mr. Horne said grimly.

"I *can't* go back," Alan snapped. "Maybe she can, but I can't. Monogamy would destroy me. I can't kill my feelings and I'm tired of lying. I can't change the way I love." Suddenly he remembered that woman on the plane. He hesitated then added: "I can't change the way I *am*."

They traded awkward looks.

"Okay," his father said sharply. "Go back to California. No place in Virginia for poly-pagan faggots!"

"I'm not a faggot!" Alan shot back. "I'm a bisexual poly; I cross-dress sometimes…" He stood up abruptly, then hesitated. He didn't want to suggest he was rejecting them. "I need to sleep." His eyes softened and he relaxed. "You know I still love you."

They headed down the hallway.

"You've stood with me all my life," he said to his mother. When you found me wearing your clothes, back in Japan…"

"But you've stood with us too!" Her voice reassured him. "We've learned a lot from your honesty. When we first got married, we thought—well… If we had felt we'd had options back then—"

"Look," he said, talking faster. "You don't have to stay in Virginia. Why don't you move to California? It's different there. It's safer and open to all kinds of things."

"This is our *home*, Alan," Mr. Horne snapped. "We've lived here, on and off, for twenty years. Why do you hate Virginia? If they lynch us—well, I'd rather die here than in exile. I don't want to move anymore. I'm tired of living among strangers."

"You make new friends, Dad. Like we did with the military."

"Maybe we *should* leave," Mrs. Horne said quietly. "People don't treat us the way they used to; the dance club is dying. We've led it for ten years; now we flirt with someone and—" She sighed deeply. "What are folks so scared of?" They'd reached the bedroom door.

"They're scared of everything," said Alan. "But us—you and I—I like how we challenge each other. No one I know has parents like you."

He reached for the doorknob but his father grabbed his arm. A smile flickered over the older man's face.

"Your lipstick is crooked; and the nail polish is…sloppy."

Alan chuckled. "I was in a hurry, Dad." He stepped into the bedroom; unzipped himself, and let the skirt fall to the floor. "Goodnight," he said, closing the door.

"Alan," Mrs. Horne said loudly from the hallway, "the skirt and blouse don't match."

"Shit!" Alan muttered. Then he started to laugh. Lavender stirred briefly.

He did fare better as a man. He'd brought *one* outfit from California, but couldn't even get that one right. Best to abandon women's clothing for now.

Alan awoke contented, sometime after nine on Monday. "Morning, folks," he said as he swept into the dining room, wearing his own old *yukata*. "*O-hayo-gozaimasu*." He bowed to his father. It was like his adolescence in Japan. He sat down at the table and reached for the newspaper.

"There's a cease-fire in Chechnya, Alan," his mother said matter-of-factly. "I know you were worrying about that."

Alan flipped through the paper and tossed it back on the table.

"I can't get over those jazz records. Armstrong and Beiderbecke. Hawkins and Basie. Ellington. I've never heard this stuff before. 'Body and Soul'—Wow!"

His parents eyed one another. Mrs. Horne cleared her throat.

"We know you want to stay here, Alan..." She glanced towards her husband.

"I don't expect Vicki to be gone the whole month," Alan answered, trying to anticipate what she was getting at.

His parents eyed each other again. It made Alan nervous.

"You can certainly stay here if you want to..." But his father's tone suggested otherwise. Alan's uneasiness increased.

"The Tarot reading changes everything." His mother's voice rang strident.

"How?" They all were tensing up.

"It appears that your soul has abandoned you," his father said. "You need to get it back."

"You need a soul."

"So Gayle does a reading..." Alan spoke very deliberately, "...and you throw me out of my home?"

"Virginia isn't your home," his father said firmly. "You aren't Christian or heterosexual or monogamous..."

"Does that matter?"

His father looked him in the eyes. "You can't possibly find your soul here."

They glared at one other. Then Alan grinned. "*You're* not Christian, heterosexual, or monogamous either, Dad."

Mr. Horne scowled. "Danny was a long time ago," he answered softly. Then he laughed. "I like it here, in spite of everything. We're not throwing you out, just making a suggestion."

"But I can dig into myself here. I can meditate and think..."

"You didn't lose your soul here," his father interrupted. "You won't find it here either."

"You know what Meister Eckhart says," his mother cut in. "*If you want to find God, look for him where you lost him.*"

"Meister Eckhart!" exclaimed Alan. He'd always wondered about the medieval mystic.

His father shot his wife an annoyed look. "We're your parents," he said to Alan. "We love you. You're welcome to stay if you really want to. But the Tarot reading…your soul… The Quest to retrieve your soul…the shamanic quest…does not point to Virginia. And just thinking will do no good. It's precisely what Jung and Campbell say: You never find the Grail where you expect it. You have to go seek."

"*Where?*" Alan growled in frustration.

His father handed him a small sheet of paper with a hand-scribbled note. "I've bought your ticket."

"Germany?" Alan exclaimed looking at the paper. "Go to Germany?"

"It's just a guess, but I think it's a good one. You went through so much in Germany! And you know the Craft—the Craft of the Wise, Witchcraft: Your experiences in the Inner World guide you in the Outer. Everything that happens holds meaning if you can decipher it: Everything you see, everywhere you go, everyone you meet. Find the places and people you need; decipher your visions—you will find what you seek. I think what you seek is in Germany."

"That's more like Ritual Magic, Dad. Or Alchemy."

His father shot him an annoyed look. "It's all connected, you know."

"I've never trusted myself to—"

"We'll be with you in spirit, Alan." Mrs. Horne reached for his hand and her husband's. Mr. Horne took Alan's other hand to complete the circle. They sat silent a moment. It felt like a Quaker meeting.

"Sweet Lord Jesus," his mother began softly, "watch over our son and bring him back to us, whole and reborn. Open him to the Inward Light, the Inner Teacher."

"Lord Buddha," his father added firmly, "watch over and protect our son. Carry him to the Other Shore of Enlightenment."

"Lord and Lady, Watchers and Protectors above…" Alan eyes were closed; the words were flowing through him. "Hermes, Aphrodite, Athene; lead me to wisdom. Protect me on my journey."

They sat silently, eyes closed, holding hands. Then Mrs. Horne broke the spell. "We have to hurry, Alan. The plane leaves at six, and it's a four-hour drive to Washington."

"It took a bit of doing to get you that ticket," Mr. Horne added. "It's been specially negotiated so you can choose your flight back. Stay as long as you need to."

But Lavender—she had shuffled in from the bedroom—interrupted them: "Dad," she exclaimed, "can we have bacon?"

FATHERLAND

THREE

Alan dragged his large new duffle through the narrow entrance of his pension room (he loved that German pronunciation: pen-see-OWN), shut the door, locked it, and sank onto the soft comforter-bed. For the first time in uncountable hours his world was quiet, dark and comfortable. He had returned to Munich after twenty-four years. Munich: The capital of the former Kingdom of Bavaria, now a south German state. He'd spoken briefly with the unnaturally friendly but rather preoccupied proprietress, a Frau Neufeld, then staggered upstairs.

It was two-thirty Tuesday afternoon. He'd arrived two hours late. It was eight-thirty a.m. back in Virginia. Alan hadn't slept on the plane. He hadn't slept since nine the previous morning: Twenty-four hours without sleep.

The airline passengers wouldn't care. They'd left Washington at six p.m., intent on enjoying the flight. As soon as dinner was over—by Hermes!—just as Alan decided to sleep, the others decided to party. They partied through a movie, the news, the business news, and the sports news. Four rows from the large screen, Alan couldn't shut out the noise or light. The screen went blank at four-thirty in the morning, European time, but the party went on—it was only ten-thirty p.m. back in Washington. Clearly none of these people had plans for the following day. But how could Alan complain? It was utterly illogical that he was going to Munich—Spiritual quests are never logical.

The plane had arrived late in Frankfurt, Alan had missed his connection, the airline had lost his duffle. But here he was, at last, safe in a comfortable room, duffle recovered, in Munich.

On the short flight from Frankfurt he'd read an article in *Der Spiegel* magazine—*The Mirror*—about Mel White. Growing up Evangelical Christian, White had been told that homosexuality was an "abomination." White struggled against his "sin" but eventually concluded it wasn't a sin at all—it was a gift from God. And he discovered a church for people like him: The Metropolitan Community Church. Alan felt encouraged to find this article in a prominent magazine right after landing on German soil; it seemed a good omen.

Still, he imagined he heard a voice—the woman beside him on the plane to Chicago?—commenting angrily: *How dare this man question the Word of God?*

Alan had dreamt of Munich for twenty-four years; fervently at first and then, less distinctly, in the recesses of his mind. Munich and the American University for Military and Diplomatic Dependents where he'd met Julia, Shannon, and Thea; the first women he'd become close to. Julia had taken her own life. The others still lived, somewhere.

He'd met Julia his first week in college and was falling in love with her when she killed herself three months later. Those memories still haunted him.

Shannon had become his first real girlfriend. She'd returned to the States after a year in Munich and then misunderstood the letters he'd sent her.

Thea had become his fiancée after their return to the States. He'd been drawn to her not only by her intelligence and kindness but also because her family was full-blooded Hungarian and had started teaching him their distinctive language. But the poly creature he didn't yet realize he was (the word *polyamory* had not yet been invented) had collided with her family's Catholicism. She remained out there, somewhere—her rejection still grieved him. Everything had started in Munich.

He dared not sleep. It was mid-afternoon, he'd been awake for twenty-four hours—yet Alan dare not sleep. He wouldn't awaken till nine p.m. or midnight. He'd suffered insomnia in California. What would he do at one a.m. in Munich? Would he roam the streets? Toss in his bed? Start a diary? Go mad?

Gayle had offered a suggestion in Chicago; an odd idea that carried its own logic. His plans for Virginia bothered her; she'd hoped he'd remain in Wisconsin. "Be careful looking for your soul," she said. "You could go mad, or lose your way on false trails. Don't linger too long, except in a place your soul might reside." When his father handed him the ticket for Germany, Alan had decided to stay nowhere more than a single night, unless—

So here he was in Munich, but afraid of staying too long. Afraid of Munich, Bavaria, Germany.

But why be afraid of Germany? This was the place to begin: where he'd started college. But suppose he didn't find anything; suppose he couldn't restring the fragments of his past.

And if he *did* find his soul? Retrieving a soul takes courage; he might not be worthy. His quest still might fail.

39

That did it; he had to get up; he dare not sleep. There were still seven hours of daylight. He had to find the University and reconnect to his student life in Munich: The past life that had meaning for him.

Hermes rose, tall and beckoning, from the stone fountain in the portico of the Residenz, the old Bavarian royal palace. Alan had emerged from the Residenz Museum, a few blocks from his pension, seen the statue, glanced about, folded his hands, and bowed to the god. *Hermes, protect me on my journey!*

The long plane flight had given Alan time to think about his quest, and he'd developed definite ideas about how to proceed. It seemed reasonable to begin at a museum. Culture was part of what Munich meant to him. Munich was also the first place he'd lived on his own. He'd been lonely that first night in the dormitory, after his parents left. But living away from home had given him the freedom to explore his own ways of living. He loved going to college in Munich. He attended cultural events at reduced rates: Museums, operas, concerts, and plays. Art, music, and literature, already important to Alan, became more so in Munich.

As a Wagner-obsessed teenager Alan had worshipped music and literature. He'd devoured Shakespeare and T. S. Eliot, Beethoven and Verdi. But Wagner had seemed the most beautiful, captivating, thought-provoking music he'd ever heard—though he admitted finding it boring at first. But he'd opened himself up to both music and ideas. He'd let Wagner in. That obsession led to Paganism. His sense of the gods grew from his emotional connection to Art. A museum was the place to begin his quest.

Alan contemplated the statue. He felt no guidance, but the statue reassured him. It seemed a good omen to encounter Hermes immediately after his arrival. He had already discovered Artemis in the Bavarian Treasury Museum. Alan's intuition had told him to start here, just blocks from his room; and here was Artemis, cast in shining silver, arrows and quivers in hand, hounds at her feet as she rode a silver stag.

His religion taught him that Inner and Outer were One: An old saying of Hermes Trismegistes. The Outer led to the Inner. If he traveled attentively through the outer physical world, the path would lead to his soul—he was certain of that. But he had to pay attention to the world and the people around him. This ritual attitude would trigger an inner vision. Tending the Outer inevitably transformed the Inner. "As Above, So Below," in the words of Hermes Thrice-Great. "As Without, so Within."

Gods—It was Lughnasadh! Alan had crossed the ocean on August first, the holy feast of Lugh of the Long Arm, the all-skilled hero who had saved the Irish divinities. Alan had already encountered Hermes, Artemis, and Lugh: Hermes—the Guider of Souls; Artemis—the patroness of solitary women witches. Lughnasadh—the great harvest feast; one of the eight great Festivals of the Wiccan year. And the moon was waxing.

Alan Horne, history professor, stood in the middle of history. He had walked across Odeon Square past the burnt-yellow Theatine Church and stood at the Feldherrnhalle, the Field Marshal's Hall. In the middle of history at Lughnasadh: The fifth anniversary of Saddam Hussein's invasion of Kuwait. Alan remembered driving Vicki to the local community ritual while listening to astonished reports of the invasion.

In two years of study in Munich, Alan had walked the downtown a hundred times; yet the only building he really knew was the Opera. Now he had touched the statues and read the inscriptions at the Field Marshal's Hall; and he thought: *Hitler walked here with his men—the Beer Hall Putsch—1923.* The Present flowed from the Past.

Alan despised Hitler but couldn't ignore him. He had known of the Nazis since childhood; they were inescapable. He had learned of the Holocaust when he was eleven, during the Eichmann trial. Hitler had swept over Europe like a force of nature; he had walked where Alan now stood. But could an eleven-year-old understand the Holocaust? As an historian, Alan had to face the specters of the Past. He might never come to terms with the Nazis, but he couldn't ignore them.

In graduate school in Virginia, Alan had been riveted by "Triumph of the Will," Leni Riefenstahl's screen documentary of the 1934 Nazi Congress. The images and sounds had seared into his memory: The grainy old footage of white smoke rising from the concrete, and the men emerging over the distant rise, like gods: The Nazi leadership. And at the end of the film, the music.

As his plane landed in Frankfurt, it had embarrassed Alan to realize that he was humming the "Horst Wessel Song," the Nazi Party anthem. The German passengers pretended not to hear. The martial rendition at the end of the Riefenstahl film had stirred him deeply: The powerful drums pounding the monumental bass for the mass singing.

As a young American student, Alan had entered a Munich bookstore looking for *Mein Kampf*, not knowing its sale was forbidden in Germany; forcing the embarrassed clerk to explain (Alan had merely been looking for historical books). Alan had learned a lot since then—but not how to track a fleeing soul.

He understood the power of simplistic ideas. He understood why some people hated others who "aren't like us," who "don't belong here"—though he himself had never belonged anywhere he'd lived.

As a young man Alan had been terribly naïve. He'd avoided anything popular. The popular things he did like— the Beatles for example—he'd stumbled into on his own, before anyone could tell him to like them.

As a boy he'd avoided war movies because other boys were watching them. He'd avoided reading about Nazis because so many boys found them fascinating. When he finally was forced to confront them, he found himself susceptible. He'd grown up without bias. He knew intellectually that the Nazis were evil—he'd read about the Holocaust by then—but he didn't feel the primal disgust he felt for the Ku Klux Klan, and he mistrusted others' disgust as a cliché. He granted everyone a fair hearing. A Unitarian before he became a Pagan, he affirmed the dignity and worth of every human being—even the Nazis, even the Klan.

Nazi spectacle had soaked into him like Wagner, Shakespeare, and T. S. Eliot. He'd heard the "Horst Wessel Lied" without knowing the German words. He learned them later—they were trite in any case. But Alan, deeply susceptible to music, had remembered the melody ever since.

He loathed the Nazis and the hatred they stood for, just as he loathed the Klan—but he recognized the appeal of their evil.

*

"*Tegernseer Landstrasse. In der Nähe von Chiemgaustrasse.* I want to go to Lake Tegern Street." The bus driver didn't understand him.

But he got there. Having stopped by the Opera where Wagner and King Ludwig II, "Mad King of Bavaria," had premiered the revolutionary *Tristan* a hundred and thirty years earlier ("No, no operas right now; not the Season"), walked the ancient downtown, passed the Frauenkirche ("Church of Our Lady") and through the Sendling Gate (which he now had *touched* for the first time, feeling the ivy grow from the old dull bricks), Alan now rode, nearly dozing, past places he'd never stopped to visit: Mariahilfplatz ("Mary's Help Square") and the Eastern Cemetery; the old church he had often passed but never entered; leaving the bus, as he always had, where the bus continued straight but Tegernseer veered sharply left. Ten minutes further on foot and he had arrived.

This was the Munich he remembered, but it had changed. The walk to the caserne, one of the U. S. Army installations in Munich, covered the same distance as before, but Alan was older and tired more easily.

The humid air made him sweat—it seemed nearly as hot as Virginia—but he'd been in a hurry and hadn't wanted to slow down. Rush hour was approaching. The noisy street disoriented him. He thought again of the women he'd known here: Julia, buried in the foothills of the Alps; Shannon who'd misunderstood him; and Thea who'd rejected him. He thought of Wagner, King Ludwig's money in his pockets, walking through Munich with his lover Cosima while her husband Hans von Bülow, conductor of *Tristan*, Wagner's ode to adultery, trailed sheepishly behind—

though this had probably only happened in newspaper caricatures. Alan thought of the short-lived communist government of 1919 and the failed Nazi putsch of 1923. The Past was flooding through him, as it so often did, reviving both nostalgia and terror. Ahead he saw the university building where he had met Julia and Shannon and Thea, and he turned left into the old campus.

The small boy was playing alone in the empty plaza.

"Excuse me! *Kleinchen*! Do you live here?"

The boy stared and said nothing. Apparently he didn't understand German.

"Have the Americans been gone long? I saw the signs in English. I used to live in this apartment." Alan gestured towards the building and walked towards the boy, who stared at him blankly. Alan had been told that his dormitory had once been an SS barracks.

A woman in a headscarf pulled back the window curtain, saw Alan and yelled at the child. The boy turned towards her, glanced back at Alan, and ran through the doorway. The woman continued screaming something that sounded like Arabic. Then the boy and the woman were gone.

The caserne seemed surprisingly deserted for a Tuesday rush hour. The former college building, where he had talked so often with Julia, was locked up. Dust on the outside wall spelled "American University" where the metal letters had been removed. Alan had come here for freshman orientation, twenty-six years before. He had sat with Julia in the third-floor library. She'd talked about the German philosopher Nietzsche and he'd talked about *Tristan*. He'd spent long evenings in the library listening to Wagner and Mahler. Ironically the Bavarian State Opera apparently now owned the building. He longed to go inside but was afraid he'd be arrested for trespassing. Stadelheim Prison, where Ernst Röhm, homosexual chief of Hitler's SA, had been shot after the Night of the Long Knives purge in 1934, lay a mile to the east. Alan had not known about Röhm when he lived in Munich. Julia had killed herself in a hospital a mile south of the caserne. Perlacher Forest, huge, dark and menacing, where he had walked one night in total darkness with his friend—just a friend—Kathy, stretched south from the city. Kathy had told him that the forest ran all the way to the Alps, fifty miles away.

Alan continued across the caserne. His sophomore dormitory, where he had snuggled with Thea, appeared abandoned as well. He'd kissed her on this street corner.

"You know, Alan, some girls like to be touched on their breasts," she'd whispered as they lay together in the darkness.

Thea was gone now. When she broke their engagement, she had asked him to stop writing. Back in America they'd been 400 miles apart, and he'd admitted wanting other lovers.

After Shannon, he should have realized he was different from other people. He had taken her to their prom in Berchtesgaden, up in the Alps. She'd returned to the States the following year. When Alan wrote that he was seeing other women, Shannon assumed they were breaking up. He hadn't meant that, but they *were* on opposite sides of the Atlantic.

Now he was back where he had met these women, but they all were gone.

Only that small boy, no more than seven years old, outside his freshman dorm.

The caserne repelled him. It smelt of smog and gasoline. Alan walked the deserted cobblestones. Here had been the Officer's Club, where he'd lunched with Kathy. In the adjoining building he'd attended the memorial for Julia.

The caserne had become a backwater. The notices posted by the Americans before they left collected more grime every day.

Only one thing lived in the caserne: The traffic. And it didn't inhabit the caserne; it passed under it.

A major commuter route passed straight through the facility, one level below the buildings. They'd been overhauling the street when Alan left Germany. Now he felt thankful he'd left before its completion. At five-thirty on this workday afternoon, the cars—noisy, smelly, and dirty—passed through on their way home from work. Was it the traffic's ugliness—the city smog, the mid-summer heat, the pavement dirt—or Alan's overall exhaustion and despair that caused him to leave without even trying to find the hospital where Julia died, or the park bench where he had lain one winter night and cried for her, or Perlacher Forest, dark and massive, where he had roamed without thought, singing to himself and to Kathy songs of Wagnerian joy and sadness?

Nothing remained. Art and Memory had failed him. The spiritual connection to Munich was broken.

From his bed Alan watched the sky darken outside the open window above and behind him. The cool night air blew across him; the fifth floor window could stay open. He'd set his alarm for seven-thirty to leave time for a bath before breakfast.

What had been the point of coming to Munich? Everything he had valued here was gone. Even the Alte Pinakothek, the great Munich art museum, was closed for renovations. Alan pulled the cotton sheet over his face and turned to the wall. The entire trip had been useless—he wouldn't find his soul here.

FOUR

"Mr. Horne, you look much happier today!" The proprietress of the pension herself sounded more cheerful than she looked. But it was true that Wednesday morning found Alan quite revived. Sleep and a hot bath do wonders.

When Alan first came downstairs past the office, he had heard Frau Neufeld talking heatedly in Bavarian on her office phone. The local dialect had always been too bizarre for him to understand. It was Germanic, but locals considered it a separate language. It sounded peculiar enough to stop Alan in his tracks. For several seconds he simply stood in the hallway listening. He could only catch a few phrases.

A son, daughter, nephew, niece—someone—was getting married. The future in-laws had flown in over the weekend, all the relatives were there. There'd been some kind of row. Alan had caught a few names, but the Bavarian was mostly gibberish.

"Frau Neufeld," he told her now, "when I arrived in Munich yesterday I was hot, I was tired, I was discouraged. Things went from bad to worse. I didn't find what I was looking for. But here, now, in your fine establishment—"

He nodded towards the short somewhat stocky older proprietress, who stood beside his table. "—I feel much better!"

He did. After a thirty-six hour Tuesday, Alan had slept solidly and awoken as refreshed as a baby in the morning. The failures of Tuesday evening were not so depressing on Wednesday morning. Alan was far from the cares of California, Wisconsin, and Virginia. He had not found the memories he had wanted to recapture in Munich, but he had found Munich. Through the second-story windows of the dining room he could see the handsome stone downtown Munich buildings and watch pedestrians pass on the sidewalks below. The blue sky welcomed him to Germany.

Frau Neufeld tried to conceal it, but Alan knew she was pleased with his remark. Alan guessed Frau Neufeld to be about sixty—perhaps too old for him to flirt with, but not too old for him to compliment.

"You're too kind, Mr. Horne!" Frau Neufeld could not help smiling. When Alan arrived for breakfast she had seemed nervous. Now she pulled out a chair and joined him at his table.

"*Gnädige Frau*, in California people lead a hectic life; We're always rushing. From work to home to the market; committees, children; wife, friends, business obligations— no time for spontaneity."

He'd been rushing for ten years, yet his words surprised him; where were they gushing from? For ten years he'd barely noticed his own alienation. Now, unintentionally, he was outside his predicament.

"But you have friends and family. A job, a home; and California's beautiful! My husband and I visited San Francisco once: A beautiful city."

"But there I could never do *this*!" He made a sweeping gesture towards the room. "This is what I need, regularly:

To stop and enjoy life. A hot bath in the morning. A leisurely breakfast."

His morning bath, in the one bathtub in the pension, on the second floor, was chiefly responsible for his change of spirits. He'd filled the large, porcelain, claw-footed tub with hot water and climbed in. He'd lain and soaked for twenty minutes. He hadn't done that for years. It must be good for his soul—wherever it was.

If he felt so happy here, then perhaps...

But he couldn't stay in Germany—he had a wife, child, parents, girlfriend, job.

His soul was not a matter of Germany or America. He needed them both: The Past and the Present. He smiled at Frau Neufeld.

"For me this is *Heaven*! Ham and sausages, German bread, cheese, and eggs. A pot of tea. Sitting and eating slowly and thoughtfully. Looking out at the beautiful Munich architecture. Sipping my tea and chatting with *you, gnädige Frau*. I could sit here forever!"

Alan and Vicki had practiced yoga and Tai Ji together when they first met, but they'd stopped long ago. Alan had studied Vedanta, the classical Hindu philosophy, and practiced meditation. He'd wanted to live life slowly and deliberately. He hated rushing; but sometimes it was invigorating to plunge into activity: The Unitarians, the Pagans, the human rights work; even his teaching at the college.

Frau Neufeld blushed. "You are too kind, Mr. Horne!" She regained her composure and added, somewhat awkwardly: "Your wife was unable to accompany you?"

What was she getting at? He smiled awkwardly. "She had business to attend to. Our daughter is with my parents." This avoided the sticky points.

"Yes," Frau Neufeld sighed. "Marriage is a complicated business." Had she sensed that Alan and his wife were having problems?

"And your husband's in Berlin, Frau Neufeld?" Frau Neufeld's face froze for an instant.

"Yes. He has some business…at a hotel up there. He grew up in Berlin. It's only six hundred kilometers."

"Really? No further than Los Angeles to San Francisco!"

"Meanwhile I handle this pension. I love Munich. I was born here."

Her eyes sparkled. Alan was enjoying this conversation. He finished his tea, smiled at Frau Neufeld, and said, very deliberately: "I have to be off. I need to finish packing, and I'd like to walk around a bit before I leave."

A cloud crossed Frau Neufeld's face. "Must you leave so soon, Mr. Horne? You only arrived yesterday; and all the way from America!"

Alan presented a look of regretful necessity. "I'm afraid so. You understand business, Frau Neufeld." He gave the proprietress a knowing look.

Alan smiled, but he felt he had exhausted Munich's spiritual possibilities. His parents' home in Nuremberg, a hundred miles north, now seemed more promising. Later, if his quest were successful, he might return to Munich.

"I'm sorry you couldn't find your old professors, Mr. Horne. You must be disappointed."

"Well, Frau Neufeld, the American military is leaving Germany, which is how it should be. We've been here too long. This is *your* country. And when the U. S. army leaves, the schools that service the army's children leave. I wasn't really an 'army' child, of course: My father worked for the Red Cross. But I grew up with the American military and now the Americans have left. I shouldn't expect to find my past here." But the Americans being gone had disappointed him.

"Well you went to college here. And your name is German. You feel a connection to Munich. Mr. Horne, if it would be helpful, leave your luggage here while you go out. You might change your mind and then you'd have to carry it all back from the train station. I can keep it in my office. You can pick it up when you actually leave."

"Frau Neufeld," Alan smiled, "you are *too kind.*"

Frau Neufeld smiled back awkwardly, hesitated a moment, then ventured: "I told you my daughter Helga was leaving for Hamburg this afternoon. But first she's taking some friends to the Nymphenburg palace here—you could go with them."

Was Frau Neufeld trying to set them up? Her daughter was attending university; she must be twenty years younger than he. And Frau Neufeld knew he was married...

"You should see Nymphenburg. It's just a few miles from here. It's a beautiful palace, and the grounds are a wonderful place to walk."

"I know. I went there once."

"You should go back then! Visit before you leave!" She suppressed a smile. "Helga and her friends are going at ten. You could meet them there." She seemed intent on a rendezvous.

And a little happier. Frau Neufeld had still looked quite distraught when she entered the dining room. He'd apparently cheered her up. If she wanted Alan to meet her daughter, perhaps he should meet her. Perhaps it could snag his soul.

*

Alan wavered about meeting Helga Neufeld and went to Nymphenburg late. Before deciding, he wandered through the Hofgarten, the large public park not far from the pension. He relaxed among the trees, gardens, and fountains; and thought of Eliot's "The Wasteland," in which the park was mentioned. He didn't arrive at the palace till nearly eleven, and sighed with relief when no one met him at the bus stop.

Emerging from the trees onto the Nymphenburg grounds, Alan gasped at the immensity of the baroque buildings, which stretched across the horizon before him.

As he approached he noticed three women walking ahead of him, all roughly in their twenties. One was blond, one red-haired, and one sported jet-black hair. The blonde wore a tank top and shorts; the redhead a white blouse and knee-length skirt; while the last wore an ankle-length, long-sleeved dark blue dress. *She must be sweltering.* The three were arguing. The woman in the long dress was apparently involved with an Arab, and this had led to some tension.

The palace itself disappointed him. Only one section was open, and no tours were offered, even in German. Alan walked through on his own.

He'd looked forward to seeing the portraits of King Ludwig I's favorite women in the Gallery of Beauties, which he had visited before. However the three Nymphenburg ladies argued so heatedly they never noticed the annoyance of the other visitors.

"It's my business who I'm involved with," the dark woman said loudly. "And my religion is my affair. I don't care what my...*brother's*...future mother-in-law thinks!"

She'd apparently quarreled with her family over the weekend.

Alan was relieved to get back outside.

The palace grounds appealed to him, as Frau Neufeld had suggested. You could walk for hours along the paths and canals. The main canal ran a full two miles out from the palace. The sun shone bright and hot, but not glaring. Here, unlike California, the light did not strain Alan's eyes. It was marvelous to walk the gardens among people who appreciated leisure. Very different from his life in California.

The gardens relaxed Alan, made him feel safe and at ease. Fragments of a Beiderbecke song he'd heard at his parents—"Singing the Blues"—popped into his head. They complemented the blue sky and warm air. He imitated trumpet sounds. He closed his eyes and sang nonsense syllables. He felt wrapped in happiness. It was as pleasant as his morning bath and breakfast had been. He could almost believe he'd found his peace, his soul.

Then a sudden commotion startled him. A voice hissed, "My mother would like nothing better: I should dump Ahmed and throw myself at some *Amer*—" Silence. Alan opened his eyes. The three women stood before him. Their faces displayed the oddest combination of expressions: Amused, appalled, and puzzled.

At first they were all too startled to speak. Then, like a statue that had come to life or a video which had been unpaused, the blond woman walked towards him and smiled.

"You'd be Alan Horne. I thought we'd missed you. We thought you were coming at ten."

With a large grin she extended her hand. How had she recognized him? Was he so obviously American or had Frau Neufeld provided her daughter a detailed description?

"Hello!" Alan took her hand. Its warmth and softness appealed to him. "You must be Fräulein Neufeld."

"*I* am Fräulein Neufeld." The dark-haired woman extended her hand. Alan felt obliged to give up the blonde's rather familiar grip. But as Alan reached for this new hand, the woman hesitated as if she had made a mistake. The coldness of her touch nearly caused Alan to pull away. It seemed that her hand immediately went limp, as though she had reconsidered and decided to withdraw all contact. Alan forced a smile.

"Nice to meet you, Fräulein Neufeld. Helga, isn't it?"

"Yes. My mother told you?"

"That you would meet me here?"

"No," said Helga, dropping his hand as if it were contaminated. "She told you my name."

Alan and Helga began walking. The blonde and the redhead fell in behind.

"It was presumptive of her. Strangers don't address each other by first names here. My mother shouldn't have told you." Helga spoke very stiffly.

"She probably didn't think you'd mind, Fräulein Neufeld."

Helga's face reminded Alan of Lola Montez in the Gallery of Beauties. They both sported jet-black hair and rosy cheeks. Lola Montez, an Irish woman posing as a Spanish dancer, had caused the downfall of King Ludwig I, amidst the scandal of their affair, in the mid-1800s. She caused trouble wherever she went.

"I didn't remember Nymphenburg being so *big*," Alan told them.

Yet he retained clear memories of his first visit, even after two decades. He hadn't realized how much he'd missed Germany.

"You've been in Munich before?" The redhead seemed surprised.

"Twenty-five years ago."

"Look!" cried the blonde, gazing towards the garden lake. "Swans!" She watched them a moment then added excitedly: "The grounds are *lovely*; I could walk here all day."

Clearly the blonde enjoyed life.

The conversation soon died, and Alan dropped behind the women. He was hoping to wander off. He'd forgotten how much classical Pagan art dotted Europe. It was everywhere at Nymphenburg. He lingered at a statue of Diana and finally bowed to the goddess.

"What are you doing?" The blonde had noticed.

He'd remained discreet in his answers, but he was thousands of miles from home—Why bother?

"There's a Temple to Diana in the Hofgarten downtown. That's why I was late. I never expected it." He attempted an endearing smile.

"It's not a real temple," Helga grunted.

"But suppose it were," said the redhead. "Would you pray?"

Alan hesitated. These women had shredded his composure. In his talk with Frau Neufeld he had avoided anything too personal. Now he felt more confident and spit out the truth.

"I *did* pray. I asked Diana for guidance."

"You pray to Diana, not to Jesus?" The redhead seemed intrigued. "In Bavaria people pray to Jesus and Mary and the saints. Even in Thuringia we pray to Jesus if not to the others."

"People don't pray to Diana," Helga snorted. They were growing flushed in the summer sun.

Alan sped up.

They were still together in the Chinese Bath—now waterless. The interior seemed rather pathetic—gaudy tile walls that hadn't been washed in decades. The blonde glanced around and grunted.

"I lived in the Japan as a teenager," Alan blurted. He was thinking of William Bao. "I always hoped to see China. But Tian An Men…"

"No one remembers Tian An Men!" the blonde exclaimed. "It's just like the 1600s! Look at this palace! The Bavarian royalty didn't care about the Chinese people; they wanted the latest fashions." Her vehemence startled Alan.

"You're from Saxony, Käthe," the redhead drawled. "Of course you insult the Bavarians. Why should I care about China, when you trash your own German culture?!"

"I'm also an artist, Inge. The Chinese and German styles clash; it's pure ostentation."

"You always complain!" Inge retorted. The blonde—Käthe?—didn't answer.

"I don't like it myself," muttered Helga. "It has no soul."

"Does everything have to be 'spiritual?'" Käthe interrupted.

"Art *should* be spiritual!" Helga snorted. She had retreated further into her garment.

Alan had grown more and more fidgety. Inge suddenly turned on him. "Why do you keep humming that?" she demanded.

"It's Bix Beiderbecke, Inge," Käthe snapped. "Jazz. The 1920s."

He would never shake them. How could he appreciate the Pagan art with these women trailing him around? Maybe he should be blunter.

"Did you know that these grounds contain a Temple to Apollo and a Shrine to Pan?"

Käthe laughed (with a glance towards Helga). "We've always respected Classical art!"

Helga glared. "They didn't *worship* Apollo and Pan."

"But *I* do," Alan proclaimed. "At the Residenz I bowed to Hermes and Artemis. Here I bow to Apollo and Pan."

"It's *art*, Mr. Horne." Helga spit out in disgust. "The sculptors didn't believe in the Greek gods."

"It's not even art!" Käthe interjected, "It's a pretty distraction. It doesn't change your life. In art school they taught me—"

"Why should it change your life?" Inge shot back. "Art is a matter of beauty, not agendas." The heat was rekindling their animosities.

"But 'Singing the Blues'—Beiderbecke," said Alan. "*That's* changing *me*." He searched for a sympathetic face.

"It doesn't change *me*." Helga insisted.

"You haven't heard the recording," Alan snapped. His eyes traveled down Helga's ankle-length dress. "You may be right," he added sullenly. "Maybe it wouldn't change *you*."

They resumed their walk.

"Jazz changed Beiderbecke," Alan went on. "It was more than entertainment. It helped keep him balanced."

"But he was dead before he was thirty; too much drinking." So Käthe knew about Beiderbecke…

"He had a dark side," Alan replied. Käthe was beginning to impress him. "At first the song seems whimsical, romantic and innocent—the Tom Sawyer. Later you recognize the darkness—the Huckleberry Finn."

"I understand the darkness," Helga said softly.

"Look!" Käthe exclaimed with sarcastic brightness. "The Temple of Apollo." Across the lake a stone gazebo on an island came into view. The god stood enclosed by columns.

"I wish I'd found the Shrine to Pan," Alan sighed.

"It's only a *name*," Inge cut in. "They were using the Greek forms as models."

"You're right. I suppose the artists *were* Christians. But for me, these older gods are alive. And here, I want to acknowledge them."

"It's pointless," Käthe cried. "Good art *can* bring back the dead. But this art, the portraits in the Gallery—Lola Montez?—they're dead and the pictures are dead. True art could make them immortal, but this art fails absolutely."

"Because it can't be Religion," Helga snapped. "It can't redeem; only God can do that." Her outburst silenced the others.

"You disagree and I don't care. Religion is greater than art. You don't like Ahmed or my going to Hamburg? You think dressing modestly is silly? It matters to *me*. I appreciate your help with the moving, but you've been trying to talk me out of it ever since you got here. I resent it." She stomped away.

They followed her self-consciously. Käthe was muttering how "Helga ought to be more thankful since we both came down at such short notice to help with her move, just because she got pissed at her family." After a moment Alan stopped as the others continued along the path.

"I'm surprised and disappointed," Alan snipped loudly, surveying the palace and the gardens. "I enjoyed this twenty-six years ago, but it's all gone to ruin. It impressed me as a student. Now I'm embarrassed."

He looked about him. Helga and her friends were gone.

Alan's agitated appearance unnerved Frau Neufeld. She quickly finished her phone call, in standard German ("No, Sándor's left for Shanghai. I'll talk to you later") and rushed back to the registration desk. *She knows a Hungarian*, Alan thought.

"How was your visit to Nymphenburg? Did you meet Helga? Are you still leaving?"

It was difficult to be polite. He wondered how desperately Frau Neufeld had wanted to interest him in her daughter. Did she despise Helga's boyfriend so much?

"It was…wonderful, Frau Neufeld. We talked about the architecture and gardens. But I need to get on to Nuremberg."

Frau Neufeld couldn't hide her disappointment, but she lit up again after a moment.

"Nuremberg? Sophie could…" She searched through the papers on her desk. "I guess I don't have a card. Here." She scribbled on a notepad then tore off the top sheet. "Ask for this hotel at the Tourist Bureau."

Alan thanked Frau Neufeld, but accepted the information with mixed feelings. After his encounter with the three women that morning, all Alan wanted was to get away.

FIVE

Alan set his duffle on the cobblestone sidewalk and stared at the large glass doors before him. He confirmed the address. Then he opened one of the doors, held it with his foot, and dragged his bag into the lobby.

Alan's train had pulled into Nuremberg, some two hours north of Munich, at three-thirty. He'd barely recognized the station, so much larger than what he remembered.

The agent in the tourist office had treated him with extreme condescension. As soon as Alan mentioned the hotel recommended by Frau Neufeld, the woman had become noticeably icy. At least he'd been able to buy a map so that he didn't have to rely on the agent's minimal directions. And the agent had agreed to call ahead for him.

Alan had carried his luggage up the street—uphill literally—to the building. In the summer heat it had seemed like more than a half mile.

He rode the elevator to the ninth floor, the hotel level, and found the registration desk but no attendant. The small photo of a young man graced one end of the counter, surrounded by flowers. The photo had an aged quality to it, as if it had been taken some time ago. A telephone sat at the other end of the desk; a small sign providing the number for the manager.

Alan picked up the desk phone to call.

"We're sorry about the commotion in Munich," a patient female voice was saying, "But I hope the conference is going well, and we're looking forward to seeing you again on Sunday."

The phone used two lines; Alan tried the other.

"I'll meet you tomorrow at noon," said a voice which was difficult for Alan to visualize. "I'll just catch a train." The voice exhibited a definite assertiveness, and yet—Alan couldn't quite decide whether it was male or female.

The first line was now free, so he tried to call the manager; no one answered.

Alan took the elevator to the tenth floor and found the proprietor's room. The sign on the door simply said "Manager." Alan knocked; no answer. Where had everyone gone?

Alan was nearly back to the elevator when the apartment door swung open.

"Are you the gentleman who called from the registration desk?" The woman looked in her mid-fifties. "I've been expecting you."

Of course you've been expecting me, Alan thought. *The tourist office told you I was coming. So why weren't you at the front desk?* Or *had* the condescending agent ever called?

"Good afternoon, I'm Mr. Horne. The Tourist Office was supposed to call you about a room."

"My colleague in Munich said you *might* be coming. I'm sorry; I'm afraid I had to finish some business with my…family."

"Your colleague in Munich seemed very interested in my meeting her daughter." He couldn't help this minor complaint.

The woman started. "I must apologize for my…colleague," she said awkwardly. "Frieda's rather concerned. Her daughter's going through some significant changes."

"Helga and her boyfriend live in Hamburg now, I take it."

The woman started again.

"I met Helga briefly this morning," Alan added, thinking it might reassure the woman.

"She's just moving to Hamburg this week," the proprietress said stiffly. "A little unexpected, actually. She and two friends are driving up today. Helga's apparently engaged. I'm sorry if Frieda inconvenienced you; she's rather fond of Americans. She shouldn't have involved you in personal matters."

She showed him to an eleventh floor room, slightly larger than the one in Munich—and much nicer. It included a private bath with shower—and a television.

"Let me know if you need anything," the woman said in parting. "My name is Sophie Neufeld."

"You're Frieda's sister?"

The woman started once more. "I'm her…it's rather complicated…"

Alan left it at that.

Four-thirty found Alan back on the street looking for the subway, a short distance down Königstrasse—King Street. There'd been no subway when he'd lived there before.

Nuremberg now struck Alan as an ordinary city—no traces of the war. He and his parents used to find damaged sections of the old town wall still black with the soot of Allied bombs. Now everything was clean.

Down in the subway, down the long steps that led out of the bright August sunlight into the artificial lighting of the tunnels, a wall map confirmed that he could ride the subway all the way to Fürth, Nuremberg's small companion city. Alan used to take the streetcar. From Fürth he hoped to reach both of his old family homes: The small apartment and the larger duplex. He had fond memories of summers with his parents in Nuremberg. He was on a train in five minutes.

Alan had forgotten that the streetcar used to take almost an hour. His attention soon drifted. The novelty of being in Germany again was wearing off. Then the train emerged from underground and sped out over the city. The Nuremberg subway followed the Berlin model: It ran *above* the city as well as *below*.

An attractive woman, probably in her twenties, sat diagonally across the subway car from Alan. She wore a white blouse and pleated skirt; makeup, but not too much. She lounged back on the seat in a leisurely way.

Alan recognized her; she had left the hotel just ahead of him, and he had followed her down the street and into the subway. But he had lost her when he stopped to look at the subway map.

Alan observed the woman out the corner of his eyes as the train sped over Nuremberg, past buildings and landmarks he remembered from his earlier life. The woman was chatting quietly with a man in the facing seat. A pretty smile she had, and dark piercing eyes…

Then Alan realized she was a man.

Nuremberg still raced past. They had traveled into the industrial area where Nuremberg and Fürth merged. Perhaps he was mistaken.

He looked again. He saw the same smile—the same skirt, blouse, eyes. But the person was a man—a man dressed as a woman.

And he—she—had a very nice conversation with the man across from her—him—until that man got off the train.

Alan had found it easy to watch the two converse. The person in question had shown no awareness of Alan watching—Alan had been careful to watch only indirectly. He'd pretended to stare out the window as Fürth grew closer.

Once the person in question was alone, Alan hardly dared look.

Then the subway rolled into Fürth.

How extraordinary that this should be happening! When he packed for Germany, Alan had considered dressing as the person he had always *wanted* to be; to dress as a woman or man or whatever he felt like being; to see if Germany could accept him more than America. But "reason" won out—suppose the Germans rejected him? He had chosen his second option: To blend in and "pass" as a German; to appear as inconspicuous as possible. He had carefully removed his nail polish. Pondering the person in the train, Alan now wondered if he had chosen wrong.

As Alan left the train, and proceeded through Fürth station, he noticed the man-woman ahead of him again, followed by five or six boys, all around ten years old, who taunted him. Alan drew closer. The man-woman seemed completely unconcerned. She walked along, head held high, ignoring the boys.

When no confrontation developed, Alan slowed his pace; and the man-woman, still followed by the boys, disappeared down the street.

*

From the center of the bridge, the Rhine-Main Canal appeared completely deserted. Alan leaned over the railing and stared into the dark silent water. No boats troubled the surface. There was no one else on the bridge, and no cars along the road approaching it. No one in the backyards of the houses along the shore—one of which must be the duplex where Alan had lived with his parents twenty-five years earlier. No other person in sight. Alan was alone.

His heart felt as desolate as the canal.

From Fürth station, Alan had taken a bus down towards his family's apartment. He'd gotten off and walked past the old American gas station and the adjoining movie theater, which looked exactly as they had twenty-five years before, as if nothing had been touched since then—except for one sign: *This facility will close permanently on September eleventh*.

Half a mile down the road, what was left of their apartment stood deserted. The window glass had been broken, the window frames had rusted. You could see straight through the building and out the back. The structure had been reduced to a metal-concrete shell.

Gods! This was where he'd first become immersed in Wagner's *Tristan*. This was where he'd considered his own death after Julia's suicide. From here he'd left to visit Shannon in Frankfurt. And now it was ruins! Was *this* what he had come to Nuremberg to find?

Dresden and Berlin, Alan thought. *Hiroshima and Nagasaki*. He'd never visited Hiroshima while in Japan; he'd lived at the other end of the eight-hundred-mile-long island. But he'd seen pictures of the Peace Memorial, the burnt steel girders arching up from the tarnished white stone building.

He'd read of the destruction of war and the homeless refugees. *He* had not been bombed out; but standing in front of his old home, he felt like a refugee himself. Was he welcome in his own homeland? Was he welcome anywhere? Could any country be home for him—Pagan and polyamorous? He felt the weight of eyes upon him: Shannon, Thea—and that woman on the plane to Chicago.

A three-mile walk along a lonely road, through the small village of Zirndorf and the even smaller village of Dambach, had brought Alan to his old duplex, off the western edge of Fürth. Here he had snuggled with Thea.

A few American families remained, but his old home and most of the adjoining houses had been reclaimed by Germans.

The Americans and Germans had fought each other in two massive wars. Yet he was part German. And maybe more than just the physical part descended from remote German ancestors. Part of his soul was German. He had loved living in Germany, studying German history, speaking and writing German.

Now Alan stared at the quiet waters of the canal. This link between North Sea and Black Sea was to have turned Nuremberg into a major port. It must have failed. One more disappointment with something he'd hoped to be proud of.

Bavaria had offered Alan nothing. He'd felt so certain that he would recover his soul here. But the university in Munich had closed, the apartment in Fürth lay in ruins, the Dambach home had been repossessed. Everything was gone.

*

In the dimming light of the summer evening, the crucifix of the Sebaldus Church confronted him. What a dreadful day! Waiting for the bus to bring him back from Zirndorf, Alan had discovered a giant blister on his foot. It was painful to walk. Luckily he'd brought his sandals and could change in his room.

Leaving the hotel for the second time in five hours, Alan had walked the lively Königstrasse, admired the sidewalk cafes, and wished for a friend to share dinner with. Sitting alone at a table, out on the street where everyone could see him, he would have felt completely cut off from the happy crowds around him.

Up the street across the river Pegnitz, the Heiliggeistspital, the old medieval hospice, still had charmed with its quaint gables. Market Square with its churches and mechanical clock had still comforted. Now though, as the sky hastened towards evening, Jesus still hung tortured on the cross on the side of the Sebaldus Church.

Chords from an *a cappella* choir pierced the evening from within. A figure swung out the front of the building, closed the massive wooden doors behind him, and slumped against the wall. The dark personage remained eyes closed: The man-woman Alan had seen earlier on the subway, dressed now in a black skirt and sweater. She opened her eyes, looked directly at Alan, sighed deeply, and approached him.

"Isn't it amazing? Bach's *Mass in B Minor;* the Catholic Mass set for choir and orchestra, the most beautiful music in the world." She paused, considered a moment, and added: "I used to lead that choir."

She shuffled about, eyes on the cobblestones, then said disdainfully: "They've thrown me out. I can't even sit and listen." She paced the cobblestones. "They said I wasn't Christian. They told me a Christian wouldn't act the way I do. Maybe it's true. Perhaps I'm no longer a Christian. But I follow Christ."

Alan's embarrassment had passed; his surprise had changed to interest. "What do you mean?"

The man-woman smiled. "It's hard to explain, and yet it's so simple. Most people have no idea… I follow Jesus, and most Christians follow…Paul…or the Pope…or the Patriarch…or…or the Bible."

Alan looked at her in astonishment. He'd read these ideas in books, but never met anyone who actually expressed them. "But—I'm sorry; what's your name?"

"You can call me Sally."

"Look, Sally. You say you're a Christian, but you don't follow the Bible?"

"Most of the Bible has nothing to do with Jesus. The Jewish scriptures; the letters of Paul—who never met him; the letters of the other apostles—who misunderstood him; a psychotic hallucination about the end-time of the world; only one sliver—the gospels—actually describing Jesus; only three gospels actually anchored in history; the gospel of John careening in from an entirely different angle."

Sally swung back towards the church. "Look at him!" She stretched an arm towards the crucifix. "Look at the Savior there suffering! Through the ages he watches as we hate and destroy one another. To each of us he asks the same question: *Why? Why do you hate? Why can't you embrace one another in love? Must I be crucified again in every generation?*"

The words struck Alan like a sledgehammer. He remembered Jesus cleansing the Temple. He remembered the *Haggadah*, the Jewish Passover story: *"In every generation we are brought again out of Egypt…"* He didn't know how to respond.

Alan turned and headed back towards Market Square. But Sally followed him.

"Imagine!" Sally's eyes glowed as she spoke. "Hitler stood on this very spot, surrounded by Hess and Goebbels and Goering."

"I've seen the photographs."

"Do you know why the Church of Our Lady, the Frauenkirche, was built on this spot?"

"No." Alan had never asked such questions when he lived with his parents in Nuremberg.

"This was the site of the Jewish ghetto, in the Middle Ages. Then came the pogroms: 1298, 1349, and so on. The Jews were expelled. The Christians 'sanitized' the city. For three hundred and fifty years—until 1850—Nuremberg was *Judenfrei*—'Free of Jews.' Jews were forbidden to live here! It didn't start with Hitler." Her voice was quivering with rage and shame. "Jesus commanded us to love! Why doesn't anybody listen?"

The only reply was their footsteps over the cobblestones.

"But Sally! The 'Beautiful Fountain,' *Der Schöne Brunnen*, in the corner of the square; the sculptures above it, the three figures on top—don't they represent the Christian, Jewish, and Heathen civilizations?"

"Oh yes," Sally sneered, "It's easy to say that now. But where were the citizens of the 'Holy Roman Empire' when the Crusaders sacked Constantinople—a crown jewel of Christendom—and slaughtered the Muslims of Palestine? They were there, leading the charge!" She spoke with absolute derision.

"Sally, have you always been so…so passionate about…history and religion? Where I'm from, people don't feel personally connected to their history. Most people don't think the Past affects them."

The Man-Woman stopped, thought a moment, then continued walking. "I have a family connection to the Middle East and Asia. It has given me a different perspective."

Alan now noticed that Sally's skin was, perhaps, marginally darker than his.

They walked east, past the Lawrence Church. After a long silence, Alan said:

"Do you always dress as a woman? Are you planning to actually become one?"

Sally stopped and turned to him. "No. I don't want to physically become a woman. I just want to wear women's clothing—sometimes. Is that hard for you to understand?" She delivered the words like a challenge.

Alan hesitated. "No," he answered in a low voice. "Not at all. I understand it completely." He paused, then added: "I do it sometimes myself."

The accumulated stress of the day swept through him. As Alan began to cry, Sally took him into his arms; and they kissed.

The cooling summer evening was perfect for walking—the moon's crescent floated above them; and in the short time it took them to cross the old medieval downtown, they opened to one another.

As a man, Sally had studied music and religion, hoping to become a minister. But the more she read, the more dissatisfied she became with Protestant theology. The alternatives—Catholicism, Eastern Orthodoxy—appealed to her even less. As she matured she realized her sexuality was fluid and unconventional and the personality of Sally evolved. She tried to remain respectful in church—she wanted to continue working with church music—but the church had finally dismissed her from the choir. She'd gone to Fürth to plead with the new director to at least let her remain in the choir, but the director insisted she dress like a man. That evening the minister himself had told her to leave

Soon Alan and Sally were holding hands in Hans Sachs Square, admiring the statue of the Nuremberg cobbler-poet so dear to the composer Richard Wagner. Alan had come to this square many times when he lived in Nuremberg, to feed his Wagner-obsession. Wagner had made Sachs, the historical figure from sixteenth-century Nuremberg, the hero of his comic opera *Die Meistersinger—The Mastersingers*. For Alan, Sachs became a spiritual teacher, a wise man.

But now this man, this...woman Sally. It had been so long since Alan had been close to another man; yet Sally was so unusual, so authentic. And what did *Sally* think of *him*?

"Ah—Sachs!" Alan exclaimed. "Sachs is wise, like an Indian yogi. He's found serenity beyond Illusion and Madness!" Sachs looked up kindly from his paper and pen.

Sachs rose from the pavement, just as Alan remembered him; the same statue. The last time Alan had seen him, the square had been under reconstruction. Now the square looked pristine—as if the War had never happened.

But Sally seemed uneasy about the statue. She seemed conflicted about something. Her vulnerability melted Alan's heart; and Alan kissed her again.

They headed towards the train station.

Alan was so happy walking with Sally. As they strolled along the street together, Alan looked at the sidewalk cafes and thought of dinner. But Sally showed no interest in eating. She was hurrying now across town.

Sally led Alan down the length of Königstrasse towards the wide stairs that descended to the underground mall next to the train station.

"I need to check the train schedule," she told him. "I'm going to Bayreuth tomorrow."

"Bayreuth? You like Wagner? You're attending the festival?"

"No, I don't like Wagner. My mother and fiancée do. I don't anymore. His family was too involved with the Nazis. I loved him till I saw the photos of his daughter-in-law and grandchildren with Hitler. He hated Mendelssohn. He hated Jews. Damned Wagner!" Sally spit in disgust. "Anyway my friend Rudi's gotten me interested in Bach. Plus he builds great cabinets, Rudi. I'd be buried under LPs without him!" They continued down the street, then Sally added: "I'm supposed to meet my fiancée tomorrow in Bayreuth."

"You're getting married?"

"Yes. A woman from Tel Aviv. Her mother doesn't approve."

"Mothers seldom do."

Alan followed Sally into the underground passage. The outside light faded, replaced by yellow florescence.

"You practice The Old Religion, you say?" Sally asked, still charging ahead. They'd dropped hands because Sally was walking so quickly, but they still occasionally patted each other's backs. "I'd love to have a Pagan priest perform our wedding ritual. All the ministers we've talked with have refused to have anything to do with it."

The underground passage was huge. When he'd walked through earlier, Alan had been preoccupied and hadn't noticed the stores stretching off in every direction. The complex must be immense: An actual underground mall.

As they walked further, Alan began to worry. Stores were closing up. It was past eight o'clock. They met fewer shoppers. Their route had veered quite out of the way.

Then Alan noticed the boys walking close behind them; four or five; some to the right, some to the left. Several were well into adolescence, and quite muscular. When Alan and Sally sped up, the boys sped up. When Alan and Sally changed directions, so did the boys.

"Sally—" Alan's cry interrupted Sally's history of the early church. "Sally, I saw boys following you this afternoon." Alan leaned closer and whispered: "I think they're following us now."

Sally's eyes blazed. Without turning her head she seemed to ascertain the position of every person walking near them. Her gaze narrowed to the wide stairs up to the train station, fifty feet ahead of them.

"Walk towards the stairs," Sally whispered. "Ignore what I do, ignore what they do. Get out of the underground as quickly as possible. Don't look back. Don't try to help me, whatever happens. I can handle this."

"Should I find the police?" Alan asked nervously.

He sensed a lunge in their direction. Sally was halfway down the corridor to the right, the gang of boys chasing her. Alan ran up the stairs and into the train station. Emerging into the well-lit spacious lobby, Alan felt suddenly alone. The station was quiet, nearly deserted. A few young people sat eating at a small café.

Alan continued to the shops—all closed—and the food stands, attended by badly-shaven, greasy old men.

"There's been a fight in the underground passage." The vendor didn't seem to understand. "A fight. A woman was attacked by a group of boys. Down there." Alan pointed towards the underground. The greasy man returned to grilling his sausage.

On the street, no sign of Sally or the boys. Night had arrived, dropping blackness on the town.

In the hotel room, later, the TV news droned on. The war in the Balkans had heated up. The Croatian army had pushed into Krajina. Serbian refugees—women, children, and old men, looking unbelievably dirty and lost—streamed down the roads away from the battle.

Music from the Balkans flooded back to Alan from long years of folk-dancing: The irregular rhythms and piercing sonorities of Bulgaria and the now-disintegrating Yugoslavia.

Alan missed his work for Human Rights International. He felt he'd achieved some good on behalf of prisoners of conscience in various countries. Now he could be working on behalf of the Bosnians and Serbs. He remembered myriad folk-dances that he and Vicki had learned, and he ached for William Bao; would anyone ever see William again?

A human-interest story about a carpenter in the German state of Saxony followed the news from Croatia. The young balding carpenter had built a table-sized Lazy Susan and sawed a large hole in the center. While he lay on his back below the table, his wife settled into the hole and rotated above him. Carpenter and wife both were naked. Something about the woman seemed familiar; but the camera angle and way the woman swayed her head in her pleasure prevented Alan from getting a clear look at her.

*

Sinking into sleep, Alan thought of Sally. What had become of her?

Alan had watched for her on his way back from the train station. He'd passed the old Bavarian-American Hotel, the first place he'd slept in Germany, twenty-six years before. Central Nuremberg had seemed totally deserted. On his way upstairs he'd knocked at Sophie Neufeld's door, but no one had answered.

Alan liked Sally, but she intimidated him. He'd probably never know whether Sally had escaped the gang. Alan hadn't asked Sally's last name, hadn't gotten a card, and had no idea how to contact her. Alan planned to leave Nuremberg the following day—but for where? He hadn't found his soul.

Or was Sally a pointer towards his soul? Should he stay and look for Sally? But how could he find her?

Something drew him to this woman—this man-woman. She seemed as heretical as he was, as unconventional. This man cross-dressed as Sally, and did so publicly. Sally seemed drawn to him too. But how to find her in a city of half a million?

And Sally was going to be married. That didn't bode well for a relationship—unless groom and bride were both poly. Alan wondered if many Germans were polyamorous; it was such an insignificant minority in America. He felt an attraction to Sally, but wasn't going to abandon Vicki and Lavender and Gayle.

If he couldn't find Sally in Nuremberg, why not go to Bayreuth?—it was less than an hour north. He'd visited once to attend the Wagner Festival and he knew his way around. Alan adored Wagner, in spite of what Sally had told him. The festival should have begun—it was always in July and August. And—who knows?—perhaps he'd find Sally again. Sally had been planning to travel there. He might even find his soul.

Before sleep finally came, the Serbian refugees confronted Alan with weary, accusing faces: Dust, dirt, and misery. Why such misery in the world? Why so much killing?

Then the naked wife of the naked carpenter, turning on the Lazy Susan.

For an instant, she looked directly at him, her blond hair parting down either side of her bare shoulders. But Alan was relaxing into sleep and couldn't quite connect to his blond memories of Nymphenburg.

SIX

Thursday morning, on the train to Bayreuth, Alan tried to understand what had happened so far that day.

He'd hurried to a bank after breakfast to cash a traveler's check. The mosaic on the wall—the final scene of Wagner's *Meistersinger*—had caught him off guard. The wall depicted Hans Sachs awarding the Master Prize to Walter, the young tenor. *"Let the Holy Roman Empire pass into dust,"* Sachs asserted via the caption, *"We still shall have Holy German Art."*

Alan had run to tell Sophie Neufeld.

"Impressive, isn't it? That was my son's doing. He convinced the bank to commission it."

"Was that difficult?"

"Some people thought it was too nationalistic: *Holy German Art*. Others thought it was silly to place Art above The Nation. But Herr Neufeld is widely respected."

"You said you were connected to Frau Neufeld in Munich. What's the connection?"

Sophie Neufeld had hesitated a moment. "Frieda Neufeld is Friedrich's first wife. I am his…second. He's in Berlin now."

"With his third?" Alan had asked, as a joke.

The remark startled Frau Neufeld; but she'd come back quickly: "Exactly. Marthe Neufeld. Friedrich…left me this pension." An awkward silence had followed, and Alan had changed the subject.

"Last night a young German I was with was attacked by gang of boys. She told me to run and I ran. I never saw any of them again." He hesitated then added: "This person…is actually a man, but he dresses as a woman. Do you have any idea where I might find her? I…thought I saw her here yesterday."

This had jolted Sophie Neufeld again for an instant. "That was my son Gustav. He's in hospital, I'm afraid. He mentioned meeting a rather unusual American. I hadn't anticipated it would be you."

Alan's mind had blanked. "Sally? Gustav? Your son?"

"Technically he's adopted. We took him in as a child. Friedrich and I have no biological children."

Now, from the train, Alan watched the Franconian hills of northern Bavaria glide by. He reached into his bag and drew forth again the envelope Sophie Neufeld had handed him as he checked out. Gustav had given it to his mother on the chance that Alan was at the hotel.

Dear Alan,

I have a big favor to ask you. Could you possibly deliver a message for me? I mentioned my fiancée last night; at the moment you're the only way I have of reaching her. She's somewhere in Bayreuth; I don't know exactly where.

I want you to know that I wasn't seriously injured, but I need to remain in the hospital a little longer. I enjoyed our talk last evening. I hope to soon thank you personally for your troubles.

Go to the Bayreuth Festival House at noon. I'm including a train pass. My fiancée Naomi Herzlieb will be looking for me there. Give her the enclosed letter.

You'll recognize Naomi from the enclosed photo. She'll be holding a sign asking for tickets to this evening's performance of Tristan und Isolde, *though I told her I wasn't interested.*

If you like, accompany her to the performance yourself; that's fine with me.

Eternal Thanks,
Sally Neufeld

"He used to love Wagner so," Sophie Neufeld had sighed, "before he discovered Wagner's virulence—the nationalism, the anti-Semitism. Now the whole business disgusts him."

"I notice he signed himself Sally."

"We named him for Gustav Mahler, the composer. Do you know him, Mr. Horne? In his symphonies, Mahler never did what anyone expected. He thought it lazy to be conventional."

"That sounds like your son."

Sophie Neufeld had sighed again. "Being unconventional, Gustav naturally had to change his name—and appearance."

As he ascended the hill to the Festspielhaus, the simple brick theater that Richard Wagner had built for the first Bayreuth Festival in 1876, Alan spotted Naomi standing with the other petitioners to the left of the building in front of the ticket office. She held a small sign: *Seeking tickets for tonight's performance.* The office wasn't open, of course. All sales were done by mail, years in advance.

As he walked towards the building, he observed that Naomi was even more attractive than her photograph: Solid, blue-eyed, blond; perhaps in her early twenties; beautiful.

"Excuse me, are you Naomi Herzlieb?"

"Yes I am." She seemed surprised, but impressed. "Do I know you?"

"I'm Alan Horne. I'm visiting from America."

Now she looked even more puzzled.

"There's no reason you should know me, Fräulein. I met your fiancé last evening in Nuremberg. He ran into some trouble, and asked me to meet you and explain that he couldn't come up today."

"Trouble?"

Should he mention Gustav's dress? "He got into a scrape with some ruffians, and ended up in the hospital."

At this Naomi lost her composure. "What? I should go to Nuremberg! Is he all right?"

"He gave me a letter for you."

Naomi ripped open the envelope and scanned the page. "Thanks heavens! It isn't serious. He can still come to Berlin on Monday."

"Monday?" But Monday wasn't really his business.

"Our wedding; and the anniversary party for Herr Neufeld and his wife."

"Number three." Alan hadn't meant this to slip out.

"Yes, they met two years ago."

Naomi's smile reassured him. She had set down her hand-made sign. She wore an attractive star-necklace.

"Any luck getting tickets?"

"None. It usually takes seven years. But in 1988, I didn't know I was going to be here." She smiled again. "Do you like Wagner, Mr.—What did you say your name was?"

"Horne. Alan Horne. I'm American, but my ancestors came from the state of Hesse."

"Really? *Mine* lived near Weimar in Thuringia for hundreds of years."

Naomi smiled with straightforward, honest happiness. Her blue eyes, wrapped in blond hair, made it difficult to look away.

"Do I like Wagner?" Alan couldn't help laughing. "I *adore* Wagner. When I was a teenager, I fell in love with *Lohengrin*, then the *Ring*, then *Tristan*. My parents didn't know what to make of it."

"Perhaps we could get tickets together." Naomi's eyes shone. "For this evening." She was studying him now, and her tone expressed entreaty and vulnerability.

"I don't expect you'll find tickets."

"Probably not." Nevertheless she was positively beaming. "But I brought my own recording with me. I have the stereo in my room." Her eyes glowed. "If we can't get tickets, we can go back and listen to the whole five hours. That's what I told Gustav we'd do. It would be a wonderful evening!"

"But I'm not Gustav. You're engaged to Gustav. You want us to listen to *Tristan* together, in your room? Will anyone else be there?" *Tristan*: The glorification of adultery.

Naomi laughed. "Did you think I'd bring my mother along for *Tristan*? I'll meet her back in Weimar tomorrow. My future mother-in-law's here—she drove us up from Munich—but we've got separate hotel rooms. She's down in the city right now." Her face grew serious. "I meant this for Gustav and me, but he had business in Nuremberg. He's turned against Wagner now anyway. And he's in the hospital...and you're not." She noticed his confusion. "Gustav says very nice things about you...in his letter. You've impressed him, Mr. Horne." She added quietly: "In fact, we'd be honored if you would bless our marriage next Monday."

She pulled a printed card from her pocket and handed it to him:

Celebrating the marriage of Naomi Herzlieb and Sally Neufeld
Monday, August 7, 1995, 7 p.m.
Gate of Heavenly Peace
Kleiststrasse at Nollendorfplatz
Berlin

When he looked back up she added: "Gustav says you worship the Old Gods."

It overwhelmed him suddenly. The beautiful blonde...and the man-woman he'd kissed the previous evening. Alan turned to walk down the hill, but reconsidered, turned back, and said brusquely:

"He wears dresses, you know. He calls himself Sally. They've thrown him out of his church." He started down the hill.

"He likes the name Sally," she yelled after him. "You've heard of Sally Bowles, in the musical *Cabaret*? We don't care about his church anymore; we want a Pagan priest."

He nearly stopped when she mentioned *Cabaret*. The musical was based on stories by Christopher Isherwood, Alan's favorite author. Alan glanced back from the bottom of the hill.

"We've planned this all together!" Naomi shouted. "You must know something about Tantra!" Then Alan was around the corner, card jammed into his pocket. Had she really mentioned *Tantra*? Did she and Sally practice sexual mysticism?

As he walked back towards the city, Alan's thoughts hurried along as quickly as his feet. He passed Tristan Alley and continued down Nibelung Street—everything had Wagnerian names. The confrontation with Naomi had opened his Inner Sight. His mind was full of music—music and myth. Themes from Wagner played in his head.

Then—unexpectedly—he saw Hitler walking up the street towards the Festspielhaus, greeted by cheering crowds. He caught himself humming the "Horst Wessel Lied" again. Earlier, on his way *up* the hill, he'd thought only of the "Rome Monologue"—that tortured narration—from Wagner's opera of conflicted sexuality, *Tannhäuser.*

It bothered him to be thinking so much about Hitler. Hitler must represent something significant whose meaning was unclear, one of those Major Arcana cards from his Tarot reading. Yet Alan couldn't think of Hitler as pure evil, as most people did. In that case he could have understood him. He couldn't consider Hitler insane or deluded like Caligula or Nero. In fact, if he tried very hard, he could imagine Hitler as his supporters must have thought of him: A talented, devoted, and energetic man utterly dedicated to redeeming Germany. It was true that in order to think of Hitler this way, Alan had to block out The Leader's flaws: The personality disorders, the irrational hatred of Jews and others, the viciousness. Blocking those out, the iron will and the ability to master endless details might be seen as the traits of an exceptional leader. But the flaws couldn't be ignored. A slight change of genetics or experience might have produced a beneficent Hitler. Then the War and the Holocaust might never have happened. But there had been no beneficent Hitler, only the demonic one. Why? Why the Demonic, not the Beneficent?

Alan headed for Wagner's villa, Wahnfried—"Peace from Delusion." The walk took thirty minutes.

Old Bayreuth enchanted him: From the train station, across the narrow river, down into the mass of old buildings; the castle on the hill above; past the old opera house (once the largest stage in Europe), all the way to the villa.

Naomi annoyed him. She'd come to the festival looking for tickets when she knew there wouldn't be any. She'd left her mother in Weimar to spend the evening—the *night*—with Gustav. She'd come with her future mother-in-law (Alan assumed she meant the third Frau Neufeld—but why had they met in Munich?).

This wasn't how a German woman should behave, how Gustav's fiancée should behave. But—he knew so little of Gustav…and Germans, actually. How should *any* of them behave?

It annoyed Alan that Naomi had invited him to attend *Tristan* with her, to listen to *Tristan* back in her hotel room. Her casual remark: *Gustav's in the hospital…and you're not.*

It bothered Alan that Naomi was involved with Gustav at all, was involved with *Sally*.

And the two were familiar with Tantra—the yoga of enlightenment via the ordinary world, including sex.

Alan was jealous. Jealous of Naomi: The tall, beautiful, blond, statuesque woman whom Gustav loved instead of Alan. Jealous of Gustav: The direct, sincere, sensitive manwoman whom Naomi loved instead of Alan.

Alan was jealous because Alan was drawn to them *both*!

Wahnfried hadn't changed in twenty-five years: A two-story stone building, the approach crowned by a bust of King Ludwig II on a pedestal.

None of this would have existed without Ludwig. Ludwig had fallen in love with Wagner's music when he was twelve (some thought he had fallen love with Wagner). The king had offered Wagner whatever he needed to complete the *Ring*, that fifteen-hour cycle of four mythological operas that spanned the world's creation and its destruction. Wagner had nearly bankrupted the Kingdom of Bavaria.

Alan was surprised to find that Wahnfried was no longer the private residence of the Wagner family. They had apparently donated the building to the city or state. Wahnfried was now a museum!

After walking behind the villa to kneel at The Master's grave, Alan ventured inside. This was no longer just a visit—it was a pilgrimage. Alan had never expected to get *inside*.

He stifled a gasp as he entered the lobby. The museum was hosting an exhibit called "Redemption Through Love." Gayle would have loved this. Gayle believed in the healing power of authentic sexuality. She had a genius for the erotic. Vicki did not—and that probably unsettled Vicki.

"Redemption Through Love" featured pictures, set-models, and costumes from Bayreuth productions, illustrating "Love in the Works of Richard Wagner."

Before heading downstairs to view the exhibit, Alan explored the main floor, where Wagner had worked and entertained his guests. Hitler would have come here to visit

Winifred Wagner, the Englishwoman who had abandoned her homeland to marry The Master's son.

Germany, America, and England were all somehow linked. The American colonists had come from England. The Anglo-Saxons had come from Germany. Hitler had won over a number of Englishmen and Americans. That suggested a cautionary tale.

Music floated in from the drawing room; but the selection ended as Alan arrived. Before him stood Wagner's grand piano, around him rose Wagner's library—three walls from floor to ceiling. Alan pictured Wagner sitting at the piano working; entertaining Ludwig, King of Bavaria or Bismarck, Imperial Chancellor; and Winifred, much later, greeting The Leader—*Der Führer*—with a smile and warm words. *The Leader has united us*—*"One People, One Empire, One Leader!"*

Americans as well as Germans seemed susceptible to the idea of Empire. Like Germans, Americans sometimes thought they were better than others. Like Germans, Americans didn't always take other cultures seriously. They weren't alone in this flaw. China, Russia, Arabia, Persia, Europe, Rome—various countries and religions—had done the same.

The music resumed: The "Prize Song" from *Meistersinger*, matching perfectly Alan's mood: The bright summer sun flooding the room with light, filling it from floor to tall ceiling with brilliance and clarity, filling Alan with energy, light, love, exuberance. *This was where it had all happened!* Perhaps Gayle and Vicki could join him here someday—attend the festival, visit the villa and the town; perhaps even winter in the Alps!

Imagining this, Alan could imagine himself happy. Here he felt connected to history and art. If he could live here, in these surroundings, with the people he loved…might he not say he had found his soul?

He hurried down to the exhibit: Rooms full of pictures, placards, models, and props. He and Gayle and Vicki would have so much to discuss here!

Then he explored the smaller rooms towards the end of the building. In one of them a video was playing the second act of Wagner's opera of self-discovery and healing, *Parsifal*, where the young, innocent, un-understanding medieval seeker encounters the mysterious woman Kundry. Kundry had mocked Jesus on the cross and endured innumerable incarnations awaiting a second opportunity for redemption. Parsifal meanwhile has wandered for years after failing to heal the Grail King, the Ruler of the Wasteland, the man whom Kundry had ruined. With the king unhealed, the land remains wasted and barren, like a shriveled soul. Kundry thinks that sex with Parsifal will somehow bring her salvation; but when they kiss, Parsifal remembers the King and his own healing mission. He resumes his quest, leaving Kundry to struggle with his rejection.

The video skipped to the final scene, where Parsifal returns to the Grail Castle to heal the wounded king. Alan, deep in thought, entered the adjoining room. Above him hung the Sacred Spear of Longinus—the spear that pierced Jesus on the cross!—from the first Bayreuth production in 1882. Below, on a small round table, sat the Cup—the Grail—which caught Jesus' blood! Both were lit faintly from above.

Ah, he thought, *the Grail! The mysterious object that resonates with every person's soul and connects it to the Universe! Both the Philosopher's Stone and the chalice Jesus drank from at his Last Supper—"Drink ye all of it." Or is the Grail Mary Magdalene and Mary Mother of Jesus—The Goddess in all her complexity?*

An older woman interrupted his musings. "Excuse me." She appeared to be in her fifties, rather well-dressed and spiffy, with fading red hair. "Can you tell me what time it is?"

"Nineteen after the hour."

"Thank you." With her eyes, she indicated the Spear and Chalice; and Alan noticed a sign on the small round table.

"The relics will be illumined on the hour, and at regular twenty minute intervals."

The woman smiled knowingly. The chalice began to glow; the cup grew brighter, as if from within. The spear glistened. "Are you one of the Chosen?" she asked.

Alan had located the source of the light: A small, brilliant lamp in a corner of the ceiling. He had missed the woman's last words.

"What?"

She repeated the question. Was she serious or ironic? Alan couldn't tell.

Then it all hit him: Naomi, Sally, this grotesque older woman. What did she mean, "one of the chosen?" Did she mean Wagnerian, German, Nazi, Aryan, Christian, White? Alan's head was spinning; he felt he was about to faint.

"Excuse me. Excuse me please." Alan rushed out of the room and up the stairs. He glanced one last time into the lobby and drawing room. The music still played, the light still streamed through the large windows. He thought of the Castle of Marvels, the Castle of Illusions, the magic castle of temptation in the Grail legends.

He had to get away. Bayreuth, Bavaria, and Germany had deranged him. He was losing his balance, he was coming unhinged. France—the museums, the chateaux, the beautiful countryside he had scarcely seen (he had visited Paris just once, only for a weekend)—perhaps it could calm him down, bring sanity back to his life. Perhaps *that* was what he needed—a place not so familiar, not so laden with memories and expectations. A place not so *Wagnerian*. The Loire valley…

SEVEN

An hour later Alan Horne found himself in a wheat field west of Bayreuth, wondering why he was there.

He had taken the first available train—a local—west towards Frankfurt. From Frankfurt he could continue to Paris, England, Spain, Ireland; anywhere. To Switzerland. To the Loire Valley in France—Alan had always wanted to visit the chateaux.

He had faced the fact that he needed to leave Germany. His old college and homes were gone. Bayreuth had raised his hopes again—he'd forgotten how intensely he loved Wagner. But Naomi and the eccentric woman at Wahnfried had scared him. From the train he had watched the German countryside, thought of Gayle and Vicki, Naomi and Gustav.

But he'd gotten off again only twenty miles west of Bayreuth. Some memory of the city gnawed at him. The local train stopped everywhere, and just as Alan lost his nerve, the train had pulled in at what was supposed to be a Franconian village; but Alan saw nothing but wheat in all directions. Farmers mounted the train as Alan stumbled off with his duffles. The engineer must have wondered what Alan was doing. The train ambled off as Alan stood by the tracks.

The question returned: *What now?* It was good he had a train pass, even if it was Sally's.

Twelve days earlier he'd been sipping wine at a sidewalk cafe in sunny California with his wife of fifteen years. Their marriage had been challenging since they were both bisexual and polyamorous; but they shared a common religion—Pagan Unitarian—and genuinely cared for one another. The business with Preston and Janie, the pregnancy, the birth of Lavender had all been tribulations—but the couple seemed to have come through. Alan hadn't thought his new relationship with Gayle would cause any major difficulty.

Then Vicki announced she was leaving with Claire and probably moving out. Gayle's Tarot reading and his parents' insistence he leave for Germany clarified nothing and introduced some truly peculiar characters.

But in France Alan could plunge into the art-world of Paris, the history, the sheer beauty; Versailles; Fontainebleau; Normandy; the chateaux of the Loire; the cathedrals: Chartres, Reims.

And his daughter, his wife, his girlfriend—his soul?

He couldn't go back to Gayle without something to say about his soul—Gayle would want to know what had happened. She was more attuned to the spiritual than Vicki was—but so far he had nothing to report. Left alone, he might abandon the quest or decide that they had misunderstood the Tarot. But Gayle would ask him how the quest had gone. So would his parents. Then again, he had to do what *he* needed—not what Gayle or his parents wanted. It was *his* soul that was in jeopardy.

He'd first met Gayle online when she emailed him for advice on polyamory. He'd been trying to start a poly support group and had been posting messages on computer bulletin boards. Within a week Alan had walked into the music room where Vicki sat reading and announced: "I think I'm in falling in love with Gayle."

"How can you fall in love with someone you've never met?"

Alan had scowled; Vicki always devalued feelings and intuitions. "We share ideas, like you and I did when we first met. You remember how wrapped up in each other we were?"

"Love!" Vicki had snapped. "Falling in love is for teenagers. After the sighing and fawning, people have to live in the real world." Since the breakup with Preston and Janie she'd become an absolute cynic.

But Alan and Gayle grew closer, though they didn't meet for ten months, since she lived in Wisconsin.

When Gayle finally came to visit, the three tiptoed around each other at first. Gayle and Vicki hadn't even met by email—Vicki hated communicating; she hated being lured out of her shell. Alan spent the nights with Gayle in the guest room, then came in to Vicki in the morning.

Alan and Gayle took a short "honeymoon" on Monterey Bay one weekend around Beltane—May Day—while Vicki stayed home with Lavender. Now it was August, just past Lughnasadh. Gayle and Alan had met face to face only three months earlier.

As for Gustav and Naomi…they were both rather strange. Gustav dressed like a woman and didn't hide it. Naomi didn't mind; neither did Gustav's mother.

Alan and Gustav shared that, then. Perhaps Gustav's parents were not too different from Alan's.

But Gustav had gone public with his identity, while Alan couldn't. It scared him too much. It wasn't just fear or embarrassment for himself; he was trying to protect Vicki, who was much more fragile than he. Concern for Vicki checked his natural inclinations. Vicki was an impediment as well as a support.

And this father of Gustav's, who'd been married three times and apparently still helped each former wife with her business. How long had he spent with each? The wives apparently knew and acknowledged one another.

Alan wished them the best for this wedding next Moonday; but he wanted no part of it. He'd be far away, in Paris or on the Loire…

They liked Wagner though, some of them. They had that in common too. But Gustav had renounced Wagner, unlike Naomi—the tall, striking blonde…

A lot of Germany would pass in front of Alan before he arrived in Frankfurt to the west, traveled down the Rhine to Cologne, and headed further west towards Paris. He could sit in the dining car drinking beer and eating sausage. German sausage almost made him forget Chinese food—otherwise his favorite.

The sun was descending towards the waving shafts of wheat. He could be in Frankfurt after all for dinner. A distant speck appeared on the tracks…

As the train approached the stop in the middle of the wheat field, Alan's thoughts bolted far away. He'd remembered something he'd seen in Bayreuth but not consciously processed. He realized now what had been bothering him.

Naomi, the student of Tantra, who had offered him *Tristan* in Bayreuth, who was marrying Gustav in Berlin in four days—who loved Wagner as much as Alan (the full impact was sinking in)…

The star-necklace she'd been wearing…had six points, not five. She wore the six-pointed Jewish star, the Mogen David, around her neck.

But of course. Gustav had mentioned Tel Aviv. The dark German transvestite was marrying a tall, blue-eyed, blond, Wagnerian Israeli Jew.

EIGHT

Alan arrived in Weimar, in the state of Thuringia, formerly part of the communist "German Democratic Republic" (DDR), at six that evening, after a lovely ride through the beautiful mountainous Thuringian Forest. He had forty dollars in German cash, no map, and no idea where to find Naomi. She'd mentioned returning to her mother in Weimar, so Alan had gone there. Now he realized Naomi was still in Bayreuth, seventy miles behind him southeast, either watching *Tristan* or listening to the recording. She'd probably return in the morning, possibly with Marthe Neufeld.

Weimar Station, in contrast to the glistening stations of Bavaria such as Bayreuth, seemed downright *dirty*. The shops had already closed.

Across the street stood a small park. A few 1940s cars passed. Depressing. He should have continued to Paris!

Alan shuddered, remembering the train station men's room: Grimy walls and a badly shaven old concierge in shabby clothes, waiting for a tip. Alan decided he'd go in later—if he got desperate.

*

Around seven-thirty, after a useless walk looking for cheaper lodging, Alan dragged his luggage to the second floor desk of the Thuringian Hope and asked in a tired voice: *"Fräulein? Können Sie mir helfen?"*

The woman's back and red hair, all that Alan could see of her as she bent over her meager supplies, swung away. As the woman turned to face him, they both froze.

"Inge?"

"Mr. Horne? I didn't know you were coming to Weimar!" Inge had turned beet red, yet still seemed friendly and outgoing.

"I didn't know you were *in* Weimar. You work here, Inge?"

Inge's face had regained its ordinary hue. Her agreeable smile and green eyes, framed by her ample red hair, appealed to him.

"Inge, I need a room for tonight. And I'm awfully hungry; I haven't eaten."

"I believe we have something available, and I can recommend a restaurant down the street. One moment."

Inge spoke with a man inside the office and blushed again. She couldn't stop grinning. *Good God*, Alan thought. *She likes me.*

"We don't have any standard rooms, but we have the wedding suite. Since it's the only room available, you can have it for the standard rate—no extra charge. Here's your key—Room 555."

She looked at him, hesitated. "Mr. Horne, I'm off work in twenty minutes. Why don't you take your luggage upstairs then meet me here? I'm not doing anything this evening. I could show you that restaurant. It's particularly Thuringian. I think you'd like it."

Alan gave her a quizzical look. "Give me a moment to freshen up... Of course. I'd be delighted to have dinner with you."

They faced each other across the table. The restaurant, a half-mile down towards the old city, was dimly lit, with only a few other diners. Thuringian musical instruments adorned the ceiling and walls.

"You live in Weimar? I had no idea."

"When I met you I was down visiting Helga. We needed to talk about...business. Käthe and I helped her move to Hamburg yesterday. I only got back here this morning."

She sipped her beer.

"It's a long way to Hamburg—clear across Germany. Why did Helga move so far away?"

Inge ignored the question. "What brings *you* to Weimar, Alan? May I...call you Alan?"

"Of course. I suppose *Herr Horne* would be too formal." He smiled awkwardly. He had never understood German notions of formality. "I'm looking for someone, Inge. A woman."

She immediately became formal again. "Mr. Horne...I wouldn't have thought...I didn't think you knew anyone in Germany."

"I don't know this woman, Inge. Okay: I met her once, this morning, on someone else's behalf. I just want to clear up something with her. A misunderstanding."

Inge leaned forward intently.

"I believe she's currently in Weimar. Her name is Naomi Herzlieb."

Inge's face went white, she pulled back. "Naomi Herzlieb?" She thought a moment. "How could *you* know Naomi Herzlieb?"

He instinctively smirked. "She's marrying someone I met in Nuremberg." He thrust his knife and fork down on the table. "I suppose there's some reason *you* know her, Inge? Ever since I arrived in Germany—Gods!—It was only two days ago!—ever since I arrived, I've encountered the most exasperating people!"

Inge's face went red and she snapped, "Perhaps, Mr. Horne, if you don't like the people here you should return to America. Or avoid meeting them."

"Return to America!" he snorted, then added: "It seems impossible *not* to have met these people." Then he relaxed and broke into a grin.

"Okay. It was pure chance that I booked a room at Frieda Neufeld's pension in Munich and ended up meeting her daughter and her delightful friends—including you, of course." He smiled sarcastically. "On the other hand, does the Neufeld family have some kind of monopoly on the tourist accommodations in Germany? I continue to Nuremberg—I used to live there—and end up staying at the hotel of a *second* Frau Neufeld."

Inge's eyes widened. "I see. Sophie Neufeld. But that doesn't explain…"

"Oh yes! By fate or whatever, I encounter, quite on my own, Gustav Neufeld—or should I call him Sally?—as I'm visiting my old home on the outskirts of the city."

Inge's face expressed total astonishment.

"Gustav was supposed to meet Naomi Herzlieb today in Bayreuth," Alan went on. "Apparently she hoped they could attend the Festival—but he had a little accident."

Inge's eyes narrowed. "Did they beat him up again—those hooligans?" She stuffed a fork-full of cutlet into her mouth and chomped on it furiously. "Was he hurt?"

"Not badly. But they kept him in the hospital and he couldn't meet Fräulein Herzlieb."

Perhaps Inge cared about Gustav; she seemed lost in memories. Alan reached over and took her hand. This jolted her out of her reverie and she shot him an anguished look. Then she apparently remembered where she was.

"Gustav and I…were seeing each other…for a time." She could barely keep back tears.

"Inge—" But she was staring down at her plate. "Inge." He raised her face towards him. "What did he *do* to you?"

She tried to speak, then looked back down. Alan stroked her cheek and wiped away a tear.

"What did he do to you?"

Inge hesitated then looked straight at him. "He didn't do anything, really." She bit her lip, then continued: "He fell in love with me."

Her large green eyes reached out from the wrapping of red hair. "He fell in love with me while he was still engaged to Helga. Yes, Mr. Horne: Gustav and Helga were engaged for a time. They had known each other since childhood. Herr Neufeld adopted Gustav about the time he married Sophie. They could never determine exactly where Gustav was from. He came to Germany as a refugee when he was a boy. Friedrich and Sophie took him into their home in Nuremberg and he's lived there most of his life. Naturally, Gustav knew Friedrich's daughter from his *first* marriage." Inge squeezed Alan's hand.

"So how did *you* meet him, Inge?" They were now alone in the restaurant.

"He had come to Weimar after the collapse of the East. He was seventeen. He'd dreamt of visiting the homes of

Goethe and Schiller, the eighteenth-century German poets. I'd been studying at Weimar University. I was interested in Goethe as a 'citizen of the world.' You probably don't know much about Goethe. He wasn't just a great writer. He was also a scientist and statesman."

"Didn't Napoleon meet him and say *Behold the Man!?*"

"Something like that." She seemed impressed—and uncertain.

"Alan…If you'd like to see Goethe's house tomorrow, I…could meet you after lunch, around one o'clock. I have some business in the morning."

Alan broke into a grin. He felt quite at ease with her. She was easy to talk to. "Inge! I'd love to!"

They followed the meal with coffee and a rich Thuringian pastry; and left the restaurant hand in hand.

"Alan, didn't you see the hotel as soon as you stepped out of the train station? We're just across the street! Why didn't you come to us immediately?"

The blood rushed to Alan's cheeks. "I saw the hotel, of course. And I saw the new Stadthotel, over there. I thought it would be nicer. From the outside the Thuringian Hope seems…rather run down. But the Stadthotel was too expensive. So I walked awhile. When I walk I get the sense of a place. Weimar…seemed pretty dismal."

They stood on the edge of the park, across from the hotel. The sky had grown dark.

"I must tell you, Alan…" She never finished her sentence, because before she could finish it they kissed. He felt a natural attraction to Inge, as he had to Gustav.

"Inge…would you care to…would you…" They kissed again. "Would you like to come up for awhile? You did give me the wedding suite."

Inge grinned. "I think I'd better not, Alan. I don't think my supervisor would approve."

Alan turned and sighed. "We wouldn't have to *do* anything," he snorted, angry.

"I know how that sort of thing goes." She took his face in her hands and kissed him slowly and deliberately. "Goodnight, Alan. Tomorrow at one, here." She faded down the gloomy street, into the night, around the corner.

After a moment warmed by the memory of Inge's kiss, Alan realized he had learned nothing about Naomi.

From his room, Alan looked out the rear of the hotel. Gazing past the adjoining building—totally dark and unoccupied—Alan saw a single streetlight and no automobiles. On the major street that ran past the train station, at ten p.m., Weimar already seemed like a tomb.

The bedroom had two king-sized beds and a dresser. The suite included a second room with radio and television, chairs and a coffee table; and a bathroom with a bath *and* separate shower.

He thought of his honeymoon with Gayle in Monterey, and their embarrassment in Chicago. Did it matter that he couldn't...?

What was Vicki doing with Claire? It wasn't that Alan was *jealous*; he was merely "concerned." Vicki was not only his wife and lover—she was his closest friend.

Alan pulled back the comforter on one of the king-sized beds and switched off the light. His fifth-floor windows were wide-open, but the oppressive summer air still hung heavy.

He had known Vicki so long...and he loved Gayle so intensely.

But who was this Inge he'd kissed? He'd kissed Gustav too, the night before. What did he want from these people? Did he want relationships? Did he *know* what he wanted?

Why was he opening himself up to them? Would opening himself up lead him towards his soul? Was it wise to let himself be drawn to them?

Touching his sweaty body, he thought of Gayle. Gods! He missed the intimacy—Gayle's understanding, Vicki's understanding.

Now—Praise Hermes!—his body responded—as it hadn't in Chicago and Monterey...

NINE

Alan felt particularly happy heading for breakfast Friday morning. Following his romantic episode, he had slept well, awoken satisfied, and only grown happier as the beauty of the morning sank in: The sky a deep blue, the air clear. Weimar in the morning sun did not intimidate him as it had the night before.

Perhaps by understanding his needs—sex, beauty, leisure, sleep, whatever—Alan could retrieve his soul.

Another perfect breakfast beckoned, such as Alan never enjoyed in California (he always ate at work). Alan had abandoned his "business" state of mind. He was doing things at his own pace now, rather than by dictation.

After sex with himself and a good night's sleep, anticipating a wonderful and relaxed breakfast, Alan felt happy. But would "happiness" lure back his soul?

Breakfasts were now a high point of Alan's days in Germany. Waking up centered and eating a relaxed breakfast meant a lot to Alan.

German continental breakfasts had apparently expanded, since Alan's college days, beyond bread and jam to include cheese, ham and deli meats; even boiled eggs.

The dining room of the Thuringian Hope had been re-modeled into something resembling a greenhouse, a sun-room extension of the main building. A wall of glass curved up over a third of the room. Side glass panels ascended to the partially glass ceiling. Sunlight from the nearly cloudless deep blue sky poured in as far as some of the buffet trays. Alan grew ecstatic: Not merely happy—*ecstatic*. Something about food: Enjoying food, eating slowly, sitting quietly, and appreciating life. A mini-illumination—a mini-satori, they would say in Zen. He felt intimacy with foods and dining.

He filled his plate with breads, meats, cheese and an egg, grabbed butter and jams, and took a seat. He breathed deeply as if inhaling the very sunlight, and surveyed the room.

Weimar, in Thuringia. The former DDR: The virgin Germany he had never before seen.

He could imagine how beautiful Weimar would be if it were all clean. No wonder Goethe and Schiller had lived here. Goethe worked on *Faust*, Schiller on *William Tell* and *Wallenstein*. But now it all was dirt and grime: Communist "efficiency." Like the coal dust hovering over his relatives' homes in Appalachia.

Dinner with Inge had given him a lot to think about. Both she and Helga had been involved with Gustav.

He felt for Inge. She cared about Gustav, and her uncertainty towards him moved Alan. There was something about Inge he could love. And Naomi?

Would he have wanted Inge to come to his room? It would be awkward to start a relationship with someone in Germany. Maybe he should he just go to bed with people! He knew this was what other people did—but he couldn't.

He wanted to *know* and *understand* the people he was attracted to. Better to keep to himself. He could always touch himself, as an act of worship to Hermes and Aphrodite.

But that nagging matter…of his soul…and his wife…and the lover he already had.

The shimmering sunlight streaming into the dining room reminded Alan suddenly of Thomas Mann's *Death in Venice*: That sun, that golden sun, awakening him from his long frigid sleep, filling him with warmth and light, taking him, possessing him, engorging him with life, ripeness, fullness, spilling over with warmth and love. It was another Wahnfried, full of sunlight and warmth.

Where *was* Naomi? She wasn't at the *Hope*, and the clerk at the *Stadthotel* had refused to tell him whether anyone by that name was there.

Inge didn't seem to know where Naomi was either. Perhaps she was no longer that close to the Neufelds.

How had Naomi met Gustav? It must have been when he still adored Wagner. Gustav preferred to be known as Sally. It was difficult to imagine Gustav and Sally together.

Inge, on the other hand, seemed an all-around nice person. Gustav, though "in your face," just wanted to live a happy life. Alan could see Gustav and Inge hitting it off. They'd both studied in Weimar, and were both interested in culture.

How could Alan find Naomi?

Alan grabbed a newspaper off the next table. The French were proceeding with nuclear tests in the Pacific. The Croatian offensive displaced more and more refugees in the Balkans. Alan thought of those haggard refuges he'd seen on the television in Nuremberg; the Serbian and Croatian folk dances he knew; how much he enjoyed dancing with Vicki.

A local story jumped out at him. A recent salmonella outbreak in Thuringia had killed several people. No one had died for several months, but the threat was not past.

"The main source of poisoning is meat that has been sitting in the sun."

Alan glanced at the ham, salami, and mortadella lying directly in the morning sunlight. He remembered the cholera epidemic in *Death in Venice*. He sat his fork and knife down. He imagined himself getting ill.

That's silly, he thought.

But he ate less than he might have.

Alan paced the lobby of the Thuringian Hope, then stared out the window at the old train station and the empty park and street.

How could he ever find Naomi? He might have been in Cologne by now—on the Rhine—if not Paris! Instead he looked out on dirty, decrepit Weimar—a once-beautiful city now covered in filth.

Then the morning clerk called him to the desk. He had a message.

Alan,

You asked me about Naomi Herzlieb. I'm not sure I should tell you this. Did you know that Naomi is Jewish?

I walked over to the Stadthotel last evening after our dinner. I don't know if Naomi is there or not, but a small Holocaust-related event has been meeting this week. Her mother may be there.

By the way, I enjoyed our dinner. You're a very nice man.

Inge

So Naomi *was* Jewish—Another matter to irritate Helga Neufeld, no doubt.

Certainly Naomi had been born long after the Holocaust. But her mother...it would depend on her age.

Alan walked the two blocks to the Stadthotel. The desk attendant confirmed the Holocaust-related meeting; it was just finishing up ahead of the Sabbath. He again refused to tell Alan whether a Naomi Herzlieb was registered at the hotel. But Alan, remembering an old movie he'd seen, took a chance and walked over to a middle-aged man who was checking his suitcases in the lobby before leaving.

"Did you see a tall, blue-eyed blond woman go by recently?"

The man nodded and pointed towards the train station. "She was heading for the bus. About ten minutes ago. With an older woman."

Alan walked to the bus stop on the edge of the park, eerily quiet for a Venusday morning. Friday: It would be Sabbath at sundown. But Alan wasn't Jewish. He had dated Jewish women. He had studied Judaism. His Unitarianism and his Paganism had made him very accepting of other faiths. But Alan wasn't Jewish, and there were no people at the bus stop. He must have missed them.

But glancing up at the sign, he had to remind himself to go on breathing: The bus went to *Buchenwald*. The old concentration camp must be just outside the city.

He remembered the Mogen David. And the Holocaust meeting.

A bus arrived five minutes later. Alan climbed on and saw Naomi towards the rear with an old woman, presumably

Naomi's mother; the only people on the bus. They must have boarded at the preceding stop.

The old woman—ancient, wrinkled and bent, with long white hair—stared out the window intently.

Alan headed towards Naomi, but she shook her head violently and mouthed a silent "No!" Alan dropped into a seat several rows in front of them.

The last time they'd seen one another, in Bayreuth, Alan had stomped off after Naomi invited him to her hotel room. She had a right to be angry. But she and her mother did not seem on good terms either.

The bus proceeded along a wooded road, with Naomi and her mother whispering heatedly.

From three rows ahead, Alan could not make out what they were discussing. In any case they were speaking Hebrew. Alan had studied Hebrew in college, but only Biblical Hebrew. This entire business frustrated him. He'd expected—perhaps because of Inge's hospitality—to be warmly greeted by Naomi. But Naomi did not seem pleased to see him at all—and she and her mother were arguing.

The bus passed beautiful wooded hills. Goethe and Schiller had probably discussed poetry and philosophy here on their walks.

Alan had always felt that Americans didn't appreciate Goethe and Schiller. Translations didn't capture their brilliance—neither the poetry, drama, philosophy, nor wit.

At the end of the route, Alan stepped off the bus as if he'd never met Naomi. The road looped back on itself with no hint of an historical area. Old stone buildings circled the loop, but they didn't look significant. Alan was heading for one of the footpaths when Naomi's mother stopped him.

"Do you know which way the camp lies?" she asked in shaky English. "I can't seem to get myself oriented."

"It may be behind those buildings. I've never been here before."

He examined her aging face. Naomi stood a short ways behind, watching apprehensively. Perhaps she was afraid he'd mention their encounter in Bayreuth; Wagner, Gustav, the upcoming wedding; and the Pagan ceremony.

Mother and daughter headed towards the stone buildings. Alan walked the opposite direction down a footpath across a field, and shortly was stumbling across train tracks overgrown with weeds. Further on he found what must have been the old camp processing area. The rail tracks curved in along a concrete platform and ended against a cluster of pylons. Alan could see cattle cars clanking up to the platform, their large doors sliding open; men, women, and children flooding out of the cars, hands above their heads. Angry soldiers pointed machine guns at them and barked orders. This was the true *Endstation*, the Final Station.

Another path from the platform led back towards the stone houses, past the gas station and the Commandant's Office. Then the camp itself appeared, with the iron gate through which so many had passed, and the words: *Jedem das Seine*: "To Each His Own."

The German seemed ambiguous. Did it mean "Let each do as he wishes" or "Let each get what he deserves?"

Alan wanted to understand this place—but how? The camp sat peacefully under enfolding hills, blue sky and summer sun; but the peace deceived. The spirits of the tortured dead hovered about. When Alan closed his eyes he felt immense anger coursing through the valley. And blood—blood, urine and feces. There had been no appeal against the SS.

Was William Bao now in a camp like this, lost to the Chinese Gulag? Could Alan do nothing to help him? Alan had helped bring people out of prisons in Russia, Uzbekistan, South Africa and East Germany (yes—East Germany!)—but his work for human rights now seemed at an end.

Plaques at the decrepit concrete camp buildings offered commentaries prepared by the former communist government, glorifying the German communists and the prisoners from eastern bloc countries. The plaques described the Nazis and their atrocities. Alan felt shame imagining the scene, shame on behalf of everyone who had been tormented here; but also on behalf of Goethe and Schiller and the ordinary Germans who knew the Nazis were evil.

Far across the camp Alan spotted Naomi and her mother slowly walking about. Prisoner barracks had been destroyed, but their foundations had been preserved and marked in outline.

Naomi's mother knelt before a stone marker, then rose and placed something on top of it. Naomi noticed Alan and turned away towards the surrounding hills. His presence apparently disturbed her.

Alan entered one of the camp buildings, now a museum. Beneath drawings and paintings by school children from across Germany, Alan signed a guest book and wrote: *We have seen.* He thought for a moment then added: *We will remember.*

But what had he seen, and what would he remember? And could it point towards his soul?

The first time that Parsifal entered the Grail Castle, in the old story, he saw the suffering king but didn't know how to respond. He kept silent. Beholding the crimes of the Nazis, Alan could also say nothing. He sensed that Naomi and her mother were in torment, but didn't know what to do.

Back outside the museum, Alan saw them walking the perimeter of the camp. Uncertain, he fled into a restroom.

Washing his hands, he glanced through the barred windows and found himself looking straight at the crematorium. Thick smoke billowed from the tall brick chimney. Prisoners watched through the barred windows of their cells as the remains of their loved ones floated into the hill-air of Thuringia.

The image seemed as real as a memory. Could Alan have been here in his previous life? But someone who had probably been here walked nearby with her beautiful daughter; and a gulf separated him from them.

When Alan reemerged into the sunlight, Naomi and her mother were gone.

But returning to the remains of the barracks, Alan ran straight into Naomi's mother again, sitting on a bench around the corner. Before he could retreat, the old woman muttered:

"It's hopeless. Hopeless."

"What is, Mother?" Alan spoke softly, hoping to put the old woman at ease. Now, unlike Parsifal, he'd at least asked The Question.

"My daughter," she sighed. "My daughter. It kills me."

Alan felt himself turning red.

"My daughter is abandoning me. She argues with me here. *Here!*"

Strangers always trusted him. Or was it her desperation? Alan sat down beside her.

"Perhaps you've misunderstood one another."

"She wants to marry a…well, I don't know how to describe him."

"You're speaking English," Alan answered carefully. He didn't want to reveal that he knew Naomi. "You can tell I'm not German?"

113

"German. German? Fuck the Germans! All week I've been surrounded by Germans! My daughter left me here alone with them all day yesterday. They tell me how much they respect me, but their fathers and grandfathers—" She stopped to collect herself. "Never mind. Forget it. My daughter—"

"Was that who I saw you with?"

"Yes. She left Tel Aviv and came here to study German culture. She listens to Wagner, she adores Wagner—*Wagner!*" The old woman was tiring. "If I'd kept her in Jerusalem—"

"You're Israeli?" he asked, thinking of the Holocaust gathering. "You were imprisoned here?"

She didn't answer. Alan extended his hand. "Alan Horne, from California. I've spent some years in human rights work. Honored to meet you."

She took his hand and smiled for the first time. "Delighted, Mr. Horne. My name is Herzlieb—Rachel Herzlieb. I apologize for getting upset."

"It's understandable. Where's your daughter now?"

"Across the camp somewhere. We'll meet at the bus. We were arguing. It's hard to come back. I remember too much, but can't forget."

She was trembling slightly. Her wrinkled face reminded Alan of a photo he'd seen somewhere. "Let me show you something, Mr. Horne." She led him across the open field.

Most of the barrack foundations were outlined in black stones, but one was marked entirely in white. Mrs. Herzlieb took Alan past the stones then turned around to face the museum, the gate, and the commandant's quarters.

From either end of the white outline, the ground sloped downwards. In the center a large stone displayed an engraved Star of David—the Mogen David—with a Hebrew inscription.

"My friends and family all died here. Can a child comprehend things like that?"

Alan placed his hand on her shoulder. "And you survived."

"I was only five or six when we arrived. I don't remember much before that—a few flashes of ordinary life. The Monster was already chancellor. I had relatives in Prague I never met. Our house was trashed. People kicked my mother and father and laughed. You can't imagine; you've never been in danger."

Yet I'm bisexual and Pagan and polyamorous, Alan thought—but didn't speak.

"Our house outside the city—Germans live there now. I was barely thirteen when I escaped near the end of the war.

"My family was gone: Parents, brother. I thought of going to Prague, but I knew they were all dead. I hated the Germans, and I distrusted the Russians; so I went to Palestine. We made it a new Land of Israel, but everyone I cared about was dead."

She looked towards the mountains. "You can't imagine...I can't explain." She sighed. "I swore I'd never come back, but my daughter..." She grunted in disgust. "During the Gulf War, five years ago... Saddam Hussein shot missiles into Tel Aviv... She got this idea...that she could understand our enemies. 'They're human beings,' she said. It was right after her father died of cancer. She started studying German. She argued with her professors in Tel Aviv. She got herself onto a computer and somehow—I don't understand all this—she met this...person..."

"She...wanted to understand the Germans?" Interesting. *Impressive.*

"The Arabs, the Germans; the people trying to destroy us. She thinks you can understand evil. And change it." She

115

shook her head, uncomprehending. "And she's going to marry this…*Christian*. But he dresses like a woman and the wedding's going to be Pagan. And the family is…how can I explain this?" She shook her head in resignation. "This isn't why Moses brought us out of Egypt! *The Lord is our God*," she cried, "*The Lord is One!*" She could barely hold back her tears. "My father and mother met on this hill when they were teenagers. They fell in love walking in this forest. And they died here."

She glanced up: Naomi had emerged across the field. "Would you like to meet my daughter? There she is. I'd love to have her meet someone like you."

But it reminded him of Nymphenburg. Did Mrs. Herzlieb think she could solve her problems by involving her daughter with an American? If she only knew what Alan was really like!

"I'm sorry, Mrs. Herzlieb. No." He shook her hand. "I couldn't intrude on family matters."

Before Naomi was halfway across the field, Alan had left the camp. Walking down the road he realized, suddenly, who Mrs. Herzlieb reminded him of, with her long, stylish, white hair: Cosima Wagner—daughter of Liszt, wife of Richard—in her old age: Anti-Semites, all.

The plain but massive bell tower rose several hundred feet above the empty Memorial Park.

Alan had walked a short ways down the road from the camp and discovered, across the road, behind tall trees, the park on the crest of a hill overlooking the city.

Along descending steps, monumental stone tablets followed a huge circular arc around the bell tower, each presenting a heroic bas-relief on one side, and an inspirational inscription on the other.

Alan walked, deep in thought. Then, looking up, he saw Weimar spread across the valley below. He felt like Moses viewing Canaan; or Jesus tempted by Satan on the mountain top.

Dachau, just outside Munich, also sat on a hill.

He'd visited Dachau once. He'd wondered whether members of the Bavarian State Orchestra or singers from the Bavarian State Opera had been imprisoned there. What a humiliation it would have been for a successful citizen of Munich to be imprisoned on a hill overlooking the site of their former happiness.

Alan wondered what it would mean if *anyone* could be thrown in jail simply for being different, or because somebody didn't like them, or because the police had a quota for arrests that day. It had happened under the Nazis, in Stalin's Russia, under Franco and Pinochet, in Argentina and China and South Africa. It had happened in the American South. It didn't take much to get arrested, tortured, and killed in a society where the police or the government could do anything they wanted.

It was not the sweeping global disaster of the Holocaust that dismayed Alan; it was the myriad small acts of personal insult and humiliation and cruelty of which it consisted— the petty and mindless cruelty of the Nazis.

From the hill he now admired, in the valley far below, the city of Weimar, once the center of German culture; where Goethe and Schiller had strolled discussing literature and philosophy; where Franz Liszt had premiered Wagner's radiant opera *Lohengrin;* where the young German Republic had written its first post-monarchy constitution after World War I.

Alan had come the full half-circle around the promenade, past the heroic tablets. As he looked towards the bell tower he noticed Naomi looking out over the valley. She saw him, and began walking towards him. Then a voice called from the road. Naomi turned, hurried away, and was lost among the trees.

Alan pondered the inscription on the door of the bell tower: *The destruction of Nazism and its roots is our duty; the construction of a free and peaceful world is our task.* Noble sentiments forced upon the East Germans by their Communist leaders. Of course the Communists believed it—they had fought pitched battles against the Nazis in the early 1930s. They had fought the fascists in the Spanish Civil War. But nobility forced becomes unwelcome and resented. Evil—or the fight against evil—must never become a cliché. How often Alan had inwardly yawned during his work for Human Rights International! He believed in human rights—but he tired of continual exhortations to noble actions.

Suddenly he noticed that the clock on the tower read 12:30. He had to get back into town for his meeting with Inge! It occurred to him that he could probably catch the bus with Naomi and her mother. He ran across the square and into the cluster of trees that shaded the forest road. But Naomi and Rachel were gone.

The fountain splashed in the cobblestone square. Alan and Inge had arrived at Goethe's house in old Weimar.

"It was good I met you at the hotel," he told her. "I might never have found this on my own. I suppose Goethe looked down at this fountain as he worked on *Faust*. He probably imagined Gretchen and Faust meeting here."

Had not Faust lost—and regained—his soul? Alan's thoughts lingered on Buchenwald.

Inge's smile, which had seemed an extension of the summer weather during their walk downtown, had worn thin. "You never answered my question, Alan: Did you find Naomi and her mother?"

He didn't know how to express the conflicts in his heart. "I found them at the camp; at Buchenwald. Naomi ignored me. Her mother complained about the wedding. I...I still don't understand what I actually experienced there. I love Germany, but –"

Inge's face seemed to wilt. After a long silence she spoke. "We've had our difficulties, we Germans. It's a burden to live with our history."

Was the Holocaust merely a "burden?"

"You don't understand, Inge. I've thought of moving to Germany. I've thought of taking German citizenship." He had never admitted this to anyone.

Inge gaped at him. "Why, Alan? America is the envy of the world. I wish I could live in America."

For an instant, he saw them together in California.

"The United States is a wonderful place, Inge. But we have a past too."

"You mean, how you treated the Indians and Blacks?"

"That's the most obvious. We're often short-sighted; we often have trouble seeing other people's points of view. We brag about our freedoms but feel threatened by nonconformity. We try to dictate reality to the world, but we're terribly unsure of ourselves."

They left Goethe's house in silence. Some minutes later Inge asked: "So your meeting with Naomi was a failure? I could have told you her mother objected to the wedding."

"I don't know what I expected."

They continued to Schiller's House.

"I can picture them strolling through Weimar," Alan said. "Goethe talking Philosophy and Schiller talking Freedom."

Freedom and Dignity, Alan thought. *We glorify Freedom and Dignity—but only for "approved" groups. I've spent so long hiding my essential self from other people; and now when I stop concealing— my contribution's no longer wanted.* He snorted, thinking of his church and HRI.

After Schiller's house, they continued to the cemetery south of downtown. Inge led Alan to the mausoleum.

"I don't understand," he said. "Do you mean that Goethe and Schiller were never *buried*?"

They entered the large stone structure. It was a delight to escape the sun and humidity. The coolness and shade inside felt refreshing after the heat.

One level down, a series of stone sarcophagi formed most of a circle. The noise of the city did not reach here. Alan relaxed in the silence and coolness. He squeezed Inge's hand.

A pair of beautifully polished wooden coffins lay at one end of the semi-circle. One bore the golden letters *Goethe*; the other *Schiller*.

"So they *haven't* been buried. They've lain here for two hundred years?"

"They were removed for safety during the war."

Inge hesitated, then continued in a lower voice. "Something rather surprising—I heard this from a friend. Some years ago the STASI—the East German Secret Police— removed Goethe's skull to measure the brain cavity."

Alan regarded her uneasily. "And?"

"Goethe's brain was larger than average. But what does that prove?"

"That the brains of the STASI were smaller."

After a moment's uncertainty they slipped into an embrace.

"You're really quite agreeable, Alan." Inge took his arm as they emerged above ground. "What are your plans in Germany?"

He tensed. He imagined himself living with Inge, Gustav, and Naomi. He'd have to abandon Vicki and Gayle; they wouldn't leave the U. S. And little Lavender! Had his parents foreseen that he might never return?

Inge was an exceptional woman, but could he be honest with her? There was only one way to tell.

"My plans in Germany?" He hesitated, lost in the vision. "Let me tell you about myself…"

TEN

The train rattled on, clanking each wooden tie as it sped along; and the thumping in Alan's brain grew ever louder, ever more painful, as Alan's eyes bore deeper into the Thuringian hills he glared at through the window.

Alan tried to stop clamping down on his teeth, but he was upset—his final conversation with Inge still infuriated him.

He had told her about his marriage, his daughter, and Gayle; and she had told him she'd had enough problems with Gustav. She'd dumped Gustav because he refused to commit to monogamy, and she found Alan's behavior even less acceptable.

"How can I get involved with you, when you refuse to grow up and commit to one person; when you won't act maturely and make responsible plans for the future?"

Alan had countered that he *was* making "responsible plans for the future."

Then the rage had swept over him. He had tried not to say things he would regret. He had thanked Inge for the kindness she had shown him, had excused himself, and had returned to the hotel to retrieve his luggage. Then he had walked across the street to wait for a train.

The trip to Weimar had failed. He'd found Naomi but she'd avoided him; and her mother—!

He'd reconsidered Paris, but Paris seemed too pedestrian now—even with its art and atmosphere. Naomi and Rachel had affected him deeply. Inge's rejection followed on top of *that*. Paris would do no good. Besides, he'd diverted himself northward. Paris would mean retracing his steps, which he meant never to do. It went back to Gayle's suggestion to never stay anywhere more than one night, unless and until…

He certainly hadn't found his soul—and would he know it when he had? Paris didn't seem the place.

Perhaps he'd put too much faith in Western Europe and Germany. He remembered the East; he'd gone there as a student: Vienna, Prague, Istanbul.

Yet Germany still appealed to him, even with his college gone, his homes gone, and the Germans thus far disturbing. Something about Germany *excited* him. He still loved Wagner, despite Naomi and her *Tristan* proposition, despite that peculiar old woman at Wahnfried, despite Sally's denunciations. He *loved* this country. He knew that Germany was flawed, deeply flawed—but it seemed to him that it was trying to address its past; whereas the United States didn't even *know* its own past. And Germany—German Art, German Literature, German history—moved him in a way that America seemed unable to. The *promise* of America—democracy, freedom, individual responsibility, human development—*did* move him; it always had. But he wasn't sure the United States could live up to its ideals, or come to terms with its own darkness.

On the bus from downtown Weimar back to the hotel, Alan had decided to head east, towards Prague and Vienna and maybe even Istanbul. But on the way he could visit Wagner's homeland in the state of Saxony: Leipzig and

Dresden were on the path towards Prague. He'd wanted to visit them as a student, but East Germany had denied him a visa. His diversion from Paris now pointed him eastward. Perhaps Wagner could still offer him something. If not, then on to Prague.

Prague: With its old Jewish Quarter, where Kafka had grown up; the old Synagogue and cemetery; the old city with the astronomical clock and the beautiful, distinctive architecture of the Church of Our Lady before Týn; the city of Mahler and Smetana; the city where Alexander Dubcek had tried to pull the country away from Moscow in 1968—until the tanks came in. As a student, Alan had visited barely two summers after the invasion.

Kafka and Mahler. Alan had been interested in Judaism once; had studied Hebrew and Rosh Hashanah and the art of the cantor. He'd dated Jewish women…and a Jewish man.

From Prague, if necessary, he could continue to Vienna, city of Mozart and Beethoven (and Mahler again!), which he had visited once in a drab November fog. Surely he could find something that might nurture a soul there. Or if necessary Budapest, where Thea's Hungarian parents had grown up; a beautiful city he'd never experienced.

And on, if necessary, into the Balkans. Istanbul must hold something for him. Athens must. Gods! If he *had* to, he could continue all the way to Jerusalem (where Naomi and her mother once lived). Or Cairo. Or India. His soul must be lurking *somewhere*!

But what if it *wasn't*? What if he hadn't found it, when he returned to California to confront Vicki? What then?

The train was entering Leipzig, in the former kingdom of Saxony, late in the afternoon, after an hour's ride. Twenty-five years earlier, Alan had been unable to travel to the city of Wagner's birth; now he was here. He had no idea where anything *was* in Leipzig; but he had arrived.

Damn Naomi and that peculiar old woman! Otherwise Alan might actually have enjoyed Bayreuth!

Alan knew his fascination with Wagner unsettled people. He'd first heard "The Ride of the Valkyries" when he was seven. He'd fallen in love, as Ludwig II had, with the swan-knight *Lohengrin* when he was fifteen. He'd memorized the *Ring* by the time he left high school. It was odd: When he listened to Wagner, he felt he was *inside* the music, *inside* the story, *inside* Wagner's head. He'd even considered the possibility that he might be Wagner's reincarnation!

For the seventh time since arriving in Leipzig Alan set down his bags, rested a minute, then continued. He'd been walking half an hour, with no sign of the *White Rose* pension. He'd just passed the Gewandhaus, home of the world-famous orchestra. Just a few more blocks, hopefully.

The woman at the Tourist Bureau had reserved a room for him and assured him it was only a ten-minute walk. He'd asked about the house where Wagner was born, but it had been destroyed long ago. So the only Wagner relic in the city of Wagner's birth was gone. But Alan couldn't bring himself to leave for Dresden that night. Saturnday would be fine.

Alan wouldn't have cared how far the *White Rose* was if it hadn't been for the luggage. Alan was carrying his original Virginia duffle plus a second bag with accumulations from his three days in Germany.

Could it really be only three days since he'd landed in Frankfurt?

Each step brought Alan more pain. The luggage must weigh fifty pounds.

He finally saw the sign for the *White Rose* above an old door surrounded by scaffolding, on a dirty and deserted street two blocks past the Gewandhaus. A thin young man greeted him as he entered.

"Good evening Mr. Horne! I am Herr Müller."

The ground floor held a small dining room of workmen drinking beer.

Herr Müller led Alan up a dilapidated staircase. "The toilet is here, your room is across the hall."

The room was smaller than Alan's room in Munich, quite a change from the honeymoon suite in Weimar. The wall paint was chipping. The dark furniture increased the glumness. Alan noticed scaffolding outside the window; workmen were painting from the window ledge. Herr Müller closed the shades. A portable shower stood just above the headboard of the bed. Workmen hammered outside. Alan guessed several hours of daylight remained.

"I'm afraid we're remodeling. I hope this is okay."

After signing the register back downstairs, Alan asked, hesitantly: "Did the composer Felix Mendelssohn really die just a block from here?"

"You saw the plaque? Yes. It was easy for Mendelssohn to walk to work at the Gewandhaus. Did you know that Mendelssohn started the Bach revival?"

"How so?"

"A lot of Bach's work was forgotten after he died—especially the church music. Bach wrote continuously for the Thomas and Nikolai Churches—"

"I passed the Nikolai Church on the way here. They were collecting money for Bosnia."

"I just returned from that event. The Balkan situation is becoming catastrophic. We're deeply involved in relief efforts.

"Anyway, after Bach's death his manuscripts were divided among his children. Some ended up as wallpaper or kindling! Two *Passions* and the *Mass in B Minor* survived, but they were forgotten. Three Passions were lost."

"And Mendelssohn?"

"He presented the *Matthew Passion*, the drama of Jesus' death, in Berlin in 1829. It caused a sensation. Otherwise it too might have been lost."

"Mendelssohn was Jewish?"

Müller's face darkened. "Wagner and the Nazis said so," he snapped. "*Mendelssohn the Jew degraded German culture.*" He grew calm again after a moment.

"Mendelssohn was Jewish by birth but Christian by choice. His father was the son of the Jewish philosopher Moses Mendelssohn and let Felix choose his own religion. When he was twelve, Felix chose the religion of Jesus and Paul."

"*Paul the Rabbi.*"

Herr Müller regarded Alan closely. "Yes, *Paul the Rabbi.* I'm surprised you know about that."

"I studied in Munich two years. I've thought of becoming a German."

Like Christopher Isherwood. Other English people had done it—not people Alan approved of, however: Houston Steward Chamberlain, Wagner's racist son-in-law; and Winifred, Wagner's racist daughter-in-law. To be fair, they had married into the family after Wagner's death. P. G. Wodehouse had spent time in Germany. Why shouldn't Alan? But the idea startled Kurt Müller.

"You'd give up your American citizenship?"

"Just an idea," Alan snapped defensively. "By the way," Alan continued quickly, "why did you name this pension *The White Rose*? Something about the English War of the Roses?"

The question astonished Müller. "You said you'd studied in Munich!" He looked Alan over again. "At the height of the War, in 1943, a group of Munich students began distributing pamphlets—"

"I remember. They—"

"Hans and Sophie Scholl were arrested, tried, and guillotined. They called their group *The White Rose.*"

"You named the pension for them?"

"When the demonstrations against the communist regime began, a few years back, I wanted to remind people that situations are never hopeless. At the darkest moment of German history, *some* Germans dissented, and paid with the Guillotine." Müller reflected. "So unfortunate. Like Tian An Men. So disappointing."

Müller remembered Tian An Men; had he heard of William Bao?

"I have to go to a meeting." Müller was shaking his hand. "Pleased to have met you." He had switched to the familiar form of address. "Please call me Kurt."

"Very good to meet *you*," replied Alan. "Have you heard of William—"

"Excuse me, I really must run. Let me know if you need anything." Müller swept out the door. "You might enjoy eating at Auerbach's Keller downtown."

"The one from Goethe's *Faust*?"

But Müller was gone.

*

That night Alan lay in darkness, curtains drawn, after the activities of the day. The curtains shut out the scaffolding beyond the window. In the darkness, Alan allowed in the thoughts that daylight and city noise had excluded.

Auerbach's Keller had surprised Alan with its dark wooden walls and clientele in business suits and stylish dresses: A trendy tourist spot. Alan couldn't imagine Goethe there. Students couldn't afford it. But Mephistopheles...

Alan now felt at the mercy of others. He might end up in Prague or other places he'd visited before, but he was going via cities he'd never visited. He'd read about Leipzig and Dresden, but in the mid-1800s, the time of Wagner. Both cities had now been overlaid with sixty years of totalitarian rule. What was left? Not Wagner's house. Not much of Goethe. No signposts toward his soul.

Yet Alan felt happy. A good sign: To notice when he felt happy. He'd eaten at a Chinese restaurant near the Train Station. The manager knew Kurt Müller. Alan felt odd talking to Chinese people in German. It tweaked his stereotypes. Not knowing the German term for *chopsticks*, Alan dredged up the Mandarin. It surprised the waiter; he'd told the owner. It surprised Alan to remember the word. But 1989 had inspired him: A million Chinese walking through Beijing calling for democracy. He'd studied Mandarin for three years. But the government crackdown had shredded his motivation. He'd forgotten most of what he'd learned. William Bao had inspired him again, but Bao had now vanished into a Communist prison. Nevertheless Chinese food had always lifted his spirits, ever since he'd discovered it in Japan as a teenager.

Alone now in the darkened room, Alan pondered Vicki and Gayle.

He'd enjoyed his "honeymoon" with Gayle in Monterey—waking and dozing in the darkness side by side; walking the shore arm in arm the next day, sharing pasts and possible futures, thinking how they and their spouses might meet and live together and share their dreams.

It didn't matter that they hadn't actually…

They'd shared orgasms. Did it matter that he couldn't…?

He wished he weren't so old!

After Gayle had returned to Wisconsin, he couldn't even make love to himself. He'd pleaded to Hermes to help him. He knew that Vicki, because of her medication, was no longer interested… The anti-depressants she'd been taking since the break-up with Preston and Janie…

The medication, their affair with the Lemons—Vicki's feelings of worthlessness. She had no energy.

Then she told him she was leaving…

Darkness. Darkness.

When Alan had first gone over to the bathroom across the hall, after his arrival at the *White Rose*, he'd glanced out the window and realized that the East German government had left whole sections of Leipzig in ruins after the War. During the fifty years that the West Germans had devoted to rebuilding, the East Germans had poured all their money into weapons. They were only beginning reconstruction now.

But—they'd expected the Americans to attack. What would *you* do?

In the darkness and silence of the dilapidated pension, Alan contemplated the destruction of a great city and his own apparent impotence. But in spite of his depression, Alan felt happy.

*

Kurt Müller did not appear downstairs for Saturday breakfast. Alan was told that he was helping with a charity basketball shoot near the Monument to the Battle of Nations, on the outskirts of Leipzig.

Alan struggled to remember the so-called Battle of Nations, fought against Napoleon in 1813. It wasn't mentioned much in the history Alan taught. Wagner had been about five months old. Wagner's mother and father had risked crossing the city to be together.

Alan took the streetcar out to the monument. After a long monotonous ride it rose massively ahead of him, unlike anything Alan had ever seen: A giant block of stone rising hundreds of feet above the Saxon plain.

It reminded Alan of the Washington Monument; but the Washington Monument resembled a slender needle, while the *Völkerschlactdenkmal* resembled a distended breast or a gargantuan pimple, mountain, or butte.

A long reflecting pool like the one in front of the Lincoln Memorial stretched in front of it. In front of the reflecting pool, every inch of paved space had been crammed with basketball equipment. Speakers blared heavy metal. Hundreds of young people, mostly boys, bounced around shooting baskets to the music. Most of the boys ignored everyone around them; but some had brought their friends. They shouted to each other over the music.

Several courts away, Kurt Müller offered pointers to a young man. Alan headed over.

Alan admired Kurt. Kurt had been involved in human rights work and the revolution that had brought down East Germany six years before. Now he volunteered at activities like this, and tried to help the refugees in Bosnia.

Kurt noticed Alan and flashed him a grin. That relieved Alan; he'd been afraid Kurt wouldn't remember him.

"What are you doing out here? Most tourists don't come to the monument. You're American, right?"

"From the United States. Sometimes I think that I'd rather live here."

"So you said. I don't know why. It's often uncomfortable being German."

"I told you—I studied German language and history in Munich." He hesitated. "And I love Wagner."

"Wagner! Really? Most of us think he's terribly out of date. He was anti-Semitic." Kurt started to say more, but caught himself. They surveyed the crowds.

"I've got to get back to the tutoring." Kurt pointed towards the monolith. "You should go up in the monument. There's a special exhibit on history. Most Americans I meet know very little about Germany."

"I'm not 'most Americans.' I've studied and studied, particularly the period from Bismarck through the Weimar Republic."

A young man ran up to ask Kurt about dunk shots.

"Maybe," said Alan, "when I come back from the monument we can talk more."

"I'm afraid I have to get back to town soon," Kurt answered bluntly. "If I'm already gone, why don't you visit the Thomas Church downtown, where Bach served as cantor? You're interested in music? Go to the Bach Museum! My partner Rudi runs it. You'll enjoy it!" *Partner*?

Alan started towards the monolith. Kurt returned to his student.

*

Dim light permeated the cool interior of the massive stone *Denkmal,* as if visitors were embedded within a mountain, entombed within a pyramid. The cavernous interior dwarfed mere humans. Huge brooding figures towered above, eyes closed, like huge German Buddhas lost in contemplation. They evoked a world beyond this world, a time beyond this time. They reminded Alan that the mundane was connected to the eternal. Had he made any progress tracking down his soul? Did Germany and the people he'd met there—Kurt, Inge and the others he'd encountered since Marsday—hold any significance for him? Did world affairs matter?

Alan paced the massive enclosure, read the displays, examined the photographs, and pondered Germany's past. Just as during the Tarot reading with Gayle, Alan felt the huge figures were trying to communicate something—but what?

The memorial had been meant to remind visitors of the destructiveness of war and the blessings of peace. It was meant to be dedicated in 1913, the hundredth anniversary of Napoleon's defeat at the Battle of Nations.

But by the twenty-fourth year of the reign of Emperor Wilhelm II, many Germans were feeling differently about peace and brotherhood; convinced of the necessity of fighting and the impossibility of international cooperation. The monument became a symbol for patriots who supported the Emperor and Germany's *Day in the Sun.*

After the defeat of the Empire at the hands of the French and their allies, the monument had become a rallying point for those who wished to restore German greatness. For those who had championed Germany then—the

Goerings and Goebbels and Hitlers—the monument represented the past and future glory of the German People.

Alan wanted to talk further with Kurt Müller, but Müller had left by the time Alan returned from the monument. Alan headed into town to look for the Thomas Church and the Bach Museum. Perhaps he could find Rudi. What had Kurt meant when he called Rudi his "partner?"

Thomas Church stood on the other side of medieval Leipzig, just past the beautiful old town hall, a half mile past Auerbach's Keller.

The steepled white building seemed a diminutive structure; no massive stone cathedral from the Middle Ages; a simple German church; modest and Protestant in design.

Baroque Catholic churches like the Theatine Church in Munich could appear unassuming on the outside yet hold glories within. But Leipzig was Saxon not Bavarian; Protestant not Catholic. Bach had championed Martin Luther and had come here every Sunday—and certainly days in between—to offer music to his god.

Alan went in. The tall-ceilinged church was anti-baroque, relatively unadorned: Some gold and glitter, but restrained. A large organ, perhaps Bach's own, occupied half the rear wall, rising from the choir loft. An ornamental pulpit in the German style rose towards the front of the church beside the central aisle. The transept displayed richly colored stained glass splashing bright summer light down upon the altar. In front of the altar, a large metal plaque lay embedded in the stone floor. Its raised words faced away from the congregation, towards the stained glass and God: JOHANN SEBASTIAN BACH. The great composer lay buried awaiting the Lord. The sparkling light contrasted with the gloomy shadows of the *Völk-erschlachdenkmal*, and Bach contrasted with the Nazis. Alan wondered again, if Hitler had been different, had he not persecuted his enemies and provoked a cataclysmic war— had his vast talents been used for good rather than evil— would he have been remembered as Germany's greatest leader and rested in a monumental tomb?

Alan remembered the Weimar coffins of Goethe and Schiller, but then the air exploded and an unseen choir implored:

KYRIE! KYRIE!
KYRIE ELEISON!

Alan recognized the chords that had burst from the church in Nuremberg; he couldn't remember what Sally had said they were.

The choir loft in the rear of the church had filled, the organist played. A fugue followed the choral introduction, then each voice re-entered in turn; creating a seemingly endless series of waves of sound and emotion, captivating Alan so completely that he sank onto a pew and lost all awareness of time, knowing he sat where this music had first been heard, a few feet from the man who had created it, in Bach's own church, perhaps where Bach himself once had sat. Bach had certainly sat in the organist's chair. Art and music often pulled Alan from the Here-and-Now into the Transcendent.

After the choir finished, the director critiqued each voice part in turn. Alan pondered the great tomb, the stained glass above and behind it, trying to fix the sight in his memory. He considered approaching the choir, but didn't know what to say. He didn't know how to communicate what he'd felt. Instead, he walked out into the plaza.

Now he felt a bit lost. He had encountered something that had changed him, but he knew that others couldn't see that change. That was it: Art changed Alan whenever he opened himself up to it. That was part of his Witch's path.

Yet people passed by as if nothing had happened. Had music ever changed them? Did they understand that something transcendent had happened in this church, long ago—and was happening still?

He looked up. Bach was standing in front of him: A large dark statue rising from a tall pedestal, a few yards from the side of the church. Bach didn't seem dead. He didn't seem like a statue. He rose up, as if on the way to something important, as if on the way to his Work. Music must have affected Bach the way it affected Alan—as a life-changing force. But Bach could create *Art*—what could Alan create?

Indeed, people walked past as if nothing had happened, with no inkling of how the statue was affecting him, of how the music in the church had altered him.

The statue faced the Bach Museum, closed for repairs. Kurt must have forgotten.

But a music shop adjoined the museum. Alan stuck his head through the door and asked: "Is anyone here?"

A cheerful, balding twenty-something man looked out from down the hall. "Who are you looking for?" His smile was infectious.

Alan smiled back awkwardly. "Someone. Anyone. Myself, actually. I'm staying at the *White Rose*, near the Gewandhaus. Herr Müller suggested I visit the Bach Museum. But it's closed."

"Yes, we're doing a major remodeling. I help with it sometimes. I'm a bit of an amateur carpenter. Many buildings in Leipzig desperately need renovation. You say you met Kurt Müller?"

"Yes, Kurt is a great host. Do you sell all kinds of music in this store, or just music by Bach?"

"All kinds of *classical* music, if that's what you mean. I'm Rudi Wagenheim, by the way." He offered his hand.

"Alan Horne. So you don't sell just Bach?"

"*Just* Bach? You make it sound so...*just*! As if Bach is...well...*just* Bach. The greatest composer in history!"

"But there *are* others. You do sell others?"

"Of course. But only the rarer material. We specialize in Bach. *Everything* by Bach, and the hard-to-find of the others."

"I'm looking for something by Wagner."

"Wagner!"

"An old recording of the third act of *Tristan*. With Melchior. On 78s."

"I'm afraid we don't carry any Wagner. *Anti-Semite*, you know."

"But he was born here in Leipzig!"

"True, true. But he was pompous and conceited. What do you say in English? *A Royal Asshole*."

"But his *music*..."

"Ah—his music...and his drama! A very *dramatic* person, certainly—but *unhealthy*. Just let me find—I thought we'd sold out, but then I found..."

He was searching among the CDs spread on a large Lazy Susan that somehow looked familiar.

"Are they preparing for a performance in the church? They were rehearsing..."

"The *Mass in B-minor*. Now *there*'s music! Ah! And *here*'s drama! Here: Read the first section while I set up." He handed Alan the booklet from a double CD:

John Passion
First Part:

Oh Lord, our Ruler,
Whose fame resounds in all lands;
Show us through your suffering
That you, the true Son of God,
At all times,
Even in the greatest depravity,
Are justly glorified!

Rudi popped the CD into the slot. Alan started to comment.

"Pretty simple. More Hebraic than I'd have expected. Almost Buddhist. Or rather…" Alan thought of something he'd read long ago. "*Though he slay me, I will trust in Him.* That's in the Jewish *Torah* or *Prophets* or *Writings*, isn't it?"

"Put on the headset. Close your eyes. Forget where you are. Listen."

Alan regarded him suspiciously.

"Just listen. Experience, don't analyze." Rudi was smiling broadly.

What a charming man!

Rudi continued sorting sheet music. An additional circle of wood, about two feet across, covered the middle of the Lazy Susan; as if the middle of the wheel had been cut out. Alan pondered it as he listened to the music. He was sure he'd seen the Lazy Susan somewhere—but where?

When the opening chorus finished, Alan removed the headset and found Rudi in the office, finishing up a phone conversation.

"Glad to hear you're back safely, Friedrich. We collected quite a bit of money. Your speech helped. See you tomorrow."

After Rudi hung up, Alan went in. "Business seems light."

"Most of the interest's in the museum."

"I hadn't realized how much I missed Germany. You don't find places like this in the United States."

"America's a big country. There must be shops like this in America—if not about Bach, then about Elvis."

"I don't mean shops, whether for Bach or Elvis. I mean people like you who care about history and culture."

"You just don't know the right people."

Alan's thoughts had drifted back to the morning. "Kurt suggested I visit the *Denkmal*. The exhibit reminded me of the U.S." He hesitated. "I visited Buchenwald yesterday."

"Buchenwald. You're American and you missed Germany? America inspires the world!"

"But Rudi. The United States doesn't *know* what it has. It doesn't know *itself*." He wasn't sure how to explain. "We Americans have committed genocide too: Against the Indians and the blacks. But we dismiss it. It's never sunk in." His tone darkened. "I worry that Americans will have to suffer something terrible like the Holocaust or Hiroshima—Heaven forbid!—before we understand the rest of the world's sufferings. Germans—and Jews!—understand what anguish is." He sighed and looked at Rudi. "And Art here is more than entertainment."

Rudi stared back, puzzled. "Don't idealize us, Sir. We've made terrible mistakes. Like Buchenwald. And Auschwitz."

He began sorting again, clearly annoyed. For a moment he seemed to ignore Alan. Then—

"Have you been to Dresden? That's the cultural center of Saxony; the capital too. If you're interested in Art you should go there. And if you want to live in Germany, Dresden also has jobs. A beautiful city. My girlfriend lives there." *Girlfriend?*

"I intended to go there this evening," Alan replied. "I've been looking for Wagner sites. His Leipzig house is gone. I thought maybe in Dresden…"

Rudi scowled. "You'd better get going. It's Saturday. The trains will be crowded."

"I wanted to talk to Kurt. I've enjoyed visiting Leipzig. You and Kurt are the most decent people I've found in Germany."

Had they helped him towards his soul? Rudi loved music. Kurt was a humanitarian. Leipzig was run down—but reviving. Something here had moved him.

Rudi smiled. "Kurt and I are rather busy the next several days. But Alan," he put his hands on Alan's shoulders, "if you think so much of us, you can always come back…"

Rudi was inviting him back! Rudi and Kurt—Alan must be making *some* progress. Why not just stay in Leipzig? But Rudi had recommended Dresden; the Art was all *there*. Alan needed something in addition to agreeable people. Perhaps he could find it in Dresden.

ELEVEN

The train rounded the hill, revealing Dresden wrapped about the river valley in the late afternoon sun, sixty-some miles east of Leipzig. Alan recognized the top of the Semper Opera, so important to Wagner; and the spires, perhaps, of the Zwinger palace, which Rudi had urged him to visit, visible even at this distance.

Rudi had recommended the Hotel Vibatron, on the edge of downtown, and even referred Alan to his girlfriend, Fräulein Gettelmann, who worked there. From the train station, Alan took the streetcar north into the city, passing St. Walpurgis Street along the way. The name surprised him. Walpurgis Night was another name for May Eve, when spirits of all sorts supposedly assembled on Brocken Mountain in central Germany. Leaving the tram and passing under the street via a vast pedestrian tunnel, he arrived at the hotel.

Judging from its Stalinist architecture, the Vibatron must until recently have been part of a huge communist bureaucratic complex. But now—the carpets were new, the walls freshly painted. The Hotel Vibatron must have only recently opened. East Germany—and Eastern Europe in general—was being reborn after the collapse of communism six years before.

Fräulein Gettelmann was out until the following morning; so Alan continued upstairs.

His room, except for the lack of a bathroom, was almost American in design. The huge fifth floor windows overlooked a deserted field and former Stalinist architectural monstrosities.

The room contained two beds with new blankets, but no sink. To wash your hands or enjoy a glass of water you had to walk down the hall to the bathroom.

Evening was approaching and Alan needed to eat. Dresden beckoned—the city where Wagner had become famous (after premiering *Rienzi*, *The Flying Dutchman*, and *Tannhäuser*)—and then lost it all: After his involvement in the uprising of 1849, Wagner had fled Germany with a price on his head.

Alan stood silent in a downtown Dresden square. A huge wooden rack with compartments towered above him, each compartment marked with a number and containing pieces of stone.

The Church of Our Lady had stood on this spot in the center of old Dresden, before being destroyed in the Allied bombings of February 1945. Black and white photographs of the old church were tacked onto a wooden board along with a description of the attacks.

The bombing had happened five years before he was born, but Alan still felt guilty. Did all those people really have to die? Did whole cities have to be destroyed? Most of the victims were women, children, and civilians—not responsible for Hitler's insanity.

What if the United States ever launched insanity upon the world? Would Americans understand if other nations bombed them, destroyed their cities, and killed people indiscriminately?

Then Alan saw the fire, felt the heat and blistering wind of the firestorm; saw thousands of people as they were incinerated, as in Hiroshima and Nagasaki. He heard their agonized cries. Could it be justice to demand that their anguish pay the debt of the victims of Buchenwald?

From the hill above the Elbe, near the Albertinum museum, Alan watched dusk approach over the deep blue river and the bridges so lovely, as the sun sank towards the west.

As he descended the hill, the Semper Opera came into view—where the world had first heard *Rienzi*, *The Flying Dutchman*, and *Tannhäuser*. As he approached and walked around it, Wagnerian themes flooded back into his head. Alan circled the building in awe, humming as though making an incantation. Wagner had been pivotal for him since his enchantment by *Lohengrin* when he was fifteen. *Lohengrin* had led to *The Ring*. Then everything from his childhood had converged: The mythology of the Greeks, the Bible stories of Moses and Jesus, the legends of Wagner. Encounters with psychology, comparative mythology, and mystical Asian religion then led him to Pagan shamanism.

Yes, Wagner had been central for him; and here Alan was, in Dresden; where Wagner had joined the failed Revolution of 1849. Wanted for treason, Wagner had wandered for fifteen years in Italy, France, and Switzerland— returning to Germany would have meant trial, imprisonment, even perhaps death.

Dresden *was* beautiful, even with the soot of years over-laying the original gilt of the buildings. Rudi had been right: Alan might feel at home here.

But could Dresden become a "home?" Could Dresden bring him closer to his soul? Had Rudi and Kurt brought him closer?

Beyond the Opera, the Zwinger Palace stood, closed for the evening. Rudi had recommended its extensive art galleries, its landscaped lawns, the wide stone stairs up to the roof; the panorama from there of the old city.

But the streets of Old Dresden, with their sidewalk cafes filled with people dining, pained Alan with memories of Vicki and Gayle. He wished they were with him to share a meal. He felt so alone. It was Nuremberg all over again—without Sally to rescue him; without the Chinese restaurant he'd discovered in Leipzig.

He resorted to American fast food on the wide main thoroughfare of the modern city. Young Germans thronged the restaurant; American fast food must be the ultimate "trend" in the East, cut off so long by the Iron Curtain. American pop culture ruled the world.

Saturday dusk descended on the Hotel Vibatron. Black night obliterated the surrounding high-rises and the field below. Alan climbed into bed and lay alone in the darkness, longing for Vicki and Gayle. He missed each of them in a different way, because his love for each was different. He loved Vicki's cold logic and wit, and Gayle's intense combination of the intellectual and the practical.

After a morning shower, Alan went down to the Sunday breakfast buffet to meet Fräulein Gettelmann, curious about Rudi's girlfriend. Perhaps Fräulein Gettelmann loved classical music too. Alan was beginning to wish he knew more artists. He'd forgotten how important Art was to him.

The dining room was as newly painted and sparkling as the hotel room, like the dining room in Weimar, but larger and without the glass wall and ceiling; and therefore cooler without the direct sunlight; much more uplifting than drab Leipzig with its collapsing concrete structures. Yet Leipzig had produced Rudi and Kurt. Leipzig was drab, but it possessed something—a soul?

Germany might offer him something after all. Perhaps the problem had been Bavaria. Everyone—including the Bavarians—said the State of Bavaria was "different." But Alan had lived there; he'd expected to find it conducive to his quest. Now he was drawn more to Thuringian cuisine and Saxon sunshine. Still: Had he learned *anything* about finding his soul? Would he recognize his soul when he found it? Would he know what to do when he found it? He tried to follow his innermost impulses, but it was challenging to stay aware of his own reactions to the world.

If he couldn't find his soul in Saxony, he would chase it east and south: To Prague, Vienna, Budapest. Vienna: The huge Prater park, the palaces, the Vienna Woods. Prague: That quaint old city, not so far from Dresden. He could be in Prague in under two hours; that beautiful view from the hilltop Fortress out over the Vltava river and Charles Bridge.

"…I would like to introduce her." Alan suddenly realized that the man from the front desk had been addressing him. Alan looked up.

"Fräulein Gettelmann?" His jaw dropped. "Käthe? I'm sorry. Did we meet the other day in Munich? My gods!"

He rose and pulled out a chair for her. The young blonde regarded Alan with an air of surprised innocence. She was only in her twenties, and he was forty-five.

"Sit down! Please do sit down! I'm sorry—I wasn't expecting *you*!"

Käthe's bright laugh revealed sparkling teeth. The laugh, the teeth, and the sheer summer dress made Käthe irresistible.

"You aren't familiar with the German hotel industry! Everyone knows everyone else, especially in the more progressive establishments." She was flaunting that smile.

"Rudi told you I was coming?"

Käthe laughed again. "Yes. We had a long phone call last night, Rudi and Kurt and I. Of course, they didn't know I'd already met you. It's quite a surprise to me too! Sally and Naomi were beginning to wonder if they'd ever see you again. We thought you might have left the country."

"But why would I see them, Fräulein Gettelmann?"

"Call me Käthe. *Fräulein*'s so old-fashioned. The wedding, of course."

"What? You mean Naomi and Gustav?"

"Naomi and *Sally*. Sally told us she wanted you to do the ceremony."

My gods—he'd forgotten ever discussing it!

"She called us all last night. She didn't know where you were. But Frieda told her we'd all met you in Munich, so she called us to see if *we* knew. Helga was quite indignant—but said she wouldn't miss the wedding now for *anything*. Inge said she'd seen you in Weimar."

"Of course. The wedding. Naomi did mention that."

"Sally says you have to do it. You're a priest aren't you? A Pagan priest? She says you're the only one who's worthy. It seemed odd to us; but Sally's odd, after all."

146

"Quite odd, I'd say. Fräulein Gettelmann—Käthe, would you go to the Zwinger with me? Rudi thought I should see it. If you'd come along…I have some questions for you…"

"But, Mr. Horne—Alan, I fully intended to show you around."

The "Green Chamber" of the Albertinum sparkled with gigantic jewels and gorgeous ornaments.

"You mean all of you have dated Gustav?"

The question dampened Käthe's smile. "Yes, we all dated him. Gustav's a charming person."

"But a little blunt at times, I think."

"His problems with his church have roughened him. I haven't seen him for six months or so. I've been here fixing up the Vibatron. Rudi helps with the carpentry."

"You do all seem to be involved in the Hotel business, one way or the other."

"Sally's father, Friedrich Neufeld, is well-known in the German hotel industry. That's how he's provided for his wives—when he divorced them. Frieda got a pension in Munich. Sophie got a hotel in Nuremberg. Inge and I both work in the hotels."

"The Neufelds and their friends seem difficult to avoid."

"But Helga, Friedrich's only natural child, has a mind of her own."

"But you and Inge aren't related to Herr Neufeld."

"We were dating his son. Gustav asked his father for favors. Herr Neufeld got us all jobs." She must have noticed Alan's surprise. "The economy in the east isn't good. We didn't want to leave home. None of that matters to

Helga. She grew up in Munich and helped her mother with the pension; she could live with her if she wanted. She *was* living with her until Wednesday, after Rachel Herzlieb arrived. The whole business of Frau Herzlieb being Israeli, and Sally marrying a Jew. So Helga decided then and there to move to Hamburg to be with her Egyptian boyfriend. A Muslim. She's thinking of converting. But she still considers herself Catholic by birth."

"She seemed pretty vehement the other day at Nymphenburg."

"Apparently she's always been independent, but cautious: Needs something or someone to rely on, I think. Not the type for Gustav, certainly. Although they *were* engaged for a while. They're not really related, you know. Gustav's adopted. Helga was very attached to him when they were younger."

They left the "Green Chamber" and continued downstairs past the statues and paintings.

"How's the Arab feel about Helga?"

"He's a nice fellow and quite patient. Helga can be very devoted. She just needs to have limits. That's probably what drove Helga and Gustav apart. Gustav's comfortable with uncertainty and new ideas. He got too unconventional for her. She's really quite conservative."

Alan turned to her. "You seem to know them both well."

Käthe laughed but looked embarrassed. "Alan," she said somewhat exasperated, "I dated Gustav for awhile! He'd travel here over weekends, sometimes. But I realized I was too…scared…I couldn't handle what he was exploring."

"The cross-dressing?"

"Yes. And then his involvement with Naomi. Sometimes I'd notice them here, on weekends, walking together along a street. Now—well, you know…people change."

"But how did you come to know Helga? I knew that Gustav and Helga were engaged, but then Gustav fell in love with Inge. Inge told me that when I saw her in Weimar."

"So—Inge didn't just see you in passing?" Käthe was discernibly blushing.

"Oh no, we…" But he didn't elaborate.

Alan put his arm around Käthe and started walking. She seemed to enjoy the attention. They arrived back on the ground floor.

"I went to Weimar to look for Naomi," he said. "You know her, I presume?"

"I've never *met* her. I imagine she must be very—"

"Gustav sent me to Bayreuth with a letter for her."

"Yes, Sophie told me he got beaten up."

"Naomi and I didn't hit it off. When I met them again in Weimar, her mother was quite vocal though."

"Yes. Frau Herzlieb objects to the marriage."

"But how do you know all these people?"

Käthe smiled sadly. "We got together, the three of us: Helga, Inge, and I. I tracked down Inge because I knew Gustav had been in love with her. Frankly, I think he still loves us all. I don't think Gustav ever *stops* loving anyone. He's a very *loving* person."

She took Alan's hand. "And I *liked* Inge, Alan. I honestly *liked* her. I didn't think I would. She was my boyfriend's ex-girlfriend, after all. I expected to feel jealous. And then we both went and met Helga, and liked her. And we wondered why on earth we shouldn't get together to talk…"

"About Gustav?"

149

"About Gustav, yes; and other things. Things women talk about. You know. And we became friends. You *could* say we formed a club, of sorts—a *Former Gustav's Girlfriends Club*."

She seemed melancholy as they left the museum.

"It turned out we all still cared about Gustav, in spite of the fact that he refused to commit to any one of us exclusively. We all knew he still cared about us, even though we all refused to acknowledge him. That's funny, isn't it? We can't accept his love, because he loves other people too. None of us felt able to love him, because he loves all of us, not just one." She thought for a moment, then added: "Pathetic."

They headed over the hilltop.

"You feel differently now?"

Käthe hesitated. "After we stopped seeing one another, I thought about it for a long time and I realized..." She looked towards the river. "Come on, let's go to the Zwinger."

They passed the Opera House.

"I wish we could see an opera, Käthe."

"Not until next weekend, I'm afraid. The season opener is *Lohengrin*."

"Wagner! I always just miss these things."

They walked towards the Zwinger Palace.

"I realized," Käthe continued, "that everything I'd ever believed about relationships was wrong. Everything I'd ever thought about myself or men or sex. The whole thing. Sally understands everything, instinctively. All I had to do was open my eyes!"

"Nothing else changed your mind?"

"That was it. I sat and thought about how I'd been raised and what I'd been taught. I'd never really thought it all through."

They were walking through the gardens of the Zwinger now, encircled by the wings of the palace on either side.

"That plaque thanks the Soviet Union for rebuilding the palace. Quite a propaganda coup. It points out that we have the Russians to thank for the restoration of the Zwinger; and implicitly reminds us that the palace had been destroyed by the Americans and the British in 1945. I'm not terribly political, but I understand *this*. Kurt views it differently, of course."

"The Firestorm must have been terrible; Hiroshima without the radiation. Churchill apparently decided to destroy the city."

"My family never spoke of it. Come on, I want to show you the paintings. Art's more important than politics."

The galleries were huge. Alan was astounded by the immensity of the palace. After two floors, he stammered: "I had no idea there would be so many levels!"

Käthe laughed and put her hand on his shoulder. "We have two more to go! You're not tired already?"

"Just a little. I'm not used to climbing stairs."

Käthe headed down the corridor, rehashing theories Alan had already heard on the lower floors.

"You see how the artist presents the figures? The men's genitals are too small for the body size, lessening their importance. Thank Goddess we left behind those portraits in the other wing; they all look alike!" Käthe laughed as she walked, supremely confident. Alan trailed wearily behind. He'd been delighted to discover Käthe worshipped the Goddess, but her approach was certainly different than his. Käthe pointed at paintings of nymphs and fauns.

"Lots of emphasis on nudity, but all selective and contrived. The paintings proclaim their political agenda. It's just a tease, intended to control your perception."

"Really?" But Käthe was hardly listening.

"They give you sensuality, but only to a point." She gestured towards a group of dryads. "All this erotic painting. Lots of breasts; but never a cunt."

Alan tensed at the word.

"Gods pursuing nymphs or women, figures lying around after love-making; superficially very sexual…"

"I don't understand what you're…"

"You never see any erections! The men are totally flaccid. And the women!"

Was she trying to impress, shock, or dominate him? Did she simply trust him enough to say this? Did she act this way with Rudi and Kurt?

"You never see the women's pussies. The women are never shown with their legs spread. Furthermore—"

"Yes?"

"—you never see the couples actually fucking." Käthe flashed a suggestive grin. "This painting isn't erotic at all. It's dishonest. As if *this* is how men and women experience love! It's prettied up. It robs the sex of its power."

Alan took a deep breath. "But don't you think," he finally got a word in, "that sexuality—relationships in general—require a little…discretion?" They were climbing to the fourth level.

"Of course Alan. But how can you enjoy a healthy sexual relationship if you aren't comfortable with your own body and its functions?"

Her face lit up in anger. "Look at these paintings! These depictions of orgies! There isn't any cum! What is fucking without cum? Or a woman's wetness. But the vital juices, the slop, the mess—the reality of physical love—are never shown!"

Alan looked at her incredulously.

"You think I'm crazy, don't you?" she said. "You think I'm totally shameless!"

"Not at all. I was considering the possibility…" He struggled for the phrase he wanted. "I'm actually considering the possibility…"

Käthe's face had assumed an ashen seriousness.

"…that you may be as crazy as *I* am."

Seeing the need for acceptance in her eyes, Alan opened his arms to her. As the two embraced, Alan decided that though the two of them were crazy in different ways, they might learn something from one another.

As they entered the final corridor on the fifth floor, Käthe glanced at her watch. Her arm dropped from Alan's shoulder.

"Gracious Goddess! We'll have to hurry to catch the train to Berlin!"

"What do you mean? I was planning to continue to Prague."

"But the wedding's tomorrow. Sally and Naomi. Tomorrow evening. We need to go to Berlin. Kurt and Rudi are already there."

"But Käthe, I never actually said I was going to do it! I don't really know Sally. I don't even know *Gustav*."

He meant to avoid Berlin; the Sally crowd had started to make him uneasy. How could Sally be so different from Frieda and Sophie? *Heaven knows what Marthe and Friedrich Neufeld are like!*

Käthe took his hand and pulled him towards the stairway.

"I told you, Alan. They want you to lead the ceremony!" They were starting down the four levels of stairs.

"Naomi mentioned that in Bayreuth; but I don't understand. Why should they even *think* of me? I only met Sally *once*, for a few hours. Is it because I told her I was Pagan?" He didn't mention the kisses. What had impressed Sally so?

"You told her you were a *priest* of some kind; that you honored the *Old Deities*. She felt you were comfortable with her gender."

"Now wait a minute!" He stopped on the landing.

"Alan, she's never found anyone as suitable as you."

"But I want to go to Prague! I don't *want* to go to Berlin. I went to Berlin once—years ago—and it was dismal and drab and dreary. And I don't think it *leads* me anywhere." *Or will it lead me where I'm not prepared to go!*

They were shouting at each other on the landing.

"Don't you understand, Käthe? I've had nothing but annoyance since I arrived in Germany. I think I should go to Prague—or Vienna, or Budapest. Or Sofia or Skopje or Istanbul. I don't know…" Had he thought it was going to be easy to retrieve his soul?

Käthe looked at him sullenly, then grabbed his hand again. "Come on. We've got to get back to the hotel, pack our stuff, and get to the station. What time of year did you go to Berlin before? The winter?"

"It was November…"

"Then of course it was dreary. It's summer now. When were you there? Before *The Change*?"

"1970."

"Come on."

He allowed her to take him back to the hotel. He always let people control him.

They entered the train station at a trot. Käthe had insisted they head there as quickly as possible. Alan had considered sneaking away, but Käthe had given him no opportunity.

She had dragged him to her room to pick up her bag, then accompanied him to *his* room and stood there while he packed; all the while discoursing on the significance of the wedding in Berlin. The Neufelds wanted Naomi's mother to feel welcome. Helga Neufeld was tremendously upset about something. Helga's Arab boyfriend... Alan couldn't follow it all.

Käthe dragged him to a large placard displaying train schedules. Alan regretted mentioning that he was traveling on a train pass; he might have snuck off on the pretext of buying his ticket (Käthe already had hers). He was agitated enough to leave with no explanations.

"Look!" cried Käthe with an aura of excitement, "Track Five. Come on, we've got just enough time!" She grabbed his hand and dragged him towards the trains. She seemed to have no problem ordering him around.

The conductor was hanging out from the train door, watching for tardy passengers. Käthe pulled Alan along and gestured to the conductor. He waved and yelled: "Come on!"

As they reached the train, a roar erupted around them. They found themselves immersed in a crowd of people carrying banners and whistles, rushing towards the street. The Dresden football team had arrived and was being welcomed by its boisterous fans. Alan jerked free from Käthe's grip and jumped onto the adjoining train. While looking at the schedule, he had realized that the train on the adjoining track was leaving for Prague in five minutes. In the commotion Käthe had no chance to turn and recapture him.

He didn't look for a seat immediately; he locked himself in the nearest restroom till the train was away from the station. It seemed he'd been hiding all his life.

TWELVE

Alan enjoyed the *rat-atat-atat-atat* of the train speeding along; but the heaviness in his head, the cramped position of his body, and the burning warmth in his closed eyes told him he had dozed off. He allowed himself a few moments of warmth and satisfaction, then opened his eyes. The sun-drenched summer countryside reassured him.

But an uncertainty troubled him. Where was he going? *Prague.*

Prague: The capital of the new Czech Republic, on the banks of the Vltava—the Germans called it the Moldau—with its quaint architecture, its astronomical clock, its beautiful hills... He'd visited Prague once, long ago.

Where were the hills? The land seemed totally flat.

Alan glanced at his watch. They had left Dresden an hour and a half ago. They should be approaching the border and going through customs. It shouldn't have taken this long. From Dresden to Prague would be eighty miles, at most.

A city appeared along the horizon. As the train sped closer, a tall tower became visible above a rapidly enlarging sprawl. This was no ordinary city. It was large—*huge*. And the land was flat.

Alan's stomach started to churn. This couldn't be Prague. Prague was smaller, with hills.

He flagged down a conductor; how could he be on the wrong train?

The conductor didn't know, and suggested that Alan catch the next train to Prague when they arrived in Berlin. If there was no train that evening, Alan could find a hotel from the tourist bureau at the Main Station. It's true they'd be arriving at Lichtenberg Station, but an S-Bahn to the Main Station was readily available; the Main Station was only ten minutes away. Alan had never realized that Berlin, like Paris or London, contained multiple major train stations.

By the time they arrived at Lichtenberg, Alan had realized that Käthe must be on the train. It was a miracle she hadn't tracked him down. Such a pain; was she always so assertive about her opinions?

Stepping onto the concrete platform, Alan spotted the S-Bahn. He also noticed Käthe further down the track, talking heatedly with two men whose backs were to him. Alan headed quickly towards the S-Bahn.

A train pulled up as he arrived. In seconds he'd hopped on with his luggage. As the train began moving, Alan noticed Käthe, Rudi, and Kurt staring directly at him. Alan didn't care. He was heading out over the vast German metropolis.

"The pension is in the West End? Isn't there anything closer?"

The tourist clerk shrugged. Alan took the slip of paper and stuffed it into his pocket. He had missed the train to

Prague, and anyway the Prague plan now was bothering him.

To get to the West End, Alan caught a second S-Bahn from the Main Station, and soared out over the central Berlin government district. The city had always had two centers: The Middle—*Mitte*—with its government buildings and museums; and the large *Tiergarten* park stretching from the Brandenburg Gate to the fashionable West End. Long before The Wall had split it physically, Berlin had been split psychologically. Alan had read this all somewhere—Isherwood? Jung?

The bright August sun poured brilliance on the *Mitte*: The tall silver TV tower topped with its giant metallic ball and revolving restaurant; Alexanderplatz—wasn't there a novel about that square?—and the Red City Hall, exactly as it had appeared twenty-five years before. It hadn't been much of a visit that Thanksgiving, but he'd spent a few hours in East Berlin. Now the S-Bahn carried him over the narrow River Spree from East to West. And he saw that The Wall was truly gone. The halves of the city had been reunited, physically if not psychologically.

Over the trees of the *Tiergarten*, Alan spotted the Brandenburg Gate. No sign of the Reichstag, once burned by the Nazis, now the seat of Germany's Parliament once more. The East German border towers and guards were gone. Germany was One—and the part of Alan that was German need feel divided no longer.

After the war, the *Tiergarten* had spooked visitors with toppled heroic statues and mythological figures peeking through the remnants of trees. Hadn't Isherwood said that too? Now the *Siegessäule*, the Victory Column, which Hitler had moved down the avenue, emerged above the trees. Alan got off at the Zoological Station.

*

Lying down on the narrow bed of the pension did nothing to calm him. Alan had realized: To take the train to Prague meant traveling back to Dresden by the same route he'd followed to Berlin. To him it seemed bad luck to go backwards. But how then could he travel to Prague? Through Dresden was backtrack! Through Leipzig was backtrack! Through Nuremberg was backtrack! He knew the routes—but they were backtracks, like backing out of a dead end. Like admitting defeat. Unlucky.

The route to Prague would have to pass through Poland, perhaps through Wroclaw (how much easier in German: Breslau. In Silesia.). Alan had passed through Wroclaw once, long ago; but he knew nothing about Poland, Polish cities, or Polish railways. Poland lay outside the European Union. He knew no Polish. He didn't know whether Poland required a visa. The Czech Republic was also outside the Union, for that matter. Alan didn't speak Czech. The situation was deteriorating. He realized that he was traveling on a German train pass which would be of no help outside Germany. He never would snag his soul!

On the street again later, Alan turned the corner back onto the Kurfürstendamm—the "Prince-Elector Road," the great main boulevard of West Berlin. He'd simply wanted to explore the neighborhood, but it had taken *forever* to walk to the *Siegessäule*!

A short ways down the "Ku" (as Berliners called the street), the Emperor William Memorial Church rose in ruins from the pavement, engulfed by a demonstration against the French nuclear testing in the Pacific. Students held long white banners: *August 6, 1945—August 6, 1995. Hiroshima, We Remember!* Some of the students held anti-American placards.

Talking with the students, Alan finally understood that the church had not been dedicated to Emperor Wilhelm II, but to his grandfather, Wilhelm I. He'd always wondered why they would erect a memorial to the Kaiser who had taken Germany into World War I!

Alan now headed towards downtown, trying to remember where Isherwood had lived in Berlin, and where the fictional Sally Bowles had lived—it was somewhere in this general area. He ate in a Chinese restaurant and thought of Japan and Beijing.

After dinner Alan returned to the hotel in the twilight of the oncoming summer night.

From the narrow German bed Alan glanced about his room. Nearby lay the snacks he'd bought at the local grocery: Potato chips, coke, an apple; and a newspaper.

The German newspaper highlighted the war in the Balkans, the collapse of the cease-fire in Chechnya, and German politics. Further back, he'd found an article on Kashmir.

Alan would read in the morning; at present he was too tired and despondent.

What was he doing in Berlin? He'd never intended to come here, though he had to admit he found the city vibrant. He could almost abandon the quest for his soul.

Then Vicki would leave him. And Gayle too probably.

Alan turned off the lamp and lay in the quiet darkness. Waning light intruded through the window: The filtered light of the city around him, reflecting down the central opening of the building. The window faced three walls of an interior courtyard.

What was he doing here?

Alan lay a long time before sleep overcame him; and he did not sleep well that night.

THIRTEEN

By Monday morning, Alan had abandoned Prague. He might still try for Paris: He'd come far enough north to catch a train without backtracking. But it would be a long ride; he couldn't convince himself. Meanwhile, he decided to take the S-Bahn to Potsdam, just outside Berlin, to see *Sans Souci*, the palace of the eighteenth-century Prussian king Frederick the Great, which he had read about in high school.

He hadn't even known German then! He'd fallen in love with Wagner already, but hadn't learned any German yet. He learned about *Sans Souci* in his French class: A story about the philosopher Voltaire visiting Frederick the Great. Did the sickness of his soul stretch back so far?

Alan caught the train from the Zoological Station south into the lovely, less populated area of southwest Berlin. After some time a time a lake appeared. The stops grew further apart. The lake revealed its full size. Along the lake the train made a stop; and Alan, staring into the tranquil water, was startled by voices he recognized.

"I disagree with you," a female voice said. "I maintain my position. There *are* sexual undercurrents to history."

"But do we need to dwell on them?" a male voice answered. "Are they really so important?"

"Yes," added another male voice. "Aren't other factors more relevant?"

Turning, Alan discovered Kurt, Rudi, and Käthe two rows away.

"Economic factors," Kurt continued. "Religious factors…"

Käthe had noticed Alan. She broke into a smile and exclaimed: "Herr Horne! I was sure I'd lost you!" She hesitated then added: "You know, I almost thought you were trying to get away from me in Dresden." She seemed disappointed and uncertain.

"Good morning, Fräulein Käthe. Have you been sightseeing?"

"We've been to Wannsee," Kurt explained sharply, "to visit the site of the conference."

"You may remember," Rudi added, "The Holocaust was planned here."

"That's what I've heard. I don't know much about it."

"It happened here," said Kurt. "On the shores of this lake, in 1942: The decision to murder millions of people." Alan thought of Rachel and Naomi.

"Is there a memorial?"

"Nothing like what there *should* be."

They fell silent.

"You know Herr Horne," Kurt said finally, "We had no idea who you were when we met you in Leipzig."

"And where are *you* going?" Rudi asked.

"*Sans Souci.* I heard about it long ago. Frederick the Great used to entertain Voltaire."

Alan felt a bit defensive. To him history, geography, and biography were not dry facts—he related to them *personally*;

he was a history professor! In some way he connected intimately to his environment, spatial and temporal. "As Without, so Within," as the Alchemists had written. He was sure his connections to the Inner and the Outer could change him—could find him his soul. He was not visiting places as a curious outsider. He had lived here; not only in the physical places he was visiting, but in the spiritual realms awakened within him by the outer facts of time and place—which he had experienced through history, philosophy, art, literature, music. These weren't external impositions of society or teacher—they were his native homeland. He'd been taught both Biblical and Greek legend by age ten, and had come to the personal experience of literature and psychology by age fifteen.

To be mistaken as a tourist always put Alan on his guard; but he felt at ease now. Rudi and Kurt seemed to inhabit the same realm of the mind. They were familiar with Alan's historical reference.

"Yes, Frederick and Voltaire were friends. The palace is closed on Mondays, but we wanted to walk around the gardens. We always do that when we're in Berlin. It's relaxing to visit the park." After a moment Kurt added: "Käthe seems a bit tense."

Käthe said nothing.

"I'm sorry to hear the palace is closed," Alan told them. "I couldn't come here when I lived in Germany before; I couldn't get an East German visa. I couldn't visit Wagner's home cities either—they were all in the DDR."

"Well, we can have a pleasant stroll," Käthe said softly. "We can walk to *Sans Souci* from the station. It's only a mile or so."

*

Alan had planned to go to Potsdam, visit *Sans Souci*, and head for Paris. The Saxon threesome derailed him. Soon they were all walking across the bridge from the train station into Potsdam.

"Friedrich says they're going to rebuild the Garrison Church."

Alan's puzzled look prompted Käthe to explain Rudi's remark.

"That's where Hitler and Hindenburg met," she said, "the Chancellor and the President, in the early days of the *Reich*. They called it the Day of Potsdam." Apparently *she* thought historically too.

"The meeting of The Old and The New," explained Rudi.

"Parliament met at a huge church service here in Potsdam," Käthe went on, "after the Reichstag fire—"

"After the Parliament building burned down," Rudi interjected.

Käthe glared at him. "Hindenburg shook Hitler's hand and said, 'Thank God we've come this far—it's taken long enough!'"

"It was unfortunate, Mr. Horne," Kurt interrupted. "Chancellor Brüning had been on the right track. The economy was improving. But Brüning wanted to reform agriculture, and Hindenburg considered *that* Bolshevism. There was no one left but Hitler, and President Hindenburg appointed him Chancellor."

"They packed the cabinet with non-Nazis," Rudi added, "in order to control Hitler. Eight or nine out of twelve, but Goering controlled Security…"

"It's always the same," said Kurt. "Whether Hitler or Castro, Mao or Franco. The people who want power just grab it and keep it—as we saw with Tian An Men."

They enjoyed the *Sans Souci* gardens at leisure. The palace, as Rudi had said, was closed. But as they walked Alan contemplated Frederick the Great, so different from Wilhelm II—or *was* he? Frederick had taken Silesia from the Poles on dubious grounds. But hadn't the U.S. intervened repeatedly in Latin America? Alan resisted pursuing the thought.

"We were going to Dresden regularly," Rudi replied to Alan's question. "Kurt and I had been together for years. He runs *The White Rose* and I run the Bach Museum and music store. We fell in love at university. But Leipzig is not so cultural…"

"It's hard for *any* city to be as cultural as *Dresden!*" laughed Kurt. "And that's where we met Käthe."

Kurt and Käthe exchanged a kiss.

"It was just about the time…" Käthe stopped for a moment, embarrassed. "It was about the time I realized that Gustav—I suppose I mean Sally—wasn't as forward-thinking as I thought. He talked about freedom, but—" She hesitated. "Well, he isn't nearly as liberated as he'd led me to believe!"

Kurt glanced towards the men uneasily. "That's your opinion, Käthe!" he answered gravely.

Rudi laughed uncomfortably. "And Kurt and I?" he said slowly. "Are *we* liberated enough for you?"

"I'd say you're *coming along.*" She tried to make it a joke, but the men weren't laughing.

"It isn't a matter of sexual shamelessness, you know." Kurt sounded more serious than Alan had ever heard him.

Alan hesitated a moment then said, very self-consciously: "I need to get back to town. You don't have to come with me…"

But of course they did. They insisted on accompanying The Visitor into downtown Berlin. During the long trip back into the city, they talked continuously, especially Käthe, hardly allowing Alan a chance to speak. The thrust of her argument was that the world could be saved if people got over their sexual hang-ups.

The closer the train approached the city center, the longer and more unending the ride seemed to Alan.

They got off at Alexanderplatz and stood below the TV tower. Alan had been unable to shake them. He hadn't even attempted to return to his hotel and get his baggage. They had sailed right through the Zoological Station, where Alan had intended to get off. He had sensed that his hosts would simply follow him back to his room. He had known from his experience with Käthe in Dresden that it would be extremely difficult to get away. On the other hand, he now wondered whether he was feeling overly intimidated. He determined to venture an escape.

"You go on," Alan told them, looking up at the tower. "I want to walk to the museums."

"But they're all closed, Alan," Käthe told him, "Just like *Sans Souci*. It's *Monday*. Museums are closed on Mondays."

"I just want to see where they are," Alan yelled back as he walked off. "Meet me there in half an hour."

"But they're *closed*. *Closed*." Käthe glared after him until Kurt and Rudi dragged her off towards the tower. It was as if Käthe's two boyfriends intentionally diverted her so that Alan could leave. Alan couldn't help wondering what they'd all told one another about him.

Rudi had described Museum Island, the huge complex on an island in the Spree, in downtown Berlin. He'd particularly recommended the Pergamon Museum. But Käthe was right: The Pergamon was closed. So were all the other monumental buildings on Museum Island.

But it was barely one p.m. Unter Den Linden, the Berlin equivalent of the Champs Elysées, the great Parisian avenue, would provide an interesting walk before he left for Paris.

A block down the avenue, Alan stumbled upon the Museum of German History. What better diversion for a history professor! He could duck in, hide from the threesome, escape to his hotel, grab his bags and head for the train station and Paris.

"This museum is amazing," the young Middle Eastern man commented. His smile was genuine, his voice inviting.

"Yes," replied Alan. "The entire history of Germany, from prehistory to the present. From the Romans to Barbarosa…"

"And the Hapsburgs to Napoleon…"

"And Bismarck to Wilhelm to Hitler."

Appreciating the gleams in each other's eyes, Alan and the stranger both laughed.

"We think the same way, you and I. I didn't know Americans thought historically."

"What makes you think I'm American?"

"Do you think I'm a typical Egyptian? Egyptians fixate on the pyramids, or Al Azhar, or Coca-Cola. *My* vision is Alexandria as it once was: The Bridge between civilizations."

The Egyptian extended his hand. "I am Ahmed," he said warmly.

Alan blanked a moment, trying to recall...something, then replied:

"Alan Horne. Delighted to meet you!"

Ahmed pivoted suddenly. Alan's eyes followed. A woman in a head scarf appeared from the next room.

"He's walked down the street. My father doesn't approve of us, I'm afraid."

"I don't think that's accurate, Helga," Ahmed answered gently. "It's more correct to say *you* don't approve of *him*!"

For an instant Helga glared. Then she lowered her eyes and replied: "You're right, Ahmed. I don't approve of my father."

Alan left before she recognized him.

On the wide Unter Den Linden ("Beneath the Lindens"), goose-stepping East German soldiers no longer guarded the classically inspired columns and grotto which once had formed the *Tomb of the Unknown Soldier*. Alan entered the dark, once off-limits interior. After his eyes adjusted he discerned a figure in front of him. Beyond the figure, a sculpture rose from the floor. The figure unexpectedly turned to Alan: A man, perhaps in his sixties.

"Yes, this *was* the *Monument to the Victims of Fascism and Militarism*. Did you realize you were talking to yourself? The *Tomb of the Unknowns* is gone. This is the *New Watch*."

"*New Watch*? What does that mean?"

"*Die Neue Wache.* The 'New Watch House,' the 'New Guard House' of the King's Guards. It was built in Napoleonic times and eventually became a memorial to the victims of war."

"But…what *is* the *New Watch*?"

Sadness crossed the man's brow. It reminded Alan of the Hans Sachs statue where he had kissed Sally in Nuremberg.

"The *New Watch* is an awareness, a vigilance. You sound American. You might not understand. You have to live through some things to appreciate them."

Alan struggled to not feel slighted. "I know," he answered, "that Germany had the first social security system in Europe, that Germany was prosperous and cultured; but within thirty years, Germany lay in ruins brought largely on itself."

But why single out Germany? Remember Lenin, Stalin, Mao, and Pol Pot. Remember the lesser villains…

"You understand better than I expected," the old man answered. "You see this sculpture? It's by Käthe Kollwitz: The mother grieving for her family. Or maybe the father. *Male* and *Female* become interchangeable. It's terrible to watch children destroy their parents' legacy."

The man stared ahead a moment, then muttered: "My children. My family! My son and daughter!"

The man fell silent, staring into the eyes of the bronze parent.

They were still together at the *Brandenburger Tor*—the Brandenburg Gate.

"The *Tor* is so clean!" exclaimed Alan. "In 1970 it was filthy."

"And now it's pristine—at least on this side. They cleaned the eastern half first. And here on Unter Den Linden, instead of students buying dollars on the black market, we have Gypsies, Romanians, and Poles selling Russian Army belts! How are the mighty fallen!"

They passed through the Gate and into the West. The man pointed left.

"Those giant tents, yellow and blue, off in the distance: That's Potsdamerplatz, one of the great squares of old Berlin. It and Alexanderplatz—like Time Square or Grand Central Station for you Americans. Unter Den Linden and the Kurfürstendamm like Broadway. My parents talked about old Berlin, when I was a child, before they died in the camps. I remember them like dreams that aren't quite real."

He's in the Dreamtime, Alan thought. *And so am I.* The old man gazed ahead as if into a vision.

"Imagine New York without Time Square or Grand Central Station—the World Trade Center or the Empire State Building. Imagine ruins, rubble, people digging in the snow for a scrap of food. That's how it was for some of us in Berlin. Those tents—the *Cirque des Étoiles*—magnificent stores once stood there."

Cirque des Étoiles! Where Vicki told me she was leaving! Alan felt a pang of desire for Vicki, and anger at her for abandoning him.

If this man was sixty-five or seventy...he must remember 1940 or earlier. *But who would attack the United States, attack New York? Why would they?* They continued walking.

"My parents wed three months before Hitler became Chancellor. They were Social Democrats, but avoided arrest for several years. By the time I was eight, though, we were all in the camps."

171

The man's eyes flamed suddenly: They'd arrived at the Reichstag—the old German Parliament.

"Look: Where Goering burned down German democracy. It could have been so different! Hitler had lost the presidential election to Hindenburg, decisively. The Nazis *were* the largest party in Parliament—but never a majority. Even with intimidation and terror, Hitler couldn't win an election. He could only pass the Enabling Act—his takeover of the government—by packing the Reichstag with his Brown Shirt thugs. But Otto Wels, the leader of the opposition Social Democrats, rose and denounced the Nazis!"

Would an American senator do the same? Alan wondered. *Would Americans behave better, in similar circumstances?*

Then the man settled onto a bench and apparently forgot that Alan was there. He seemed to be sinking into sleep. After five minutes, Alan stood up and slowly walked away. The Lehrter Station was just a few blocks to the north.

Alan couldn't go to Paris now; he'd need an overnight train. And now Alan wanted to understand Berlin. Helga hadn't recognized him at the History Museum. Ahmed must be her Arab boyfriend.

The strange old man had depressed Alan with his talk of the old Germany. Alan knew that nations could collapse overnight. But he couldn't imagine New York being destroyed.

Another fact had moved him, deeply; he hadn't realized it at first. The memorial plaque at the *Neue Wache* had mentioned the usual victims of the Holocaust: The Jews, the Gypsies, the Unions. But it included a group Alan had never seen mentioned on a public memorial in the United States. It honored the *homosexual* victims of the Nazis. Germany respected its queer citizens in a way the United States didn't.

One final fact unsettled Alan. It hit him as the S-Bahn was pulling out of Lehrter Station.

The inscription at the *Neue Wache* specifically thanked Herr Friedrich Neufeld of Berlin for his generous support of the project. Friedrich Neufeld was an important person after all. Whoever this man was, with his extra wives, sullen daughters, and adopted transvestite sons, he had made a significant contribution to German society. Alan wanted to know more.

FOURTEEN

Alan paced his room, not knowing what to think or feel. He'd been back at the pension for an hour, thinking about Sally and Naomi's wedding. What a strange couple they were!

He'd eaten a few egg rolls in Potsdam, but nothing since then. Shortly before six p.m., he dressed and headed for the Ku-Damm. The restaurants he saw were too expensive, or too crowded, or serving the wrong kind of food.

A sign on Kleiststrasse mentioned Nollendorfplatz straight ahead.

That's it! he remembered now. *That's where Isherwood lived. The birthplace of Sally Bowles!* And connected to Sally Neufeld, because she'd named herself for Isherwood's most famous character.

Nollendorfplatz seemed ordinary enough. But a dark stone mounted in a wall of lighter granite caught his eye, beneath which Alan read the words:

Beaten to Death.
Silenced to Death.
To the homosexual victims
Of National Socialism.

Towards the bottom of the plaque Alan saw the name *Friedrich Neufeld*.

And *Kurt Müller* and *Rudi Wagenheim*.

These prominent people (Kurt had helped bring down the East German government) supported homosexual rights. It was refreshing to see this marker after the diatribes of the American Christian Right and people that Alan knew personally, who could only think of homosexuality as "an abomination condemned by God."

Alan sighed and stuffed his hands into his pockets. Something was there: The card Naomi had handed him in Bayreuth—the invitation to her wedding.

Kleiststrasse. Nollendorfplatz. It couldn't be far away.

Alan entered the Gate of Heavenly Peace as gray evening approached. It was not a church, as he'd expected. It was a Chinese restaurant. Alan was nervous and hungry.

"Mr. Horne," said a middle-aged Chinese man in a business suit. "We were wondering where you were. Please follow me. The party is gathered in an upper room."

An upper room like Jesus' last meal.

"Have I met you before?"

"You may have met my brother. I am Herr Lin. My brother Herr Lin owns a Chinese restaurant in Leipzig, and Kurt Müller says you visited Leipzig recently. Herr Müller helped us start our business when we arrived here five years ago." Herr Lin led him up the narrow stairs.

"You were expecting me?"

"Fräulein Neufeld told us to expect you. We thought you'd gotten lost."

"How did you know who I was?"

"You're hard to miss." *How was that??*

He ushered Alan into a banquet room with sofas and reclining chairs.

"Alan. I was wondering where you were."

Sally kissed him on the cheek and led him to a man whose back was to them, talking with Ahmed. "Father, this is Alan Horne." It was the man Alan had met at the *Neue Wache*.

"You're Mr. Horne! I had no idea."

"You've met already?"

"Mr. Horne and I ran into one another just after...after Helga and Ahmed and I left the German History Museum."

"I saw them briefly," Alan said. "I didn't realize you were there too."

"Sally admires you so much, Mr. Horne. May I introduce my wife?" But Marthe Neufeld was absent.

"She's taking a call from Sándor," Sally said under his breath. "They're still negotiating in Shanghai." They exchanged significant glances.

"Ah," exclaimed Friedrich. "Well, my wife will be back in a moment."

"But you have three wives," Alan replied without thinking.

Herr Neufeld gave him an odd look.

"I mean...you've been married three times."

Herr Neufeld smiled awkwardly.

"Yes, I see...you know...my wives...are here. I don't see them just now. Let me introduce you to some other..."

"My gods!" exclaimed Alan. "I think I know everyone already!"

Kurt Müller and Rudi Wagenheim were curled up on a sofa together. Käthe was walking away from them. Rudi sang softly:

Nehmet, esset, das ist mein Leib.
("Take, Eat, This is my body").

He lingered on the final note. Kurt laughed and sang:

Trinket alle daraus.
Dies ist mein Blut des neuen Testaments…
("Drink you all of it. This is my blood of the New Testament…")

Kurt and Rudi kissed.

Alan thought they were singing Bach. He wondered whether Rudi and Kurt had met through music or social action.

"We thought you weren't coming, Mr. Horne. We thought we'd lost you! Do you recognize the music? You aren't familiar with *Bach*, eh? You're the grand *Wagnerian*!" Rudi nearly snickered.

Alan couldn't suppress a laugh. "The *Matthew Passion*, isn't it? The only vocal Bach I know. It's—"

"*The Last Supper. Take, eat. Drink ye all of it.* It seems so appropriate."

"For a wedding?" But Alan thought a moment and sang:

Da ging hin der Zwölfen einer,
Mit Namen Judas Ischariot,
Zu den Hohenpriestern und sprach:
"Was wollt ihr mir geben? Ich will ihn euch verraten."
("Then one of the twelve, by the name of
Judas Iscariot, went to the high priests and said: 'What will you give me? I would betray him.'")

"Yes, yes," laughed Kurt. "Judas and the High Priests!" Rudi clapped his hands. What had put *that* into Alan's mind?

Then Friedrich Neufeld placed his hand on Kurt's shoulder and whispered: "The situation in Krajina's becoming catastrophic."

They withdrew to a corner with Sally and Naomi. Alan wondered where Käthe had gone. Then he noticed Rachel Herzlieb sitting alone, worried and distraught, and went over to her.

"Mr. Horne," she smiled disconsolately, "A pleasure. I understand you met my daughter after all."

"I'm glad to see you, Geveret Herzlieb. I wanted to talk with you more."

"These circumstances," she replied. "I must make the best..."

"I know you don't approve of this marriage. But Gustav is a good man—loving and conscientious. I'm sure they'll be happy."

Rudi came over, smiling.

"Have you visited the Synagogue downtown, Mrs. Herzlieb? The restoration is complete. I've heard some wonderful cantor music there. Fascinating how the German Enlightenment interacted with the Jewish Enlightenment—Goethe, Schiller, Lessing; Moses Mendelssohn, and so on. And the interplay—if you'll pardon the pun!—of the Jewish cantor tradition with the Passion music of Bach."

Rachel Herzlieb's eyes brightened. "I don't believe we've met. I'm Rachel Herzlieb, from Tel Aviv."

"Rudi Wagenheim." He extended his hand. "An honor to meet you!"

"Mr. Horne?"

Alan recognized the voice. He turned and accepted Ahmed's offered hand.

"*Ahalan wa Sahalan, ya Sayid. Tcharaft b-marifatak!*" Alan tried not to grin as he spoke.

"You speak Arabic?" Ahmed's eyes lit up. "You're an unusual American!"

"I've been studying Arab culture a long time. I visited Cairo once, while I lived in Munich. Hospitable people!"

"When did you learn Arabic?"

"During the Gulf War. I studied it over my lunch hours."

Ahmed frowned. "A depressing time. The Iran-Iraq War had been terrible enough!"

"And now the embargo, and Iraqi children dying!" Alan welcomed the chance to talk. Another human rights disaster, but Americans had lost interest in Saddam Hussein.

"I wish my Arab brothers weren't so insular. Some have lived in the West, but many simply hate."

As opposed to Americans? Alan thought.

Ahmed sighed. "We must learn to respect one another, or we are lost! You must understand that, Helga!"

Helga had walked up, head covered, looking nervous and pre-occupied. Inge and Käthe followed behind her, apparently finishing a conversation.

"You're wearing a headscarf, Helga. Why?" Alan asked; but Helga turned and walked away.

"I told her it wasn't required, but she feels strongly about it." Ahmed seemed apologetic and a little embarrassed.

"She gets on my nerves," Inge whispered. "She's so dogmatic now. Doesn't it bother you?"

"Of course it does," said Käthe. "We all used to be so close."

179

*

He felt a hand on his shoulder. It was Friedrich.

"Mr. Horne, I'd like to introduce my wife Marthe. Tonight is our second anniversary."

Alan and Marthe Neufeld stared at each other a moment. A series of expressions passed across both their faces. It was impossible to tell what they were thinking, but something extraordinary was apparently going on inside both of them.

"You were..." Alan was nearly choking. "Aren't you..." The sentence hung unfinished a long moment. "Did I meet you last week...at an exhibition?"

"Mr. Horne?" Friedrich asked, concerned. "You haven't met my *wife* before?"

"I'm sorry, Friedrich." Marthe Neufeld started to laugh. "In Bayreuth..."

"We were both at the exhibit at Wagner's villa." Alan was laughing too. "She asked..."

"A display of the props from *Parsifal*, Friedrich. I was waiting for the Grail and Lance to glow. The light was shining down as if from Heaven." She turned back to Alan. "I never understood why you ran out of the room."

Friedrich kissed his wife's hand. "You're a Wagnerian too, Mr. Horne? Truly astonishing. You Wagnerians all seem so strange! Why can't you all simply like Handel?"

Alan had retreated to the restroom. Sitting in the stall, eyes closed, he heard the bathroom door open.

"Helga may have followed through this time." It sounded like Inge, agitated.

"You think she told them? Why?" Käthe's voice.

"She said she couldn't stand the humiliation. She wants to start a new life with Ahmed. She said her father and his adopted son ought to learn—" The voice broke off. "Oh my God! We're in the wrong—" The door slammed and the room was silent again.

Alan could understand Helga's annoyance; he understood shame. He himself felt shamed in the United States. He suspected the homophobes might never understand. At least his family accepted him.

Sally's unconventional life might certainly have offended Helga. Islam clearly appealed to her. Perhaps it had drawn her to Ahmed. But Ahmed, apparently, did not reject the West.

Alan had been taught, through Unitarian Universalism, that "all things are connected." Then perhaps by not rejecting Helga outright—or the homophobes—he could learn something about his soul.

Back in the banquet room Alan found Frieda, Sophie, and Marthe gathered around Friedrich. They seemed comfortable with each other and affectionate—not rivals at all.

With regret Alan remembered his life with Vicki, Preston, and Jane. More recent memories of Gustav and Inge completed his plunge into gloom.

FIFTEEN

Mr. Lin brought in the appetizers, and the guests sat down around the large table. Sally had announced that the ceremony would follow the meal. Alan was seated near Sally and Naomi. He tried to discuss the ceremony with them, but they simply asked him to picture them all in the middle of the Universe and bless their union based on everything he intuited at that instant. Alan had no idea what to do.

Meanwhile the conversations of Friedrich and his friends, here in the Chinese restaurant, did nothing but depress Alan. Everything he heard reminded him of William Bao.

"Bosnia is deteriorating every day," Sally said. "Thousands are being killed, and Sarajevo's cut off from the world. I'm not a Muslim, but I *am* a human being!"

"And Chechnya," Kurt added. "Why is everything so unsettled?"

"There was a bombing in Paris last week," Rudi added, taking Kurt's hand. "Chaos everywhere. The Tokyo subway attack in the spring, the Oklahoma City bombing, the bombing of the Jewish Center last year in Buenos Aires..."

"Are you familiar with William Bao?" Alan finally asked.

"Of course," said Kurt. "Marthe's boyfriend Sándor…"

Herr Neufeld shot him a reprimanding look. "Let's talk after the ceremony," Kurt whispered. Friedrich Neufeld returned to his previous appearance, as if he'd never noticed Alan's remark.

"We have to help the Bosnians and Chechens," Friedrich said. "Just as the Scholls had to speak against the Nazis."

Alan's anxiety increased. Helga had ignored his question about the headscarf, Friedrich had cut off any discussion of Bao. But now Helga returned to the table so Alan tried again:

"Helga, could I...?" he hesitated. "Why have you started wearing a headscarf? Ahmed says it isn't required."

"It's not strictly required, Mr. Horne," Helga answered him calmly, "but I want to wear it. It's a matter of my own self-dignity. I'm tired of the way men look at women here. I'm more than just a body with female parts. I want to be respected for who I am, not how I look. So I've decided to cover myself."

"But the body," Käthe broke in, "the body is a path to the soul. We ought to be proud of our bodies, female and male. That's what I've learned through Tantra."

"Tantra!" snorted Helga. "Promiscuity and perversion!"

"How did you and Ahmed meet, Helga?" Alan tried to sound calm, but he was beginning to tremble inside. "I've never heard your story."

"He came to the pension when he arrived in Germany. He'd never been in Europe."

"My father," said the Egyptian, "had suggested that I come and study in Europe and compare European culture with the Islamic ideal: Medina after the Hijrah, when Muhammad fled from Mecca."

"Ahmed," Alan asked (he was thinking of his own journey), "concerning the idea of *hijrah*—can a *hijrah* ever be personal? I feel sometimes like I'm on a *hijrah* myself."

"It usually refers to the flight of the Prophet from Mecca to el-Medina. But it's also symbolic: It means to abandon an inferior life for something better."

Naomi's face lit up. "Like the flight of the Jews from Egypt!" Ahmed beamed.

"Oh for Heaven's sake!" Rachel Herzlieb muttered into her soup.

"Of course, Naomi," Ahmed replied. "The Jews were fleeing persecution at the hands of the ancient Egyptians, who were idol-worshippers."

"It's possible," Alan interrupted with a smile on his face, "that the Jews may have been followers of Akhenaton, the monotheistic pharaoh."

But Ahmed was growing enthusiastic. "Islam, you see, thinks of society as a family. We should love one another as Allah loves us."

"It's a beautiful vision," Alan replied smiling gently at Ahmed, "but the Qur'an is terribly confusing—and least for me! I suppose I should study it more seriously. Since I'm already forty-five—"

"Forty-five!" Inge gasped blushing, her voice beginning to tremble. "I took you for thirty-five at most." Her face turned a deep red. "You wanted to date me, but you admit you're married, and you're twenty years older than I am. Alan—!"

"But if people care about each—"

Inge stood up and left the room. Alan sat stunned.

*

The main meal arrived: Mandarin, Sichuan, and Cantonese dishes. Alan tried not to brood about Inge—he noted the broccoli beef was exceptional. But it was impossible to relax.

"I'm not going back to Tel Aviv," Naomi growled at her mother.

"Jerusalem then. At least live in *Eretz Yisrael*."

Alan suddenly felt tired of all intransigence. "You know," he interrupted, "the earliest inhabitants of Palestine weren't Muslims or Jews, but Pagans"

The table went silent. Helga tried to sound pleasant:

"Has anyone seen the exhibit on Frederick II at the Pergamon?"

"Frederick!" Alan exclaimed, "My history professor idolized Frederick! He called him the most enlightened leader in Europe! During the Crusades, he respected the Muslims as no other European did. He gained more through diplomacy than all the Crusaders!"

Sally beamed. Helga turned to Frieda.

"Mother, I know you think I don't respect the Church. I do. It's just that I've found peace and community in Islam. And Islam comes from the same source."

"I understand," said Alan.

"I can't do things just because society says so. I have to respect myself. People told me to make money and dress well; I did what people told me. But meeting Ahmed and discovering Islam changed me."

"But Helga," said Sally, "*I* believe in integrity, so does your mother! We really aren't so different."

"You're wrong," Helga insisted gravely. "We're very different."

Then Inge returned to the room, eyes swollen and red.

"I'm sorry I upset you," Alan told her.

Inge glared at him, looking exhausted. "Alan, I like you; but you don't seem to realize… The more I like you, the more it hurts me. It isn't your fault, but *the way you are* hurts me."

She started crying again. "I just—" Then she buried her head in his shoulder.

"There's nothing to do about it, really," she said finally. "You seem to need several people—and I need to have just one. I care about you, though; I think you're wonderful. But we couldn't be happy together; we need different things."

"Have some dinner, Inge," Alan said gently. "The chicken's amazing."

Mr. Lin beamed.

Everyone agreed about the food; but the longer they all sat there together, the more they antagonized one another. Alan started to explain himself to Inge, but after a few sentences—

"I won't live in the 'Promised Land!'" Naomi yelled at her mother. "I'm as much a German as a Jew." She saw Alan look up at her. "You can do that in America, can't you, Mr. Horne? Be more than one thing? The Germans called us 'foreigners,' but we lived and died here! We became model citizens, some of us."

He realized now that Naomi was inspiring him—and felt it must say something about his…soul.

"Being Jewish," Naomi went on, "it doesn't mean locking ourselves in Israel. We ought to be *opening* ourselves to the Universal. We're all one family, like Helga said. The Nazis were our brothers, our sick brothers and sisters. Saying we're 'chosen' doesn't mean we're superior—it means realizing that we really *aren't* special. My Jerusalem," she stammered, "my Jerusalem…is in the heart—and open to everyone."

Yes, Alan thought, *it's all in our hearts. Jerusalem—the City of Peace—the Soul! It dwells in our hearts.*

Alan marveled. Was this the same Naomi who'd invoked Tantra in Bayreuth and invited him to her room? She seemed so sexual then, so spiritual now! Was it Tantra that had reconciled these apparent opposites?

But Rachel Herzlieb was infuriated. She practically spit at her daughter: "Where do you get these ideas?"

Still Naomi glowed with inner conviction. "*My* Jerusalem," she reiterated, "is not a physical city. It is the Jerusalem of the Heart to which I bow, where all may live in community. We are one family—*one family*—as Ahmed said! I am a citizen, not simply of Israel, but of the *world*."

The room fell as silent as a tomb. There seemed no way to reconcile Naomi and her mother. But Friedrich Neufeld stood, walked around the table, and gently touched Rachel Herzlieb's shoulder.

"Geveret Herzlieb, I understand how uncomfortable you feel being in Germany, surrounded by Germans. God knows we Germans have committed crimes for which we can never atone. But Germans aren't all Nazis and never were."

"But you allowed it to happen, Herr Neufeld. You let it happen."

Ah, thought Alan. *The point is to have someone to blame.*

Friedrich Neufeld, saddened, did not answer. He seemed to be staring at his own arm. Rachel became alarmed.

"Herr Neufeld? Are you all right?"

Still Friedrich said nothing. Alan walked over and shook him.

"Herr Neufeld! What's the matter?"

Friedrich silently removed his jacket, unbuttoned his shirt sleeve, and pushed it up his arm; where a series of blue numbers appeared.

Rachel stared at the tattoo, then looked up at Friedrich.

"You may know, Geveret Herzlieb, that the great Synagogue here in Berlin was saved on Kristalnacht, the Night of Broken Glass, through the courage of a single policeman. You probably don't know what became of him and his family—his wife and young son."

Rachel started to speak; but Friedrich raised his hand.

"It was so long ago, Rachel; I barely remember. But I know there were righteous Germans because I know my father was one."

The tension was broken. Herr Lin brought in dessert. But Alan heard whispering behind him.

"We have to leave, Ahmed—now!" Helga's voice sounded pleading, insistent.

"By why, Helga? Why?" Ahmed sounded quite content. "The fruit looks delicious—and you can have ice cream!" No answer from Helga. "Why would we leave?" the Egyptian went on, "The wedding is still to come."

"It's not a legal ceremony. It's not even Christian! Don't you understand? Herr Horne is just an American who calls himself a priest—a pagan priest! Don't you understand what 'Pagan' means? Alan Horne is *kafir*."

This is what she thinks of me?

"I think he's charming; I want to talk with him more. I'm staying for the wedding."

Ahmed returned to the table. Helga did not.

SIXTEEN

Herr Neufeld tapped his fork on the wine glass, startling Alan out of a reflection. Alan had just noticed that only twelve other people were present. Earlier he had counted thirteen. He realized that Helga Neufeld had left the room. Ahmed was sitting back down, looking troubled.

Friedrich stood to face his guests.

"Ladies and Gentlemen, I would like to introduce the person my daughter has chosen to perform the Handfasting (that's what you called it, Sally?)—Mr. Alan Horne, from California. Alan, I think I may be the only person here who hasn't actually met you before today! But I'd like to know you better. Could you tell us something about yourself? Are you really a Pagan priest? My daughter says you're absolutely fascinating."

Alan rose, acknowledged the applause sweeping the table, smiled broadly, waited for the applause to end, then turned to Friedrich.

"What would you like to know about me, Herr Neufeld? I don't know what Sally has already told you."

"Sally says you're the most authentic person she's ever met—an example of how to be honest about one's soul. Be honest, Mr. Horne. Tell us who you are."

189

Honest about my soul? Alan hesitated. Everyone was watching. What could he say to them? How could he be honest? *What the hell.*

"I don't know what to say, my friends. Talk about souls? I live in California with my wife of fifteen years and my daughter, who's almost four. Frankly, I came to Germany to search for my soul. If I tell you I'm bisexual, polyamorous and pagan, I'm not sure you'll understand what I mean. I've fallen in love with both men and women, and I can't seem to be happy with only one partner. In addition to my wife, I have a girlfriend I've been seeing for about a year. As a child I was baptized as a Christian, but I abandoned both Christianity and Rationalism to study Wicca—which you may know as Witchcraft. My wife is now thinking of leaving me, I'm incapable of having sex with my girlfriend, and she's told me I've *lost* my soul. I thought I might find it with my parents, but they sent me to Germany because I'd gone to university in Munich. I haven't found *anything* in Germany—other than all of you. I've come to care for you all, even though I've known you less than a week."

Alan glanced around the table. Mrs. Herzlieb looked ashen, Inge and Käthe seemed intrigued, Ahmed curious, the Neufeld wives pleased. Sally and Naomi were beaming; Rudi and Kurt were grinning. Only Friedrich's face remained inscrutable. And Helga's seat was empty.

"I don't know what else to say," Alan said at last.

Sally stood and acknowledged him. She and Naomi had changed into identical white dresses during dessert.

"You've done well, Alan. Excellent. I knew I'd chosen the right person to bless our wedding."

Feeling reassured, Alan turned to Friedrich and said, nonchalantly:

"I want to know *you* better too, Friedrich. I've met your children and wives. Are *you* bisexual or poly? Are *you* Jewish or Christian, or agnostic? What are *you*?"

The question startled Herr Neufeld, who looked embarrassed. Alan lost his nerve.

"I'm sorry," he snapped, "I shouldn't ask personal—"

"No, no. It's perfectly natural," said Friedrich. "You've told us about yourself. Now you want to know about us."

The room had grown silent.

"You want to know who I am," Friedrich went on, sounding a bit angry. Alan heard whispers now: Apparently Friedrich didn't often raise his voice. Was Friedrich mad at *him*—or someone else?

"Distinguished guests," Friedrich continued, with a bit of a laugh, "Mr. Alan Horne wants to know: Am I Jew or Christian? Muslim or Atheist? Am I straight or gay or bisexual? Who am I? *What* am I? Pacifist? Nationalist? Happy, sad—*what*?"

He paused a moment to collect himself.

"My friends," he continued, a bit calmer, "none of us can ever know when calamity may strike, when death may come—and when we may be taken away from those we love."

He surveyed the table then turned to Alan.

"Alan, you want to know who I am. I will tell you, Alan. I am a human being!"

After a long pause, Sally stood and drew Naomi to her.

"Are you ready?" Alan asked.

Naomi nodded.

"I think we can begin. Would the blessed couple join me here?" Alan stepped a bit away from the table.

"Lords and Ladies, Manifestations of the Universe, Purveyors of Love, Respect and Dedication, bear witness for us: That this couple, Sally and Naomi, has freely chosen one another to love and care for; to live with; to perhaps make children and a family together; to cherish and learn from one another. *So Mote It Be.*"

"*So Mote It Be,*" answered the two women.

"Sally Neufeld, do you offer yourself freely and with love to Naomi Herzlieb, to love and support?"

"I do."

"Naomi Herzlieb, do you offer yourself freely and with love to Sally Neufeld, to love and support?"

"I do."

Rachel Herzlieb started to cry.

"Then in the name of the Goddess who gave us all life, and *Her* Consort who rules as Lord of the Animals and of all Wild Things, I now acknowledge you before the Universe as—"

A loud banging burst from the doors in the rear of the hall. The assembled turned in surprise. The knocking repeated, then the doors flew open. Five policemen stepped in, surveyed the room, and approached the table.

"Are you Herr Friedrich Neufeld?" one of them asked hesitantly.

"Indeed, I am Friedrich Neufeld. Why have you disrupted our celebration?"

The question caught the officer by surprise. "Excuse me, *mein Herr.* I'm sorry to interrupt your party, but I have a warrant for the arrest of Herr Friedrich Neufeld of Neukölln, on charges of a morals nature."

"What are the charges?" Herr Neufeld shot back with an air of defiance. Then, breaking into a shout, he repeated: "What are the charges?"

"Bigamy, *mein Herr;* or, more properly, trigamy. You are accused of keeping three wives: One in Munich in the Free State of Bavaria; one in Nuremberg, also in the Free State of Bavaria; and one here, in the State of Berlin."

The hall fell silent. As the policemen handcuffed Friedrich Neufeld, Sally whispered to Alan: "I suggest you leave the country as quickly as possible. But try not to attract *die Polizei*'s attention."

Alan looked at Sally. "What do you know about this?"

Sally motioned for him to keep quiet. Ahmed had intercepted the policemen and their prisoner. "Friedrich, I am so sorry!"

As the policemen led Herr Neufeld away, Alan quietly slipped out a side door.

Alan went straight to his hotel. It was past ten o'clock. He couldn't go anywhere else, except to roam the streets or haunt the train stations or airports.

Alan began throwing clothes into his suitcase but eventually his pace slowed. Why should he worry? What could the police arrest *him* for? Sally was a man, so the wedding would have been legal. As an American Wiccan priest, Alan probably held no legal status—even in the U.S he didn't have legal recognition—and the police had arrived before he'd actually *married* them—so they couldn't accuse him of *performing* a marriage. But these were all technicalities.

Could they arrest him because of Friedrich Neufeld? No—he had nothing to do with Herr Neufeld's marriages to former or current wives. What should *he* be afraid of?

Alan began flipping through the newspaper he'd purchased the night before. An article caught his attention. A priest during the "Burning Times" of the sixteenth century had defended people accused of witchcraft. It had endangered the priest, but he had saved many of the accused.

Alan reread the article. They had not arrested the priest. People had been imprisoned, tortured and killed; but the priest had saved some of them. And *he* had not been killed.

So victims could sometimes be saved—though you can never assume they will be. Even during the Holocaust, some Germans—like Friedrich's father—had helped individual Jews.

Alan got into bed and turned off the light. He wanted to sleep, but his thoughts kept returning to the long-anticipated wedding that had not been consummated. Sally had suggested leaving Germany.

He considered once more: The priest in the 1500s had saved lives, and the priest had not been killed. What did this mean for Alan's soul?

Pondering this, Alan fell asleep.

SEVENTEEN

Alan lunged up from the bed. He'd been watching…Gayle and Vicki making love. A voice kept repeating "Who are you? Who are you?" If Alan could answer…he might regain his soul. He heard Wagner, Bach, and Serbian folk music. He saw Friedrich Neufeld and his three wives; and Helga, head to foot in a black robe—like a witch, or a woman in an Afghani burqa. Soldiers fought, and Sally Neufeld led her new wife Naomi through the rubble of fallen buildings. They were trapped in fighting and chaos. Rudi conducted an orchestra and choir in the middle of the devastation. The buildings looked like New York, but the devastation was that of World War II. The music became disjointed, disconnected, like Schoenberg. A merchant from the Cairo bazaar offered Alan tea and invited him to sit and chat—he didn't seem to care how long Alan stayed: Total hospitality and politeness. Bulgarian music, Israeli music, Arabic music. Ahmed argued with Israeli soldiers while Rachel Herzlieb looked on—Justice and Humanity—Survivors. A few feet from Rachel and Naomi's destroyed home in Jerusalem, Frieda, Sophie, and Marthe stood in the street wailing. A body, presumably Friedrich's, lay face down covered with filth. *Death to the despicable scum!*

A reporter interviewed Kurt. Käthe and Inge stood locked in an embrace. Where was Alan watching from? Was this foreordained or only what *might* be? Scrooge and the Spirit of Death.

Where am I? What was I doing? A dream. A vision. *Pull yourself out of it!*

Nothing looked familiar. This was not his bedside table with the lamp and alarm clock. *This is not California, and I am not at peace.*

He picked up a newspaper from the bed. The paper was in German. *A story about witches!* He looked around again. His clothes on the chair. Where was Vicki? *Not California.*

The unexpected dresser—he was in Germany, Berlin. And it was evening and it was morning, as in the Torah: The second day. The third day? What day *was* it?

He'd woken here before; he'd gone to Potsdam. That must have been yesterday. Faces appeared: Two men and a woman; an Arab, and a woman who wanted to be Arab; a mournful elderly fellow, the Brandenburg Gate, and the Reichstag.

Policemen. A wedding.

Alan flopped back and stared at the ceiling. Was it *Marsday*? He'd come to Berlin…*Sunday*? He'd been in Berlin…?

Two days! In Berlin two days! I've slept in Berlin two nights.

I shouldn't have stayed here. I was not to remain more than a day. Now what? Where is my soul?

But if he was still in Berlin…why rush to leave?

He wanted to leave. Sally had told him to leave. *I presided at a wedding broken up by police. Sally suggested I leave the country.*

Too groggy. Figure it out over breakfast.

*

Alan remembered the impersonal dining room from Monday morning. How strange to know in advance what breakfast would be. He'd been rushing, day by day, to new places. Now…

"Is Frau Neufeld in?" Alan thought the question straight-forward, but the waiter seemed confused.

"Frau Neufeld? We have no Frau Neufeld here." They were denying the Neufelds as Peter had denied Jesus.

"No Frau Neufeld? Don't the Neufelds own this hotel?"

The waiter repeated: "I told you, *mein Herr*, there are no Neufelds here."

Was he for once in an establishment the Neufelds didn't own? But then he'd been sent here by the Tourist Office!

Alan collected cheese, rolls, meats, and eggs; sat down and ate in silence. Had it all been an hallucination? Could he have been trapped in some Magic Castle, like Parsifal on his Grail quest; some illusion from which he'd unknowingly awakened? Or was he still sleeping?

I'm not supposed to be here: Nowhere more than one night, until I find my soul. Did I bring on the disaster by staying? Paranoid. Where were the Neufelds and their friends?

A phrase from the *Matthew Passion* leapt at him: *Und alsbald krähete der Hahn.* "And immediately the cock crew."

"Though I should die with Thee, yet will I not deny Thee." Where had they gone? The Neufelds and everyone who knew them seemed to have vanished like the alluring maidens in Klingsor's Magic Castle in *Parsifal*.

Alan began to tremble—*I suggest you leave the country as quickly as possible*—and walked out with his breakfast untouched.

*

On the bus to Tegel airport, a tabloid story caught his attention.

WOLF IN SHEEP'S CLOTHING?
PHILANTHROPIC DISPLAYS MASK LURID LIFE OF LUST AND WITCHCRAFT

Noted hotelier and philanthropist Friedrich Neufeld was arrested Monday evening on charges of trigamy.

Neufeld was taken into custody during a bizarre witchcraft ceremony in a restaurant on Nollendorfplatz.

According to initial reports, Neufeld's son, Gustav, dressed as a woman, was about to be married in a pagan ceremony when the police entered the room.

Gustav Neufeld, along with his three alleged "mothers," followed officers to the local station. The women declined to speak with reporters. The junior Neufeld nearly caused an incident at the station. He was dressed as a woman and insisted on being called "Sally." He asserted his father had done nothing illegal, and demanded that the elder Neufeld be released on bail, which the police refused to do, explaining that decision will be made today by a judge.

It has since been revealed that Gustav is not Friedrich Neufeld's natural son. It appears that the elder Neufeld may have adopted Gustav as a child in the early 1980's.

A police spokesman also reported that Gustav Neufeld is apparently not a German citizen. His actual nationality is as yet unknown. The police suspect he was born in the Middle East, perhaps Turkey or Iran.

This suspicion has been bolstered by the comments of Friedrich Neufeld's natural daughter Helga, formerly of Munich, now of Hamburg, who has broken with her family and was eager to speak with the press.

"We all knew Gustav was not my father's natural son," Helga told reporters. "As for my father's 'wives,' they all knew about and tolerated one another. Since I became old enough to understand the situation, I have found it increasingly humiliating. Such sham marriages demean our Judaeo-Christian-Islamic traditions."

Unidentified sources suggest that Helga Neufeld had once been engaged to Gustav—suggesting that Gustav had never been legally adopted.

Gustav Neufeld is currently unavailable for questioning. After being allowed a brief meeting with his father, Gustav—a.k.a. Sally—vanished, along with his fiancée, Naomi Herzlieb, formerly of Tel Aviv.

The three "wives" will not be charged with a crime, police spokesmen said. In such cases the women are never charged, since they are considered victims. All three vehemently defended their 'marriage.'

Friedrich Neufeld is known for his significant contributions to human rights causes in Germany and abroad. He is a charter member of the Neue Wache, and a major contributor to the Holocaust Memorial Fund here in Berlin. He also provides substantial financial support to a foundation for peace and reconciliation in the Middle East. Shortly before his arrest, he had arranged a massive donation of clothing and food for refugees in Croatia and Bosnia. Were it not for his unfortunate proclivities, one could consider him a model person.

At Tegel, Alan went straight to the airline ticket counters.

"Where are you going, *mein Herr?*" The expression on the clerk's face somehow disturbed Alan.

Alan excused himself and sat down on the nearest bench. Lufthansa, British Air, Swiss Air, Air Lingus…. Where did he want to go?

He realized this was his chance. He could go *anywhere* with no danger of passing back through a place he'd already been. He could fly to Prague. He could fly to Paris. But where did he *want* to go? Where would he find his soul?

He wanted to be with Vicki. They'd been married fifteen years. Alan loved cuddling and discussing philosophy and music with her. He wanted to run to Lavender and spin her above his head, like he had when she was a baby. He thought of Gayle and the husband he'd never met. He wanted to hold her and make love with her. He thought of his parents in Virginia. They were probably taking Lavender to the Zoo or the amusement park. He desperately wished he could be there.

Alan knew where to find everyone he cared about, but he didn't know where to find himself. Was it because he'd so often done what society wanted instead of what *he* truly wanted? Did he even *know* what he wanted?

What would Alan say when Gayle asked him about his soul, when his parents asked him? But surely part of his soul lived in his relationships with the people he loved!

Alan picked up his bags and started walking. He walked past all the counters in Tegel Airport. Then he walked past them again, and then a third time. He thought of how he would like to return to places he'd visited as a student: Paris, Rome, Istanbul, Athens, Cairo, St. Petersburg. He'd travelled so much while he lived in Munich! But he'd missed places: Spain, Scandinavia, England. How was he to choose?

When he finally sank back into a chair, feeling he'd been walking in circles—he realized he *had* been walking in circles: Tegel Airport is *circular*. You can walk and walk and never come to an end. His airport walk was exactly like the quest for his soul: He was going around in circles!

In his mind, Alan caught an image of Gustav Neufeld as Alan had seen him in Nuremberg, in the subway walking away with the group of boys behind him. Now, after Friedrich Neufeld's arrest and Gustav's disappearance, Alan could only have said: *Where are you going, Gustav?*

But as Alan asked this, the image swung round to face him. Alan now realized what was bothering him so: The face of the man at the ticket counter had resembled Gustav's. Now the face that Alan had held in his arms in Nuremberg turned to face him and asked: *Where are you going, Alan? Quo vadis?*

Quo vadis! The words Jesus had asked Peter, as Peter fled Rome to escape imprisonment and death. Peter had returned to Rome to bear witness. Should Alan return? But how? And where?

Alan was back on his feet. He left his baggage with a storage checker, and caught the next bus downtown.

Alan had intended to return to Nollendorfplatz and the Gate of Heavenly Peace. If he could find Herr Lin…

But the bus he'd taken didn't go to Nollendorfplatz, and he'd left his map in his bag at Tegel Airport. He hadn't planned to spend so long in Berlin and hadn't studied the map. He found himself downtown again on Museum Island.

Tuesday now, and the Pergamon was open. Alan walked through the large doors into the cool lobby. Perhaps the exhibit about Frederick and Islam could help him understand Helga and Ahmed. Alan had always remembered what his history professor had told him about Frederick, and how much the professor had enjoyed studying in Beirut. Of course that was before the Lebanese Civil War.

Ahmed had grown up Muslim, but spoke highly of ancient Alexandria, where people of different backgrounds exchanged ideas.

Helga, on the other hand, seemed to want her world as constricted as possible. She wanted to convert and had begun wearing a headscarf. What would happen to those two? Alan himself had a weakness for the Arab world, ever since he'd seen *Lawrence of Arabia* as a teenager.

The Pergamon looked huge and the exhibit on Frederick was upstairs. Alan decided to explore the ground level first.

The first exhibit immersed the visitor in statuary from classical Greece. The second hall...brought Alan to a stop. A Greek temple, or the façade of one, filled the entire room: Remains from the Temple of Pergamon in Turkey. The façade contained only about five percent of the entire complex. Turning towards the other wall, Alan found himself in the presence of *Them—The Holy Ones*—Athene, Hermes, Aphrodite, Zeus.

Alan brought his palms together and bowed to the images, then reached into his shirt and brought out his silver pentagram. Why did he always feel he had to hide his faith? He kissed the pentagram, whispered *Forgive me*, and let the star and attached rings drop onto his shirt. Then he approached the Deities.

He remained silent before them for several minutes, then remembered where he was. The museum was not crowded—it was late Marsday morning—and the other visitors seemed not to have noticed the eccentric figure frozen in front of the statues.

Then Alan turned back to the temple: Those marble columns, facades, steps—such a small portion of the original. A realization overwhelmed him: What it would be like to worship his divinities in freedom, unconcerned for the opinions of his countrymen, without the fear of losing his job or children, without the danger of having his private backyard altars vandalized, as some had been. Why was it still unsafe to be a Pagan in most of the United States? Gustav's voice returned—a statue of Dionysus resembled him—with the question again: *Where are you going?* Then a second question, from the medieval *Parzival* poem; the young redeemer asking the sick old king: *Uncle, what ails you?* Sally now seemed a redeemer or guru or guardian angel for Alan.

Alan fingered the pentagram. *I don't know. I don't know!*

The adjoining hall stopped him completely once more. Before him and above him, of the fairest blue and gold, rose the Ishtar Gate of Babylon. He saw his path, but it frightened him.

"Oh Queen of Heaven, oh Star of the Morning, oh Mother of Earth and Sea!" Alan spoke aloud and quickly turned to check whether anyone had heard him. But the chamber was empty; why should he be so afraid?

The exhibit on Frederick described the Empire of the 1200s—the Holy Roman Empire of the German Nation. No matter how powerful the Emperor was, the Bishop of Rome was always more powerful. The Western Church hounded Frederick, insisted he wage war in Palestine, insisted he threaten the Palestinians, Muslims for six hundred years, with torture and death. Frederick, recognizing the humanity and greatness of the Islamic world, resisted the Pope and suffered for it.

Alan left in a daze, his head swimming with confused thoughts and feelings, pentagram and rings tucked back into his shirt. He could return to Tegel Airport, but then where? Could he act according to his beliefs? Could he live by his convictions? Should he find Nollendorfplatz?

On the subway west from Unter den Linden, Alan tried to remember the parks, palaces, and museums of the West End, hoping for some clue to Nollendorf; but his mind was full of everything that had happened over the past seven days and his vision of the Old Ones at the Pergamon.

He asked directions but ended up in a section of the city that seemed totally unfamiliar. Filled with despair, he wandered the sunny tree-lined streets of Charlottenburg far to the west. He was afraid of his destiny, like Jesus in Gethsemene. If only he could find the restaurant!

Then he stumbled on Charlottenburg Palace, which he had heard of so often. *How strange!* Alan thought. *For forty-five years, East Berliners could not come to Charlottenburg; just as West Berliners could not visit Sans Souci. The fashionable members of Berlin society, who had wintered in the Bavarian Alps or attended the Festival in Bayreuth or the Mozart Festival in Salzburg, were suddenly forbidden to do so. The businessmen and intellectuals of Hamburg, Frankfurt, and Munich were unable to visit Dresden or Potsdam or half of their former capital. A wall encircled West Berlin. Armed guards stood in watchtowers over a no-man's land that ran through the middle of this city, precisely where I walked this morning and yesterday. Fifty years ago, Berlin lay in ruins, Alexanderplatz destroyed, Potsdamerplatz destroyed, like the Church of our Lady in Dresden, like those old photos of Nuremberg I saw when I lived there. All because a brilliant and hypnotic Leader was also deranged and diabolical. And how many people died for his pettiness and spite! And couldn't this happen to the United States, under a certain type of leader?*

Alan entered the Palace. Italian tourists crowded the ticket counter.

Charlottenburg seemed larger than Nymphenburg. But Nymphenburg had gardens, unlike Charlottenburg; and while Nymphenburg lay a few miles from Munich's dense downtown, Charlottenburg sat squarely in the center of Berlin's vast expanse.

Alan remained tense. He imagined the security guards watching him. They frequently reprimanded the Italians for examining vases and portraits too closely. The guards were also on edge. Alan thought he heard them mention the name Neufeld. He swore two guards had been looking right at him. He imagined he caught them turning away, as if to conceal that they were watching. He got the distinct impression that more and more guards were following him. He sped up and left, as the guards pulled out walkie-talkies. Alan rushed to the nearest subway station and took the first train north. He recognized his own paranoia—he kept thinking of Peter after the arrest of Jesus.

He began to wonder whether he was hallucinating. The police must be looking for him. The entire Neufeld family knew Alan's full name; Helga must have reported him!

Later he seemed to recall passing Richard-Wagner-Platz. He glanced up during a brief subway stop and saw mosaics depicting Wagner operas. Although it did nothing to anchor Alan back into reality, he felt a bit calmer when he arrived again at Tegel Airport.

But his thoughts lingered on Charlottenburg, somehow associated with Emperor Wilhelm II, who'd led the Germans into World War I. Hitler was an obvious lunatic, but how to describe Wilhelm? If America could not produce a Hitler, could it produce a Wilhelm?

The medieval German Empire had fallen apart in the centuries after Frederick II. The Thirty Years War, in the 1600s, destroyed what was left of "Germany."

Then Bismarck, the Prussian Prime Minister, pieced it back together in the mid-1800s.

But then a new Prussian King, young Wilhelm...Wilhelm wanted none of old Bismarck's caution. He wanted renewed glory for Germany, and fast. He dismissed the old Chancellor and brought the world to one crisis after another.

But he wasn't to blame for the Great War. When a Serbian murdered the heir to the Austrian throne, Austria struck back and Wilhelm supported it. Wilhelm paid for defeat with exile in Holland. Later Hitler spoke of Germany's "greatness" but never brought the old Emperor back. Hitler declared *himself* Leader, and simply began destroying everything he hated.

Where could Alan flee? He retrieved his baggage and walked the airport once more, terrified of circling aimlessly again.

He thought of Wilhelm heading west into exile. He thought of the German tribes sailing west over the seas—and he remembered Friedrich Neufeld's off-hand remark, when he discovered that Alan and Marthe had met in Bayreuth:

"You Wagnerians are so strange! Why can't you all just like Handel?"

Handel: Another of Alan's childhood loves. Bach's contemporary Handel had left Germany, while Bach had stayed behind. Handel had abandoned his patron the Elector of Hannover to live in London—then the Elector was invited to England as King George I.

King George and Handel; the Angles, Saxons and Jutes.

Alan could go to London. At least he spoke the language. Wicca came from the British Isles. A British Airways flight was leaving at 5 p.m.

As the plane lifted off, Alan looked down at the city he was leaving: The Brandenburg Gate, the television tower, the green swath of the Tiergarten. Somewhere down there, Friedrich Neufeld sat in prison. Somewhere, Frieda and Sophie and Marthe discussed their husband. Had Helga and Ahmed returned to Hamburg? Where were Sally and Naomi? Had Naomi left her mother alone, in the vast city that had once resolved to exterminate their people? Or had Rudi and Kurt and Käthe perhaps decided to look after her? They had a conscience. Did Alan?

The plane rose higher. Alan turned to the British Airways stewardesses, in their funny blue uniforms and hats, and sank into his seat with a sigh of exhaustion and relief. Berlin was dissolving into the mists of the August clouds, and Alan was heading, nevertheless, he hoped, towards home. But was he any closer to his soul?

PARADISE ENOUGH?

EIGHTEEN

The flight to London rejuvenated Alan. He enjoyed being in the air again, after the noise and commotion of the German trains. At some point he noticed the Frisian Islands passing below them and realized he was off "the Continent." After a modest dinner, he grabbed a newspaper from an empty seat.

The government of Zimbabwe had launched a campaign against gay people, calling them corrupt and sinful—a decadent import from "The West." President Mugabe hoped to leverage the issue into a grand anti-Western crusade. So human rights abuse continued as ever, and what was Alan to do? Many Westerners would agree it was decadent!

After a nap, Alan looked down to see the desolate marshes of east Britain.

Approaching London after almost two hours in the air, the plane descended directly over Windsor Castle. This surprised Alan; a plane crashing into the castle could wipe out Queen and Family—like a plane flying into the White House.

*

He'd just pulled his baggage off the conveyer belt when he heard a familiar voice.

"Alan?"

It isn't possible.

"Alan!"

It *was* possible. His wife was walking towards him across the terminal. She had no luggage. She looked good.

"Vicki? I thought you were in the Northwest with Claire."

"Claire. Claire and I... She wanted...but I met... It's a long story." She looked at her husband, laughed, and sighed. "I've got a room in London. Do you have plans? Why don't you come over? I was on my way to the car."

"How long have you been here?"

"Ten days."

"Ten days! How long were you with Claire then? A week?"

"Not even a week. That was more than enough, really."

More than enough?

"Look, Alan, come into town with me. I'll tell you over dinner."

He grabbed his bags and followed his wife towards the parking lot. She was a good-looking forty-year-old. But what was she doing in London?

Alan lowered his fork, chewed, appreciated the flavor, and swallowed.

"I never expected good Indian food in London," he said. *India, the great Pagan Land. Why do Christians and Muslims belittle it?* Vicki's melancholy appearance worried him. "You left Claire in Yellowstone to come to England with a Morris Dancing team?"

Vicki scowled. "I met *Ian* in Yellowstone, but he flew back to Chicago. Claire drove me to Billings so I could fly to Chicago myself and join the Morris team there. I toured with them for a week but now they're gone. And Ian's gone—I just put him on the plane."

She stroked his cheek. "You know, you might as well stay with me—unless you have other plans. We *are* still married, after all." She stated this as a simple fact, no feelings either way.

Alan could not decipher the contradictory looks on his wife's face. Did she care about him, or Claire? Was she leaving him, or returning? And who was *Ian*?

And her bisexuality. And her polyamory. Had she accepted these things about herself, or was she determined still to fight them? After everything they'd been through— what was holding her back? Could Alan be wrong about it all?

NINETEEN

By Wednesday afternoon Vicki had led him around Buckingham Palace, Westminster Abbey, and the Tate Gallery. She had apparently left the United States in roughly the same mental state as Alan. Whatever had happened between her and Claire in the Northwest, it had driven her abroad. She'd always felt drawn to Art and History, just like Alan; but her obsession was England, not Germany. She hadn't lived there the way Alan had lived in Germany; but everything about England fascinated her, though she'd never visited. The dancing tour had kept her out in the country though; now she was free to discover London.

"The Abbey was interesting," she ventured. "All those memorials."

It was late afternoon. They'd walked most of the way back along the Thames from the Tate to the Houses of Parliament.

"But who is actually *buried* there?" Alan asked. "T.S. Eliot isn't; he just has a plaque. The same with Byron. Handel may be there…" Alan had always liked Eliot and Handel and Byron. He'd often toned this down for his wife; she didn't approve of his intensity.

"They wouldn't even *acknowledge* Byron till *years* after he died in exile," Alan went on. "He was too controversial to *honor*—being gay or bisexual or whatever he was, disdaining societal norms."

"Societal norms…" Vicki's tone carried a hint of spite. "And who was this woman you met in Dresden?"

"Käthe." He was sorry he'd mentioned her—an offhand remark had slipped out. He hadn't mentioned the other Germans. He wished he *could* talk about them.

"You 'got together,' I suppose?" Vicki must have thought he'd mentioned Käthe to spite her. She never seemed to realize that he simply wanted to talk. But of course she was more sensitive now about polyness. It was her bias to believe that her husband was hopelessly promiscuous.

"Nothing happened," he growled. "I tried to get away from her. She was too intimidating for me."

"I thought nothing intimidated *you*." Her voice now suggested sarcasm.

They walked on. What could he say? She had the right to bitch if she wanted.

"The Thames is beautiful," she said, looking towards Lambeth Bridge.

"I'm glad we went to the Tate," Alan sighed. "I've always wanted to see the Pre-Raphaelite paintings. They were darker than I'd expected." The Pre-Raphaelite women haunted Alan. Their intensity called to his soul.

The Tate has been Alan's idea. It was as if he and Vicki were beginning the journey again, as he had begun it in Munich, by visiting a museum.

The couple had turned onto Whitehall and were approaching Parliament Square when Vicki unexpectedly took his hand.

"Alan, do you think our life together's been worth it?" She stood just inches away.

"Yes, Vicki," he replied after a hesitation. "I do. I'm glad I married you. Our marriage is important to me."

He leaned forward to kiss her, but she turned and resumed walking.

"I'm not convinced it was a good idea." She'd expected a normal marriage and he'd given her something else. He felt he'd failed her.

She took her husband's hand again and they continued up Whitehall. She wasn't leaving him yet.

In front of Parliament a young bearded man, seated at a small folding table, asked them to sign a petition.

"On behalf of Bosnia," he said. "The situation is very bad. The Muslims of Bosnia are being subjected to 'ethnic cleansing' by the Serbs."

"Ethnic Cleansing?" exclaimed Vicki.

"A new term for genocide," Alan snapped. He turned to the bearded man. "I've just come from Germany. I've seen footage of the war. Horrible."

He turned back to Vicki. "People have abandoned everything just to escape."

"Then you will sign our petition, *al-Hamdu'llah*?"

"We're not British citizens. Does that matter to you?"

"Sir," said the man, "the situation is so desperate… Sign…please."

Alan and Vicki signed. Alan was thinking of Rudi and Kurt and Friedrich.

*

The couple ate dinner at the worst Italian restaurant in Leicester Square, in the Theatre District. The miserable service merely worsened their mood.

"I slept with him, alright?" Vicki snarled. "I got involved. But it's over. Ian flew off on some emergency—at least that's what he said. It doesn't matter."

"But don't you understand? I don't care what you did. It makes no difference, like you said: It doesn't matter."

"That's what annoys me about you, Alan," Vicki snapped. "It matters to everyone else, but not to you."

Alan stared at his wife. "As far as I've ever been able to determine, Vicki, it doesn't matter to *you* either. You don't care about exclusiveness. You're just afraid of what people might think. You're afraid to be judged for your convictions. You're afraid of your own desires."

"And *you're* always so damned self-confident, Alan. You completely ignore my feelings."

"That isn't true, you know it isn't. I care a lot. But I won't deny what I believe to please you or anyone else." They glared at each other. "Maybe I should just leave."

He shuffled in his chair, raised a fork of pasta, then set it down again. It hurt that she wouldn't agree with him. But he didn't want to lose her.

"And where would you go, Alan?" his wife asked sarcastically. "You don't know anything about England." She always belittled him.

"I could go to Scotland…or Ireland. I'm partly Scots-Irish."

Vicki took her husband's hand. "Alan, don't leave me. I need you."

"Why? So we can tidy up our divorce arrangements before *you* leave *me*?"

"No, Alan," Vicki answered, her eyes growing moist. "I need you to help me figure out who I am. I don't know what to do."

It was odd: Alan had spent a week in Germany determined to spend no more than a day in any one place, until he found his soul. He hadn't found his soul—as far as he knew—but somehow now he had to stay with Vicki, regardless of how long. He loved her. He felt comfortable with her—even when she challenged him.

Five minutes later they left again for her bed-and-breakfast.

TWENTY

By Thursday lunchtime Vicki had coaxed him to the Tower of London. The idea had seemed so clichéd to him. But they'd seen Sir Walter Rayleigh's cell, and were now standing above the canal entrance to the Tower.

"Lady Jane Grey was brought in from here," she told her husband mournfully, "and Anne Boleyn. They both knew they'd never leave."

"Traitor's Gate." The place was rife with victims of the Tudor period.

They walked onto the green lawn inside the Tower walls. Alan struggled not to despair about William Bao—in prison himself in China. A grim wooden block sat squat to one side of them on the grass.

"Queen Anne Boleyn knelt here," Alan said. "Her head would have fallen there. We'd see the neck with the spine and muscle exposed. Would the eyes be open and moving? Would the mouth gasp? Or would death be instantaneous?"

Vicki always claimed he had a flair for the gruesome—but he'd read too many human rights reports not to wonder.

"I'd rather not think about the details."

"But—you might be able to look into the mouth and see light coming in through the neck!"

"I don't want to think about it! It's disgusting!" She walked away. Alan pondered the execution block for some moments—executions were common in China—then they entered a small chapel adjacent to the green.

"Most people weren't killed here, you know," Vicki whispered. "They were executed outside on Tower Hill. Only the special ones were brought here."

"You mean," Alan snapped, "the ones the government was afraid to kill publicly." He was fuming. "This British nation we revere as a model of democracy—cutting off heads in what we consider its greatest time!"

"But everyone did it!"

Other visitors were noticing. "Best to discuss this later," Alan whispered.

The chapel—"Saint Peter in Chains"—held the remains of distinguished victims who'd been killed on the block outside. *Strange*, Alan thought: *We kill them, then—eventually—honor them.* His thoughts had shifted to Friedrich Neufeld and his son…or daughter.

"Jeez!" he exclaimed under his breath. "Anne Boleyn and Lady Jane Grey—both resting right here!" Another place of pilgrimage.

They left the Tower and descended into the Underground—that is, the subway. Alan insisted, as they hurried into the Tubes, that the Beefeater in the Tower had been biased against Richard III.

"He *may* have killed the princes in the Tower, but you can't prove it." It seemed a basic human rights issue: You can't convict someone without a trial.

"Alan! They found the bodies inside the wall. What proof do you want?" But something totally different had annoyed her. She moved closer and whispered:

"Look at these proper British businessmen, rushing home on the trains, all dressed in dark ties, black suits and vests; grim and preoccupied." This wasn't the England she adored: The land of folk customs and dancing; the old rural non-Christian England.

They reached the tracks just in time for their train. After a short ride, they emerged—according to Vicki—near the Barbican (whatever that was).

"The Museum of the City of London is somewhere nearby," Vicki explained. "We just have to find it." Alan sighed; his wife seemed confident of everything except her own nature.

"I saw the Museum of German History in Berlin," he told her. "Everything laid out chronologically. All well-organized." So very German! He wanted to talk about Germany but didn't know how. He'd explained that Lavender was in Virginia, and she knew about Käthe. That was all he'd told her.

Even as he spoke, Alan realized that she was so excited about the museum that she was paying no attention to him.

But the Museum…was not really helpful; interesting—but not enlightening. They returned to Leicester Square and a Chinese buffet. Their moods were not improving.

"You brood too much," Vicki accused him.

"And you run from anything serious. Escapist."

"I don't like dwelling on pain. There's enough without making it worse."

They seemed so different: Alan obsessed with reality, Vicki obsessed with avoiding it. The sites of London had intensified their antagonism.

"How long do you plan to stay in the City?" Alan asked.

Vicki scowled. "I don't know. This didn't turn out quite the way I'd expected."

What had she expected? She had come to England with a stranger, on a whim; then the man had left her. Of course she felt abandoned. Alan squeezed her hands.

"Because of Ian? Because he left you?"

Vicki looked disgusted. "I don't want to talk about it."

Alan sat down his chopsticks. "You always assume people have a hidden motive."

"Alan!"

His hurt look softened Vicki's expression. "Look. I admit Ian was nice to me. He paid my airfare to London."

"He must have liked you a lot."

"I'm sure he did. It's just...he liked me too much. We'd only known each other a few days."

Alan looked her in the eyes. She'd gone along with the man after all.

"*Why* was Ian in Yellowstone?"

"His Morris team was invited to dance in England. He wanted to relax before the trip, so he flew to Yellowstone for a few days. I saw him practicing his dance steps outside his tent, alone. He was beautiful, leaping into the air and swooping. Later I met him and found out he had a spare ticket for England—Someone on the team had broken their ankle. After Claire and I argued, I went to Chicago and joined the tour flight. I got there just in time to get on the plane." She stopped suddenly, thinking but saying nothing.

Alan pondered the explanation. "How convenient he found you—an experienced dancer." He tried not to sound sarcastic. "And what was the problem with Claire?"

Vicki turned red. "She wanted to make love. She wanted to have an affair. But I wouldn't do it."

"Why not?"

"Claire wanted to hide it from Tomie. She didn't think Tomie would suspect *me*."

"And you didn't want to hide?"

"I didn't want to piss off a Sicilian." They both laughed.

"You've fantasized about Claire."

Vicki was turning redder. "Fantasies are fantasies, Alan," she snapped gruffly. "People shouldn't take them seriously. We live in the real world, not the world of our delusions."

"You never take your dreams seriously, Vicki, because you never expect anything good will come of them."

Vicki scowled. "This food is terrible." Then she relented. "I know *you* like the buffet, Alan—the Chinese food. You've lived in the orient, you cared about Tian An Men, and you're worried about William Bao. But I don't like it. It's just too greasy; just another mediocre ethnic food."

She stood up. "Come on. I want to walk around Leicester Square. It's so pleasant this evening."

After a long walk around Leicester, Piccadilly, and Trafalgar Squares, the heart of London, with the bright full moon rising above them, the married couple returned to their bed and breakfast, barely speaking. They lay in bed watching the news from the BBC. The war rolled on in the Balkans, the situation deteriorated in Chechnya, but Alan and Vicki hardly noticed. They were each trying to understand how the other could hold such an opposite attitude towards the world. How had two people, once so much in love, come to this?

TWENTY-ONE

Vicki opened up about Ian as they rode back into town to see St. Paul's Cathedral on Friday morning.

The chance to go to England had seemed the answer to Vicki's longings. Vicki had been doing English dancing for years, and her Wiccan religion connected her to the English soil and folk customs. She thought of England as her spiritual home, and English dancing as a religious practice. When she first saw Ian, in Yellowstone, practicing capers, leaping high in his kit.... Alan understood the appeal.

But St. Paul's did not please her.

"The most patriarchal place I've ever seen," Vicki griped as they wandered inside, not far from the tombs of the Duke of Wellington and Lord Nelson. "Monuments and tombs and national heroes. Pompous. Pretentious." She'd never shown much tolerance for crap.

"It's all very English," Alan retorted. "Nelson and Wellington: The glory of England." But he knew what Vicki meant. Did "glory" help the common people?

"The architecture's overwhelming," Vicki retorted, "but these heroes, stuck on pedestals!"

It was true that Americans would never glorify the military in this way; and for modern Germans it would be unthinkable. But Alan tried to rationalize it.

"It makes *us* uncomfortable," he told his wife, "but the English respect their heroes." But Vicki would not be pacified.

"The *Empire*," she blurted out, "the bloomin' *Empire*: Claiming the right to civilize the rest of the world because they thought *they* were better!" She swirled round with a grimace. "I love England—but not *this* England! It isn't the military that makes a country great! It's other things; intimate, personal, fun."

They stumbled upon the busts of George Washington and Lawrence of Arabia—one a rebel, one a misfit—in a side room where both could be overlooked; then she led him out of the cathedral and headed north.

"Here!" exclaimed Vicki suddenly, twenty minutes later. "The Temple of Mithras; what's left of it." She'd struggled to find it from her map.

She did not worship Mithras, the imported Persian god of Roman soldiers—she didn't even like Him. But His temple was a welcome change from the Christian sites. She was searching for what was left of Pagan England.

England meant something for Vicki that it couldn't mean for Alan. English folk customs resonated with Vicki, they nourished her soul. Morris Dancing had first drawn Vicki to Ian—it was only later, during the week of dancing, that she'd learned Ian was married.

Alan surveyed the crumbling foundations of the Temple. "It's amazing that any of the building is left!" He reached into his shirt, pulled out his pentagram, held it and the rings between his two palms, and bowed quickly to the smooth stones. They both felt the strain of living as Pagans in a Christian culture, and they knew most Christians didn't understand.

He whispered "Blessed be!" then slid the pentagram back inside his shirt.

Alan lured Vicki, after lunch, back south across the Thames. He had heard that the Globe Theater—Shakespeare's own theater—had recently been reconstructed in downtown London. Following directions he'd gotten at the City Museum, they were amazed to find it was true.

"It looks just like the original!" Alan gasped.

Alan could bond with the past by visiting places of historical significance, and bonding with the past enabled Alan to bond with people from the past. It was a bit like channeling the Dead. And the Globe brought him closer to Gayle, since Gayle idolized Shakespeare.

"I wish I could find something for Gayle," he blurted out.

Vicki tensed. *I shouldn't have brought her up*, he thought

"How *is* Gayle these days?" Vicki asked.

"Oh, she's all right." He hesitated. "I saw her on the way to Virginia." He held his breath.

"Why *did* you end up here, anyway? Why did you end up in *Germany*?" After three days with his wife, he still wasn't sure he was ready for this.

"I thought I'd spend some time with my parents; I told you."

"But you ended up in Germany! Is *this* what you do when my back is turned?" Was she teasing or serious? Did she think she could travel around with her girlfriend, and he'd just stay home and wait for her?

"You said you were leaving me. I needed support from someone." The simple truth.

"So you went to Gayle for solace. My, my!" Anger and mockery. Because of Preston and Janie.

"You said you were leaving me!"

"And Gayle consoled you!" Mocking frustration. Did she have any idea how difficult it was for him to be so different from other people?

"No. Gayle did a tarot reading, and we decided I'd lost my soul. I went on to Virginia with Lavender, but my parents sent me to Germany."

"Why?"

"They said I wouldn't find my soul in Virginia. They said I should go back to my old college campus. A lot happened to me when I lived there."

"And?"

"Nothing. No campus. Nothing but weird people. I've told you some of it."

"Did you fuck her?" The question caught him off guard. "What?"

"Did you and Gayle fuck?"

It took Alan by surprise. He hadn't told her much about the "honeymoon"—and nothing about his "problems." He stepped closer to Vicki.

"This is hardly the place to discuss *that*," Alan said in a whisper. "I'll tell you somewhere more private." He was still the withdrawn little boy he'd always been.

"I thought you weren't self-conscious about sex. Well, well!" The mocking—she *was* still bitter about Preston!

"I'm *not* self-conscious about sex. But I've come to appreciate my *privacy*!" She couldn't accept that explanation, of course. She was convinced that he was deluding himself. He merely wanted "attention."

They left the Globe to look for a bank; they needed to cash a travelers check.

"You see, Vicki," Alan continued under his breath as they walked, "I physically couldn't fuck her. I couldn't stay hard. We cuddled—that's all. Perfectly enjoyable." He felt embarrassed but honest.

"Guilty about my leaving you, Alan?" Rubbing salt in his wounds.

"Not at all. I always consider your feelings."

She remained silent the rest of the way to the bank, determined to concede nothing.

The bank visit turned into a disaster. They got the money; but as they were leaving, the British clerk insulted them, apparently because Vicki was using a money bag attached to a cord around her neck. To the British woman, this somehow embodied all the sins of Americans. Back on the street the bank manager came running after them.

"May I apologize for Mrs. Hayle! Her daughter-in-law ran off with an American last week. A Virginian. Harold Somebody. They've gone off north somewhere. I'm afraid her son is devastated. Most awfully sorry."

Vicki and Alan accepted the apology and hurried away.

They descended upon the British Museum just after four-thirty. Vicki had expected to find the key to her deepest yearnings in England and now, after so many disappointments, Alan had grabbed onto the idea that the British Museum must offer her *something*. He remembered well how notables like Karl Marx had done their research there. After the disaster with Ian, Vicki had thought she might find what she needed in London. But London had so far disappointed her. In desperation she leapt at Alan's suggestion;

but the British Museum was also not what she had expected.

"There's hardly anything here!" Vicki sighed in exasperation. "Where are the Celts and the Picts? They ignore Stonehenge and Avebury. They don't even value their own pre-history! Suppose Egyptians ignored the Pharaohs and talked only Christianity and Islam!"

"They have everything *else* though!" Alan replied, trying to encourage her. "All the rooms we walked through on the way in: Egypt and Greece; India and China."

"It's the *British Museum*, Alan. I wanted to learn about *Britain*!" She could barely contain her frustration.

They wandered for forty minutes, then Vicki announced: "I'm leaving London."

"Why?"

"Why? Alan! Look around!" She drew him off to a corner. "Look how this museum is arranged," she whispered. "Don't you see the attitude behind it?" She was radical in her own way—Wiccan, feminist, matriarchal. She loved the ancient customs, but the thought of "The Empire" offended her.

"I don't think I follow your logic."

"Everything takes the superior attitude of a cultured visitor to an exotic place. *The English gentleman amuses himself with the subspecies.* Don't you see that? You heard the woman in the bank: We're all inferior. The only people who *really* matter are the British. And Americans think the same way about themselves."

She paused to collect her thoughts.

"London is crowded and dirty, people forever rushing in and out of the Tubes. I want to go somewhere quiet. I want to get out of 'The City.'"

"Where are you going then?"

"You mentioned Scotland. It must be quieter, more primitive. There must be more *room*. I want someplace I can *think*, where I can *hear* myself think, where I can find my feelings again. I don't know what else to do. Maybe I'll find *my* soul there. At least I can lose myself in the British countryside. I've seen a lot since I got here; I love the countryside. I saw a lot from the bus, during the tour; but we had no time to explore and the other dancers weren't interested. There are places I want to see, sacred places. On this island: My ancestors' home. I've seen London now—and I'm sick of it."

They found their dinner downtown in a Tibetan restaurant. Alan was surprised to find meat; he'd somehow expected vegetarian. Afterwards they returned once more to Leicester Square.

A crowd had gathered around a sidewalk mime. He moved from person to person, making faces and gestures, then returned to the front of the crowd.

"He's *marvelous!*" Vicki exclaimed.

"Amazing." Somehow the mime suggested props and costuming. He brought the invisible to life under his spell.

The crowd grew—an appreciative audience that laughed and applauded more and more.

Then a police car drove up. The officer rolled down the window and spoke to the mime. The artist nodded. Policeman and mime whispered for several minutes. The policeman didn't want the crowd to hear, and the mime seemed determined to stay in character.

At the end, the mime offered apologetic faces and sad gestures to the crowd, then packed up and left. The police car drove off. The square had been cleared of Art. The crowds remained, dumbfounded that their idol had been taken from them. Vicki and Alan headed for the Underground—the Tubes.

"I keep thinking about that mime in Leicester Square," Vicki said back at the bed-and-breakfast, after the lights were out. "Why did they make him leave?"

"He probably hadn't registered. There's probably a fee and paperwork for performers. Or maybe he hadn't paid his taxes."

Alan snuggled up to his wife in the narrow bed.

"But couldn't they let him finish? No harm in that. No injury to anyone."

"It's a wonderful city, full of monuments and magnificent buildings and churches. But where is its soul?" He stopped abruptly. "Gayle said I'd lost my soul—I told you. Based on the Tarot reading." In the darkness he could just hear his wife's slowing breathing.

"Claire said something like that, too. She said sometimes she worried I'd lost my soul and that she could lose hers. Something about her and Tomie…"

"What did she tell you?"

Vicki sighed. "She's frustrated because of Tomie. She's afraid he could never accept her…being…how she is."

"What is there to accept?"

"You know she's bisexual, Alan. What can she do?"

Alan thought a moment before answering. "And she's poly, isn't she, Vicki? You can tell sometimes. When she rests her arm on my thigh or pats my butt. Did she tell you?"

Vicki lay silent a long time. "It doesn't matter. Claire is a reasonable person. Whether she's bisexual or poly-amorous, it doesn't matter. She promised Tomie there wouldn't be any others, and there won't be. She's reasonable, and I'm reasonable. We can manage our feelings. She asked me and I refused. And then while we were driving to Billings, she wondered if we'd lost our souls."

They both lay silent a long time; Alan thought Vicki had fallen asleep. He watched the moving patterns of light on the window curtains. He couldn't quite believe what she'd told him. She seemed more troubled by this encounter than her description allowed for.

"Alan!" His wife's sudden shrillness startled him.

"What's the matter, Vicki?"

Silence. Perhaps he'd been dreaming. His eyes grew heavy.

"I'm leaving London tomorrow."

He was awake again, for certain. She sounded determined.

"I'm tired of the city. I want to get away from people. I want to go somewhere empty. I want to get away from judgments." She was always running away.

She lay quiet again for awhile, then added: "You can do what you want." So he could have his freedom? She didn't still love him? Vicki could not see his grimace in the darkness.

"Vicki," he began, "I always said I'd stay with you, no matter what; forever—if you'll have me. Can I go with you?" He wanted her to understand his commitment to her.

Alan thought she was starting to cry. He rolled onto his side and wrapped his arms around her.

"I never meant to leave you, Alan," she said between sobs. "I thought of it, but I couldn't. When I saw what

Tomie was putting Claire through, I appreciated you all the more." Yet she put him through...

"You came to England with Ian's Morris team."

"It seemed like such an opportunity. I've always wanted to come to England. And Ian was so...But then he 'had to leave.' 'Had to leave'—Shit!"

"Where'd he go?"

"Abroad somewhere. 'An emergency,' he said. 'Spur of the moment.' I never believed it." She clung more tightly to Alan. "I want to go somewhere I can be left alone. I'm tired of people disappointing me."

"Well, Scotland then. It shouldn't take long—a day or two. Gets us out of the City. I hear it's pretty empty there; I hear it's beautiful. It would give us time to think." Given time, she might settle down again.

"I've thought already," Vicki snapped. "I'm tired of people who treat me no better than their used condoms. I'm tired of societies that condemn people for loving."

The words startled Alan. She *agreed* with society...didn't she?

"We leave tomorrow then," he said decisively. "Right after breakfast."

Vicki hugged him closer. "It was never *you*, Alan," she said just before they nodded off. "It was the way people treated us; exploited...misinterpreted...mocked...belittled... betrayed."

The final sentence—had Alan imagined it?

"I wound up despising society for the way it insisted we live."

TWENTY-TWO

Saturday morning they headed north through Cambridge, sixty miles off, stopping in the town to buy two ritual goblets and mourning the fact that they might never see their coven again.

It was sad—they'd grown to love their spiritual nest. But they'd never felt truly accepted. Though they all professed the Wiccan Rede—"An it harm none, do what you will"—their fellow coveners could never overcome the suspicion that polyamory must inevitably hurt people—a common-enough opinion. Alan and Vicki had never felt completely at home.

"They *do* care about us," Vicki said. "They're just not *like* us. They can't imagine our being happy the way we live." That was it, of course. The others were convinced that in polyamory people must get hurt, that it must be "bad for children," that it exploited people, that it was shallow and selfish.

The couple continued another eighty miles north through Nottingham, stopping at Byron's home in Newstead Abbey. Financially unable to restore the ceremonial hall, Byron had used it for target practice, shooting his pistol into the wall.

"Stranger than I thought, Byron!" commented Alan.

In the chapel, Vicki rebelled against the English guides' continual admonition to "treat this place of worship with respect."

"I'm not a Christian, Alan. I don't see why they have to belittle non-Believers."

Then Sherwood Forest, a bit further on. So strange, to be immersed in trees. In a week and a half Alan had barely set foot outside urban areas—only that wheat field near Bayreuth, and now the stop at Newstead Abbey. But now he and Vicki were abandoning the cities to flee into the wilds of Scotland, with only the Ordinance Survey maps she'd picked up as guides. Nevertheless, Vicki had been travelling several weeks in Britain already and knew her way around. The motorway signs for Sherwood Forest were confusing, but Vicki located what she was after: A gigantic tree, with huge trunk and branches spreading in all directions, supported by wooden supports added beneath them over the years.

"So Robin Hood hid in this tree?" Alan asked.

"That's what they say, but it's impossible."

"Why?"

"Because in 1200, this tree would have been a sapling—the size of a bush. A cat couldn't have hidden in it." What Vicki knew about England continued to amaze him.

"So he hid in a similar tree; one that was large at that time. And the Sheriff rode up from Nottingham…"

"Yes. Nottingham."

"I don't know how we got lost there. I thought we were following the signs. This is like *The Divine Comedy*, or the Grail Quest. Here we are in a Dark Wood. Might as well 'charge in where the bramble is thickest,' as Campbell says!"

"Whatever. We still got to Newstead Abbey before they closed, and we've made it to Sherwood Forest while it's still light."

"And Charles I hid here, when the Puritans were searching for him?" Alan didn't know much about the English Civil War in the 1600s—except that it had influenced the U.S. Founding Fathers.

Vicki shook her head emphatically. "No, Alan. That's the *Royal* Oak. I don't know where that is. This is the *Major* Oak. And it was Charles II." How'd she know all this stuff? It was like his own knowledge of Germany.

"How could I get confused?" He laughed to soften his sarcasm.

They walked around the Tree.

"This historic marker's very interesting," Vicki said after they'd circled back around. "It even mentions the Green Man." It included a drawing: The face embodying the abundant God of Nature—mouth spewing forth leaves and vines.

"I guess for the British it doesn't seem as strange as it does to Americans."

"Oh no," Vicki snapped. "I imagine Americans can handle it just fine; like the British themselves in the British Museum. They'd think it was a quaint old folk custom, totally unrelated to real life and the modern world. Certainly not on par with Jesus or the Resurrection. Unlike *us*. We *honor* the King of Nature."

Vicki surveyed the tree one final time. "We'd better get going. It's getting dark. We'll never get to Scotland at this rate."

*

A few hours later, after dinner at a rest stop, Vicki and Alan could say that they had "seen" York. They'd driven into the city around 9 p.m., having decided that York would be the best place to stop for the night. They had come two hundred miles from London. Scotland turned out to be farther than they'd expected; they'd barely made it halfway. Alan had missed the first exit for York, and they had driven directly into the city. A gas station attendant, whom Vicki could barely understand because of his accent, had recommended a bed-and-breakfast on the edge of the Old City; Vicki had phoned and gotten directions. But the directions proved inadequate. They were to follow the old Roman wall until it ended, then turn left and cross the bridge over the river.

But the wall disappeared and there was no bridge. They had turned left anyway.

For two hours, they had crossed and re-crossed the old medieval town center, a mere half-mile across. Every time they were close to their destination, the street changed to one-way going the wrong way; or they faced a barricade. They passed the huge cathedral several times. The Dark Wood had become a Dark City.

It was Saturday night, and huge crowds of high school students roamed the streets. Alan finally had pulled into a bus stop, and Vicki had flagged down a student. The student had described an elaborate algorithm for escaping the city center.

"They don't want tourists in here, you know. Not in autos anyway. They made it complicated on purpose. Lots of roads in, only one road out, you know." The students around them laughed. Vicki and Alan had been caught in the labyrinth like ants in an ant trap!

Ten minutes later, with the algorithm, they arrived at the bed-and-breakfast. In the previous two hours it had never been more than three-quarters of a mile away.

"This is wonderful!" Vicki said as she shut the bedroom door. "Very pretty."

Alan surveyed the room: Pink wallpaper, flowers, embroidered curtains; and a large wooden bed. Un-American Feminine—but peaceful.

"Very quiet," he replied. "I appreciate that. Quiet after the noise of London and the humming and vibration of the highway. Whew!" Silence renewed him. He'd always been impressed by his mother's Quaker friends.

He pushed his luggage against the wall and lay down.

"What are we doing, Vicki?" he asked, reaching for her hand. "What are we doing in York, England? Why are we here? Has either of us found what we need?"

His wife stroked his cheek.

"I don't know if I have or ever will," Vicki said quietly, "but either way, I'm glad I'm with you." She lay down beside him. "You've stayed with me through everything."

"Think of all the people we've dated, Vicki, over the years. Will we ever find *the Ones*?" He wasn't even sure his wife still wanted to.

Vicki snuggled closer.

"Lilly and Wayne," Vicki sighed. "I was in love with him, but he told me to give all my devotion to *you*, like a proper wife should. He was *so* monogamous."

"And Lilly flirted with me, but it was only a game. When you tried to create a real connection, she got frightened."

"Stanley and Mary?"

"They invited us over for a backrub…"

"…And the four of us ended up in bed."

"And they said *What do you want from this?*" Alan buried his head in his wife's chest.

"And you said *I want friends to spend my life with.* And they looked at you oddly and didn't answer. They thought we were only after 'kicks.'"

"We had some good times with Stanley and Mary. But you got involved with Tony, and I fell out with Mary…"

"It all fell apart." Vicki was clinging ever more closely to him. Desperation. No one understood them.

"You've been so kind to me, my love," Alan said. "I really enjoyed those times we spent with Holly—especially the weekend we all went down to the ocean. We rented that condo, like anyone would do with a boyfriend or girl-friend. But when *we* do it, the monogamous don't under-stand."

"I liked that weekend too."

"We made a dinner, then snuggled in. You and Holly watched TV, and I read Hermann Hesse. Then we went to bed and it was beautiful—but society calls us perverted."

Vicki smiled. "We left the window open. You could hear the waves on the beach."

"It was a full moon. The next morning the fog had come in, remember? We walked along the beach, the three of us; holding hands and dreaming… We wanted a future together; but Holly couldn't take it seriously."

"She wanted a *normal* marriage and children. She *settled* for us in the meantime. Then she latched onto Eric and had no use for us. And monogamists call *us* untrustwor-thy!"

"Those Saturndays we stayed over and drove to church together the next morning…and sometimes had lunch to-gether…"

"Those were some days—beautiful days."

They lay silent a long time. Then Vicki said: "Do you hear that, Alan?"

"What?"

"That noise. Somewhere downstairs."

"I don't hear anything. What do you hear?"

"People making love. Don't you hear them?"

Alan listened in the darkness. "I don't hear anything. Goodnight."

TWENTY-THREE

"Amazing!" The young man smiled at Alan after breakfast Sunday morning. "You went to the University of Virginia?"

"*Wahoo-wa!*" Alan answered with a scant smile. "For graduate school." *Wahoo-wa* was the unofficial university cheer. "How do you like England?" he asked the man. "Have you been here long?"

"Flew into London a week ago. Saw the sights. Got to York yesterday. In York for the weekend. Scotland tomorrow."

The man reflected. "The British are all right, I suppose. A bit behind the times. Don't understand air conditioning—or private baths. A little odd trying to buy things like toiletries. Nice people, though. Great breakfasts! Have a nice day!"

The young man flew out the front door.

"*Wahoo-wa!*" Alan yelled.

Vicki and Alan started to laugh.

"What an asshole!" Vicki exclaimed.

"Harold, wasn't it?"

*

"The Minster is huge," Vicki said. They had realized over breakfast that the drive from London had totally exhausted them. They had also discovered that York Minster was one of the largest cathedrals in Europe. They had decided to spend the day in York, recovering. They had joined a morning tour and were now standing on the path that ran atop the old city walls. The gigantic Minster towered nearby.

"And the guide is an asshole," Vicki went on. "Constantine-this-and-Constantine-that."

"I never knew that Constantine was proclaimed Roman Emperor *here*. Of course they have to say he became a Christian out of conviction…"

"When it was mostly politics."

They stared out over the city. The Roman walls of Erobocum—Ancient York—dropped off on either side of them.

"And all that crap about the Pagans," Vicki went on. "How barbaric they were. These people are driving me batty! The 'barbarians' who overran Rome were mostly heretical Christians." They'd both been holding in their feelings. "*Heretical*!" Alan snorted. "Meaning they disagreed with the Bishop of Rome or the church councils! The 'sacking of Rome' was pretty tame." He was getting angrier.

"*The Christian Britons were attacked by the pagan invaders*," cried Vicki. "They were the Angles and Saxons! They created this fucking nation!" The simple truth.

"And they're always telling us that 'the churches are still in use,'" muttered Alan, still mulling over Newstead Abbey. "Of *course* we couldn't trot into the Minster in the middle of Sunday service! But they repeat this everywhere." He thought a moment. "*The Ladies do protest too much, methinks.*"

They walked along the wall, hanging back from the group.

"It *is* a beautiful morning."

"What really *pisses* me," interrupted Vicki, "is that they build all their churches on Goddess-sites! They seal up the holy wells and sacred springs to build *their* churches and fill them with dead people. The Emperor Julian was right, two thousand years ago. As Gore Vidal said in his novel."

"Come on," said Alan. "We're going to miss the guide's next pretentious speech." Then he laughed, realizing how pretentious they sounded sometimes themselves.

"Nice," Vicki said as they walked through the crowded medieval alley that afternoon. "The Shambles are nice." But was the bustling old medieval market area more picturesque than San Francisco?

"It's *atmospheric*," Alan replied. "I'm surprised we found a Unitarian church in York. Didn't see any in London."

"Yeah. I forgot they were here in England."

"But not like American UU's. You didn't tell them we were *Pagans*. Feeling a bit *self-conscious*?" He smiled anticipating her reaction.

"No need to get into *that*. We have more in common as Unitarians. These folks are probably still *Christians*. They've simply thrown out the Trinity. Like American Unitarians two centuries ago. We'd probably shock them. Like the Unitarian who was visiting from Romania, when Preston told him we were Pagans. The Romanian didn't know what to say! Paganism—one of the foundations of Western Civilization; but most people have no idea we still exist."

"Preston and Jane!"

"The English Unitarians would *never* understand polyamory. They don't even get it in California!"

Alan sighed. "And I was church president." He stared vacantly ahead. "Sally," he sighed and went silent.

"Let's get some tea," said Vicki. "It's been awhile since lunch; who knows when we'll have dinner?"

"Thank the gods for tea!" Alan exclaimed. "A blessed repose in the midst of trouble! A pause from the world."

After tea they headed for the Minster. But they stopped abruptly on the sidewalk at a perfect chalk copy of Botticelli's *Venus*.

Alan had brought his palms together but caught himself before bowing to The Lady. He'd remembered the crowds around them. He still didn't feel safe as a Pagan.

The artist had reproduced every detail, line, and color, exactly.

"What did you think of the Manor House?" They'd stopped there earlier. It was supposedly haunted.

"Don't know. Interesting stories. Perhaps there *are* more ghosts in York than other places. I imagine the guide was exaggerating. The story of the saint…"

"Margaret of York. 'Pressed' to death for remaining Catholic. She just wanted to practice her religion—like us. Crushed under a door laden with stones, here in 1586. And she was pregnant."

"Tudor justice," Vicki muttered. "Let's go in the Minster."

They wove through the tourist-crowded plaza towards the two rising towers. The massive stone structures unsettled Alan. He imagined them collapsing, as if in free fall—but why? What was he seeing?

The Minster itself did not impress them—except for the large octagonal room with Pagan ornamentation.

Later they discovered a museum of Danish York—the Danes had once controlled the north of England—and Alan bought a postcard for Gayle: a Pre-Raphaelite painting of a knight and a lady with long blond hair (like Gayle's). Then Alan and Vicki attached themselves to a group visiting sites connected with hauntings. By the time the group broke up, it was after dark.

"I never thought we'd eat in a burger joint," Vicki sighed. It was late now: After nine in the evening.

"I ate at one in Dresden," Alan said as they tossed out their paper wrappers and left. "Europeans love American fast food. They've never had it before."

Soon the couple had passed Bootham Bar—the old Danish gate—and walked up the narrow lane towards their lodgings.

"The guide was too nonchalant about the Gunpowder Plot," Alan said as they reached the bed-and-breakfast. His work for HRI had darkened his attitudes towards many "amusing" local customs.

"Well it *is* the most famous plot in British history," Vicki replied as they opened the front door. "I guess he *did* over-enjoy it. And what they do on Guy Fawkes Day—'A penny for the old Guy'—grotesque!"

"It wasn't enough to execute the conspirators," Alan went on more quietly now as they climbed the stairs to their room. "They had to 'draw and quarter' them—Rip them apart, cut them open, drag out their intestines—while they were still alive. Enforce *justice*? *Inflict* justice; *terrorize* their own people and hold onto the power they thought they were entitled to." He thought a moment. "But then," he went on, "suppose someone plotted to blow up the White House or Capitol building."

"I'm glad things have changed," Vicki said, shutting the bedroom door behind them. "I'd have hated living back then. Now we know better."

Alan gave her an odd look. "It's really no different now," he said. "We just don't think about it. Remember the guide's story about the Landlord? That was only a hundred years ago."

"He hid dead bodies in the wall?" asked Vicki.

"He wanted the subsidies for the orphans he took in. More children meant more funding. When a child died, he just stuffed it into spaces between the walls and went on taking the subsidies."

"And the ghost woman at the Manor House," said Vicki, her eyes glowing. "Do you suppose a ghost really lives there?" They didn't believe in ghosts—though many Pagans did—but they left open the possibility. The ghosts of the Dead held such sorrows. And where were their own spirits?

"That building *could* be haunted," said Alan. "I sense pain in this town. The ghost-soldiers marching along the Roman road."

"Only visible from the knees up," whispered Vicki, "because the ground is higher now." Most Wiccans believed in reincarnation, but Alan and Vicki were also Unitarian Universalists—natural skeptics. They would need a personal experience before they believed.

247

"Scotland tomorrow," said Alan, crawling under the covers. "Out across the moors."

"Heathcliff and madness," sighed Vicki. "Misguided Romanticism." She crawled in beside her husband and turned out the lamp.

"Misguided Reason," Alan replied. But is it Feeling or Reason that leads us astray?

TWENTY-FOUR

Monday morning they headed north. As Alan guided the car out of the city, Vicki raved about the Japanese student they'd met over breakfast.

"Isn't Saito amazing? He's taken lessons in English but never actually spoken it. Never! Then he decides the best thing would be to fly to England and practice—for two weeks!"

"I guess he has lots of money," Alan replied smiling. "He might have done better just getting a tutor."

Soon they were out in the country. It was a beautiful morning. *Nearly a week since that wedding in Berlin.* Alan had still not told Vicki much about Germany. He didn't know how to explain his experiences. He didn't think she'd understand. He trusted his wife in a lot of ways—but he didn't trust her to understand him. He was careful what he told her. He'd mentioned several people in passing; but not that Sally was biologically a man.

"I miss the Germans I met. They seemed so sincere and courageous." He glanced over at Vicki. "Don't you miss the Morris team?"

"It was certainly an experience: Riding all over England with a bus full of Morris dancers. Dancing and singing all day. Hanging out afterwards at pubs with English teams—beer, bangers and mash. We stayed up too late and got up too early. Ian knows so much about England!

"When you and I lived in Virginia, I never thought I'd dance on a Morris team. Then in California I was suddenly doing Morris dancing, English dancing, Contra dancing—on top of the folk dancing. I say I'm Wiccan—but my religion is really dancing. If I couldn't dance—I don't know what I'd do."

"Where does Ian stay when he's in England? You say he does research?"

"Folklore and such. South of Bristol, near Yeovil, not far from Glastonbury. Crewkerne, in Somerset. Way to the south. Out in the country. We danced there—at the end of the tour. After all of southern England."

She lapsed into thought. Awhile later she cried, "Look: The moors! This road will take us straight across the Lake District. It's supposed to be spectacular. We didn't get this far north on the tour. I've always wanted to see this."

"I miss the Germans I met," Alan repeated. "An Israeli woman marrying a German. A Catholic woman converting to Islam." Vicki could have grasped only the barest sense of who any of them were. He'd avoided mentioning Friedrich Neufeld and his three wives—and the aborted wedding.

Vicki looked over grimly. "I'm sure you wonder about what's-her-name, the one who talked about sex."

Alan couldn't tell whether his brief remarks about Käthe had amused or threatened his wife. "From what you've told me, Vicki," he continued after some thought, "I'm surprised Ian left you, just like that."

"Well you trust people, and I don't. I'm not surprised at all. Men always want sex, no matter what they say. Afterwards, they don't care what happens." She noticed his pained look. "Except for *you*, of course." But did she believe it?

"You don't think Ian might be an exception? He paid your way to England."

"He had an extra ticket. One of the dancers had to cancel."

"It was still nice of him to invite you. He didn't have to."

"He needed a dancer."

They drove on. Alan dared not say he had faith in his wife's lover.

"This has been an amazing trip," he said after a while. "To meet them all and then leave them. I even miss that Muslim woman, the convert."

"You shouldn't get involved with shady characters, Alan. At least Ian was respectable—even if he did abandon me. Too bad he was married. He asked me to stay with him here after the rest of the team returned to the States. He wanted a week to recover. We saw the team off at Heathrow, then went back to Somerset together. I finally asked about his wife; I'd heard people talking. He started to explain, but a call came in and he said he had to leave right away for the continent. Some kind of emergency. I think he staged it all."

The moors flew past. They'd been driving an hour.

"It must have been the ghost stories," Alan said. "I'm remembering so much now. The people I met in Germany; and Lavender, Bao, Gayle. Everything that's happened. I meant to send postcards to Gayle, but so many things came up. I wonder how she's doing."

"At least she's honest about being married. Honest to you and to her husband." She scowled to herself, then snorted: "Ian."

251

"Maybe he *did* have an emergency. Things *do* happen." Alan mistrusted his wife's facile judgments.

"No, not like *this*!" Vicki snapped. "He claimed some friend had been arrested. He stammered something about wives and cross-dressers and weddings. Utterly incoherent and unbelievable. When I met you at Heathrow, I'd just seen him off."

The car lurched to the side; Alan had slammed on the brakes. Vicki jerked around to him, horrified. Cars were honking everywhere. Alan pulled off the road. After staring blankly into space a long moment, Alan slowly turned to his wife.

"Where did you say he was flying?"

MOTHER HEART

TWENTY-FIVE

An hour later they had stumbled on an old American diner in the middle of England.

Vicki slid onto the red vinyl seat and Alan slid down the other side of the table to face her. He reached across the red and white checkered tablecloth, took her hands, and laid his head on them.

"It's a fabulous restaurant, Alan." She freed one hand to stroke his graying hair. Alan wondered whether she was being sarcastic. But it *was* fabulous—just the sort of diner Vicki would like—when not distracted.

"Where the hell *are* we, Vicki?"

"You said we were passing Birmingham. Is the traffic bothering you? Do you want me to drive?" Vicki did care about him.

"We're in *England*, right? At an *American* diner near *Birmingham*? And *why* are we here?"

Vicki withdrew her hands. "You said you wouldn't take me to Scotland. You insisted we turn around. You said we had to find Ian." Her voice betrayed annoyance. No doubt she thought it silly to look for Ian—what would they do if they found him? Better to run away. But—suppose she were wrong?

Alan lifted his head. "I've never seen traffic so bad," he said. "The highway is clogged with trucks, all driving eighty. There are no smog or emission standards here. We've only come maybe a hundred and fifty miles…" The noise…the dirt. A nightmare.

The waitress brought Vicki's hamburger and coke; and Alan's hotdog, fries, and milkshake.

"It's funny," Vicki said. "They have fake juke box selectors mounted on the walls in each stall. They don't actually *work*. The buttons aren't even real; they're painted on." It was all pretense.

Alan was devouring his hotdog—that was real. Alan trusted his appetite.

"Did you get a hold of Ian?" he asked her.

"No one at home. I get the same message I got when we called from Leeds."

"We can't get there today. I don't think we're even halfway to Crewkerne, and it's already afternoon." He sank back onto his hands. He was fretting again. For a while, in England, he had managed to relax, but now…the history, the culture, the travel…everything was dragging him back to his quest. Somehow his shamanic intuition connected to Time and Place, to the "mood of the times"—and the mood of the past. And now, this mad dash southwards…

"I don't see what the rush is, Alan. Let's take a break and rest. The clerk in the snack shop said we're near Warwick Castle. It's in perfect condition—unchanged since the War of the Roses five hundred years ago. Ian isn't home anyway."

"He may still be abroad. The wedding and arrest were a week ago, but who knows what kind of legal complications were involved? Do you have directions to the Castle?" At last they had told each other everything, he thought.

Walking out to the car, Vicki watched her husband in amazement.

"You really think he's with your friends in Germany?" That was nice—she called them his "friends."

Alan started the engine and zoomed onto the motorway. Somehow, he had to control and channel his obsession.

They descended the stone stairway and emerged from the stone tower of the castle back into the afternoon sun. They didn't quite follow the details of the life and death of the Earl of Warwick, only that he had played a major role in the War of the Roses.

"He manipulated both sides to increase his own power," said Alan. "But his luck ended here."

"The army broke through the walls and slaughtered the whole family. Wasn't that what they said?"

"Another place of death."

Vicki started down the stone path. "Why are you always thinking about death?"

"It's everywhere, Vicki. In the Balkans and Chechnya and Iraq. Death and destruction. I saw what we did to Dresden and what the Nazis did to the Jews. Here, in England, I see how Catholics and Protestants tortured each other. When I think about Naomi and Rachel, and Ahmed and Gustav and Inge, I think: *What's going to happen to them?* Everyone hates everyone else: The Catholics and Protestants and Orthodox; the Muslims and the Jews; Chechens and Russians. I suppose Bao will die in prison. People hate people who are different. Everyone feels threatened. Death…"

Alan struggled for words. "I love the United States, but I never feel safe. I never feel accepted. Do you? My *family* accepts me—but I don't feel comfortable being myself there. Too many people feel threatened by my existence. Too many people feel uncomfortable. I never feel welcome." He was remembering the woman on the plane to Chicago, and the look on the maid's face at the hotel there with Gayle.

They walked down into the dungeon. Not a torture chamber; but the low dark room did display a few tools used to punish prisoners or make them "confess."

Neither Vicki nor Alan spoke. They examined the instruments. Finally Vicki said: "It's hard to believe that anyone actually used these things."

"Well," Alan replied dryly, "they thought they were protecting the Church or the State or themselves. They had reasons for doing it."

"But gouging people's eyes out? Asphyxiating them? Boiling them alive or burning them? Aren't people worth anything?"

Alan frowned. "They weren't and they aren't, Vicki. Even democracies torture to keep the world safe. People will do anything to feel secure."

"But nothing like this!" Vicki exclaimed.

Alan stared at her for a moment. It was funny—Vicki was cynical, but in small ways. She didn't trust people, but didn't think they were evil—just petty and weak. *No one wants to admit what's happening.* Alan boiled over.

"No, no—nothing like this happens now," he sneered. "People are shot, people disappear; deprived of sleep, shocked with electric wires; burned with cigarettes; shoved bound into freezing water; drenched with boiling water; butt-crammed or cunt-crammed with broomsticks or barbed-wire or —"

"Alan! Alan!"

The other visitors had turned to listen. Alan's voice had grown loud, his tone desperate, his expression an anguished fever.

"Alan! Calm down!" Then again, softer: "Calm down."

Alan's contorted face relaxed. The frenzy drained from his eyes. He told himself to calm down, relax, get under control.

But as they went out he thought: *Dear Gods, don't ever let my country do these things!*

He remained calm the rest of the visit. As they walked down the long hill from the Castle, Alan's thoughts dwelt on the victims of the past, the young and the innocent. Some had known what they were doing; others had done nothing to deserve their fate. Henry VI had mental problems. Edward V and his brother Richard, the "little princes" of the Tower of London—Edward V was thirteen when he was killed; Richard was ten.

His thoughts drifted back to the Tower, where Edward and Richard had been killed. Lady Jane Grey, Anne Boleyn and Catherine Howard—all beheaded in the Tower; all denied their rights. And William Bao? And Friedrich Neufeld?

TWENTY-SIX

From Warwick—they'd found another Unitarian church there—they continued south to Stratford-on-Avon: Shakespeare's house, but still no souvenirs appropriate for Gayle. Vicki found a statue of the Fool in the main square. The Fool: Her deity. It connected her shamanism to her Morris Dancing.

There was no point rushing to Crewkerne until Ian resurfaced. After Stratford they looked for Chipping Campden. Alan had heard of it as a child— it was supposedly "quintessential England"—but all they did was drive in circles for an hour without ever finding it. They felt like they had entered an alternate world. It was the Grail Quest as Joseph Campbell described it—a bit like looking for Brigadoon.

"I suggest we stay in Stow-on-the-Wold," Vicki said after they'd abandoned Chipping Campden. They'd already driven over two hundred miles back south that day, off to the west of London.

"Stow-on-the-*what?*" Had she been planning this all along?

"A little town maybe eight miles from here. Down this road." How'd she know about all these places?

"Sounds like you've done a little research."

"We're entering the Cotswold Hills, Alan; the Morris tour came here too—it's the Holy Land of Morris Dancing. Lots of places of interest to Morris dancers—and Wiccans. Lots of pre-historic sites." She *had* planned this. But she couldn't have done it consciously—she'd meant to take them to Scotland.

"You knew this when you detoured me to Warwick?"

Vicki smiled and ran her hand along her husband's cheek. "Alan, I spent a week in a bus full of Morris dancers. We drove all over southern England, but all we did was drink and dance. Now that I'm back, I want to visit a couple places that interest me as a Pagan. Can you be patient? That's all I ask. Who knows?—Maybe we'll find our souls. If Ian turns up we can head straight to Crewkerne."

"Looks like we're coming to Stow-on-the-Wold. What a coincidence. My, my. Okay—let's see what we can find." Why couldn't they trust each other? What made them so uncomfortable?

"The folks in Stratford said we might find a Bed-and-Breakfast out on Evesham Road, once we get into the village."

"You've figured out everything, haven't you?" She *was* manipulating this trip—but at least they were heading towards Ian. And after his own week of traveling around Germany, how could he deny her England?

They found the pub in Stow-on-the-Wold nearly deserted. Vicki and Alan were the only people at a table. While they ate dinner, the few men at the bar left. The television remained on, the cricket game continued. Alan watched the bowler hurl the ball towards the batsman. For the first time in many hours, Alan relaxed. The man in the white uniform and little hat threw the ball over and over. Alan was fascinated.

"What's he do before he lets go of the ball? Some sort of running hop?" The game seemed utterly alien—but appealing.

"It's a strange game and a strange country," Vicki replied, "but I love it."

"Love it?"

"Well, not cricket; but England. At least the English countryside…and the customs. I don't get *cricket*." Why was his wife so drawn to England? To Alan it seemed a peculiar country. But Wicca came from here.

"I wish I were back in Germany," he said. "I miss the people I met."

Vicki smirked.

"You disapprove of Germany, don't you? And the people I met."

"You always gravitate towards the most questionable elements. Why can't you just be normal? What has behaving differently ever gotten us?" She looked at her husband with a pleading look. *Please*, her expression seemed to be saying, *please let's go back to acting like everyone else.* Why did she worry so much about what other people thought?

"The problem with *you*," Alan said slowly, "is you run from your fate, while I embrace mine. I cherish myself, peculiarities and all. And I embrace *you*. And you don't. You run from who you are. I *love* the way *I* am. You're always *avoiding* growth, while I thrive on it."

He thought a moment. "This pub reminds me of that pizza place where I met you and Brett near Washington, during the fantasy convention."

"What place?"

"You remember? It was *Fantacon*. You spent the weekend with Brett in his hotel suite. Saturnday evening you called to see if I wanted to meet you two for pizza."

"You remember that?" Of course he did. But she'd put it out of her head.

"Yeah. You and Brett were there, and another woman. I tried to act particularly nice to Brett, and he ignored me the whole time. It's good the other woman was there; it gave him someone else to talk to."

"Yeah," said Vicki. "Later she kept asking us who you were. Brett kept pretending not to hear, and I kept saying you were a friend, and she kept looking skeptical." It always galled Alan how the monogamous despised polys. But maybe Brett was merely embarrassed about being involved with a married woman.

"He kept acting like I wasn't there. It annoyed me."

"He was in love with me, Alan. We've been over this before. He wanted me to leave you, and I said *I'm not leaving my husband.*"

"Good for you! That must have made him bonkers. Wasn't Brett the one who thought jealousy had a biological basis?"

"He was very self-righteous about it. '*Jealousy is beneficial and necessary,*' he would say. '*Monogamy is the foundation of society and evolution. People* should *be possessive of their mates.*' And he told me: '*If you were* my *wife, I'd kill any man who tried to flirt with you.*'"

"A real charmer. And you question *my* tastes in lovers? It seemed so obvious that I should be nice to him: My wife's lover; the friend of my friend. But given his attitudes, I guess he couldn't respect me."

"He despised you. Because of *you*, he couldn't have *me*."

"Because of his own attitudes, you mean. We made it clear I was willing to share."

The thought hung incomplete, as Alan sipped his beer. He swirled the liquid around his mouth, swallowed decisively, look straight at Vicki, and added:

"But some people don't share."

They finished the meal in silence. When they left the pub, Alan could not decipher the expression on his wife's face. He thought sometimes that they were total opposites.

"Ian still doesn't answer?" Alan asked as she returned from the bed-and-breakfast office. They turned and walked down the road. The sky was nearly dark. The couple glided along silently. Occasionally a car sailed by.

"You're hopeless," Vicki said finally. "You always expect the happy ending. You trust Ian even though you've never met him. Like you trusted all the women who have ever exploited you, and all the men who have ever betrayed me. We've both been betrayed, you know—over and over." He hated the way she berated him for believing in people. She thought it was so foolish.

Vicki clicked off the television on the dresser. "What is it, Alan?" It was time for bed.

"The news report. The story from Kashmir."

"The story about the hostages? What about it?"

"There was something wrong with it. Something not quite right." Shamanic intuition?

"*What* wasn't right? *What?*"

"I don't know exactly. The news said the hostages had been decapitated, but…I don't know." He went on removing his clothes. Something—he couldn't pin it down—was bothering him.

"Honestly, Alan. You always think you have some kind of secret insight, beyond the grasp of the real experts. You always think you know better." That was true—he acknowledged that. Sometimes he intuited matters of significance, without knowing precisely what they were or how he knew them. And sometimes…he was wrong.

"The reporter," Alan started again, "he was vague about why the Westerners were in Kashmir; why the rebels kidnapped *them* specifically; why they *killed* them; and—and why they killed them so *brutally*." For some reason these deaths seemed particularly significant—he didn't know why.

"But they emphasized that it was brutal. The commentator called it *barbaric*."

"So decidedly *Western*. Label Kashmiri militants *barbaric* for doing what British monarchs did four hundred years ago. When we were at the Tower of London, no one called beheading *barbaric*." He didn't expect Vicki to understand. He saw connections other people didn't see, between different places and times. And he didn't take reactions for granted. The barbarism of the murders didn't necessarily give The West an excuse to dismiss the militants as subhuman.

"It was just a brief report, Alan. It probably was incomplete."

He crawled into bed and switched off the light. He was startled to feel his wife's hand running along his torso.

"Vicki?"

"I haven't been fair to you, Alan. You've always loved me, even when I intentionally misunderstood you. I want to make up for that…" Vicki felt suddenly warm and needy—it had been a long time.

Her hand slid down into his crotch. He felt himself beginning to throb.

"Besides," she added, taking him firmly in her hand, "I think *I* deserve you at least as much as Gayle and that German woman." Alan scowled in the darkness. What did she think Käthe had done?

"I never got close to Käthe, Vicki. She preached sexual freedom, but she also preached sexual responsibility."

He pulled away from her. "Vicki, do you understand that people can be frank and honest about sex—and their feelings and opinions for that matter—without giving up a reasoned control of themselves?" He'd turned soft again.

"As for Gayle and myself," he went on, "I'm never at ease with her, because I'm never sure how *you* feel. We've finger-fucked and mouth-fucked; but I never stay hard enough to go into her. I'm always worrying about *you* and *your* feelings. I haven't fucked anyone but *you* since we broke up with Jane and Preston." It embarrassed Alan to admit this. Did it mean anything to Vicki? Did she feel any less hurt or betrayed? Did it make any difference at all?

Vicki said nothing. He'd probably pissed her off. Her hand remained on his crotch. Then it glided over his hips and up his back. He felt her warm cheek against his, and her hand swept down and grabbed his butt.

"Vicki?"

She planted her open mouth onto his neck and then his chest. Her breasts pressed softly against his stomach, and her warm abdomen set his cock a-tingling. Her hands pressed hard against his back.

"Vicki!"

Her tongue prevented further comment.

TWENTY-SEVEN

"It's rather strange, don't you think?" Mrs. Hollingsworth lifted the empty teapot from the Tuesday morning breakfast table. "The wire on the frame apparently simply *broke*—and the picture fell from the wall. No obvious reason. Never happened before. How odd."

Alan and Vicki smiled, though rather awkwardly, at their hostess. They'd had a good night—but hadn't slept enough.

"You don't think you might have bumped the wall?"

Alan nearly laughed, caught himself, and attempted a charming smile. "It would have taken quite a jolt to cut the wire clean in half, don't you think?"

"Yes, quite. *When* did this happen?"

"We were asleep," Vicki answered with a smile. "We heard a crash and turned on the lamp. We didn't see anything at first..."

"Then we noticed the picture had fallen down," Alan interrupted, a little nervous.

"Curious," Mrs. Hollingsworth sighed, and headed to the kitchen for more tea.

269

Vicki and Alan finally grinned. "Next time, not so *exuberant,*" Alan whispered. He imagined he was glowing as much as she was.

"Remember that time at your parents', when the mattress collapsed through the frame?" Vicki spoke softly, but her smile was a mile wide.

They were soon packed and off again. Alan's discomfort was returning—the picture shouldn't have come down...

"Wait, wait. Pull over," cried Vicki. They'd been driving the deserted country road for half an hour. "There's a piece of paper attached to the fence there."

"A piece of paper can't be the sign for the Stones," Alan replied with annoyance. "Neolithic stones marked by a handwritten paper sign tacked to a fence post? You're nuts!" Alan trusted his wife's knowledge—but she did make mistakes. In the case of the Rollright Stones—which he'd never heard of before—his confidence was low indeed.

"They're around here somewhere," she insisted. "They're on this road!"

"We've been back and forth on this same stretch three times!" Alan's frustration was mounting. He slowed the car and switched on the emergency blinkers. "You can't even tell me what these stones are. Why not just give up?"

He stopped the car and jumped out. Walking over to the fence, he lifted the limp piece of paper and read the handwritten scribble.

"Someone left a note for a friend," Alan yelled to his wife, who was walking towards him along the road. "They must have missed each other."

Vicki walked up but didn't answer. She was staring at something behind him. Turning, Alan saw, beyond the fence and the hedgerow, a huge stone rising out of the soil.

"Great Goddess!"

The stone lunged up bent and rough, defying gravity, abnormal. "It ought to topple right over," Alan gasped as they walked towards it. It stood in the middle of a vast field, which stretched off towards the horizon. "How on earth would anyone find this?" he asked. Yet they had found it—as Alan and Vicki had found one another. As ancient seekers had found the Grail, by some mysterious grace, when conscious seeking yields nothing. As Alan and Vicki hoped to find their own souls. Something in the English landscape was beginning to speak to them.

"They say you never count the same number of stones twice." They'd crossed the road to a circle of smaller stones down a short path.

Alan stared at his wife, looked around the circle, and started counting. For some reason it was impossible to concentrate. He counted two thirds of the circle twice, then lost interest.

"It's good we walked across the road," he said. "To think I wanted to rush off." He took his wife's hands. "You're quite a navigator. I don't see how you ever found this. And then you insisted we look over here. Thanks!" Vicki was quite a companion. The sex had brought them closer.

Vicki could barely wipe the grin off her face. She enjoyed the attention Alan was paying her. She'd enjoyed the love-making too. "I've talked with people about the

Stones, since I got to England. They're marked on the Ordinance Survey Maps, after all."

"This must be fifty feet across," Alan said, walking along the circle. "Think of the rituals we could do with the coven!"

"The coven!" sighed Vicki, "Eight thousand miles away!" She followed her husband around the circle. "Preston and Janie and Claire. They love us as much as they can; just not as much as we'd like. They don't understand."

"This should be the northern edge of the circle." Alan pointed towards a stone.

"I miss the coven." She placed her hands on his shoulders "We're so alone now."

"You've lost the Morris teams and Ian. I've lost my German friends."

"But *you* think that Ian will come back...right?" She clearly didn't believe it but hoped she was wrong.

"He has to come back sometime. If we go to Crewkerne and wait, he has to show up. How long can he be gone?"

"But Alan—what's the point—if he doesn't want to see me?"

"But it's *you* who don't want to see *him*."

Her face flushed with embarrassment. He took her in his arms. Sharing the truths they disagreed on was probably the most valuable gift they could offer one another—even if it embarrassed them.

"I guess we'll find out when he gets back—assuming it's soon. I miss the coven."

They kissed.

"Alan, you've never really explained what you found so appealing about those people in Germany. Yesterday you said you still missed them. Is that all over? What did it mean for you?"

"Let's talk about it while we drive, okay?"

Vicki started towards the gate.

"Vicki!"

"What?"

"This *would* be a nice place for a ritual, wouldn't it? I suppose they'd arrest us. But I haven't done a ritual since California."

"The plaque said entrance was granted solely for viewing the stones. I don't think that includes casting circles. I doubt non-Pagans would understand."

"If only we could *buy* them!" Alan blurted out. Surprised at his own presumption, he added: "I mean…you know…we could *live* here. Start a Pagan community." He thought a moment. "Community is important to me. That's why it hurts to feel excluded."

"Where would we buy our food, Alan?" Vicki snapped. Then she softened. "It's a nice fantasy, though. I assume this is run by the National Trust." She took her husband's hand. "I wish I were as mellow as you are. I always end up cynical."

"Vicki!" Alan repeated sharply an hour or two further down the road, "This isn't the motorway to Swindon." As before his wife didn't answer, just smiled suspiciously.

They'd stopped at Blenheim to see if Winston Churchill's family home could give them any insights on their quest, but all it did was send Alan into another mild rant like the one at Warwick Castle, triggered by the guide's description of a tapestry supposedly depicting the sufferings of the common people in wartime. Alan suggested that governments always found ways to justify their wars and ignore genocide. The Holocaust, Bosnia, Rwanda, Armenia, Cambodia. He'd come to despise the rationalizations.

They'd eaten lunch and headed further into the country-side.

"Vicki!" He braked to a stop now on the side of the road. Vicki went on smiling. "Why aren't we on the road to Swindon? That's the road we want, isn't it? The road to Crewkerne?"

Vicki looked at him, then back at the road.

"There are places I need to go, Alan. The Morris team wasn't interested—I told you that before. I have to find them now; it's a matter of my soul. Like the places you went in Germany."

"What about Ian? What about Crewkerne? You have to find *him*."

"We'll get there soon enough. Ian's still not back. If he arrives, we can get there quickly. We're not that far away now." Her eyes returned to the road.

"I understand," answered Alan. "Some things can't be rushed. Some people wouldn't understand, but I do. To find him, not as quickly as we can, but at the pace that the Quest requires. And finding our way back to him may require that we find our way back to something else—the Sacred Land." He pondered a moment. "T. S. Eliot…E. M. Forster…" He stared into the blue skies.

"I'll check for Ian every day," Vicki added with a hint of mockery, eyes still straight ahead. "You're right. You understand me. Everything at the right pace." She followed his gaze into the clouds. "Come on, we'd better start driving."

"Can I see the map?"

"I'll give you directions, like I've been doing."

"Give me the map."

"No."

"Vicki!"

"Alan, even if I give you the map, you won't be able to read it and drive at the same time. If you like, *I'll* drive—but I'll drive where *I* want to. I can find a lot from memory now."

Alan gawked at her.

"Honey," Vicki said, reaching over and cupping his neck in her hand, "Didn't you like that treat I gave you last night? Wouldn't you like some more? You can have more, my Love, as soon as we see my stuff—I promise." She leaned over and kissed his neck. "I have plans for you, Sweetie." She reached down and rubbed his crotch. "Come on, Lover." She started to laugh. Was she teasing or serious?

Alan pushed her away; she'd made him grumpy. "Where are you taking us?"

She pointed ahead. "There. Just over that hill. Come on. I want to surprise you."

She planted her lips on his. Alan felt her mouth open and her tongue prying against his closed lips.

Almost against his will, he relaxed and opened his mouth.

TWENTY-EIGHT

Alan walked back and forth along the crest of the hill. "It's difficult to tell what it is. The angle from here is so skewed…"

"We had a better view with the Morris team. I don't know which hill it was. Even then it didn't look like the photographs. They must take the photos from the air. There's no place to see it from the ground."

"You can tell it's a horse though. Wow. The White Horse of Uffington. Thousands of years old. Never thought I'd see it."

"It's strange how they stretched it across the hill," Vicki mused. "Not like a *real* horse—a *psychic* horse, a *spirit* horse. The type of Spirit Animal we need."

What sort of spirit entities could they call on? Alan wondered. What lay in the Universes—Inner and Outer—to help them, to guide and protect them?

Vicki put her palms together and bowed to the ancient Figure. Then their eyes followed the elongated chalk-tracings across the green grass glistening in the oppressive afternoon sun. If you weren't familiar with the ancient psychic landscape of Britain, you wouldn't know you were looking at the image of a horse, etched in chalk across a

lengthy stretch of grassy hill. Vicki and Alan did know—
and that compensated for the stifling heat of the British
summer afternoon.

Vicki took her husband's hand. "Let's get back to the
car. I want to show you something else."

"But why do you miss them so much?"

Alan shifted in his seat and glanced out again at the
passing landscape.

"You *know* why I admire Gustav, I presume."

"Oh yes—that's obvious. You probably traded ideas
about nail polish." She turned to watch the passing hedgerows. Vicki could be closed-minded. It felt demeaning.

After a long silence, Alan answered. "No, we didn't. But
I think we admired one another. I certainly admired *him*.
And he must have admired me, because he asked me to do
his wedding."

"Oh Alan, Alan. Who's going to recognize *you* as a
priest?" She laughed derisively out the window. She was
convinced that society would never accept either of
them—why bother trying? But he wanted her to respect
him—and herself.

"*He* called me a priest. And so did Herr Neufeld. I admired *him too*. He's worked so hard for cross-cultural understanding."

"And pretended to marry three women at once." Of
course she would say they'd only pretended—it could only
be real if society approved.

"But he loves them all. And *they* love *him*, I think. They
genuinely care about one another."

"But they'll never be accepted; you know that." She considered herself a realist. He thought she had simply given up.

"Sometimes being accepted isn't the point. Sometimes you have to stand up for what you believe. Sometimes you have to bear witness." He didn't care what society said—he knew what he believed.

Vicki turned towards her husband. "But that's the point, Alan. Sometimes it does no good to bear witness. Some things will never be accepted." She'd lost hope long ago.

They remained silent awhile.

"I thought it might be different in Germany," Alan went on eventually. "I love Germany—I always have, ever since I discovered Wagner when I was fifteen. People don't seem so judgmental there—despite what non-Germans tell you."

"It's because they aren't Puritans. They don't have the Puritan heritage we have in America."

"But they have the Lutheran heritage. Now, after Berlin, I'm not sure about the Germans. To cart that poor man off to jail…"

"I thought it might be different in England, I admit it. Even if I couldn't be happy with you—or Claire—in America, I thought I'd feel freer here. But Claire re-ignited all my insecurities about women, and Ian re-ignited all my insecurities about men. And England!" He was surprised she was sharing this.

She drew a deep breath, held it, then began again. "I *love* English folk customs, but the English are so *peculiar*! I can't imagine ever feeling *at ease* here. I mean, Americans are *afraid* of lesbians, pagans, and polys. Here…Here they'd just think you were a little crazy. I mean…I don't think they'd ever actually *respect* you. They'd merely tolerate your eccentricities."

"Maybe they'd only give you the respect granted the Fool."

"The Fool—my spiritual teacher!" They fell into their own thoughts again. Then Vicki cried: "Look!"

Alan followed her pointing finger to a huge stone peeking over a hill. A second stone appeared. The car sailed over the crest and Avebury spread out below them in the mid-afternoon summer sun.

"Good Goddess!" cried Alan.

The road led them down to a group of old buildings, enclosed in two circles of gigantic stones.

"There are six prehistoric sites at Avebury," Vicki said. "I persuaded the Morris team to stop here—we were passing so close. Only Ian seemed interested at all. But we could only stay here an hour.

"I want to see the sites now, one by one. It may take a while—probably the rest of the day. You don't have to come along."

Alan had pulled into the parking lot.

"Are you laughing at me?" she asked as he grinned at her. "You think I'm being silly?"

"No, no. It's just—"

"What?"

"What did you expect me to do if I *didn't* go along?"

"Wait in the car, I suppose." *Not in this heat!*

"Vicki," he said, taking her hands, "I told you I would travel with you through life. We're both Pagans. You're my High Priestess. *Thou art Goddess.* I *want* to visit these sites with you. We are Goddess and God together. I've committed myself to you—for life." He paused. "Unless you don't *want* me to come along."

He closed his eyes and sank back against the driver's seat. Then he felt his wife's arms enfold him; and her kisses on his cheeks and neck.

"Thou art Horned God to my Goddess," she whispered. "Come on. I want to show you the stones."

"What amazes *me*," said Alan, "is the shapes of the stones. As weird as the Rollright Stones. They stick out of the ground at odd angles. They aren't uniform. They bulge or narrow or tilt. They're clumsy, rough, unfinished."

"Yes," said Vicki, "I used to wonder why they didn't make them neat and uniform; why they didn't polish the stones smooth, like any stone mason would now. But that's the point: The rough stones make more of an impact. The off-kilter angles create more effect. They're disturbing. The stones…speak to me spiritually."

Alan looked back at them. "If they stick up this far, they must be anchored way down." Something still bothered him.

"I'd hate to knock one over," said Vicki. "Of course a single person couldn't, really. Can you believe they pulled some down to build a road in the 1700s?"

"They create an eerie effect, especially with the sun coming down in the west."

Vicki led him away from the main circles, across a road and through a wooden cattle fence.

"See up ahead? This was the avenue that led to the Sanctuary."

"The Sanctuary?"

"Another site. We'll get to it later. Two miles away."

As they moved farther into the fields, rows of huge stones rose on either side of them.

"Amazing," said Alan. "There's Silbury rising in the distance." A mile away, volcano-like and green: Silbury Hill.

He was heading towards the next pair of ragged columns when Vicki stopped him.

"No point walking any farther. The rest of the stones haven't been excavated. But at one time, these stones would have continued two miles."

"Amazing!"

"Come on," she said taking his hand, "I'm not sure how easy this next part will be. I studied Avebury back in California. If I'd known I was going to be here... I'll have to see what I can remember."

TWENTY-NINE

Alan pulled the car off the road and stopped, then threw his wife a disgusted look.

"Here?" he snorted. He'd been driving all day...and gotten impatient.

"Here."

Alan shut off the engine, opened the door, and got out. His eyes scanned the fields of grass and came to rest on the tall cone of Silbury Hill, now behind them. His eyes narrowed.

"Here?" he asked Vicki again across the car roof. "Are you sure?"

"I think so. Over that ridge. Come on." She headed into the field.

Alan's gaze was fixed on Silbury Hill. "Five thousand years old, some of it," he said loudly, rushing to catch up to his wife. "As old as the pyramids and about the same size. Here—in England!"

He followed Vicki along the path. Now and then he turned to stare a few more seconds at the huge mound hanging in the mist, stark against the late afternoon sun. Something about it drew and focused Alan's attention.

"There it is!" cried Vicki. She'd stopped on a small rise. A long low mound crossed the horizon ahead of them.

"Bigger than I expected," said Vicki.

"So *this* is a *long barrow*? What does that mean?"

"A burial site. They buried important people here, back in the days of Silbury."

"Here? In long low mounds? Not under a mountain of earth like Silbury? Or huge stones like Avebury? So Silbury wasn't a tomb like the Pyramids?"

"No evidence of burial there. Scientists have analyzed Silbury to death. Early archaeologists were convinced that there *had* to be something there: A royal burial chamber; a vast treasure. But they found nothing. Nothing."

She looked back towards the great hill.

"They know it's man-made," she said, fixing her eyes on the distant hump. "They know it was built in stages, over hundreds of years or longer. But no one knows why."

They stood silent.

"Look, Alan." Vicki raised her hand towards Silbury and the lower lands behind it. "You can't see it from here—maybe you could with binoculars—but down past Silbury is Avebury, and the circles of stones we visited. We aren't more than a few miles away. We came from down there, behind and to the right of the hill, then behind it, and then out around to the left, there." Her hand traced the path.

"We can't see the avenue of stones from here either. But it would have traveled the two or three miles from the Avebury stone circles to the Sanctuary further up this road. There must have been a massive temple complex: The Avebury Temple and the Sanctuary, with the two-mile monumental avenue joining them. The sacred burial area *here*. And then—out past Avebury, on the other side—I remember it all now—Windmill Hill."

"Windmill Hill? That doesn't sound prehistoric."

"It's called that *now*. No one knows what *they* called it. This was long before the Angles and Saxons, or even the Celts. Long before any of the *known* people who have inhabited this island. Whoever they were, they've long since *gone*."

"Gone." Alan repeated the word with an air of finality.

The air had grown cooler, a breeze now noticeable. The sun was descending into the western haze beyond Avebury.

"Excuse me, please." A voice from behind startled them from their reverie.

Vicki stepped into the high grass to allow the stranger to pass. Alan too stepped aside and watched as the lone woman headed down towards the road. The woman, alone in the tall grass, grew smaller then vanished over the next rise.

Vicki took her husband's hand and walked towards the mound. It was farther than it had first appeared. Now and then they met another person leaving the site.

Finally they arrived at the head of the mound. The opening to the barrow was sheltered by two large vertical stones a bit smaller than the stones at Avebury. Above the entrance, they could see along the length of the barrow, several hundred feet along the ridge—a massive barrier of soil and stone.

As they passed through the entrance it became dark and cool. Their eyes had to adjust to the interior dimness.

"It's so refreshing in here," Vicki said, "after the heat of the day."

"They say it's the hottest summer in a century."

Vicki continued further into the barrow. On either side of the main passage, smaller passages branched out. As Vicki went on Alan ducked to the side.

He found a small chamber that might have held four or five people. The stone felt cold. The chamber was utterly still except for the echo of Vicki's footstep.

People had been buried here, the entire length of the barrow. How many bodies could they put into three hundred feet? A single family in each chamber? Possibly forty chambers? Two hundred people altogether? The skeletons long since gone.

Returning to the main passage, Alan passed four or five chambers on each side. Then, in the dim light, he saw the silhouette of his wife.

"Apparently they only excavated this far. Look."

A small votive altar had been carved into the stone in front of them. Flowers and coins lay on its rough surface.

"Other worshippers must come here," Vicki whispered.

They contemplated the fading light and flowers. Vicki's arms slid around her husband's waist, and her head sank onto his shoulder.

"The Lord is in His holy temple," she said to him under her breath. "Let all the earth keep silent before Him."

Alan stared at the fading flowers on the altar. *Life from death. The Living to the Dead.* Then he realized his belt had come loose: Vicki was opening his zipper.

"Vicki! What are you doing?"

His pants had fallen, and Vicki had taken him completely into her mouth.

"Darling!" he cried. "Sweetheart!" He desperately tried to lower himself onto the dirt. He tumbled backwards nearly bumping his head against the stone.

"I welcome my Lord into my holy temple," she cried, lifting off him a moment. "I long to suck his essence into me."

"Vicki! This is hardly the place. Someone might come in." He realized that he was aroused in spite of—or perhaps *because* of—the danger.

"I want my Horned God to come in," she gasped. "My thighs are wet for him." She hoisted herself over his face.

He could smell her through her jeans, close against his face. Her mouth was like hot syrup over his cock. She was moving her tongue up and down the length of his shaft.

He reached up and unbuttoned her jeans, unzipped them and pushed them down her legs and reached into her dark moist hair. Her cunt was soaking and hot; Alan's finger slid easily into her. Her whole body shivered as he thrust his fingers in. She was chuckling now and gasping. Her mouth clamped tightly onto him. His own mouth stretched upwards towards her pungent smell.

Then he saw them above her.

"Vicki!" He tried to push her legs away. They tumbled over. He tried to stand up, but her mouth still locked firmly onto him.

He saw her eyes open and the shock register.

"Goddess!"

Alan ran down the passage pulling his pants back on as he ran, checking each side chamber as he ran past. He reached the entrance and continued around the protecting stones. He looked across the fields—to the right and left—and along the top of the mound.

"Do you see them?" Vicki had caught up.

"No. Nothing. No one."

"But where could they go?"

"I don't know. It's as if they were phantoms." He took his wife in his arms.

"My gods, Vicki. You're trembling all over."

"Did you see what it said, on the ceiling of the vault? I noticed as you were running out."

She led him back down the passage. On the rock under which they had lain, the words stood out in white paint: *Know Thyself!*

"Some recent devotee must have painted it," Vicki whispered. "I can't decide whether I'm pleased or disgusted."

"Let's get out of here."

THIRTY

Alan let out a deep breath, rose from a squat, and walked around the edge of the markers sticking up from the grass of the field. They had driven a little further up the road. He gestured discreetly in the direction of the couple walking back towards the other car.

"I thought they'd never leave," he said quietly. "I couldn't tell if they were Pagans or non-initiates."

"You understand what we're going to do, right? The Sanctuary isn't really visible anymore, but we can do this. It's circular and it's ancient. The markers show us where the stones used to be. If anyone comes here after we start, we'll close the circle *mentally*, understood? We can talk later." Vicki's knowledge of the site amazed him. He was privileged to have her as his magickal partner—they worked well together.

Alan pulled a packet of salt from his pocket and picked up the bottled water from the ground beside him.

"At least we have this. I kept it from breakfast just in case. Okay. Let's begin."

They walked into the middle of the markers, which formed concentric circles on the ground.

"*Salt and Water*," Vicki said softly, "*Earth and Sea. All is one—and the World is reborn.*"

She walked to the edge of the circles then continued clockwise around the site.

"*Through Water and Earth I hallow this space, and with my hands do sacred work.*"

She returned to Alan, who bowed to her. He carried a small flashlight to the edge of the circles, turned clockwise and began walking.

"*Through Fire and Air I charge this space, and with my feet walk holy ground.*"

They faced one another in the center of the markers, took the water and salt, and touched each other's foreheads.

"*Through Water and Earth, come to new birth.*"

They held the flashlight between them.

"*Through Air and Fire, find your desire.*"

They had blessed the site and themselves now with the sacred elements. They went to opposite sides of the markers and walked clockwise across from one another. Then they began casting the magickal Circle—creating a holy area for the practice of their Magick.

> "*Now I cast the circle 'round.*
> *In this circle we are bound.*
> *All for Good and naught for Ill.*
> *Raise the power of our Will.*
> *Safe inside, from Evil free,*
> *Work the Craft for Thee and Me!*"

They returned to the center and sat on the ground. The circle had been blessed and consecrated—it was now Sacred Space. They could begin the Magickal Working.

"So what do you think?" Vicki asked. "Who did we see in the barrow?"

"Let's try to find out."

He took Vicki's hands and they closed their eyes.

"Hermes, Guider of souls, Teacher of Wisdom." Alan paused to think. *"Oh Spirits who joined us in the barrow—who are you and why did you visit us?"*

For a minute Alan was silent. Then he started to hum. He continued for some time, then faded out. They sat silently awhile. Then Vicki said, *"So mote it be."*

"So mote it be," Alan repeated—"So must it be!"—opening his eyes and looking at his wife. "So, what did you see?"

"I saw two people, rather young," Vicki said. "Two women."

"What did they look like?"

"One of them looked rather masculine, and somewhat dark—possibly middle-eastern. The other was tall and striking. She wore a Star of David."

"Was one of them blond, with blue eyes?"

"Yes."

"Which one?"

Vicki thought for a moment. "The one with the Star of David. She was tall and blond and blue-eyed."

"Listen Vicki," Alan continued after a moment, "Did you notice anything unusual about the shorter, darker woman?"

"What should I have noticed?" She looked into his eyes. "You almost act as if you recognized these people."

"Just tell me, Vicki—Focus on the shorter woman. Visualize her. Was there anything unusual about her?"

Vicki concentrated a long moment. "I think…she was actually a man."

Alan exhaled a long sigh. "Sally and Naomi. The couple I met in Germany."

This agitated her. "Why should you see *them now*?"

"I don't know, Vicki."

They stared at the central marker. Then Vicki stood up. "Let's go."

"What about Cakes and Wine?" The Sacred Feast of the Goddess and God.

"Not here. It's too public," she said. "Maybe at Windmill Hill." He understood immediately and caught his breath—she intended the Cakes and Wine to include the Great Rite between them.

"Shall we uncut?"

They went to opposite sides of the circles.

"Now we travel back around.
Sacred Circle be unbound.
The magic that we wove inside
 In our hearts shall now abide."

They had gathered the Circle back up, like a rope they had earlier unwound.

They stood silent again, then headed back to the car.

"As the Athame is to the Male…"
"So is the Cup to the Female."
"And conjoined they bring happiness."

The athame—the protruding male object; and the cup—the opening female object; joined together.

One spoke, then the other spoke; then the two spoke as one. They smiled, kissed, and relaxed onto one another. Then they rolled apart, alone between the "Windmill" hills. Alan remembered Naomi's words as he was walking away from her in Bayreuth: "You must know something about Tantra?" And of course they did. Wicca was strongly Tantric: The sexual union of Lord and Lady—Priestess and Priest—creates and recreates the world.

"Thou art Goddess."

"Thou art God."

"Drink deep, and never thirst," they whispered together.

Alan swung around, lowered his head between her legs, and licked the sticky sap from her thigh. His tongue followed the whitish line up to where it entered her moist hair. Then he sank his tongue deep into her, drawing their combined fluids into his mouth.

As Alan drew in the last bit of jelly, Vicki shifted position and took his cock into her mouth. Her lips continued down to his crotch hair. Sucking him firmly, she drew her mouth up his entire shaft, drying him. Alan smiled, and they kissed, swirling tongues around one another.

"Take. Eat. This is my body," Alan said without thinking. Vicki's brow darkened.

"Blessed be," he quickly added. But he thought: *Nehmet. Esset. Das ist mein Leib.*

"Great Zeus!" he exclaimed. "Look how dark it's getting!"

He grabbed his clothes and started to dress. Vicki had swung around to pull on her shirt.

"Look at Silbury catching the last rays of the sun." She grabbed her jeans.

"Nestled between the breasts of the Lady." He looked to the hills on either side of them.

"In her very cove," she said. "On his towering peak."

"Best get back to the car."

*

But the car was surrounded by a small crowd—about eight people.

"Excuse me," said Alan as he and Vicki climbed back through the wooden fence. "What are you doing?"

"We've been camped here four days," said a tall man with a neat beard. "The authorities have just expelled us; said we were trespassing and had to leave. Barely five minutes before you arrived."

Alan remembered the difficulty he and Vicki had had finding Windmill Hill. They'd driven in the general direction, become confused, and asked directions at a filling station; followed those directions to the pub, to the barn, along the gravel road climbing the hill, to the gate and the *No Trespassing* sign—then further up the dirt road to the fence. He recalled they *had* passed *one* car.

"You were here when we arrived?" Vicki looked embarrassed, and Alan guessed why—the people might have seen what they'd been doing between the breasts of Windmill Hill.

"Yes, ma'am. We've been here four days. We were packing to leave when we saw you drive up and walk through the fence. We didn't think it right to follow you. We didn't know what business you had on Windmill Hill. People come here for all kinds of things, if you know what I mean. Isn't right to spy. Just waited for you to come back." Perhaps they'd seen nothing—and knew the wisdom of respecting people's privacy.

"Ma'am," said a second man, young and gaunt, "Do you think you could spare a little change? We don't know where we'll be sleeping tonight. It'd be mighty helpful…if you could spare a little something."

Alan examined the young man's face. "Have I met you before? Have you ever been in London?"

"Yes. Worked there till last Friday. Made my living miming. In Leicester Square and so on. Till the Bobbies chased me off."

Vicki's face lit up. "We saw you in Leicester Square! The police car drove up and asked you to leave! You were the Mime!"

The man's expression changed immediately. He fell into character as a humble servant addressing an eighteenth-century noblewoman. He bowed; he opened the huge double doors of a palace; he led her down the corridor to the ceremonial reception hall; he presented an elaborate birthday cake, complete with mechanical ornaments. Then, just as suddenly, he was an ordinary, unemployed, homeless and penniless mime. He had mastered his Art—but had no money.

Vicki glowed with appreciation, but the bearded man broke the spell.

"Do you think you might spare something, ma'am? Sir? We don't know where to go."

Vicki and Alan exchanged whispers, then Alan unlocked the car and reached for his wallet. "Here," he said. "This ought to be good for something."

"Oh, sir!" stammered the mime. "Twenty pounds! Are you sure you want to give us that much? We didn't expect..." Alan was genuinely moved.

"No," said Vicki. "You take it. It's for all the people who enjoyed your performances in London but gave you nothing. You deserve it." This meeting had affected her as well.

As Vicki and Alan swung the car around, the mime called out:

"Sir! If you remember and ever have the opportunity…"

"Yes?" Alan was growing impatient. His sympathy went only so far.

"If you ever meet up with the National Trust, you might ask who appointed *them* to kick people off the Land that gave us all life."

"Are you going to tell me where you're taking me?" Alan asked as they drove down Windmill Hill. "I presume you're *not* taking me to Crewkerne." He would follow her wherever she went; that was part of his commitment to his wife. But he didn't trust her to take him to Crewkerne—at least not directly. She didn't seem in any hurry to find Ian.

"We couldn't get there tonight, Alan. The last fifty miles are two-lane backcountry roads. No fun driving *those* after dark, with the hedgerows folding over us! And Ian still wasn't back when I called this morning." So at least she'd *tried* to reach him.

"So we're spending the night…where? We're not going to sleep in the car, are we? We're not getting in trouble like those people on Windmill Hill? You have a plan?"

In what remained of the fading dusk, Alan could see his wife grinning.

"Relax, Alan. Relax and trust me, Darling. I've phoned ahead." He could only smile in reply.

Then came the darkness. Along the road they seldom passed another car. Alan drove onwards into the night. Now and then, ahead of them in the blackness, he imagined he glimpsed Sally and Naomi.

*

"Vicki?" Alan spoke from the darkness. The bed-and-breakfast had grown quiet and they would both be asleep soon.

"Are we going to Crewkerne tomorrow?"

There was a long silence.

"Maybe. I want to see Bath first. It calls to me somehow. That's why I brought us here."

"Why?"

"Ian said it has a Roman museum and baths. And Jane Austen lived here."

"I don't read Jane Austen."

"She's very funny."

"And she liked Bath?"

"Despised it."

"Oh goody."

Alan lay awake. He thought he heard his wife beginning to snore.

"Vicki?"

"Hm? What?" She was groggy.

"Don't you think our host's kind of strange?"

Vicki grumbled, shifted position, and tugged on the sheet. "No more than any of the others. Go to sleep."

The thin sliver of light from the city split open the dark silhouette of the curtains. Alan lay quiet, fearing that Sally and Naomi lurked in the distant unseen corners of the room.

THIRTY-ONE

The stone figures moved up and down over the doors of the Abbey in downtown Bath, as if walking the ladder of Jacob back and forth between Heaven and Earth; taking messages between humans and gods; coming down and going up; maintaining the connection; sustaining the communication: The Messengers, the Angels; the Message. *Only connect, like E. M. told us*, thought Alan. It was a bright Wednesday morning.

Vicki followed her husband's gaze towards the church. "I've seen so many cathedrals," she said. "Every city where the Morris team danced. Did you know you can't call yourself a *city* here unless you have a *cathedral*? I'm cathedraled out."

Alan continued gazing towards the sculptures. "Look how the figures go up and down. Who goes up and down? Who communicates with the Gods?"

"In Christianity," Vicki answered, "it's the Saints, the Martyrs. They set an example, they bear witness, they show us how to live."

"But for *us*," Alan interrupted, "for religious Pagans, it's the shamans, the dreamers, the witches. They fly between

Heaven and Earth—and even down into Hell—if you believe in such things. So mustn't it be *us* then; the ones who travel back and forth and bring the good truths from Heaven; who willingly offer ourselves for dismemberment in the depths of Hell, for the sake of the Community?" Alan thought a moment. "Why did Sally and Naomi visit us? What did they need to tell us? Why did we run away?" *Run away—like in Berlin.* He realized that sharing his thoughts and his doubts with his wife brought him closer to recovering his soul—wherever it was.

They turned to one another. "'*Here on earth,*' he quoted, '*God's work must truly be our own.*' That was JFK, wasn't it?"

Vicki took him into her arms.

"I see the path that you're on," she whispered. "I don't know if *I* can follow it—but I'm proud that *you're* trying." She took his face in her hands and kissed him all about his forehead.

"Thank you, Vicki. I need to be able to talk to someone about this. It's important to me. Thank you." He felt they had married each other all over again—on Windmill Hill.

They clung to each other as tourists and children passed by. *It must be wonderful to be a tourist—to have no worries, to relax.* If only the two of them could do that! Vicki kissed her husband's forehead and said: "Come on. I want to see the Roman ruins."

Dim light diffused through the lower level of the Temple complex. The chamber remained cool and quiet in spite of the tourists.

Closing his eyes, Alan sensed the water surging upwards from deep within the earth. He sensed divinity around him. He recalled the statues they'd seen in the museum, one level up: Images of the Sun and Diana, Lady of the Hunt; effigies of Horned Cernunos, Lord of the Animals; and the image of Holy Minerva, the Lady of Wisdom, the Mistress of the Spring. He felt the presence of the Holy Ones surging through him, from his feet up to his head. The burst of energy swept him along.

"Holy Minerva, Sacred Athene, Divine Wisdom, Hagia Sophia—teach me your ways, teach me to act nobly, to live with integrity. Teach me to follow my heart, my head, my intuition. Teach me to serve the Community and the world."

He dropped a coin into the pool.

Vicki walked up and kissed him on the cheek. *"You are the salt of the earth,"* she said quietly.

"And you—*you are the light of the world.*" He was still glowing from the Great Rite. He could tell Vicki was also.

They stared into the water, then took hands and walked into the sunlight of the courtyard, open to the sky, which enclosed the larger pool. Vicki led him along the edge of the water.

"This pool was heated from below," he said. "Not a bad accomplishment for Roman times."

Alan knelt at the edge of the water and pulled the pentagram from inside his shirt; lifted the chain over his neck, and dipped it and the rings into the water three times. Then he kissed it and returned it to his neck.

"I haven't taken that out since Berlin, when I saw the Ishtar Gate."

"No," said Vicki. "You took it out in London, at the Temple of Mithras. But I noticed you didn't glance around this time, before you took it out. In California, you always seemed afraid. I realize now that embarrassed me."

"I just like to be sure…"

"That no one's looking? Honestly, Alan. That always astounds me. You talk about being honest, then you cringe at the slightest anxiety."

Alan couldn't hide his embarrassment.

"But you didn't do it this time," she went on, emphatically.

"Didn't do what?"

"Look around first. You didn't check to see whether anyone was watching. You simply did what you did. That's good. I realize now that I need that."

"You need—"

She put her hand over his lips. "I need you to challenge me," she said softly, "by living up to *your own* standards. When you do that, it challenges me to live up to mine."

"You need…?" he stammered, "…My own…? Challenge you?" He had never felt that his own struggle to live with integrity mattered to her. Perhaps it hadn't, before.

Vicki grinned and took his hand. "Let's go upstairs to the Pump Room."

"I had no idea," he mumbled, "no idea."

As he followed his wife up the stairs, he thought to himself: *Is it possible? Is it remotely possible? Could I have found my soul?* And the realization settled on him, that It had indeed returned.

"This water's pretty horrible," Vicki said, making a face. They'd accepted a sample of the Pump Room water. "All the sulfur."

"Maybe my nose is clogged up. I don't smell much sulfur. Tastes tolerably good to *me*. I could drink another."

"Yuck!" Vicki mock-grimaced, curling her nose. "No thank you!"

"Why did Jane Austen hate Bath?" he asked. "Seems a nice enough place."

"It's precisely the type of place *you* would have despised. Jane Austen hated it because everything here was pretense and insincerity. That was in 1800. There was no place for the heart. People came to show off how important they were and who they knew. You could be stupid and cruel, as long as you were rich. You remember Beau Nash?"

"The Master of Ceremonies? The man the guide mentioned?" Vicki's words had reminded Alan of Naomi's idea of a Jerusalem of the Heart.

"He ruled Bath like a presiding deity. It didn't matter who you were. If he didn't approve of you, Bath society snubbed you. He refused to extend the evening balls beyond their customary ending time, even when the royal princess begged him to. His rigidity permitted no exceptions. He had brains and refinement—but no heart."

"The Pump Room doesn't seem so intimidating now."

"It would have been in Austen's day. The Ball season must have been like the Inaugural balls in Washington. The attendees wore their most expensive clothing. Everyone would be on 'best behavior.' Nash provided the best food, the best wine, the best musicians. The room sparkled with jewels and gold and silver. Jane Austen must have felt so alone—a modest, soft-spoken, intelligent, educated woman who knew exactly what social standing was worth—or not."

"I always thought you liked glitter and sparkle, Vicki." Now he could appreciate his wife's quiet side.

A little while later…on a neglected street in Bath…

301

"I don't get what's special about Sally Lund bread," Alan said. They'd stumbled on the house where the famous bread originated.

"It's just a bun, Alan; but it's known all over the world..."

"It must have been horrendous to bake bread in the summer heat."

They read the information on the wall. "I knew she'd come here from France..." Vicki said cautiously.

"Her family was Huguenot," Alan said with surprise. "Protestants persecuted in France. Her real name was *Solange Luyon.*" He thought of the refugees in the Balkans and Chechnya. "Guess things were the same in the 1600s," he added finally.

They continued reading. "Alan, I never realized there was still so much intolerance in the world." This sent an anguish through him. An awareness of evil was burrowing into her heart. And he realized he was afraid for Sally and Naomi.

"Everywhere, I'm afraid. The people I met in Germany knew what was happening and what it meant. Maybe because of the Nazis. They seemed more aware of human suffering. Americans don't have the feeling in their gut."

"So the world knows about Sally Lund's *bread* but not about her *life.*"

"Her bread is her legacy, Vicki. Curious she took the name Sally." After a moment he added: "*Take. Eat.*" Bach, communion, the feast of the gods.

THIRTY-TWO

Yes, food meant something to him: The Communion of Food. Alan had found another Chinese restaurant. He and Vicki handed their menus to the waiter.

"After dinner," Vicki said, "I'm calling Ian one last time. I'm not waiting any longer. It's over a week since he left. I've been away from home almost a month." Alan presumed she was going to remain with *him, Alan*—but he couldn't be absolutely certain.

"Yes," he said, "my folks will be expecting me back. Last Venusday was Lavender's birthday—did you remember?" Alan missed his daughter. He hoped Vicki did too.

"I remembered it a day or two ago, strolling around York. Poor thing. She didn't get a party." Vicki did care about them both.

"My folks were planning to give her one. Probably took her to the zoo."

"I miss her," said Vicki. "It seems so long ago."

"Well, if we can't find Ian…"

"I knew he'd dump me," she grunted. It pained Alan to see how much emotional energy Vicki invested in believing the worst about people, and how much power she still gave up to Ian.

303

"You don't know that. Not at all."

"He never cared. He was only flirting. Damn." No—she didn't know that. She clearly still hoped to be proven wrong.

"If you really want to go home, we can try to get a flight this weekend." Still, the quest for their souls…for their sanity…for their mental welfare… Wouldn't she be abandoning hers?

They ate in silence. Alan was thinking of William Bao. Vicki tolerated Chinese food but thought it overly rich and salty. She ate it out of politeness. He'd been enjoying dinner, but now the conversation had soured him.

Then he noticed a conversation across the room. An oriental man was trying to explain something to the waiter.

"That man over there," Alan said. "I think he's Japanese. He's trying to order something, but he only knows the Japanese word—and the waiter only knows English and Chinese."

Vicki glanced around, then returned to her broccoli beef.

The waiter whisked past them, grabbed a notepad from the register, and returned to the table. He handed pad and pen to the Japanese man, who wrote something.

"Well why didn't you *say* so?" exclaimed the waiter.

After they were outside, Alan smiled at his wife. "You realize who that was?"

"No. Who?"

"Saito. The Japanese student we met in York. Remember? He came here to learn English."

"I guess his English still needs work. Come on. I think I see a phone booth."

*

Alan paced the sidewalk. Vicki was talking heatedly on the phone. But of course she had a lot to settle with Ian. At least they'd finally tracked him down. Alan glanced into the ice cream shop. The clock had advanced five more minutes. Hopefully Vicki's phone confrontation would not last much longer.

Alan stepped into the shop and examined the thirty-one flavors. He wanted something exotic with cherries. But he'd wait for Vicki. They could sit in a booth and watch the tourists go by. Soon, he hoped, when they'd recovered her soul as well as his, they too could relax.

"We're leaving on Sunday." Vicki's words pulled him from his reverie. "It was a struggle getting the tickets."

"Sunday? From Heathrow? You weren't talking with Ian?"

Vicki's face went crimson. "I don't want to talk about Ian."

"No one answered the phone?"

Vicki glared at her husband. "I said I don't want to talk about him! Someone answered all right. Some woman. Probably another of his bimbos."

The color drained from Alan's face. "What did she say?"

"She didn't say anything. I hung up the phone." So most of her talk had been with the airline.

Alan considered a moment. He knew how angry Vicki could get. "Have some ice cream. Let's sit and cool down."

"It *is* kind of funny." After dessert they'd continued up the street to the entrance of a bookstore. "To fly to England then get ice cream from an American ice cream chain."

"It was good, though. Made me homesick. I'll be glad to see Lavender."

They exchanged uncertain looks. Alan couldn't believe they were going to quit their journey with Vicki's soul still unsettled. What would their future together be? What would become of Lavender? Vicki started into the bookstore.

"Aren't you coming in?" she asked. "I've never seen you pass up books."

Alan looked at her oddly. "Give me a minute. I want to stay out on the street a little longer. I'll join you shortly."

He could tell Vicki found it unusual, but she let him go.

Alan stood a moment, soaking in the ambience of the phone booth. He saw Vicki lifting the receiver, dialing the number, listening to the ringing, ringing... Then the voice...and the silence.

Then the voice again. And Vicki slamming the receiver down. The scene played over and over. He knew his wife's temper. And he had a way of divining people's feelings.

Something caught his eye: A bright yellow piece of paper crumpled on the ground. He stepped out of the phone booth and bent over to retrieve it. Another trait of his—noticing details other people overlooked.

He unfolded the little square. The name *Ian* leapt towards him, with a British phone number. He recognized Vicki's handwriting.

He could see it all in his mind. Vicki expected no answer. The other woman's voice startled her. Vicki didn't know what to say; then anger and jealousy blinded her. She slammed down the receiver, crushed the slip of paper, and hurled it into the street. So she *did* love Ian.

Alan looked at it now: The yellow paper, the blue ink. What could the voice have said? The icy silence from Vicki's end could not have warned of her rising fury. The voice couldn't know Vicki's temper.

What might the other voice have said? What did it know? He was drawn again psychically into feelings and the past.

The thought began like a tease, then grew: *What would the voice have confided, had it been asked?*

Alan returned to the phone booth.

"Alan!" The voice was loud, insistent. It broke Alan's focus. Part of him was still in the phone booth; part of him had travelled somewhere else.

"Alan!" The voice repeated itself close by. Where *was* he now? He had entered into trance, but the voice was pulling him back.

"Alan!" Someone was shaking his shoulder, and the voice had become more annoying. It was Vicki, her face red and contorted. He was ripped from the psychic world back to the physical one. They were standing in a bookstore.

"What is it, Vicki?" Alan said softly. "What's the matter?"

"What's the matter?" snapped Vicki. "I noticed you standing here, and you were just staring. I came over to talk to you, but you didn't hear a thing I said. You didn't seem to realize I was here. You weren't moving. You just stood here, staring at the bookshelves—but not *at* anything; just transfixed or something. Not moving at all. Not budging. You stood like a statue a good five minutes. It scared me."

This was why he'd never told Vicki much about his trances; he knew they made her uncomfortable.

"Vicki," he answered softly, "Do you know the story of Muhammad, how he traveled to Heaven and back? How he traveled around the world, in the blink of an eye? Joseph Campbell talks about it."

"Are you okay?"

"I think I saw Aphrodite: Aphrodite and Hermes and Dionysus. See?"

He gestured towards the bookshelves. "Christopher Isherwood and Edmund White, the chroniclers of male love. Armistead Maupin—the chronicler of the City in all its facets. Jack Kerouac and Alan Watts—the Bodhisattvas of immanent joy."

"Alan, I think you may have a fever. We'd better get back to the bed-and-breakfast." Their paths were very different, and he knew it. She tolerated his eccentricities and knew that a little rest would usually calm him down. He needed to demonstrate he wasn't crazy.

He hurried down the row of books, his eyes glowing. "Not only sexual love," he called out as she tried to catch up to him. "Look!" Vicki's eyes followed her husband's finger towards a single title.

"*The Bridge Over The Drina?*" she asked, puzzled. "What's *that?*"

"When I was visiting Bosnia, twenty-five years ago, on my way back to Munich from Istanbul, we stopped by the river in Mostar, and the tour guide said: *That's the bridge in the book that won the Nobel Prize.* Turns out it was a different bridge—but that doesn't matter. The bridge I saw in Mostar *was* historic." Even after all the years of folk dancing, Alan hadn't realized until this moment how much the Balkans personally meant to him.

Vicki stared at her husband, uncomprehending.

Alan turned to his wife. "The bridge I saw is gone now," he said with great excitement. "The Bosnian Serbs destroyed it last year."

"Alan, Alan. What are you so worked up about?" She had never understood how his moments of exhilaration kept him connected to the cosmos.

"The bridge," cried Alan, putting his hands on Vicki's shoulders. "The *physical* bridge I saw is gone, but *The Bridge* lives eternally in the *book*. Understand? And the whole world can see it *there* forever, even if the *physical* bridge is destroyed." He may not have created art himself, but he knew the power of art to transform people.

"I suppose…" muttered Vicki, who seemed to be gauging her husband's sanity. "So what?" She stared at him with a concerned look. "I mean, you said it wasn't even the bridge…"

"I'll tell you on the way back."

Vicki took a deep breath. "So you're telling me that there's *nothing* wrong with us?"

"Exactly." Alan tossed his shirt onto the lid of his suitcase and pulled off his socks. "We're exactly the way we were meant to be, the way the gods intended us, the way we can most serve our community, the way we can best love our friends and families and children—the way we can nurture our souls." He tossed his shorts onto the side table. Yes—he knew his soul had returned—would hers?

"Because?"

"Because we're offering them *who we really are*—honestly, truthfully—and in love."

Vicki stared at her husband. "They'll think you're crazy," she sighed.

"For telling the truth?"

"Yes. What on earth did you see back in the bookstore? All *I* saw was you standing lost in thought." But she knew this happened to visionaries.

"All I saw was the truth," he said quietly. "That people need love to flourish, and that sex can express love. I want my friends to be happy, with love—and sex. I want *you* to be happy. It's stupid to be possessive in matters of the heart." He paused and thought a moment. "That's it," he added finally. "Stupid to be possessive in matters of the heart."

"But letting go—that's what always hurt me," Vicki cried in frustration.

"No," Alan shot back. "What hurt you was your refusal to stand up for what you knew you needed and knew you wanted and knew *you* knew was the truth. What hurt you was the culture that refused to acknowledge and provide for your needs. We have a *right* to the people we love."

Vicki had pulled off her clothes. Alan, reaching for the lamp switch, for a brief moment admired his wife's large breasts and the fuzzy fog-hair between her thighs.

"I'm too scared," she said as the lights went out. "I've always been abandoned when I was honest. I can't." She'd always been afraid—always. She'd always been mocked for her ideas. Throughout their years of marriage, Alan had tried to help—but she'd already been wounded by the time they met. She'd been punished in ways he couldn't imagine. He'd never known what to do.

For a moment the dark room was silent.

"Oh, by the way, Vicki," Alan's tired voice cut the stillness, "I got through to someone at Ian's."

The room fell silent again. "You *what?*" Vicki replied with a rasp.

"I went back to the phone and found the number, after you threw it away. Ian should be back tomorrow afternoon. The woman on the phone with you was a neighbor."

Silence again. Then Vicki took him hard against her skin, clutching him, trembling as she gasped: "My gods!" Then tears fell on his shoulders.

THIRTY-THREE

The English countryside glistened in the bright Thursday morning sun.

"Our innkeeper was a charming gentleman." Alan's eyes followed the curves of the narrow road as he spoke. "But a little *too* charming—and a little strange."

"True."

"I knew he'd lived in Southeast Asia. Who else would wear shorts and knee-high socks? And when he said that Hirohito was a war criminal and should have been hung…" He caught himself. "Well, I've lived in Japan, I remember Hirohito…"

"I'd forgotten it's been fifty years since the War ended. Looks like we'll miss the celebration."

"Fifty years next month since the end of the *Big One*," mused Alan. "Was it worth it? Would we do it again? Or would our horror of violence make us give Hitler whatever he wanted? I was in Berlin on the anniversary of Hiroshima. I saw the revulsion against the atomic bombing. I'm not sure we would ever do that again, even to save the world from evil."

The car sped on. The air was already heating up.

"What he said about Glastonbury…" Alan resumed.

"That it's been overrun by hippies and New Agers? There, you see?" She shot a scowl at her husband. "The man was a charming host. I loved the bed-and-breakfast. But you see, Alan—this is why we can't be open about ourselves. Not here, not in the U.S. People refuse to understand us. It's as if their ears are plugged and they can't hear what we tell them." She was right about these people, he knew that. But Alan hated having to hide—it made him feel ashamed—and he wasn't ashamed.

"He must think they're all crazy: Them—all of *us*!"

"Who knows what he thinks, Alan? He probably thinks the New Agers in Glastonbury stay up all night smoking pot and staring into crystals. He thinks they're all just Hippies! The point is, no matter how clearly we demonstrate that Paganism is a religion of nature and nurture and responsibility, no matter how often we explain that polyamory is about relationships not sex, most people won't understand us—or believe us. For whatever reason." Vicki was a realist, that was all. He preferred visionaries.

"Prejudice," muttered Alan.

"Whatever."

Signs for Glastonbury came into view. They would be there soon.

"You've been here before, right, Vicki?"

"We danced here during the Morris tour. But we didn't have much time to look around. It was the same pretty much everywhere. I've been all over England with Ian and his Morris team—but I wasn't looking for my soul, because I thought I'd found what I needed. I thought Ian…" Her voice trailed off.

"We should have plenty of time today," Alan said as he slowed the car. "Only twenty miles to Crewkerne, and here we are at ten-thirty in the morning. Ian won't be back till at least six p.m., the neighbor said. Where do I park the car?"

Vicki pointed him to the parking lot nearest the Chalice Well.

The narrow stream of water flowed down the side of the hill, cascading from pool to pool, through the garden: A beautiful green of trees and bushes and grass. Under the dazzling blue sky and vibrant sun, the foliage glowed. Vicki walked to the lowest pool of water, reached in with both hands, and splashed the water over her face, dripping for several moments. Then she started up the hill, past the yew trees. Alan followed.

"This is called the Chalice Well," Vicki explained, "because it's associated with the Grail. Joseph of Arimathea, who offered his own tomb for Jesus' body, is said to have brought the Grail to England. They say he buried the Grail here in Glastonbury, and that it feeds this spring with reddish water—maybe the blood of Jesus that fell into the cup, maybe the blood of the wounded king who bleeds periodically, whose wound never heals. Or maybe the woman's monthly blood. They say the White Spring nearby flows with water the color of a man's seed. And the two springs blend together at the bottom of the hill they call the Tor. They say that Arthur and Guinevere were buried here."

They came to a long rectangular pool beside the path, and walked on in silence. Vicki sank deeper and deeper into reverie. She bent down and splashed her hand along the water as she walked.

Alan watched her. She seemed unusually thoughtful. Vicki was not naturally inclined towards introspection. Alan followed her on to the Well itself.

Vicki sat down on the stone beside the Well, then looked up at her husband.

"Did you notice what they said after we bought our tickets to come in? *May you find here what you seek.* But what am I looking for, Alan?"

Apparently she expected an answer, so he spoke.

"Your soul, I presume. Sometimes I think you'd rather be abandoned by Ian than face the possibility that he may actually care about you. Sometimes I think you'd rather abandon your soul than risk finding it."

Vicki said nothing. She peered into the depths of the Well then remarked: "They say there's a pentagonal chamber off to the side there, inside the Well. I can't see anything. No one knows why the chamber was built. It may have been used for initiations."

She looked up at him. "I've always thought a part of me was waiting to be discovered in England. Now that I've tramped back and forth here, I'm not sure. I saw lots of towns and people during the dance tour, but I didn't learn anything. I felt deeply connected to Ian—but he ran off." Her voice faltered. "The trip you and I have had so far..." Her voice wavered again.

She squeezed his hand and led him to the Lion's Fountain, where a stream of clear water flowed from a small lion's head. She took a glass from the shelf, filled it under the flowing stream, and handed it to her husband. Clearly she expected that the spring water would taste better than the mineral water in Bath. It wasn't red, he noticed.

"Thou art God. Drink deep, and never thirst. You've been the one great constant in my life, Alan. I've always thought you'd abandon me, but you never have." She'd never trusted him; she'd grown up being told to trust no one. He'd grown up differently.

315

"You deserve to be loved, Vicki. You've always deserved to be loved. All the men who betrayed you were fools. You thought *you* were worthless, but *they* were."

"I guess we'll find out tonight whether there's one more to add to that list, eh?"

Alan held up his hand to stop her from saying more. He refilled the glass.

"*Thou art Goddess.* Drink ye all of it." He realized with satisfaction that he had combined the Pagan and the Christian in his offer. He thought of Rudi and Kurt and Sally.

Tears welled up in Vicki's eyes. He drew her to him and cradled her in his arms.

"I want to climb the Tor with you now," Vicki told her husband. He remembered Windmill Hill.

Panting from the steep climb up the oblong hill called The Tor, they turned and surveyed the surrounding English farmlands, and Glastonbury below them.

"Somewhere off that-a-way," Vicki said, "is the stone circle of Avebury...and Silbury Hill."

"And Windmill Hill," Alan added.

Vicki smiled. "Somewhere off *that* way," she said, turning around, "is Stonehenge."

Alan regarded the ruined Abbey that crowned the Tor.

"Henry VIII went all the way when he decided to take over the Church," Vicki said.

"Yes. He not only burned the Abbey, he had the abbot drawn and quartered, and the quarters of his body sent to the four directions." It was the Tower of London and Warwick Castle once more. The Victors always destroyed the Vanquished. "Barbarians," muttered Alan.

He walked into the narrow ruins of the devastated abbey. Vicki followed close behind. Then Vicki burst into tears.

"Vicki! What's the matter? Are you ill?"

"No, no," she answered, leaning against the old stone of the church. "It's just that…I kissed him here—Ian—when the dancers were finished. The day was so lovely. I couldn't help it. Forgive me." He could see how much she had loved Ian.

Alan kissed her full on the mouth. "Forgive you?" he asked. "For what? For loving someone who'd been kind to you? For kissing someone you loved? I will always rejoice in your lovers, if you truly care for them." An image flashed through his mind—he saw how beautiful this life could be. He remembered Sally and Naomi—how happy they'd looked in their wedding gowns. Where were they now? Were they in danger? Why had they appeared to them in visions?

He began to walk the hill lengthwise. "It quite befuddles me," he muttered as he walked. "They insist this hill is natural, yet it looks so man-made!"

"You can still see the terraces around the curves of the hill," Vicki said and pointed. "The terraces made the labyrinth. But do you *really* suppose this was used for *initiations*?"

"I don't suppose anyone really knows," said Alan. "It certainly would be nice to imagine so. This place is *magical!*" But how would you convey this to non-initiates?

After lunch they were driving again, down a dirt road which was growing narrower. Alan was getting worried.

"Are you *sure* this is the road you meant us to go on? It's getting worse and worse."

"No," snapped Vicki, "I've been here before." She caught herself. "Well...I have directions. I know the way."

But the road continued to worsen. It had started off good enough, then narrowed to two lanes, then less than two. The pavement had deteriorated to dirt road, then dirt path, which veered erratically through woods and grew fuller and fuller of stones. Then they came to a small creek. The usual Grail-Quest entanglement, perhaps.

"Go on," Vicki cried. "We can get across."

Alan looked at the water tumbling past. "It's no good, Vicki."

Vicki threw her husband a nasty look—a look Alan usually yielded to.

"Okay," Alan said softly. "Here goes." He drove the car slowly into the water. The creek was no more than half a foot deep. As they crawled forward, they could hear the water splashing off the tires. The current swept over the stones, but the car only skidded twice.

"There, you see?" said Vicki. "Not a problem."

But a solid wall of bramble confronted them on the other side of the stream. They could find no further path. Therefore the Grail must certainly lie ahead—or not.

"How could you think this was the right road, Vicki?" Alan snapped. "Where the hell *are* we?" The gurgling of the stream annoyed him.

"This isn't the way to Crewkerne, is it? Hell—this isn't the road to *anywhere*. This isn't a road!" He seldom lost his temper. He drooped over the steering wheel, then started to laugh.

"What's so funny, Alan?" Vicki snapped; but he went on laughing.

"It's like the Grail myths. Or Dante's Dark Wood. To find the Grail, you have to plunge into the forest where the bramble is thickest. Pick any place—it doesn't matter where—you can't escape arriving there eventually—if you are meant to arrive. If not, you will never find it. But Fate cannot be outrun or outwitted, try as you may. You cannot escape it. So let it happen. Accept it. Embrace it. Love it."

Vicki stared out her window looking disgusted. "Alan," she said in a peeved tone, "You produce the most illogical pronouncements." How could she not understand him? The explanation was straight out of Campbell!

They stared into the bushes ahead of them.

"So where *were* you trying to take us, Vicki? I know we were heading for Crewkerne when we drove out of Glastonbury. We went through Yeovil, but—" For some reason, he thought of T. S. Eliot…

"I wanted to surprise you, Alan." Vicki spoke in a voice not quite convincing. "*The Cerne Abbas Giant.*"

"The *Who*?" It did sound vaguely familiar.

"The huge figure of a man, etched into the side of a hill. Like the Horse at Uffington—but a man."

Alan looked at her. "You're right. It *would* have surprised me." He looked into his wife's eyes, trying to guess her thoughts. He wouldn't have expected her to want to see these things. She was such a skeptic, really.

"So why did you really want to come here—I mean—come to see the Figure? It wasn't really to *surprise* me, was it? Was this a way to avoid meeting Ian?"

Vicki turned red.

"That wasn't it, Alan; I *swear*." Alan thought she was going to cry. "I wasn't running from Ian. I—"

She sank backwards into her seat. "I just wasn't ready to meet him again, *yet*." She closed her eyes and drew a few deep breaths. Then she looked intently at Alan.

He took her hand. "But why come to the Figure?" he asked. "Why not at least take me somewhere with a *road*?" He eyed her suspiciously. "Or is this even the way to the *Giant*?"

"Oh yes, Alan, it is. I mean, more or less. I must not be remembering it quite right. And the Figure *is* rather out of the way."

She sighed and stared down at the floor.

"The truth is, Alan—" she turned slowly to face him. "The truth is I wanted to pray."

"*Pray*?"

"Pray, meditate, do a spontaneous ritual—whatever. You remember Avebury?"

"Oh yes. I certainly remember Avebury: The Long Barrow, the Hill. I won't forget those soon." Now they were snuggling—as well as they could in the cramped front seat of a car on the edge of a running brook. They turned towards one another and kissed, tongues probing each other's mouths.

"People think," said Vicki, "that the Figure represents Lugh. He's holding a very large club."

Vicki went silent. She was biting her lip and blushing a bit. Alan watched her with curiosity.

"And?"

Vicki struggled not to smirk—or giggle.

"What is it?" Alan asked, drawing Vicki back into his arms.

"Oh," she whispered, laughing, "it's just that…well…" She giggled softly again. "It isn't just his…*club*…that's gigantic."

"I see."

"It isn't easy for me, Alan. I grew up being made to feel guilty and afraid about sex. When I started doing it, I only felt worse. A lot of women feel this way."

"And you let men exploit you in college—I know." Alan was maneuvering the car around to re-cross the water.

Vicki said nothing. When Alan had gotten the car back across the creek and onto dry land, he turned and saw a woman with the look of a wounded, cornered animal. If Vicki felt this way all the time, he thought, it would be horrible.

"Vicki," he began—and then she burst into tears.

"I told you, Alan, I never want to talk about college again. Never. To anyone. Not even you." The pain in her voice was terrible, unendurable. Then she added: "At least, not yet." He knew something about her past, and wished she would confront it—but he couldn't he force her to.

"Okay." He stopped the car, turned on the emergency blinkers, and took her in his arms.

"Why do you think Ian frightens me so?" she asked, sobbing. "Because of the chance—it sounds so ridiculous!—that a *second* man might actually care about me.

"But now I know I *won't* know until I've taken the chance with him, opened up to him, made myself vulnerable. And I know he might be like those men in college, and he *might* hurt me. And sometimes I just want to run—"

"But you'll always have *me*. Always. Unless you don't *want* me."

They were cuddling now, parked on the deserted dirt path.

"Thank Hera I have you," she cried; half laughter, half sob. Perhaps he was of some use to her after all. After fifteen minutes, she felt well enough for them to go on.

THIRTY-FOUR

After Alan turned off the engine, they realized how profoundly quiet Crewkerne was: No sounds but their own breathing and the car engine cooling.

"No one here," Vicki said. "Maybe the person you talked to was mistaken." Alan wasn't sure what to say—he was surprised Ian wasn't home; disappointed.

"He was supposed to be back. And it was such a mess getting here!"

Dusk was coming on. Surrounding features grew less and less distinct in the fading light—approaching nine o'clock.

"Maybe I could check with the neighbor," Alan said, glancing around. "But *where*? *Which one*? Hell, I don't even know whether the person I spoke with really *was* a 'neighbor.' She could have just been a friend who checks on the house. Damn!" He laid his head on the steering wheel. They were both exhausted.

"I guess we'll have to look for a hotel," he went on. "I doubt they even *have* hotels in Crewkerne. We may have to drive back to Yeovil—or even Glastonbury. Damn!" Then he heard the car door open.

"Where are you going?" Vicki walked to the door of the house and pulled something from her pocket. Alan jumped out and ran to her.

"You have the key? You have the key to his house?"

The door swung open. Vicki reached around and switched on the ceiling light. If Ian had abandoned her, why did she have the keys to his house?

The living room was furnished with simple, well-made wooden furniture. A brick fireplace dominated one end. The mantle displayed photos and small ceramics. The opposite wall displayed a medieval-style tapestry with a German (German!) inscription:

Ehret die Frauen,
Sie flechten und weben
Himmlische Rosen
Ins irdische Leben.

"Nice house," Alan said, glancing around the room. "How can Ian afford it, along with his place in the States?"

"It was a gift to him," Vicki said, "from the university. In appreciation for some work he'd done. That's all he told me. Either he isn't back yet, or he's gone out for something. Let's get the luggage." Apparently Vicki felt quite at home here. Alan stared at her, dumbfounded.

"You think we should just *move in*?"

"Well what do *you* think, Alan?" Vicki snapped. "You insisted we come to Crewkerne. You insisted we find Ian. What do *you* want us to do?"

Alan considered a moment. "It doesn't seem right," he stammered. "I thought we'd meet him… go to a pub… talk…"

"And *then* we'd move in? Alan! He knows we're coming, right? You said he was *expecting* us."

"Expecting *you*. I didn't say *us*! I only talked to the neighbor. Ian hadn't returned yet. He must have mentioned you; she recognized your name."

"Hell, I might even have *met* her." Then, with clear sarcasm, she added: "So what are we doing, Alan? Are we getting the luggage or driving off to look for a bed-and-breakfast? And looking for Ian in the morning?"

"Ian gave you a *key*," he muttered.

"Well we *were* kind of...*intimate*...Alan."

"Let's get the luggage," Alan said, and started out the door.

"Alan! What do those words on the tapestry mean? I always meant to ask Ian..."

"It's a quote from Schiller," he said softly, thinking of Inge. "*Honor Women; they braid and weave heavenly roses into earthly life.*"

Ten o'clock and Ian had still not arrived. They'd settled into the guest room.

"Might as well get undressed," said Vicki. She loosened her skirt.

"I feel funny about this, Vicki. Suppose he really wasn't expecting us. Suppose he only thought he might be getting a *phone call* from *you*? You said you never told him that you were married."

He lifted his wife's skirt off the chair.

"At least there was food in the kitchen," she said. "Best to get ready for bed. It's been a long day." She'd made herself right at home. She and Ian must have spent quite a while here earlier.

"To think we walked the Tor today. It seems so long ago." Alan was still taking it all in. "It seems strange to be

324

sleeping in a strange bed, in a strange house, in a strange town, in England."

Vicki switched off the light.

"It's so quiet here," he went on as they lay side by side in the silent darkness. "For me, our travels through England have been an increasing withdrawal from the modern world, back into the primordial mists of the past." That was as close as he could express how the trip had affected him.

He stared out into the darkness of village England.

"Well you know, Alan, this bed and this room, this house and this village, this country—none of them are strangers to *me*." She *had* been living here with Ian!

Sometime later, Alan realized that a car engine had been switched off; that the front door had opened and shut. He couldn't judge the time. It could have been thirty minutes—or several hours—later. He was too tired to make sense of it. Later still, he realized that Vicki no longer lay beside him. Then he slept soundly until the morning; when, with the bright sun streaming in through the cracks of the window blinds, he realized that his wife was wrapped around him.

He lay still awhile, enjoying her warmth. Vicki breathed slowly and regularly. He could hear shuffling in the other room; someone was neatening up. Then Alan smelled bacon. Vicki slept undisturbed. Twenty minutes after her husband, she opened her eyes.

He realized she was looking at him—but staring; not seeming to notice him. Her eyes looked sad; her mouth turned downwards. She seemed unaware of her husband.

Something must have disturbed her during the night. He stroked her cheek.

"Did you talk with Ian?"

She closed her eyes and held them shut as though remembering an unpleasant incident. Opening them again, she replied: "I saw him but didn't speak to him."

She closed her eyes again, as though seeking to recover from a nasty shock. Alan cradled her head in his arms, rocked her a few times, and said: "I heard him drive up, get out of the car, and come into the living room. I remember you went out to him. I was barely awake. What happened?"

"Oh, I walked down the hallway towards the kitchen. He was sitting at the table looking through papers with his back to me. He'd peeked in to see if we were here, and I thought we'd talk. I threw on my shirt and jeans. But when I saw him looking through the papers, I hesitated. The way he was holding himself, his posture, struck me as peculiar. I just stood and watched him. Then he began to tremble. Something awful came over him and he started to cry. I've never seen him unhappy, never once on our dance tour. He's always been the perfect visitor—reticent, considerate, and calm. But he was shaking all over and crying. *Crying*, Alan! I've never seen Ian cry. Gods! He was sobbing! He went on for a good ten minutes. As if the whole world had died.

"I came back to bed and just lay here, staring at the ceiling; trying to get back to sleep. I kept thinking of him. I could hear the crying from here. I must have been awake for hours. Athene!—I hope he's all right." Her voice was trembling now. She sounded exhausted.

They lay silent as the aroma of the bacon grew stronger. A faint knock at the door jolted them from their lethargy. From outside a muffled voice asked, "Are you awake, Vicki?"

"Yes, Ian."

The door swung open. A short man in his forties with thinning hair and a black beard appeared through the gap.

"I'm sorry I was so late getting back last night, dear. I really wanted to see you. I've been away so long, but it was unavoidable." His voice was shaky.

Then he noticed Alan. "What's this? A man? I'll leave you two alone…" He apparently hadn't noticed Alan when he first glanced in. He backed away. "There's breakfast if you like," he said in a tense, cold voice and started to pull the door closed behind him.

"Ian," Vicki yelled desperately, "I'd like to introduce my husband."

Ian's head popped back in. "Husband?" he cried harshly. "You didn't tell me you were married, Vicki."

Vicki turned red. "I was preparing to leave him. I *did* leave him back in the U.S. But he showed up in London after I dropped you at the airport—completely unexpected."

Ian's eyes grew less suspicious.

"Vicki's told me a lot about you, Ian." Alan tried to sound confident and friendly. "She said you know a lot about British folk customs and dancing. It sounds very interesting." But who was this man, and how'd he come to be involved with English folk-traditions?

Ian's demeanor softened. He broke into a grin. "Mr. Horne, did Vicki tell you that we're romantically involved?" So there it was—but was he *poly*?

"It sounded more than *romantic*… She intended to leave me, after all… I don't think she will now, though… It doesn't matter. She can go on seeing you, I don't mind. You're a long way from California. You can visit if you like, now and then." After he spoke, Alan realized that he might be sounding dismissive.

Ian and Vicki exchanged a significant glance. "Come on out and have breakfast," Ian said.

THIRTY-FIVE

"You're listening to Beiderbecke," Alan said, walking over to the table where a tape was softly playing. "Bix Beiderbecke. Where'd you find him?" He wanted to know more about his wife's lover.

"My wife gave me the tape," Ian replied. Odd. He mentioned *his* wife. Ian didn't seem to be concealing his marriage at all.

"I heard that song in Virginia," said Alan. "At first it seemed tongue-in-cheek, but it's grown on me."

As they sat down, Ian said: "It's nice to share a meal with friends in the morning. I really appreciate new friends." Very poly. He turned to Alan. "I'm sorry, what was your name?"

"Alan."

"I know we've just met, Alan. But I'm so glad you're here. There are times when I need friends." He sighed deeply and stared out the window. "It's been such beautiful weather. Beautiful on the continent as well." He lifted his fork. "We should go somewhere; why stay in all day? Any place you'd like to visit?" He seemed to actually want a suggestion.

"We tried to find the Cerne Abbas Giant yesterday," Vicki ventured. "We followed a dirt road that ended in a stream. Could you take us today?"

"I've been there," said Ian. "It's a little tricky, but we can try it."

The prospect appeared to calm him. They ate in silence. Afterwards Ian turned to Alan.

"You recognized Beiderbecke. Are you a jazz fan?"

"Not really. I'm just getting into jazz. My father lent me some records before I left the U.S. last month. I don't know much about it. I'm more of a classical fellow. Wagner..."

"Wagner." Ian sighed. "My wife likes Wagner."

Funny, Alan thought. He mentioned his wife again.

"She likes jazz too, my wife," Ian went on. "People say there's a connection between Bach and jazz. Sometimes I listen to Bach and feel like I'm listening to jazz—and the other way around. Thelonius Monk seems terribly *classical*. It's hard to explain. For me, there's a connection between music and how I relate to the world."

Ian related to the world through music?

"We'd better get going," Ian continued. "It'll take us awhile to get to the Giant and back. And I don't want to..." He stopped suddenly.

"What, Ian?" Vicki asked. He was staring at the carpet.

"I have to go back to London tomorrow. I want to relax this evening—and get to bed early."

Alan could read the disappointment in Vicki's eyes.

"London?" she said. "But Ian! Why?"

"What's the matter, Vicki? You can both come with me if you like—but I have some business to attend to; I doubt you'd enjoy it. After that..." He paused. "I may be taking some friends to Scotland. Would you like to come with us?"

Vicki's faced twisted into a grimace. "Ian, Alan and I are leaving on Sunday."

Ian stepped back. Surprise and disappointment clouded his face.

"I didn't know if you were coming back," Vicki snapped. "I've been away from home almost a month. I ran into Alan and realized I love him in spite of everything. I miss my home and family and daughter. Alan was with me and you weren't. So I booked a flight." Funny, Alan thought: In Bayreuth outside the Festspielhaus, Naomi had said *You're here, and Gustav's not.*

"Vicki," Ian said with a tinge of resignation, "I know you were disappointed when you realized I was married. And I admit I could have told you sooner and probably in a better way. But you didn't tell me about your own marriage, either. I think we were both afraid to bring it up. I already said I was sorry. Let's not ruin what we've got. Let's enjoy the time we have before I go back to London."

Ian *had* discussed his marriage with Vicki. But what were his own love-ethics?

"And *that*," Ian concluded, "is how I met Friedrich Neufeld."

Alan had dozed and half reawakened. Vicki and Ian were talking in the front of the car.

"Alan has been good to me," she said, "but he doesn't understand how I feel about all this. Polys don't understand. Haven't they heard of AIDS? It's embarrassing. Alan has no sense of propriety. He makes the most inconsiderate statements. He has no idea what people think of him. He has no idea how he comes across. When I try to explain, he says I'm being silly."

But, Alan thought, she'd been involved with other people since their marriage. And the two of them together had dated other individuals and couples. Alan had always considered Vicki polyamorous; her misgivings had come after the disastrous breakup with Preston and Janie. But Ian was talking…

"I know what you mean. Wendy's brought up this polyamory business too. She's got a boyfriend out west. They've been emailing each other, obsessing. So I said *Wendy, if you need to have an affair, why don't you just go and do it? Why do you have to tell me all about it? Do it, get it out of your system, then get back to normal for once.* And she looks at me like I'm crazy."

Alan observed them from the backseat. He could see them being pulled closer again already. Was Wendy so hard to understand? Did Ian really think that polyamory was about having "affairs?" Did Vicki find Alan so unsophisticated?

Friday was hot and the drive monotonous. Alan fell back to sleep.

"I love Alan," Vicki said, "but he's embarrassed me so much." Alan had awoken again, barely, and listened as his wife went on. "He's so impractical. He thinks people will be reasonable. And they won't be." Vicki's words stung him.

"You were going to leave him," Ian said.

"I didn't want to be reminded of…how I've behaved. I know I'm attracted to more than one person. I know I'm attracted to women and men. But I don't see how I can have what I want, so why not just keep quiet about it?" This was Vicki through and through. If she could just keep her queerness "under control," she wouldn't have to face the consequences of what she was. Alan remembered the article he'd read about Mel White on the plane from Frankfurt to Munich. White had tried to hide—until he realized he had to be what God had made him.

Ian tightened his grip on Vicki's hand. "But now that's *not* what you want?"

"Claire changed my mind," Vicki answered. "Claire wanted to sleep with me, but insisted we hide it. We made love in Yellowstone, then she started to worry: *Suppose Tomie finds out?* And I realized I respected Alan a thousand times more than I could ever respect her—because she seemed so *ashamed* of what we'd done. But I was afraid too. I thought I could never be honest the way Alan was—not in the U.S., not with my friends from work, in the Unitarian Church, or my family. And I'd *have* to do that if I went back to Alan." So Claire and Vicki had made love after all. And they both felt ashamed of it.

Vicki gripped Ian's arm. "Then I found you, and I saw my answer: *I'll go to England with Ian—and maybe stay there.*

"And I fell in love with the way you leapt in your Morris Dancing, the way you talked about dancing and the English countryside and the old customs. I thought you were my salvation: I'd run away with *you*." She sighed deeply. "But it turned out you *weren't* English; and it turned out that you *weren't* single. And your wife is apparently one of *them*—one of *us*—I suppose I should say."

She *did* know what she was.

"Then I ran into Alan, fleeing America too; and I thought: *We can disappear into Scotland, into the Highlands where no one can find us or bother us.* But my daughter—and Alan— and you—pulled me back. And I see there's no point in running. Wherever I go, I'll *still* be…the way I am. I can't change *that*. And why abandon my country and my family?

I deserve them. And Alan will always be poly and bi and a little transgender. Why should I allow ignorant bigots to take my birthright? I may be Pagan, but I'm American too. I won't renounce my heritage. Why should I die in exile?"

As my father said.

Ian pulled the car off the road and took Vicki into his arms.

"I'm so glad you said that," Alan said quietly from the back seat, "because I'd come to the same conclusion about myself." He leaned forward and rested his head on theirs. They seemed to welcome his touch. Alan thought they must have become more comfortable with their poly feelings: They hadn't pushed him away.

"Vicki," Alan told her, "you didn't have to lie about making love with Claire. I always assumed you'd become lovers. And you don't have to lie about Ian." Perhaps she'd *needed* to lie before. Now she seemed willing to admit she was a sexual person—and concede the type of sexual person she was. But before Vicki could answer, Alan turned to his wife's lover.

"Ian, you mentioned a Friedrich Neufeld..."

Ian looked at Alan with a strange, questioning look. "Wait—You're Alan...Horne." He glanced at Vicki, then Alan. "Now I know who you are! You were in Berlin...with the Neufelds." He didn't seem happy about it.

Vicki stroked his arm. "What is it, Ian?"

"Let's get on with the Giant."

Unease swept over Alan. They talked little the rest of the drive.

The actual road to Cerne Abbas was only slightly better than the one Vicki and Alan had driven the previous day.

It deteriorated to a dirt road, not quite as rocky as the other. It crossed a few minor water flows, nothing like the stream that had nearly stranded Vicki and Alan.

They saw the chalk figure now on the hill ahead of them, and Ian pulled to the side.

"You can't get any closer," he said, "unless you walk."

They stepped out and surveyed the Giant.

"He certainly has a *large*...' Vicki's voice trailed off as a wide grin spread over her face. The grin surprised Alan. Ian and Alan leaned on her from either side.

"No sin to love," Ian said gently. He seemed more comfortable now with his own feelings—clearly he hadn't always been.

"No sin to enjoy your lover," Alan added. He felt certain now that Ian and Vicki were both born polys, whether they admitted it or not. He wouldn't insist that they were, but he'd help them see it when they were ready.

Ahead of them and above them, the huge chalk man sprawled upwards over the grass, a gigantic club grasped firmly in the hand upraised over the skull-like face. The other arm flowed smoothly off the other way. The figure displayed strong legs, firm calves, and sturdy thighs. But though the Giant possessed prominent nipples, what held the gaze of the three Americans were the taut balls of the figure's crotch; and, sticking straight up for what must have been several yards, the Giant's straining, bulging white cock.

Back home, the conversation turned to Ian's recent trip.

"I went to Berlin because Marthe Neufeld called and said that Friedrich had been arrested. I'm a friend of his and respected in Germany because I worked on behalf of

East German dissidents during the communist regime. I could provide some international support and comfort to his wife."

"Don't you mean *wives*? I thought he was arrested for trigamy. I read it in a German newspaper." That long, mocking article on the way to Tegel Airport.

Ian reddened. Then he broke into a grin. "That's what actually saved Friedrich. He wasn't *married* at all."

Alan's face went blank. "But I met his three wives!"

Ian laughed. "His unions were blessed in private ceremonies. Friedrich never applied for legal recognition. He didn't believe the state had any business regulating private relationships."

They stared at one another.

"The funny thing," Ian went on, "is that it had never occurred to me that there was anything unusual about his marriage. I always just thought he had married and divorced each wife in turn. Everyone else apparently thought so."

"So what happened to Friedrich?" Vicki broke in. "Is he still in prison?"

"No," Ian exclaimed. "He's in London with his three wives. I'm going there tomorrow to see them. They couldn't prosecute him for trigamy, because legally he wasn't even married to Frieda, much less to Sophie and Marthe. They let him go."

"Friedrich in London? Thank the Gods!" Alan cried. "I like Friedrich a lot."

Ian regarded him grimly. "Apparently we crossed paths, Alan. While I was flying *to* Berlin to save *Friedrich*, you were flying *from* Berlin to save *yourself*."

Alan didn't reply.

"He met me in London, Ian," Vicki snapped, defensive. "We drove around England together."

Ian looked surprised. He started to speak but Alan cut him off.

"No," said Alan. "I appreciate what you're saying, Vicki, but Ian's right. Let's be truthful." He turned to Ian.

"I didn't know Vicki was in England, much less in London. I believed she was back in the United States with Claire." He lowered his gaze. Vicki reached over and put her arm around him.

"I left Berlin because I didn't know what to do," Alan went on, looking at Ian. "I was scared. And besides," Alan added after a long awkward moment, "Sally suggested I leave."

Ian shot him an unexpected, anguished look. "Yes, I know. Sally told me. Let's go eat dinner."

THIRTY-SIX

They ate at the local pub. Whether because of Vicki or Alan or the beer, Ian kept bringing up his wife.

"I didn't understand what was happening with Wendy. She's always been more outgoing than I am. I like staying home and reading or working on my projects. Wendy does too—but she needs interaction and friends. She's always been that way. But it was like some kind of metamorphosis. She'd been shy about sex, really quite reserved. I guess the books she was reading made her feel more comfortable with her sexuality. She began wanting to be sexual with other people. I said *Okay, I guess*. It didn't matter to me—I was more interested in my work: Folk-cultures, human rights... She started going out in the evenings, and not coming back until early morning. I began to feel distant from her. She wanted to tell me about her 'dates'—but I didn't care about the guys she was seeing. I just wanted her to be happy. But the guys she went out with always disappointed her. I don't think any of them understood her."

Of course they didn't, Alan thought. And clearly she didn't know what she was doing. Society doesn't tell us about polys...

"She met some guy in San Diego during a conference— all he did was screw her and then avoid her. Now she's seeing some other guy out west. I really don't know where it's going. I just know I still love her." He snuck an awkward glance at Vicki. "And Alan, I love Vicki too."

So Ian loved them both; but did he understand them— either Vicki or Wendy? Of course Ian was concerned; he wasn't convinced that polys could ever be *happy*.

"I know what you mean," Alan said. "I used to be shy myself. In high school I always kept to myself, hardly had any friends. In college, I loosened up—but I was still afraid of people. I even invented a word for it.

"But I overcame it somehow. I learned not to be afraid. I got comfortable with myself. I even got comfortable with my body. I'm not sure how it happened, but I'm not afraid anymore. The way I am doesn't frighten me. What scares me now is the way other people *view* me; the way *American society* looks at me and people like me."

It was odd. Alan had never shared these thoughts with Vicki, but something had made him more confident. If only Vicki could talk about herself!

"I know," he went on, "that you both have trouble understanding people like me. But believe me: *I'm* not the one that's threatening you. It's *society* you should be afraid of. Society is what keeps us all down." He hoped he was making sense!

"Why do you think I came to Europe? I wasn't running from myself, the way you and Vicki were. I was running from my country. I love my country, but it considers me an enemy.

"When Vicki said she was leaving me, I thought: *Why is she doing this? Is it because she doesn't love me? No—it's because she's afraid; she's under pressure from her friends and family and coworkers. They pity her. They're embarrassed by her. They assume she must be ashamed of me. They* want *her to feel ashamed of me— and herself.*

"And what's Vicki got to be ashamed of? The fact that she's associated with me? The fact that she's shared my attitudes? She hasn't had the experiences that I've had that enabled me to break free from my conditioning. Shamans have to break free from normal society's point of view. She was susceptible and frightened. It wasn't her fault. I couldn't hate her. But I could hate the culture that made people this way." *Be careful,* he thought. *With the beer you might say too much.*

Leaving the pub, Alan tried to ask Ian more about the Neufelds, but Ian refused to discuss them until they were in the car. Even in the car, though, he hesitated. He didn't seem to feel comfortable explaining until they were home. Alan realized that Ian had used dinner to delay the discussion.

Back in the living room, Ian locked the front door and said, very agitated:

"Alan, I apologize. I didn't know how to say this: Sally's dead."

Alan stared at him then stammered: "Dead…? How?"

Ian looked deep into Alan's eyes. "Let's sit down."

"I don't get it," Alan blurted out. "Was it a hate crime? Was it the police? I know he went to the police after Friedrich was arrested. I was with him when he was attacked in Nuremberg."

Ian struggled for the words. "After I got to Berlin and spoke with the police and Friedrich's lawyer, I told Sally and Naomi I thought everything would turn out all right. In fact, Friedrich was only in jail a few days—"

"But that was over a week ago."

"Precisely." Ian did not appreciate being interrupted. "I called back here, but no one knew where Vicki had gone."

Alan noticed the hurt in Vicki's eyes. So did Ian.

"That was okay," Ian continued. "I *did* say you should go out and see things while I was away. I was just surprised you didn't tell anyone where you were going." Ian apparently had no idea that Vicki had decided to abandon him, or that she'd felt abandoned herself.

"Since I didn't know where Vicki had gone, I stayed in Berlin a few extra days to visit Friedrich and his family. I saw Naomi and Sally before they left on their honeymoon."

"Honeymoon?" Alan asked. "They actually went on a honeymoon? Where did they go?"

Ian hesitated. Apparently he needed to prod himself to go on.

"Sally—of course in those days it was Gustav—" He paused. The statement must have spawned other memories. "Gustav had always wondered where he came from. He never knew his biological family. Friedrich and Sophie tried to help, but all traces had been lost. Gustav had emerged out of the conflicts in the Middle East. In a way his history *is* the history of the modern Middle East. He knew some Arabic, some Farsi, some Urdu. He even knew a little Bosnian and Albanian. Eventually he was picked up by German aid workers, and that's where Friedrich and Sophie found him, in the early 1980s, during the chaos of the Iranian revolution and the Iran-Iraq war. He always hoped to unravel who he was.

"So they planned a honeymoon in Kashmir. Sally thought he might find something there. Kashmir had been relatively peaceful. Everyone told him how beautiful it was—Paradise on Earth.

"We warned them to be careful. Friedrich and I had done casework there for Amnesty International, years ago. They promised to be cautious. They were both familiar with the politics and culture. We didn't think that Naomi being Jewish would be an issue; India's extremely tolerant."

"Naomi," Vicki whispered. "Sally's bride?"

"Yes," said Ian. "She's dead too."

Another long pause.

"What happened?" Vicki finally asked.

Ian came over and she gave him a long hug.

"Have you heard about the hostages in Kashmir?"

"Good Gods!" exclaimed Alan. "Do you mean that Sally…"

"And Naomi. They were two of the people beheaded."

"*Two* of the people?" said Alan. "How many *were* there? I thought there were *only* two. We heard the BBC report."

"The media didn't report Sally and Naomi. It'll all come out, I suppose."

"But Ian," Alan said, "if the media didn't report Naomi and Sally, how do we know what happened?" He definitely liked Ian now. Ian cared about people—and the rights of people.

Ian sat down beside him. "An Arab named Ahmed, who was dating Friedrich's daughter, went with them."

"Ahmed? I met him."

"I suppose you did. I heard about the wedding. Sally was familiar with the Middle East from his reading. Naomi had grown up in Israel and lived there until after the 1990 Gulf War. But Ahmed suggested he go with them since he was actually *fluent* in Arabic and Farsi and Urdu. And Ahmed thought it would be good for a Muslim to go with them, in case they encountered any difficulties. Kashmir's majority Muslim. The day after their arrival, the three were taken."

"Kidnapped?" Vicki asked.

"Precisely. It was totally unexpected. Kashmir had been relatively calm." Ian reflected a moment. "It's a strange thing, too. The group that claimed responsibility—no one's ever heard of them. Ahmed said they all spoke Arabic. None of them seemed to come from that area. Let's hope they're just another incompetent group that won't cause major trouble."

"So Ahmed escaped?" Vicki asked.

"Oh no. They let Ahmed go. They told him they were releasing him as a fellow Arab and Muslim. A bad sign. They could be aiming at something more world-wide."

"So why did they kill the others?" Alan asked.

Ian hesitated. He tried to speak but seemed disturbed, embarrassed, and ashamed by what he had to say.

"You know I believe in the dignity and worth of every human being..." Ian faltered again. "People like this...challenge my beliefs..."

Vicki put her arm on his shoulder. Alan moved closer.

"They wanted..." His voice trailed off. His eyes stared far away. "They wanted..." He couldn't say the words. Finally he spit out: "They simply wanted to kill Westerners. Sally and Naomi's attempts to 'dress native' didn't fool them for a minute. The attackers knew they were from Europe." He inhaled deeply. "They wanted to kill Westerners. That was it, pure and simple. They wanted to kill Westerners...and Jews."

They talked late into the night.

"I'm so ashamed of how I've acted," Vicki said. "I thought you were leading me on. I thought you weren't

343

coming back. I thought you were using me. And now, you've been so kind to everyone…"

"I left you the keys to my house," Ian stammered. "I left you the—. How could you possibly…?"

"I was confused, Ian. I…I… My mind was all worked up and…"

"She wasn't in a normal state of mind," Alan cut in. "Some of us… I get that way too sometimes, under pressure: Paranoid. Agitated. Utterly disoriented."

Ian hugged her. "I admit I was uncertain about you, not sure what to do. But I wouldn't have abandoned you. I saw something in you, at Yellowstone; something I liked: Honesty, caring about people, dedication and conscientiousness about doing the right thing. When you told me about Claire and Alan, I could tell you cared about them. I could tell that you didn't know what to do. I saw you had principles. So do I." He glanced at his watch. "We'd better get to bed. I'm going to London tomorrow."

He led her towards the staircase, but she pulled away and walked towards Alan.

"What?" Ian asked, then added softly: "Oh, of course."

He and Vicki whispered to each other; Alan couldn't hear. Vicki turned and looked towards him, mouth open; but no words emerged. She looked horribly self-conscious.

"She's too embarrassed to ask you," Ian began. "She thinks…since you're her husband, that it would be rude…"

"Oh!" Alan exclaimed. "Darling!" He went to his wife, hugged her and kissed her forehead. "Do what makes you happy, Love. Do what *you* need to do." He took her hands and whispered: "I love you."

"Alan," she replied, "I don't know…I'm not sure…I'm scared. I've felt so exploited…" She was clutching his hands. "What should I *do*?" Her voice had grown desperate.

"Do you love him, my sweet? Is he good for you?"

Vicki was in tears, but managed to stammer: "Yes—yes, yes!" She seemed to need to make a commitment to Ian—and to Alan.

Alan drew her close. "Go with him then. I…need to be alone just now anyway—to think. Go with him."

Ian and Alan regarded one another awkwardly. Then all three of them came together and hugged. Ian took Vicki's hand and led her up the stairs. Before they went into the bedroom, Vicki turned, smiled at her husband, and whispered "I love you." Then Vicki and her lover were gone behind the bedroom door.

Later that night, unable to sleep, Alan turned on the lamp. *At least Vicki and Ian are happy, I hope.* He smiled, though painfully tired. *Sally and Naomi. Fuck.*

He looked for something to read. The guest room was one huge library, every wall crammed with books. Alan's eyes wandered over the titles and fell, suddenly, on the small photograph of a blond woman. Her hair tumbled in great tufts down to her rear.

His eyes narrowed. He lifted the photo and read the inscription: *Deepest Love, Wendy.*

"Gods!"

He couldn't sleep after that.

THIRTY-SEVEN

"Alan!" The female voice waited.

"Alan!" The hand shook him again.

He realized with embarrassment that the volume of T. S. Eliot still lay across his face. He instinctively reached for the tape recorder, but the tape had long since stopped playing. "Singing The Blues" began again in his head. He felt self-conscious about the art he loved.

"It's getting late, Alan," the male voice added, as the female voice giggled. *They sound married already.* "Come out and have some coffee."

Alan reached for the book, but Vicki lifted it from his cheeks.

Vicki and Ian grinned broadly. Sunlight streamed through the now open blinds. *They're trying so hard to hide it.* And he wondered: *Could she have found...*

"We let you sleep in because Vicki said you liked to. We're cooking bacon and eggs."

Alan was not smiling. Ian glanced uneasily at Vicki. "I'll go pour your coffee," he said and left the room. *Ian thinks I'm upset.*

When Ian was gone, Vicki bent down to her husband. "Are you okay, Alan? Have you changed your mind about last night?"

Alan looked puzzled.

"That I slept with Ian."

Alan frowned. "Not at all. I was up late. I haven't quite woken up."

They kissed.

"So you're okay with it? You're not going to turn on me now that I've gone and…" She was looking into his eyes for misgivings, uncertainty, or doubt.

"I *am* okay. It's just…" He closed his eyes. "I'm not awake yet." His face was full of fatigue. "I was awake most of the night. Couldn't sleep. Something bothering me…but not this. Can't remember." Had he had a dream? Something had disturbed him…during the night.

Vicki ran her hand along his cheek, caressed his ear. His eyes opened again.

"Come on out. You don't have much time to get ready. We need to leave for London. You need all your stuff for Virginia. And I want to stop at Stonehenge. Better get your shower. It's a beautiful Saturnday."

He rolled out of bed. "I'll be quick. Save me some bacon."

Vicki left, and Alan stared out the window at the summer morning. What had been bothering him?

He picked up the T. S. Eliot and closed the pages on *Little Gidding.*

A king, a defeated king—hiding in a chapel by night.

He put the tape player back on the desk. Something…he'd misplaced something.

As he hastily neatened the bed, a small object tumbled onto the floor. Retrieving it Alan recalled, suddenly, the pang of longing it had provoked; the sudden, intense desire

347

to caress what turned out, after all, to be only a small flat photograph of Gayle; and how longing had yielded to surprise—amazement; and a disquiet that had thwarted any attempt at self-arousal; then he had noticed the tape recorder and the volume of poetry; and finally, close to dawn, had fallen asleep at last, the book over his face; clutching in his hand the picture of the woman—one of the *two* women—whom he loved.

Alan entered the dining room with hair still wet from the shower.

"We're going through Salisbury," Ian was saying, "past Old Sarum and Stonehenge." He and Vicki were bent over a map.

"Feeling better, Alan?" Vicki asked. "More awake now?"

"Much better. Vicki—"

Ian folded up the map. "Vicki says you've never seen Stonehenge."

"Come on, let's get going." Vicki's voice expressed eagerness to be on the road. She smiled at Alan. "And you don't have to drive."

"It's nice to have my car back," said Ian. Then he was out the door with a suitcase.

"Vicki!" exclaimed Alan. "Look what I found in the other room." He sat the photograph in front of her. Vicki seemed puzzled. "Don't you see who this is?"

"Alan, we have to go. Am I supposed to know this woman?"

"Vicki, this is a picture of Gayle. I know you've only met her once or twice…"

"Gayle! That isn't a picture of Gayle! I know what Gayle looks like. Remember: I met her. She's stockier than this. Her face is fuller. Her hair's much longer. And why should Ian have her photo?"

"I don't know. Maybe they've met somewhere. Maybe they've even been lovers."

"Oh now you're just being paranoid," Vicki snapped. "Why does the photo say *Wendy*? Now you think he sleeps with everyone. Hurry up. Let's not take forever."

"Ian's still putting the luggage in the car," Alan answered calmly, glancing out the window. He sat down to breakfast.

"The coffee's nearly cold," he mumbled. He finished the bacon quickly.

"Look," he said, finishing the eggs and standing up, "I know what Gayle looks like, and better than you, certainly. Photographs of her always miss something. She looks different in different pictures, quite different. You couldn't recognize her from a photograph. But that's her picture, I swear it. And I don't know *why* Ian has it."

They stared at each other. The door swung open.

"Everybody ready?" asked Ian. Then he was gone again.

Alan swallowed the last of his coffee and sat the cup down. "Did Ian just say that was *his* car we've been driving? You never told me it was *his*. I thought you'd *rented* it! What were you planning to do when we got to Scotland—*abandon* it? *Keep* it?" Vicki blushed.

"I hadn't decided, Alan. I hadn't figured that out. I just wanted to get away. I thought I might have it shipped back later. It's his *second* car, after all." Quickly going outside, she added: "It doesn't matter anymore now, does it?"

"A lover loans you his car," he muttered, watching her walk away. "No conditions, no time-limits…" She was too far away to hear him; and besides, she'd started a conversation with Ian.

Alan stepped out the door and checked that the lock had been set. "Got your keys, Ian?" he yelled towards the two glowing figures.

"Got them!" Ian replied, holding them up.

Alan looked at the two of them.

Yet she didn't trust that he was returning. She preferred to believe he was using her for sex.

He watched them laugh as they stroked each other's cheeks. *Perhaps she* has *found...*

Alan sighed at the picture he held in his hand, and pulled the door shut.

Riding alone in the back seat in the Saturday summer sun—Ian and Vicki up front—Alan drifted into thought. He pulled the photograph from his book bag, studied it again, and lay it back beside his wallet. Outside the window, the hedgerows flew by.

This is the old country, the ancient, timeless land. His thoughts ran back to the poems he'd been reading the night before. He was drifting into the Dreamtime...

The Present the Past the Present the Future the Future the Present the Past.

He thought of Mary Queen of Scots, and Sally and Naomi.

In my end is my beginning –

The motto of the Queen of Scotland—and her last words on the scaffold.

"Vicki!" he yelled. "Vicki!"

350

"What, Dear? What's wrong?" She'd been enjoying Ian.

"Did you notice a sign for *Coker* the other night—when we were driving down from Bath?"

"I don't recall, Dear. Is there a reason I should know about Coker?"

"They're little towns outside Yeovil," said Ian. "Not very big: East, North, and West Coker. Why, Alan?"

"The book I was reading last night."

"What?" Vicki broke in. "The T. S. Eliot?"

"Yes."

"Oh—the *Eliot!*" exclaimed Ian. "My wife said something about that. She's a big fan of Eliot. She said Eliot put East Coker in one of his poems. When I first came to live in Crewkerne, she noticed it was near East Coker." Alan had been glad when Gayle had said she liked Eliot.

"Alan likes Eliot too," Vicki remarked dryly. She'd never liked Eliot herself.

"Actually," Ian went on, "Wendy said there were several English locations in Eliot's poems. Was the poem *The Third Quarter*?"

"The *Four Quartets*," Alan said. "They're named for four locations; three in England, and one in New England. I don't know exactly where they are."

"Maybe Ian knows."

"I don't remember. It's been awhile since Wendy and I discussed it."

"We know where East Coker is," said Alan. "The other two English sites would be…Little Gidding and…Burnt Norton."

"Right," said Ian. "We tried to find them on the maps once. Little Gidding is somewhere to the east. Somewhere between London, Cambridge, and Nottingham."

"Vicki and I must have passed by it then! I didn't know! Where do you think Burnt Norton is?"

"I think it's in the Cotswolds. We never found it. An old Tudor manor that was destroyed long ago by fire. A ghost house." Ghosts…

"Vicki and I went through a ghost *village* trying to find Chipping Campden."

"But Burnt Norton is only a mile or two from Chipping Campden! They both seem a bit like Brigadoon. Maybe they only appear every hundred years!"

"A bit like the Grail Castle!" exclaimed Alan.

"Eliot lived in Chipping Campden, I believe," Ian said.

"Have we gone through East Coker yet?" Alan asked.

"Oh, quite a ways back. Just a few miles out of Crewkerne. *West* Coker, actually. This road doesn't pass through *East* Coker."

"Then Vicki and I just missed three of the four sites."

"The fourth is in New England, you say?"

"Yes. A group of rocks off the coast of Massachusetts. *The Dry Salvages*—The Three Savages."

"Well, we haven't passed by *those*, certainly." Vicki's tone suggested relief.

"But I *flew over* them!" Alan exclaimed with a sudden certainty. "Because my flight from Washington took me up the east coast. But I had an aisle seat: No chance of a view."

He sank into the rear seat. A few moments later he muttered: "I've missed them all—*my* sacred British sites—while Vicki found *hers*!"

THIRTY-EIGHT

Alan looked down from the walls of Old Sarum, five thousand years old—the oldest remains of Salisbury; fifty miles and a third of the way back to London—and Ian stood beside him. The two men had grown closer, certainly. If Ian were bisexual...

"When we visited Warwick Castle," Alan said, "I was torn by such strong feelings." Vicki was stepping over the ruins below them. "Children were slaughtered when it was overrun. Prisoners were tortured in the dungeon. Why?"

"People seem to think it's necessary. To maintain order, to keep the world from chaos. It's up to us—you, me, Friedrich—and others like us—to convince people they're wrong."

Vicki was balancing atop an old wall fragment, as childlike as Lavender had been in Chicago. She was in love with two men; they were in love with her. Her joyful quiet acceptance surprised Alan.

"So Friedrich and his wives are in London," he said. "I never expected to see them again."

"Hopefully they've recovered from the shock of what happened to Sally and Naomi. I just hope Ahmed's okay.

He's about to become Friedrich's son-in-law." So Ahmed was still engaged to Helga.

"Ian! Alan!" Vicki was waving to them from below. "Come down! I want to show you—!"

Alan and Ian regarded each other.

"You think Ahmed's holding something back?"

Ian recoiled from the question and only replied halfway down the steps.

"Perhaps not. He watched his friends being murdered. Maybe that's all he saw. It just seemed… I thought I caught something in his eyes, something he wasn't sharing. Don't know what it would be." They arrived at ground level.

"Your wife's name's Wendy?" Alan blurted out suddenly.

"Yes."

"How long you been married?"

"Almost fifteen years. We met in Philadelphia."

"Look!" cried Vicki. She'd lain down on a large stone pedestal that resembled an altar. Ian stood above her.

"I'm yours," she cried, looking at him and laughing. She motioned with her lips, as if to kiss him. "I feel like offering myself to you. Would you like to receive an offering, My Lord?"

Ian raised his arms over her. "In the name of Ian…"

"Best not have any of *that*," Alan interrupted, unusually serious. "Bad press."

"But I'd so like to *offer* myself," she said, taking both their hands.

"Best save *that* for Stonehenge," Ian muttered, and headed towards the exit. *Still worrying about Ahmed.*

"Anything wrong?" Vicki asked. "He seems a little down."

"We were discussing Sally and Naomi. It may have been worse than we thought."

"How? They're both dead. Ian! Honey!" she cried as Ian reached the exit. "Can we spare another ten minutes? I want to ask the ranger about the ruins. To your left. Thanks!"

Alan remembered the picture he'd left in the car and thought: *Wendy?*

Stonehenge—just ten miles to the north—looked just like the pictures. The stones rose, huge and immovable. Across some tops lay stones nearly as massive; giants confronting them on the plain. Why was this built, and how? It made Alan proud of his ancestors.

But it seemed artificial: *Too much* like the photographs. It might have been a theme park back in the States. It might be a deception.

"Look!" exclaimed Ian. "The tumuli!" Vicki followed his hand as it swept across the horizon. "The burial mounds of the ancient Britons! There. And there. And there!" he said, indicating raised mounds on the horizon.

"All tombs?" asked Vicki. "This must have been a very special place."

They walked around the stones. Sometimes Vicki held Ian's hand, sometimes Alan's. One huge stone stood on its own, away from the others.

"Quite a rock!" exclaimed Alan, examining the massive slab that seemed of particular significance.

"Probably points North," said Vicki.

"Actually not," replied Ian. "It's more esoteric. If you stand in the center of the temple on the morning of Litha—the summer solstice, when the sun is farthest north—the sun rises over this stone—straight through those arches."

Looking back towards the main temple, they could see the two rings of stones that formed the main site, and the huge circular ditch that marked its perimeter.

"It doesn't seem right," said Vicki. "These tourists trampling holy ground."

"And," added Alan, "that passage coming from the parking lot under the highway! The audio recordings: *Imagine walking out of a forest into a sudden clearing of massive stones.* Those crude paintings on the plywood walls! Encouraging tourists to gawk at our heritage."

Ian laughed. "They're catering to the public. It's supposed to create 'atmosphere.' They're trying to entertain, not lecture. It's supposed to be popular art. And anyway— the tunnel is only temporary, until they can build something more imposing."

"Still," grumbled Vicki, "These people have no sense of *space*, no sense of *reverence*. They're simply...visitors, just...*tourists*."

"But remember all the places *we* complained, where the Christians wanted *us* to be 'reverent'—Westminster Abbey and York. I can see it both ways."

"People still stereotype this place," Ian added. "They imagine Druids and human sacrifice."

"But Julius Caesar," Alan countered. "Didn't he say that the Britons sacrificed prisoners? When *did* the Stone Age end here? How did the ancient Britons compare to tribes in Africa or Polynesia? When did they start using metal?"

"Ah, the Romans," Vicki interjected, "who crucified people and laughed as gladiators hacked each other to bits! Fine ones to talk about 'civilized!'"

"I think," Ian suggested cautiously, "that here the Bronze Age began around 2300 BCE."

They continued around the stones.

"This bothers me," Alan said. "It's massive and unforgettable, but I was more impressed by Avebury—or even the Rollright Stones."

"The Rollright Stones?" Vicki asked. "They moved you more than *this*?"

"I resonated more with them, perhaps because we were alone. It was more private. I felt more comfortable there." He thought a moment. Yes, he could say that his *soul* had resonated then. Even though he had still been searching at the Rollright Stones and Avebury, he'd felt his soul calling even then. The silver cord had been drawing his body and his soul back together ever since he'd left on his journey.

"And of course there was the Long Barrow," Vicki added sadly.

"Long Barrow?" Ian asked.

"West Kennet," Alan said. "We had a visitation. The spirits of Sally and Naomi—inside the burial chambers."

"Among other things," Vicki added with a glint in her eye. "Windmill Hill."

"I've always found Avebury particularly intriguing," Ian replied without elaborating. "I hope to take Wendy there."

Leaving the gift shop, Vicki could only say: "Well, that was particularly tacky."

"Didn't you like the little models of *Stonehenge Restored*?" Alan asked sarcastically.

"What did you expect, Vicki," Ian added. "What would *you* put in a gift shop here?"

"I don't know," Vicki sighed. "Something not *tacky*. This is a holy site."

"*Tacky* is in the mind," Alan said. "At least you enjoyed Old Sarum."

"Except for the *heat*!" Vicki exclaimed. "They say this is the hottest summer in a hundred years!"

As they swung the car doors open, Ian noticed a small picture on the rear seat.

"Now how on earth did *this* get here?" he said. "I've been looking for this for weeks."

He picked up the photo as if he were going to kiss it, but caught himself and sat it back on the seat.

"I found it in our bedroom," said Alan. "You must have forgotten you put it there." He glanced at Vicki.

"I've been unpacking awhile," Ian said. "Why did you bring it along?"

"It...reminds me of someone I know." That was as much as Alan dared. He felt like Parsifal in the old legend: His politeness prevented him from asking intrusive questions. He waited for a response, then blurted: "Is this an old girlfriend?"

Ian looked at him curiously. "No old *girlfriend*," he said emphatically. "Allow me to introduce my *wife*!"

Vicki shot Alan a knowing, victorious glance.

THIRTY-NINE

The ninety miles from Stonehenge to London went quickly—not much over an hour. As they left Stonehenge Vicki turned and gave Alan a look: *I told you the photo wasn't Gayle.* Alan watched his wife rest her hand on her lover's shoulder—how strange it all seemed.

As Ian had predicted, the cars on the motorway were all going over seventy. Many flew along at eighty or ninety. The landscapes swept by.

Passing Reading, Alan exclaimed: "Poor Oscar!"

"What?" asked Vicki.

"Oscar Wilde, imprisoned in Reading."

"A lesson to us all," commented Ian.

Vicki looked at him curiously. "Why?" she asked.

"He thought he could get away with it—being gay, I mean."

"Or at least bi," Alan added.

"Or at least bi—you may be right. Oscar thought he could pull it off. He tried to make it a joke. He couldn't believe anyone actually cared. Why should anyone mind if he and Douglas were lovers? But they did. Society destroyed him. Exactly a hundred years ago. A warning to us all."

"What's the warning?" Vicki's voice quivered.

"No matter how harmless you believe your sexuality is, someone will feel threatened. No matter how noble you believe your love is, someone will call it disgusting. Very few people are comfortable with their sexuality. Most find it disturbing, one way or the other."

"Oh Oscar!" cried Alan.

The cars flew past. The heat, the traffic, the dirt, the noise. A lethargy rendered them pensive.

It was nearly six o'clock when they hit the London suburbs.

"Damn!" cried Ian as he exited the motorway. "We're supposed to meet them at seven."

"But an hour is plenty of time, surely," Vicki said. "We're near Windsor, aren't we?"

"We're in Slough, near Heathrow. We still have to get into London. Probably only an hour, even in traffic. But I was hoping to get our room and settle in—maybe have a shower—before dinner. At least it's Saturday. Friday would have been bad."

"The three wives came?" Alan asked.

"Yep. All three. I brought them all to London. They wouldn't come any other way. They've been in seclusion since Thursday."

"The four of them get along?" Vicki asked.

"Yes. Sally's death has brought them even closer."

"He was Friedrich and Sophie's adopted son," Alan said.

"Before he became their *daughter*," Vicki replied.

"I don't think Gustav ever wanted to be their daughter," Ian sighed. "He only wanted to dress like a woman—

but it was easier to just assume a woman's personality. Society wants you to be one or the other—not a mix! One or the other: Then people think they know how to treat you."

They arrived at the hotel well before seven. While Ian was inquiring at the front desk, Vicki was startled to see the Virginia college student they'd met in York. He was with the Japanese man.

"You two again!" Vicki cried. "Harold and Saito, yes? Returning to the States? Or Japan?"

Saito listened with a curious smile.

"We're leaving tonight," Harold said.

"I didn't know you were together." Turning to Saito she added: "Have you learned much English?"

"I have learned much English. Mr. Dalton… is… a… marvelous instructor." He grinned.

They were joined by a very attractive young woman. "Are you ready, Saito-san?" she asked. Then she noticed Vicki and Alan.

"I remember you! Didn't we meet in York, about a week ago?"

Vicki and Alan exchanged puzzled looks.

"Did we?" asked Alan. "You look vaguely familiar. We stayed near Bootham Bar. Were you there?" He turned to Harold. "I know we met *you*! You're the guy from U. Va."

"Exactly. *Wahoo-wa!*"

"Yes. *Wahoo-wa.* I remember Saito-san of course."

"I have learned…much English…since Sunday."

"Harold and I met in London and decided to go to Scotland," the woman said. "Rather a whirlwind romance; upset Mummy I'm afraid. I hear she's told everyone at the

361

bank. No matter. Mummy was always over-excitable. Now we're off to Japan…"

"Japan!" exclaimed Alan. "Why?"

"My idea!" said Saito. "I have invite them to visit my country. Stay with me. See sights."

"We thought we saw you in Bath a few days ago."

"Yes," said Harold. "We ran into Saito there. Charlotte and I spent most of the week in Scotland. All looks pretty much the same. People said *have to see Bath*. Got there Thursday, ran into Saito. Bored with the architecture. Saito said, why don't we visit him in Kyoto? Came back here this morning."

"Kyoto!" gasped Alan.

"So we're off tonight. What about you two?"

"We're flying back to the States tomorrow," Vicki answered. "Tonight we're meeting friends from Germany; Alan's friends, actually."

Harold's eyes narrowed. "From *Germany*?" he asked coarsely. "An older man and three women? I noticed them as soon as we got here. They sit together holding hands, pawing one another. They're sharing a suite. Disgusting!"

Ian was about to reply, but Alan grabbed his arm. "Herr Neufeld is a respectable businessman and supporter of human rights. His son and his daughter-in-law were recently murdered, and he's come to London to grieve."

"Oh," Harold said sarcastically. "Well, I hope he goes back home soon. Thank God we don't have people like him in America."

"Like…like *what*?" asked Vicki, growing redder.

"Sick old perverts."

Alan drew in a loud breath, hesitated. "I remember now; why I left Virginia." He held back a moment, then spit out: "It's full of people like you."

"And where do *you* live *now*, sir?"

362

"*California.*"

"You smoke pot and go naked?"

"What if we do?" snapped Vicki.

"Honey," said Charlotte, "we'll be late to the airport."

Harold nodded, turned to Saito and snapped: "Come on, Saito!"

"Have a nice trip," Charlotte offered as they headed towards the door.

Vicki began to thank her, but Harold turned and yelled as they swept out the door: "You're a disgrace to America and the Commonwealth of Virginia. A disgrace to the Academic Village." That's what the people at the university called themselves.

"Come on," said Ian. "The Neufelds will be waiting for us."

"But wait," said Vicki, suddenly nervous. "Do any of the Neufelds speak English? I don't speak any German…"

FORTY

In the dining hall Alan immediately spotted Friedrich and his wives.

"Mr. Horne!" the German exclaimed. "What are *you* doing in England? You came here from Berlin?" He sounded different in English.

"It hurts to see you, Friedrich. I could have stayed in Berlin when you were arrested, but I was afraid and flew to London. Forgive me."

"Ach, Alan; what could you have done? You were a foreigner. No point mixing you up in all that. And Sally told you to leave. You've heard about Sally and Naomi?"

"Yes. I'm sorry, Friedrich."

The waiter added another table and they sat down.

"But how do you know Ian?" Frieda asked. "Is this your wife, Alan? Or the new girlfriend, Ian?"

"This is my wife Vicki," Alan declared to the whole table. But after realizing what Frieda had said he added: "To tell you the truth, she's both."

"I happened to be in England, visiting Ian, when Alan arrived," Vicki added.

Ian smiled. "I met Vicki at Yellowstone, in the States, and invited her to join my Morris dancing team on its tour of England. We've grown quite close." After a moment he added, with a smile: "Alan didn't know she was here."

The Neufelds seemed to expect a further statement.

"They've gotten very close," Alan said finally. "Vicki's spent a week with Ian and ten days with me, and a few days with both of us; and I believe she's decided—"

"That I love you both and want to live with you both. Or, at least, share my life between you." It was a straight-forward declaration of polyness. She smiled, then her courage failed. It all still embarrassed her; she couldn't entirely own up to it. Her face turned red and she curled into her husband's arms. *She* has *found her soul.* Alan looked around the table.

"*You* understand that, don't you?" A smile spread across his face. He felt by now he understood the Neufelds.

Friedrich and the women all nodded. Ian kissed Vicki as the two hugged. Alan hugged her too. Alan and Ian took hands, and the three dissolved into a snuggle. Then they remembered they were in public.

"We'll have to discuss our plans," Alan told Ian. "But we'll do that later."

The seven chatted over appetizers. Ian was continuing a long friendship, Alan renewing acquaintances, Vicki making new friends. But the tragedy in Kashmir hung over everything.

"It was Friday a week ago," Sophie said, "when we got the news. It had taken all Tuesday to get Friedrich out of jail. We'd seen Sally, Naomi and Ahmed off on Wednesday. I don't know how we would have managed without you, Ian.

"They were abducted; then we heard nothing—until Ahmed turned up in Srinagar on Sunday."

"Apparently," said Frieda, "they were killed soon after being taken. Ahmed provided a good bit of information; but of course he wasn't in the best of state of mind."

"Where *is* Ahmed?" Alan asked.

"He's in Hamburg with Helga."

"But Helga turned Friedrich in."

Frieda and Friedrich exchanged pained glances.

"She was confused," said Friedrich. "She never got over losing Gustav. She'd always expected to marry him—they weren't biologically related. She never accepted Sally. She blamed me. Ahmed is hoping to help her sort things out." He squeezed Frieda's hand. "We didn't all talk like we should have. Helga isn't easy to talk to, the way Sally was. It was hard on her, having two step-mothers—and knowing how much I liked her adopted brother-sister."

"We thought we treated her so well," said Sophie.

"But she always resented us," added Marthe.

"Ian told us," Vicki said, "that the four of you aren't legally married."

"That's right. So technically, of course, Helga's illegitimate. I suppose I should have married you," Friedrich said, nuzzling Frieda.

"But then *we* would have been bigamous—or at least adulterous!" Sophie exclaimed, as Marthe nodded. "It's the damned law! They don't understand how some of us love!"

"Whatever Helga claims," Marthe added, "she listens to other people too much. She believes other people more than her own heart. No matter what she says."

"But her heart must be aching," said Vicki. "I've never met Helga, but I can sympathize with her. For a long time *I* sneered at polyamory. Alan and I had horrible experiences: We were dumped by people we cared about."

"It took years for Vicki to realize," (Alan tried not to sound superior), "that our lovers had their *own* issues; it wasn't about *her*."

"And I still didn't believe," Vicki added, "that polys could survive in a hostile, monogamous society. I thought we were doomed—condemned—rejected and condemned by society. As helpless as the Jews under Hitler. Which is why," she said turning to Alan, "which is why I was leaving you."

They gazed at each other, then fell into a long hug.

"Any news about the Saxons?" Ian asked Friedrich. "Rudi or Kurt or Käthe? I didn't catch their plans."

"Käthe's taking care of the Leipzig and the Dresden homes. Rudi and Kurt are back in the Balkans, trying to set up a relief effort in Croatia. Thousands of refugees are being massacred." How could anyone answer that?

"Rudi and Kurt will do what they can," Marthe said. "We need more people like them."

"I'd like to go back to the Balkans someday," said Alan. "When I visited as a student, I didn't stay anywhere long except Istanbul. An hour here, a day there; Ljubljana, Zagreb, Belgrade, Sofia, Skopje. But I loved what I saw: The endless hills of Bosnia and Macedonia, Diocletian's palace in Split, the Bridge in Mostar—and Sarajevo. Beautiful."

He was lost for a moment in memories, then turned to Vicki and said, with particular emphasis: "The bridge in Mostar that was and always will be."

Then the memories stopped him again. Sophie broke the spell:

"Forget Sarajevo. The Bosnian Serbs have cut it off from the world for three years. And killing everywhere. There was a huge massacre last month near Srebrenica, in eastern Bosnia—thousands killed."

"Horrible," Frieda murmured.

"Nothing to do," Ian said after a long moment. "Nothing to do but continue the work." Ian's attitude impressed Alan.

"That," Friedrich muttered, "that's the problem with human rights work. Whatever we do, other people tear it down; we're bailing water from a leaking boat." He leaned on Marthe's shoulder.

The waiter took their orders. As they waited for their food, Marthe asked: "How long will you be in England, Mrs. Horne?"

It was Vicki's first look at the Marthe Neufeld: A lively woman with fading red hair, an endearing smile, and sparkling eyes.

"I'm afraid we're leaving tomorrow. I've been here over two weeks."

"First time here?"

Vicki nodded. She seemed quite comfortable with the Neufelds. Was it because, after so many years, she'd learned to accept herself?

Alan was glad Vicki was getting along with the Germans. But she seemed to grow sad, and Alan worried his wife might have been offended by something. As the meals arrived, Alan asked discreetly: "Do you like the Neufelds, Vicki? Do you approve? I can't quite tell."

"They're wonderful," she whispered in his ear. "I was afraid I wouldn't like them. I was afraid they'd make me uncomfortable. I'm not as self-confident as you are, Alan. I've been afraid of my own orientations. I expected a stereotype: A doddering old man, surrounded by gold-digging bimbos; a *leering* old man; pathetic. But I misjudged."

"So you like them?"

"Yes. I'd like to stay in touch with them."

"No problem there," said Ian, who'd heard the end of Vicki's remark. "Friedrich and I have known each other for years—mostly through correspondence, although we'd met several times at conferences. Funny, if Friedrich had never been arrested, I never would have understood his marriages—or my own. I'd felt uncertain about Wendy—and about Vicki; but learning the truth about Friedrich's relationships—and his innate dignity—convinced me."

"He honestly loves them all?" Vicki asked quietly.

"Yes," Ian answered under his breath. "He's provided well for them. He helped Frieda and Sophie start their own businesses, and for two years he's training Marthe."

"How's he do it all? This work in the Balkans—"

"Vicki," Alan interrupted, "you wouldn't believe! In Berlin, every time I turned around, I stumbled over another plaque honoring his work."

"It's inspiring," replied Vicki. "I'd like to–"

"Not *his* work," Ian cut in. "It should be *everyone's* work."

Vicki seemed embarrassed. "What?" Alan asked.

"I was about to say, *I love you when you're pompous*. But Ian's right. I've been cynical so long. It feels good to be *released* from that."

Alan and Ian stroked Vicki's arms from either side.

"I know we've discussed this before," Vicki said to Alan. "And we signed that petition in front of Parliament, but—what's going on in Croatia?"

"The same thing as in Bosnia," Alan answered, a little embarrassed. "You missed it because you were touring—in Yellowstone and England. I saw it on German TV. The Croatian army is sweeping through Serbian Croatia, throwing out the Serbians and killing whoever won't leave."

"Meanwhile in Bosnia," said Ian, "the Serbians are exterminating the Muslims. The U.N. does nothing. Either it *can't* or it *won't*."

"At least the Middle East is improving," said Ian. "Israel and Palestine have signed an agreement. And the war may be ending in Chechnya, thank God! I was afraid the Russians might start acting like the Serbs."

Towards the end of dinner, after several whispered exchanges with his wife, Alan turned to the Neufelds and said: "Vicki and I have been wondering...but weren't sure how to ask..." They glanced at Ian, who smiled and encouraged them. "Friedrich, you have three wives—however you want to describe them. Have the women ever wanted...other husbands?"

The women glanced around, a little embarrassed.

"Sophie and I have discussed having *girlfriends*," Marthe said. "We respect each other as co-wives of Friedrich, but we don't quite click as lovers. There's a man I've known since before I met Friedrich. Sándor's flown to Shanghai on business. His work can be rather sensitive..." She glanced at Friedrich as if to ask if she'd spoken properly.

"I'd be interested in another partner." Frieda said thoughtfully. "It would be nice to have someone around when Friedrich's off with Sophie or Marthe. But I'm awkward at starting new relationships, especially at my age. And right now I'm more interested in making sure Helga's happy. I'd want someone she could accept—and that seems so unlikely now."

There followed a long pause.

"And how do you feel, Sophie?"

Sophie Neufeld looked at Vicki sadly. "I've had two husbands before." Her voice seemed laden with melancholy. "When I met Friedrich I was married to a young man, an architect. He loved Wagner, Alan. That's how

370

Gustav got so interested in music and art. I met Friedrich and fell in love. We all lived together. Paul would teach us about art and music, Friedrich taught us the hotel business. We opened the hotel. We took in Gustav. It was beautiful." Her voice trailed off as she stared into space.

"What happened?" Vicki hesitated, uncertain.

"He died of colon cancer eight years ago, at thirty-nine." She wiped her eyes. "I encouraged Gustav to study art, music and history. When he talked to us about it, it reminded me of Paul."

She laid her face in her hands. Friedrich and Marthe reached out to comfort her.

"It was fascinating," Sophie went on, "to watch Gustav develop *his* relationships."

"Yes," sighed Frieda. "He was much too *peculiar* for Helga."

"He challenged himself," said Sophie. "He always wanted to understand himself better. Helga wanted stability."

"So of course," continued Frieda, "when Gustav told her about *Inge*…"

"Wait, wait," Vicki interjected. "You mean Sally—Gustav—was poly too? Besides being—" She stopped, uncertain what to say.

"*Transgender*," said Alan, "I think you mean. Or…I don't know."

"Gustav wanted to remain a man *physically*, but dress and act like a woman." Friedrich spoke as the father who'd watched his child grow up. "He didn't like the way society dictated how men were expected to act. When he told us this, it completely unsettled Helga. She wants everything in its 'proper place.'"

"She found it repulsive," Frieda added.

"I don't know that he actually called himself *poly*," Sophie went on. "He just…thought *differently*. He had a different *outlook*. Friedrich and I had never raised him to be…exclusive. He remembered Paul and just assumed most people were selfless and loving."

"And look where it got him," Alan sighed.

"But why," asked Frieda, "has Helga become so reactionary? I remember the Sixties. I never expected this to happen."

"But Käthe was just as bad for him," Marthe cut in. "She misunderstood him just as much. Of course *Gustav* was *Sally* by then. Käthe was as dumbfounded as Helga and Inge had been. But after they broke up, she was damned impressed with his transformation—Sally Bowles and all that. Knowing Sally changed Käthe. She became more radical than *he* was. She wanted Sally to be 'liberated'—sexually free; but Sally wasn't that kind of person. She only had sex with people she cared about."

"But Marthe," Vicki interrupted, "what was the problem with…" She turned to Alan. "…that woman you met in Weimar?"

"Inge," Alan answered. "Very nice woman. Can't imagine her with Sally. Inge at heart is conventional. Very nice, though. Very stable." He hesitated, then added: "I like her a lot."

"What happened," answered Sophie, "was that Inge realized how difficult it would be to stay with Gustav, because he took his vision seriously. He wasn't just *talking* about his feminine tendencies. And he wasn't going to keep quiet about his polyness or whatever either."

"It's scary," added Frieda, "to know someone who takes their conscience seriously. It made Inge uneasy. And scared the hell out of Helga. Though I believe Sally's example must have encouraged Helga to try it too—to live according to her beliefs—without the same confidence in herself."

"Sally," said Friedrich, "intended to follow the implications of her thinking and integrate the flesh and the spirit, the traditional and the radical. She intended to do it with absolute honesty and openness: The Tantric, left-hand path."

"And I suppose," said Alan, "that none of his prospective partners—Helga, Inge, or Käthe—could handle both the physical and *spiritual* implications."

"But Naomi could," said Marthe. "Or at least Sally thought so. I think she was right. When Saddam bombed Tel Aviv during the Gulf War, she decided it was insane for people and countries to cling to old grudges. She decided to learn from the Jews' old enemies in Germany."

"Sally was quite impressed with *you*, Alan," Sophie added after a sip of tea. "The two of you might have hit it off."

Alan blushed. "We got quite close that evening in Nuremberg." A warm smile had settled on his face. He was remembering that kiss in Hans Sachs Square.

FORTY-ONE

But the mention of Helga provoked other discussion.

"Americans seem so uninformed about Islam," Friedrich said, "It doesn't spook us here. The Crusades are long passed. No need to fight again."

"But they tried to blow up the World Trade Center in New York, two years ago." Ian was pressing the point. "Of course, they didn't succeed; how much explosive would it take? But it shows they're motivated, and what they have in mind."

"Nothing to do with Islam," countered Friedrich. "Just a few bad apples. Some Muslims, it's true, use religion to further their politics—but so do some Christians in the U.S. Ahmed's a wonderful fellow."

"Exactly," Alan replied. "The New York bombing was a fringe group. Like the Oklahoma City bombing in April. A hundred and seventy people dead. Much more threatening than the World Trade Center attack. And the bomber was *American!*"

"But look," added Vicki, "at the whole American mindset since last fall's elections. Newt Gingrich strutting around like a king. Republicans out to get Clinton. Falwell and Robertson denouncing the godless pagans. If terrorists massacred a bunch of Witches, I'm sure some Christians would try to justify it!"

Ian and Friedrich seemed shocked.

"Fringe or not," said Alan, "a small group of radicals of any sort can cause a lot of trouble." He turned to Friedrich. "Aren't you frightened by Ahmed's story?"

The room went silent. Friedrich had turned pale. "Of course I am," he answered testily. "But the people who…killed my son—" He faltered a moment. "I believe they're an isolated group—non-representative. A small group of sick individuals. No reasonable person would have done this."

He returned to his food and his wives.

"Alan, you wanted to talk about something," Ian said as they drank coffee and waited for dessert.

"I just wanted to point out, in connection with Vicki," (Alan lifted his cup towards his lips) "that you also have a wife, and I also have a girlfriend."

"Oh you can both meet Wendy. Just come and visit. I'm sure she'll like you. Will your girlfriend object?"

"Oh Gayle's very reasonable. Quite open about relationships."

"She's in Silicon Valley?"

"No. The Midwest."

"Wendy has a boyfriend too, you said." Vicki smiled. "We could make quite a household. The three of us, Wendy…Gayle…Wendy's boyfriend. Six altogether. Imagine! You've met the boyfriend?"

"No, he's out west somewhere. She's been to visit, but I haven't met him. Maybe in December."

"Won't it be freezing?" Vicki asked. "Does your area get as windy as Chicago?" She turned to Alan. "Ian lives in Wisconsin—he just comes here for his research."

"No," said Ian. No gale winds. Not very windy."

"What's the boyfriend's name?" asked Vicki.

"Don't know. She mentioned it, but I've forgotten. Anyway, might not be his real name."

"Why not?" asked Alan.

Ian looked surprised. "Wendy uses a pseudonym online. Maybe he does too. Safer."

"Funny," said Alan. "That picture of Wendy."

"You said she looked familiar?" But before Alan could answer, Vicki's fork dropped on her plate with a loud crash.

"Where *is* that picture?" she asked quietly—as if dazed. It surprised Alan—and apparently Ian.

"Why do *you* care, Vicki?" Alan laughed. "You said Wendy looked nothing like—"

But before they could look for the photograph, three people strode up to the table—so suddenly that it frightened Vicki.

"What the—?" she cried. "An attack!" She seemed disoriented.

"Vicki, calm down," Alan said under his breath. "Just a few more German friends."

Vicki looked skeptical, but Ian added: "Ahmed, Inge, and Naomi's mother Rachel. Only one German, really."

Friedrich had risen to welcome them. "Geveret Herzlieb! What a surprise. When did you arrive in London? I thought you'd left for Israel!" He shook her hand.

"Fräulein Inge. Always a pleasure. How are you?" They shook hands.

"Ahmed," he said in a quiet voice, taking the Arab's hand. "How are you doing? You've been through so much. I hope you're feeling stronger. Are you staying in this hotel?"

Friedrich hesitated then added, in a nervous tone: "Is...is Helga well? Is she...here too?" He sounded apprehensive and sad. "I'm surprised you found us!"

But the three newcomers stood silent. Then Inge turned to the Americans and said: "Alan?"

Friedrich ordered coffee and dessert for the new guests.

"What brings you to London, Ahmed?" Ian asked. "And the three of you! I thought you'd gone to Hamburg to see Helga. I thought Geveret Herzlieb had left for Tel Aviv. And Inge! I never expected to see *you* here! How'd you all end up together?" He apparently anticipated an unusual explanation.

"You know I left Berlin after the funerals," Ahmed began. "I couldn't bear to stay. I had suspicions about Helga. I went to Hamburg.

"I wanted to believe in her. I loved her. She always impressed me with her interest in Arab culture—and Islam."

He lowered his eyes. Inge put her arm around him.

"He and Helga are finished," Rachel said. "Ahmed walked back into the hotel as I was making my plane reservations. I'd spent some time with the Leipzig folks, but Rudi and Kurt had left for Croatia. Ahmed asked about *you*, Friedrich." Rachel's voice suggested a new tenderness.

"He looked terrible," she continued. "He hadn't slept. I said you'd left for Scotland. I told him you'd invited *me* but

I'd declined. When Ahmed said he was coming to find you, I decided to come along after all."

"Helga doesn't think I'm observant enough," Ahmed blurted out loudly. "Me—raised in Egypt with an uncle at Al-Azhar. She tells *me* what the Qur'an means." The outburst surprised them—none of them had ever seen Ahmed angry.

"Based on what?" asked Alan.

"Based on students she's met in Hamburg, Muslims who want nothing to do with the West. They'll come here to study engineering then use it against us. They loathe Western culture—loathe it." Alan noticed he'd said "against *us*."

"And Helga's become their friend? They'd associate with *her*?"

"Because she's converted!" Ahmed cried. "Because she proclaims the *Shahada*: *There is no God but God, and Muhammad is his Prophet.*"

He looked at Alan. "You saw her wearing the *hijab*, the scarf, in Berlin. I told her it wasn't required. 'But the Qur'an *does* require it,' she shot back. And prayer! Five times a day now; hours every day. She thinks she understands Islam better than I do!"

"But your uncle at Al Azhar," Friedrich cut in, "When he comes to visit, with his wife. Surely it's the same."

"It sits differently," Ahmed answered, eyes blazing. "For my uncle it's natural and easy. For Helga—it's the negation of what she should be." Why wrong for Helga, Alan wondered? Why wrong for *her*?

No one knew what to say. The Neufelds looked as though they might simply jump up and leave.

"Ahmed," said Vicki, "does this have anything to do with Sally and Naomi?"

*

The look Ahmed gave Vicki shocked everyone. It expressed such horror, contempt, and disgust that Friedrich intervened and invited them all to the Neufeld suite for more coffee.

On the way out of the dining room, Vicki asked Alan whether everyone in Europe learned English.

"Educated people generally know several languages," Ian answered in a subdued voice. "They have to. Whereas, in large countries like the U. S. or Russia or China, people can get along without knowing much about the Outside."

Entering the hotel lobby, they were astounded to see it full of parents and children. Earlier it had been deserted. Children (and even a few parents) clutched small, inflated toys—roly-polies in yellow and red plastic.

In front of the assembly, a man in a yellow and red clown suit ran frantically back and forth across a stage, emitting a high-pitched squeal: "*Bloopy bloopy bloopy bloopy bloopy!*"

He repeated this, at tremendous volume, as he crossed the stage.

"What the hell is *that*?" Sophie muttered under her breath. The clown was making so much noise, and the crowd was so riveted to his performance, that no one heard her.

"Oh!" cried Ian. "That's Mr. Bloopy! One of our recent British phenomena."

They'd turned into the hallway as he said it. The parents shot Ian horrified glares.

"Mr. Bloopy?" Marthe asked.

"The latest British craze," Ian repeated. "A television celebrity."

"How can *he* be a celebrity?" gasped Vicki.

"As a dull skit is presented in the foreground, he runs across the rear of the set, screaming *Bloopy bloopy bloopy bloopy bloo*—"

"Be quiet!" snapped Alan. The expression on Ahmed's face during Ian's outburst had frightened him.

"—at the top of his lungs." Ian finished in a tone of apology. "This must be a benefit performance," he added, more subdued. The diners proceeded to the Neufeld suite. They returned to their own rooms very late.

The three Americans lay on the bed staring towards the ceiling. They couldn't sleep. Nobody spoke. Then Ian let out an anguished sigh.

"Sally must have given a stellar performance, a tour-de-force," Alan said in a shaky voice.

"They thought he was Naomi's sister," Vicki mumbled.

"Wearing the veil was a master stroke," Ian went on. "Though he couldn't shave, they couldn't see his stubble. She had passed as a woman after all."

They lay silent again.

"To think," Vicki said after a long pause, "it was only when they tore off their clothes—"

"The Star of David came loose from Naomi's neck; they realized she was Jewish," said Alan. "They lectured Ahmed for traveling with Jews—and women who weren't his relatives."

"They raped her for disgracing him," said Vicki.

"They intended to rape her sister," Ian went on, "but they tore off her clothes—"

"…and the *sister* was a *man*. *Sally* was physically still *Gustav*." Alan sighed heavily.

"And the sudden collision of everything—the secular Muslim, the Jewess, the man in the sari—"

"—drove them mad." Ian cut Vicki off. "They thought they'd abducted some ordinary westerners in native costume. They couldn't figure it out. They raped her again and killed him. The second rape was so violent she was probably dead when they beheaded her. The police found them dumped in a field, after Ahmed had dragged himself, bound and gagged, to a road to accost a farmer. The parchment was crammed into his mouth. *As a Muslim Brother, we are releasing you. Purify yourself—or face the wrath of the Righteous!*"

They curled more tightly around one another, trying not to think about Ahmed's story; but it was all they *could* think about. It reminded Alan of the Klan.

"To mock him as they killed him," Vicki said. "To humiliate and mutilate him."

"*Be a woman, then!*" gasped Alan, "as they raped and sliced."

"So he died unmanned," Ian sighed. "Not at all what he wanted."

"But more of a man than any of them." Vicki's words drew both men more tightly to her; and the three consoled themselves a very long while.

FORTY-TWO

At breakfast Sunday morning, the three Americans were sharing coffee with the Neufelds when Ahmed, Inge, and Rachel walked in.

"That's extraordinary," Frieda was saying to Ian.

"And Vicki figured it out," Sophie added, "not the men!" The whole table laughed.

"These two were clearly dunces," Vicki said, raising her cup. "They're raving about their other lovers and don't realize they're the same person!"

The three new guests exchanged quizzical looks.

"So what is this extraordinary incident?" Ahmed finally asked. He'd seen the sparkle in Marthe's eyes.

"Ian and Alan," said Frieda, "they're both in love with Vicki, which was obvious to us before she'd said a word. What we didn't know–"

"And they were too *stupid* to realize—" chimed in Ian.

"They're both in love," cried Sophie, laughing, "with *Ian's* wife—Wendy—as well."

"Except," added Vicki, starting to laugh herself, "that Wendy uses *another name* in her email; which is how she and Alan met. So *he* only knew her as *Gayle*." She laughed again. "It was only last night, when we were in bed cuddling, something made me connect *Gayle* with *Wendy*. And I pulled out this picture, and we started to talk, and it all came out."

Indeed the picture now lay on the table with the extensive British breakfast.

Ian looked at Alan. "We were *dunces*," he exclaimed. "Why didn't we see it?"

"*Idiots!*" Alan replied. "Absolute idiots!" He patted Ian's arm. "Both of us!"

"And of course," Ian added, "you didn't associate *me* with your girlfriend, because she always calls me by my *Irish* name: *Sean!*"

The three new guests had remained standing next to the table. "I'm sorry," Vicki said finally. "Please sit down. I'm sorry. Please!"

"I still don't get it," Ian said to Ahmed as the three settled into their chairs. "How'd you all arrive together? We had no idea you were coming. You didn't explain it last night. How'd you two meet Inge?"

The three new arrivals exchanged awkward looks.

"It was in Berlin," Ahmed began. "Several days ago. I'd gone to Hamburg to try to talk to Helga and ended up arguing with her and her friends. They'd heard about the hostages in Kashmir, but didn't know I'd been involved. I didn't tell them. I didn't want to know what they thought about it. I can imagine. I came back from Hamburg and ran into Frau—into Rachel. We were strolling around the Tiergarten talking about our lives. I noticed a young woman sitting alone on a park bench. She looked terribly unhappy. When we came closer, I realized it was Inge."

"I'd left for Weimar—" Inge hesitated. "But I couldn't go back. Something seemed unfinished. I went back to Berlin, back to the hotel, and just walked around the city. Berlin is *so* large. I had to unwind. I thought about Gustav and Naomi, how they died, just being themselves. And I thought *What have I ever done?*"

"You've been yourself, Inge." Alan took her hand. "That's all anyone can do. You do it well."

They exchanged awkward smiles. Alan remembered the time they'd spent together in Weimar. Their kisses seemed so distant now. Then they'd argued, and he'd stomped off in search of Wagner.

"We invited Inge to dinner," Rachel said. "As we talked, we realized we shared a lot of attitudes and feelings. With everything else that had happened, we'd never had a chance to notice."

"What I always wanted," Inge said, "I just wanted to live; a home to come back to every night; a place I could relax and be myself; someone I cared about—who cared about me." She glanced towards Alan, embarrassed.

"Which I wanted too," Ahmed added. "I'm sorry, Friedrich—I've left Helga to her new friends." Inge smiled as Ahmed took her hand. Ahmed's voice had grown soft and silken; his face seemed lit from within like ivory. People who nurture their souls, thought Alan, glow from within: The Jerusalem of the Heart.

No one replied to Ahmed's last statement. Alan sensed an energy around the three of them—Ahmed, Inge, and Rachel. They'd look down or up, together, as if on cue; but Alan saw no cue. He realized again how much Vicki meant to him: He and Vicki communicated the same way. He took her hand and noticed how radiant his wife looked with Ian beside her. "Lit from within"—like Ahmed. They were a good match, those three. And then he thought: *Gayle!* He and Vicki and Ian and Gayle. Somehow the four-way interaction nurtured their souls.

"It's strange," Rachel said, "that I've found not only another daughter—though nothing can bring back Naomi—but a son as well—an Arab one!"

"So what will you do?" asked Ian. "You can't adopt them both. If they marry, that would be incest."

Friedrich Neufeld chuckled.

"And who should I adopt," Rachel exclaimed, "the Muslim or the Christian? Better to simply make our family and let the State be confounded! Or rather"—she must have remembered Friedrich's attitudes towards the government and marriage—"if the State thinks it its business to meddle in private matters, let it support *all* loving, committed relationships!"

Friedrich Neufeld chuckled again.

"Where do you plan to live?" Vicki asked.

"In Weimar," Rachel whispered. Ahmed and Inge, from either side, rested a hand on her arms.

"But Rachel," Alan said cautiously, "do you really want to return to Weimar—to Germany?" They exchanged glances. "Won't it be difficult for you?"

Rachel reflected a moment. "I've learned a lot from Friedrich."

"We decided on Weimar," Ahmed said, "where German culture achieved its heights: Goethe and Schiller."

"Yes; and *Lohengrin* too," Alan added under his breath. Then, louder: "I missed seeing it by a week in Dresden. I remember our walk around Weimar, Inge."

Inge smiled back. "We'll keep Rachel's house in Israel."

"And live part of the year in Alexandria," said Ahmed. "God knows what my uncle will make of it. But God *is* compassionate and merciful. With His help, we cannot fail."

"If the Jews and Arabs can negotiate peace, as Arafat and Rabin seem ready to do; and if Christians like Clinton can work with both of them; why can't *we* make a family?" Rachel's voice rang full of hope. "Naomi would like this. She said we were one family." Then all the events of the previous week seemed to sweep over her, and she turned away with a look of regret.

"Anyway," Ahmed went on, "we wanted to affirm a new beginning. We wanted to share it with you and your loved ones, Friedrich. So here we are. Rachel said you'd come to London. Your secretary in Berlin told us which hotel."

"We're glad you came." Ian's voice brimmed with appreciation. He turned to the Neufelds. "Have *you* enjoyed London so far, Friedrich? Has it been any help?"

"It's calmed me down." Friedrich did seem more relaxed. "London is a marvelous place. It can't undo what's happened, but it comforts my grief."

"And for *us*," Sophie added, "it's a great experience. We seldom travel off the mainland."

"When's your plane, Alan? You're leaving today, aren't you?" Frieda asked with a trace of melancholy. "It seems like ages since you first walked into the pension in Munich—alone in a strange country. Well maybe not so strange, after all, for *you*. Even then, I sensed you were different."

"We leave at two p.m. We need to get going."

"Are you going with them, Ian?" Marthe asked. "You were such a help with the funerals. I don't know how we'd have managed. And the mess with the wedding."

"I'm not going anywhere. I said I'd accompany you wherever you liked, and I'm perfectly glad to."

"Oh, Scotland should be wonderful!" Sophie exclaimed. "The land of Burns and Stevenson. The mountains and the lochs. That's right, isn't it, Friedrich? *Holes*! That's what they call them?" Sophie's eyes sparkled.

"In German, *Loch* means *hole*," Alan whispered to Vicki.

"But you must want to see Vicki a little longer," Frieda said to Ian.

"I intend to see Vicki much more very soon, back in the States. If that's okay," he added, looking at Vicki.

Vicki blushed; then gave him a long hug and kiss.

"We'll go to Scotland sometime, if you like," he said. "Or somewhere else. There are lots of places I'd like to visit with you—with both of you—and with Wendy."

Through the window they spotted a marching band in uniform coming off a tour bus.

"They're gearing up for the fiftieth anniversary of The War's end, in a few weeks," Ian sighed. "Look at them."

"I wonder," said Vicki, "whether our host from the bed and breakfast in Bath will be attending."

"He was disappointed we hadn't put Hirohito on trial for war crimes," Alan explained.

"Some people are always ready to be patriotic," Friedrich sighed. "But some of us are citizens of the world."

"I'm proud to know you, Friedrich," Vicki said unexpectedly. "I wish I'd met Sally and Naomi."

Ian looked at his watch. "You'd better get going," he said.

"There's one thing I don't understand," Alan said to Friedrich. "We saw the news about Kashmir—but they never mentioned *women*. The newscasts only mentioned *men*. Am I remembering wrong?"

Friedrich shot him a look that he first took for embarrassment; then he realized that it was more an expression of sadness. Friedrich was about to answer when Ian said:

"You heard the reports correctly; they only mentioned men. As I said, Alan, there were *two* hostage incidents in Kashmir. One was Sally and Naomi; one was a group of tourists in another part of the province. All the hostages were killed—except for Ahmed, of course—but he was a special case. You saw the reports on the other group. Sally and Naomi…were not reported."

Vicki's face turned serious. "Why?"

Ian took her hand. "A German man dressed as a woman, traveling with a single woman—Jewish—through Muslim territory. The German government wouldn't touch *that*. Neither would the German press. Neither would the British press. Besides, there was no British connection." He turned away. "They didn't matter. The Establishment was too embarrassed to stand up for them."

"Which was just as well, Ian," Marthe said. "We didn't need more publicity after Friedrich's arrest. With Sándor nego—" she caught herself. "With Sándor in Shanghai. We were under such stress. Our children were already dead. It didn't matter what the press was reporting."

"Have a good flight," Friedrich said, shaking Alan's hand and bowing to Vicki.

"Thank you."

"Come on," Ian gestured. "Let's find my car."

Alan watched Ian and Vicki kiss good-bye.

"Does this bother you?" Vicki asked when she noticed Alan watching.

"Not at all. It's just—" He left the remark unfinished.

"You look rather lost," said Ian. "As if you don't quite know what to do."

"I came to Europe to find my soul, and I feel like I've found it. But what do I do now? This trip wasn't an end, it was a beginning. I *think* it was a beginning." *In my end is my beginning.*

"I'm sure I've found at least *part* of my soul," said Vicki, arms still wrapped around Ian. "Maybe the major part. And that's enough for now. I can grow that portion larger."

"I can't wait to see my folks again, and Lavender. I miss being away from them."

"I'm looking forward to meeting Lavender," Ian said, still clinging to Vicki, "and your family. I'm getting more used to the idea of children…"

Alan looked at Vicki nervously. "I don't imagine you'll want to tell *your* family."

Vicki released Ian. "They'd never understand. They'd disinherit me."

Alan sighed. "Vicki believes there can be no honest exchange of ideas between her and her family. Honestly, Vicki. You don't believe they'd still love you?"

Vicki lowered her eyes. "Oh, they'd still *love* me—or claim to. But they'd feel we were lost. They'd never forgive us. They'd feel dishonored, disgraced. I can't do that to them."

Alan sighed again. "Perhaps the rest of your soul is tied up in that. And a future vision quest."

"Have a good trip," said Ian, extending his hand. "See you in a few months—in Wisconsin…or California."

The two hugged. Then Vicki joined them.

"Let's see what we can create," Ian told them. "I'll talk to Wendy soon. I'm sure she'll want us all to get together."

"I'll be talking to *Gayle*," Alan answered; and they laughed. The "Gayle-Wendy" confusion still astounded them.

*

The plane sailed high over Ireland. Alan admired the green traces of land below the clouds outside the window. Then Vicki shook him. "Alan! Look at this!"

"What?"

Vicki thrust a newspaper onto his tray table. A headline mentioned an American student, a Japanese student, and an English woman.

"You don't really think…" He was missing his chance to see Ireland.

"Read it, Alan."

Alan scanned the article.

American student causes havoc on plane. Suspects Japanese friend of affair with British girlfriend. Claims to have bomb. Threatens to crash plane into Parliament.

Alan remembered his descent over Windsor Castle. His eyes ran down the column.

Japanese student…returning from studying English in the UK…American student…native of Virginia… British citizen Charlotte Hayle… Jealous outburst… bizarre bilingual argument… finally subdued…

"He made quite an impression, it seems," Alan said finally. "Jealousy and death—the hazards of monogamy!" He continued reading.

The American, a student from Virginia, was outraged at the behavior of his friends. The woman, daughter of a London banker, was unable to calm him. The Japanese man—who knew no English until two weeks ago—couldn't follow the American's outbursts or the Brit's explanations.

"He must have gone nuts," Alan commented, handing back the paper. Vicki couldn't help smiling.

"Thank Athene," she said, "we know what *we're* doing! At least we know how to *begin*."

The airline movies followed: The first about selkies, the second about immigrants. The selkie film was set in remote Ireland—which by then had long since vanished from the window. Alan had missed his chance to see *that* Ancestor-Land. But he'd seen Germany and England.

"*Wahoo-wa!*" thought Alan. He was returning to Virginia—the birth-land he'd left behind.

HOMECOME

FORTY-THREE

"Lavender! Honey!"

Vicki picked up their daughter, kissed her, then continued walking towards the Dulles baggage area.

"Mommy! I'm four years old now!"

"Yes you are, Sweetie! Did you have a nice birthday?"

"Grandma and Grandpa took me to the Zoo. We saw peacocks and leopards…"

"It's good to see you again, Vicki," Mr. Horne said. "But how did *you* end up in Europe?"

"It's a long story, Dad," Alan said, lifting their bags from the conveyer belt. "We can talk on the drive home." It was four hours by car back to Tidewater.

"We've missed you, Alan," said his mother. "We were worried about you. We hadn't heard a thing until the telegram. But who is Friedrich Neufeld?"

That evening, after putting Lavender to bed, Alan and Vicki recounted their adventures. Alan's parents were shocked by what had happened in Kashmir; but delighted to hear about Ian and Gayle—though the fact that Gayle's real name was Wendy rather confused them.

"We'll have to see how it goes when we all get together," Vicki told them. "You can never be sure. Is it true that…that you…feel you might be…poly yourselves?" Alan had asked Vicki not to sound *too* curious.

"Yes," Mrs. Horne sighed. "But things haven't worked out."

"You're not seeing them anymore?" This surprised Alan. "What happened? They couldn't handle jealousy?"

"No," said Mrs. Horne. "Neither of them was jealous."

"So what then? Did they stop liking you?" asked Vicki.

"No," said Mr. Horne. He hesitated a long moment. "They said they couldn't be open about the relationship; they said we had to hide it. They begged us to be discreet."

"Oh Alan," Mrs. Horne said, noticing his grimace, "Look at it from their perspective. They've lived here all their lives. They'd probably be kicked out of their church and shunned by their family and friends. Don't think too ill of them."

"I told you," he snapped, "what happened to *me* at *my* church. What did you tell them, Dad?"

Mr. Horne couldn't hide his discomfort. "Alan, I can't live dishonestly. I want partners I can be proud of. I lost my temper; I told them to go to Hell."

A few nights later Alan shoved open the door into the darkened kitchen of their California home, switched on the ceiling light, and dropped the suitcases in the corner by the china cabinet. "It's good to be home!" he sighed. They'd arrived several hours late, after midnight.

Vicki followed, sat the smaller bags on the kitchen table, then swung into the hall and turned on the air conditioning. The house, locked up for three weeks, felt like a sauna. "I thought," she said, "I would *die* on that plane by the time everyone ahead of us had gotten off."

Lavender walked in like a zombie.

"Sit your stuff down, put on your pajamas, and get into bed," Vicki told her.

They brought in the other bags. Then, sitting at the table, they could do little but toss aside the note that Alan had left for his wife ("Gone to my parents for a while") and stare at the last paper they'd gotten before Alan left: Friday, July 28, 1995.

"Wasn't that the day the Archduke was assassinated—in 1914?" Alan's mind was still racing from the flight. Conscious of history, Alan sensed cataclysmic events lurking around them.

"Huh?" said Vicki blankly.

"When World War I started. No, wait—that was June. Or was it?" In his exhaustion, he couldn't remember the dates.

"I don't know, Alan."

Lavender peeked around the corner.

"Get in bed, Lavender. Would you like me to read you a story?"

Vicki took Lavender into her room, and Alan checked the answering machine. When Vicki emerged, she found Alan waiting in the hallway.

"What is it, Alan? You look like a ghost. The flight must have finally caught up with you."

"I think you'd better hear this." She followed him into the office.

He played a long sequence of phone messages—a string of confused voices: Preston and Janie.

First: "*Alan, Tomie's flown to Montana to join Claire—Vicki's left her there for some reason. Do you know where Vicki is?*"

Second: "*Alan, we got your card; are you back from Virginia yet? We still can't find Vicki. Why didn't you leave any contact info?*"

And finally: "*Alan, where are you? Do you know what's happened to Vicki? Claire and Tomie's van went off a cliff into the Snake River.*"

"*As the Athame is to the Male…*"
"*So is the Cup to the Female.*"
"*And conjoined they bring happiness.*"

Vicki lifted the knife from the cup and licked the wine from the blade. Alan licked it as well. Then Alan offered her the cup, she drank, and they passed the chalice to the others.

"*Drink deep and never thirst.*"

Each person drank then passed the cup along the circle.

As they passed around the cake, Vicki asked: "But why did Tomie fly to Montana?"

People exchanged awkward looks. Finally Jane said: "Claire had driven back to Yellowstone after you left. Apparently she wanted to drive around Idaho but didn't want to do it alone. So she asked Tomie to fly up."

"Do the police know how they went off the road?"

"They were both probably pretty tired."

Driving home afterwards.

"You don't think it was an accident, do you?" asked Alan. "That they went off the cliff?"

After a long pause, Vicki answered: "No."

"Why not?"

"Claire and Tomie were excellent drivers—very careful. She drove us all through the mountains—in Oregon and Idaho. Narrow roads along mountain crests when she took me to Billings to get on the plane for Chicago. She was totally competent."

"Mechanical problems?"

"She got the van a complete checkup before we left."

"So they were tired."

"They're morning people, Alan—Early to bed, early to rise. Plenty of sleep. They alternate drivers."

Alan glanced around. Lavender had passed out in the rear seat. He lowered his voice. "So why do *you* think they crashed?"

Vicki thought a long time. "I think she told Tomie what happened between us. Or he pried it out of her. He reacted more violently than she'd expected. Something happened in that car, and they lost control."

In the bedroom with the lights out.

"I don't think they took it well."

"Who?"

"The coven," said Vicki, "when we told them about Ian and Wendy."

"Jane and Preston are jealous," snapped Alan. "Maybe they wish they hadn't broken up with us now."

"*Aren't you concerned about Lavender?*" Vicki mimicked sarcastically. "Our daughter's gaining two parents—and we're supposed to be *concerned?*"

399

They snuggled closer.

"Don't forget to call Ian tomorrow," Vicki reminded him. "We need to arrange the visit."

"Don't you think it's curious, Vicki, that William Bao was released by the Chinese this week; and his release seems to be linked to the activities of a German who had supposedly gone to Shanghai on 'business?' Marthe Neufeld's boyfriend Sándor was in Shanghai on business!"

"Probably just a coincidence, dear. Lots of people travel to Shanghai on business these days. Though I must say, when it comes to your friends nothing would surprise me."

"Sándor's Hungarian, you know; son of a Freedom Fighter. Did I tell you that?"

"Well then, he isn't *German*, is he?"

Alan knew his wife was smiling. Sándor was probably naturalized, but why argue? He reached down and cupped his wife's ass in his hands.

"You feel good," he said, and kissed her.

"So do you. You feel mighty good." She reached for his cock.

Their mouths and tongues played.

FORTY-FOUR

Alan's voice trailed off following his recitation; after a respectful silence Ian said: "An interesting poem, *Little Gidding*."

"Evocative," added Gayle. "Too bad you didn't look for Little Gidding when you were in England."

Alan glanced out the window of the cabin. Snow dappled the Sierra foothills, not surprising for February. Before driving to Grass Valley, they'd celebrated the Feast of Imbolg, their first festival together. Six months since Germany and England. Ian and Gayle had moved to California; Gayle was starting her new job on Monday.

"The snow's stopped," said Vicki. "The moon's glowing through the clouds. The ground's beautiful in the moonlight. It's so still—as if we're absolutely alone on earth; surrounded by white."

The four stepped out onto the porch.

"It was generous of Preston and Jane to keep Lavender while we're here. A whole week together in the foothills. And snow. I've always loved snow." Gayle's voice trembled with the same wonder that glimmered in her eyes.

Vicki said: "They were our lovers, you know."

"Alan told us. But they broke up with you."

"They couldn't handle it. They insisted on discretion. They were so afraid someone would find out. And they didn't want children. Some people are like that."

"Not me, I love children," said Gayle, smiling. She drew Alan into a long kiss. Watching them, Vicki and Ian snuggled closer.

"The moonlight *is* beautiful on the new snow," said Ian. He stroked Vicki's neck. "What say we turn in?"

"I'm so glad we could come here, Ian," Vicki sighed. "We've gotten so busy: Pagan ministry, human rights work, the poly support group starting. Who knows if anything lasting will come from all this?"

"You can never be sure what will last," said Ian; and from the way Vicki smiled at him Alan could see how much Vicki wanted her new husband.

"Let's turn in." Vicki's voice was playful and mellow.

Vicki and Ian headed for the back. Alan and Gayle stayed in the living room on the sofa bed.

"I can hardly believe," Gayle said, turning out the light, "that it's been six months already: Six months since we fell in love. You and me and Vicki and Sean. Six months since England."

They kissed and snuggled. Alan sighed. "And look what's happened in the meantime: Rabin murdered; Chechnya in turmoil *again*, in spite of elections. And the Unitarian church set on fire, because some disgruntled person read that it accepted 'polygamous pagans.'"

Gayle put her hand across his mouth. He moved it aside. "It's sad about the church, but I'm not going to hide who I am."

He held her, close to tears, then recovered.

"But the four of us *married*, Alan," she said. "Think of it: *Married!* The world may be a mess, but the four of us are *married*."

"*Handfasted*, Gayle. And only in our own eyes, and—we hope—the eyes of the Gods. Not in the eyes of the government or Jerry Falwell. Society isn't going to take our marriage seriously."

He could see Gayle's face now, looking towards the window.

"The snow is beautiful in the moonlight, isn't it?" She pressed her body against his.

"Beautiful." They were both transfixed by the scene.

"Thank the Gods for the Coven," he went on. "I never thought Jane and Preston would perform our Handfasting."

"They were very honest, I thought. They got involved with you as an experiment; just a diversion, really. They never thought of children or family—or *commitment*. *They* thought you were just 'mate-swapping.' They still love you and Vicki—but as friends not lovers. In *their* universe, marriage is only for *two*. Anything more—from their perspective—could only be happening for kicks."

Alan turned from the moonlit window and the glimmering snow-covered tree branches into Gayle's embracing arms and legs.

"Thank the Gods, *our* polyverse is larger!" he whispered, before planting his mouth on his wife's. Soon they both wanted more.

"Oh Alan!" Gayle gasped as he entered her. "What a wonderful honeymoon!"

Snow was falling outside. The four had bonded as one.

SOUL

FORTY-FIVE

Five-and-a-half years passed, and the world moved on. Bombings devastated two American embassies in east Africa and an American destroyer in Yemen. The United States led NATO in a bombing campaign against Yugoslavia on behalf of the Muslims in Kosovo, and Yugoslav President Slobodan Milosevic was arrested for crimes against humanity. Closer to home, an American dissident bombed the Atlanta Olympics, two abortion clinics, and a lesbian bar; President Clinton was impeached but not convicted for his relationship with a White House intern; and George W. Bush was declared President of the United States after a disputed election in which Vice-President Al Gore received more votes. "Gore Got More," as Alan told his friends. The government lurched to the right. In California the foursome, in a new home, awaited a visit from the Neufelds. The busy lives of the Germans and the Americans had kept them apart all those years.

*

Gayle and Alan lay pensive on the living room carpet. The opera recording, continuing after their climax, had masked their love-sounds.

"The bordello!" cried Gayle, continuing her fantasy. "The Harem!" She pulled her petticoat down to cover herself. It was all she was wearing.

"The *Bacchanale*!" Alan, naked, rolled over and grabbed the small towel from the sofa.

"*Samson and Delilah*!" Gayle exclaimed. "Incredible!"

"My love," Alan murmured. He was sucking her nipple when Vicki's voice startled them. They hadn't noticed her coming down the stairs.

"You seem to be having fun," Vicki said playfully. "Gods! We could hear Gayle from upstairs. '*Oh! Oh!*'" She simulated moans. "Tone it down, woman!" Vicki laughed good-naturedly. Her rough edges had softened. She'd become light-hearted, no longer jealous or threatened. But Gayle turned beet-red.

"Oh," Ian smirked, just behind Vicki, "Wendy's always been rather...*demonstrative*."

"Sean!" Gayle—annoyed, affectionate—threw her pillow at him. Vicki came over and kissed her.

"Don't let The Boys unnerve you," she said. Alan shut off the music. The silence calmed everyone. Then the doorbell rang and they froze. The children had returned.

"It's good we finished when we did." Alan winked, wrapped a skirt around himself, threw on a tee-shirt, and opened the door—Preston and Janie with the children.

"You two look pretty tired," Gayle said to Jasmine and Lavender. She'd thrown on a chemise. "You'd better get to bed. Up the stairs you go." A warm-hearted mother.

Gayle and Alan took the children upstairs. The girls could barely stay awake. It was nearly eleven, and a school night. They shouldn't have let them go to the movie; but it was so nice of Preston and Janie to offer…

"They were so well-behaved," Jane said after Alan and Gayle returned. "So grown up for ten and four."

Gayle had always liked to believe that Jasmine was conceived that night in the Sierras…

"I like your new house," Preston said. "I even like…" (he glanced at Alan's skirt and hands) "your nail polish, Alan." He laughed nervously and grinned, hoping Alan would appreciate the joke.

Preston would probably never lose his slight homophobia; but he was too good a friend and too kind-hearted for Alan to make it an issue. Besides, though Preston still showed some discomfort around Alan and Ian, he accepted their relationship intellectually.

"So the Neufelds are coming?" Preston asked cautiously. "You've told us so much about them! Did you really consider emigrating to Germany?" He'd lived in Germany once himself but been glad to come home.

"Yes, Preston," Alan answered. "And Vicki thought of emigrating to Britain. But we realized our home's here. It's a beautiful country, the United States; it's flawed but well-meaning. We belong here. Even if other countries sometimes enchant us, I don't want to die in exile. We're all connected anyway. No reason to isolate ourselves and think we're superior—or inferior!—to the rest of the world. We're just who we are. We've birthed both slave-traders and abolitionists; Native-killers and Native-wanabe's; the Klan and the Freedom Riders. This is *our* story and place." But something made him uneasy—he'd been feeling unsettled all day.

*

"You know," Gayle said after Preston and Jane had left, "you used to look ten years younger than your age."

"And now," Alan replied, "I look ten years older. I know."

"Not so bad, dear," said Vicki. "Your hair's just showing more silver."

"Quite distinguished, actually," said Ian, kissing him on the forehead.

The four snuggled closer on the sofa.

"So the Neufelds will be here on Venusday," said Ian. "After six years—finally!"

"Six years and a *month*," added Gayle. "Lavender's ten."

"Amazing," said Alan. "Ten years and a month tomorrow. September already!"

"Good gods! And Jasmine's five in November!" Vicki's voice trembled at the realization. "Lavender was only three when we met the Neufelds."

"What will they be doing in New York?" asked Alan. "I presume Friedrich knows people there."

"Oh gods, yes!" replied Ian. "Human rights folks, business folks, art folks…"

"It's too bad he's always so busy," sighed Vicki. "But then, so are we. It'll be nice to see them."

"I suppose they'll visit the Statue of Liberty," said Ian. "See the U.N., go up the twin towers, visit Central Park…"

"The view from the Towers is amazing!" said Vicki. "We'll go there sometime."

"They've heard from Helga," said Ian. "They told me on the phone. She's more deeply into it than ever. She ran into Ahmed and Inge and gave them quite a lecture on Islam, the West, and the Jews. Didn't even congratulate them

410

on the baby. But maybe she didn't know. Ahmed blew up at her. *This is not Islam!* he yelled. *This is what Sadat was trying to tell us. Not Islam! Islam is compassion and mercy.* He accused her friends of corrupting his religion."

"I'm sure Helga loved *that!*" exclaimed Alan. "Is she still with that boyfriend in Hamburg? Friedrich said he was creepy."

"No. Apparently the boyfriend dumped her; thought she was rather unstable. She refused to discuss it with Ahmed—She claims the West has ruined him."

"Poor Friedrich," said Vicki. "He's nearly seventy now."

"His only natural child," said Gayle. "Terrible."

"She's made remarks about Rachel," Ian added. "Oh, she's all on about the Jews and the Westerners. *You'll see!* She yelled at her father. *You'll soon see!* Friedrich tries to laugh it off. Ahmed tries to be patient. Rachel doesn't dare say anything. Helga hates the Jews. It reminds Rachel of the Nazis. But Ahmed and Inge and the baby are doing well, though Rachel doesn't get out so much now. And the Leipzig crowd comes to visit: Käthe, Rudi, Kurt—*they're* quite happy too. If it only weren't for Helga..."

"They've all disappeared, you know," Vicki said suddenly. "That's what Frieda told me on the phone. Didn't she tell you, Ian? No one knows where they are."

"Who?" asked Alan.

"Helga, the ex-boyfriend, the whole group she hangs around with in Hamburg. Helga hasn't answered her phone for weeks. It's as if they've all vanished."

"They probably went on vacation," said Ian.

"Maybe in August," answered Vicki. "Not mid-September." None of them had an explanation.

"Well," said Ian, "Time to turn in. Getting late. A hell of a Moonday today. Goodnight, Dear." He kissed Gayle on the cheek.

"No, it's *our* night, silly. Have you forgotten?" She smiled and stroked his arm. "Look at the calendar." Ian went off to check.

"Ninth...tenth... Right." Ian chuckled from the kitchen. "Only the tenth. Okay." Gayle stood up and collected her clothes.

"I loved the music, Alan. It was a nice change from the jazz." Alan smiled at Gayle, and just caught Ian and Vicki rolling their eyes. Gayle and Alan slid into a goodnight cuddle.

"So the poly meeting is Saturnday," Alan said, turning from Gayle back to the calendar.

"And *Human Rights Now!* is Moonday," answered Vicki. "We were so lucky that Ian could get you that job. Of course William Bao helped too." She noticed the kitchen clock. "Midnight already!" she exclaimed. "September eleventh. In just eleven days we'll celebrate Mabon—the autumn equinox. I'm glad the Community's growing. The Unitarians may not accept us, but at least the Pagans do. And we're recognized clergy now, thanks to the Federation of Witches."

"Who knows?" Alan answered from Gayle's side. "Someday the Unitarians...who knows? Give them five years! Meanwhile....I'm just glad I have you—all of you!"

Ian and Vicki smiled; Gayle held him closer and kissed him.

"To think," Alan added, a little teary, "to think that without you two, Vicki and I might never have found our home."

"Our Pagan, poly home," Vicki added, patting Alan's butt and taking his hand as they all climbed the stairs to the bedrooms. Alan felt happy, but unsettled. The Neufelds were coming, planes were taking off—for Boston or New York or Washington… What had put that thought into his head? He felt uneasy about the Neufelds; the Bush government made him nervous. He thought of Kaiser Wilhelm— why? He knew he worried too much. He wished he could decipher his visions! He'd had the dream about the airplane and his office building again. Or maybe it was the…?

In any case, he had Vicki and Gayle and Ian. He had love and his home and his soul.

About the Author

Trained in physics, astronomy, and mathematics, William Albert Baldwin has always enjoyed music, literature, and languages. Baptized as a Lutheran but never confirmed, he attends both Unitarian Universalist and Pagan/Wiccan celebrations (he serves as clergy for the Covenant of the Goddess). A long-time volunteer for Amnesty International, he also hosts a monthly polyamory forum. Because of his father's work with the American Red Cross (for the U. S. military), he has lived in Japan and Germany as well as Virginia and New Hampshire. He and his family now share a home in Sunnyvale, California.

Email: baldwinwa@gmail.com

Twitter: @wabaldwin

Facebook: William Albert Baldwin Author

Blog: Grail and Wand (grailandwand.blogspot.com)

Website: www.wabaldwinauthor.wordpress.com

If you enjoyed this novel, consider reviewing it on Amazon or Goodreads and recommending it to your friends!

Additional Background

Some of the universe that gave birth to *Soul Flight*.

Amnesty International
www.amnesty.org

Unitarian Universalist Association
www.uua.org

Covenant of the Goddess
www.cog.org

Loving More Nonprofit
www.lovingmorenonprofit.org

Covenant of Unitarian Universalist Pagans
www.cuups.org

Unitarian Universalists for Polyamory Awareness
www.uupa.org

Intersex and Genderqueer Recognition Project
www.intersexrecognition.org

The International Association of Richard Wagner Societies.
www.richard-wagner.org

Country Dance and Song Society
www.cdss.org

Folk Dance Federation of California
www.folkdance.com

Made in the USA
San Bernardino, CA
20 November 2019